"I WANTED THE TIME
TO BE RIGHT FOR YOU."

Logan's wonderful leonine eyes held hers. His voice was intense as he continued. "If you don't love me, say so now. Because it's almost too late for protests."

In answer, Nicola held out her arms, drawing him beneath the crisp white sheets. His aroused body pressed urgently against hers.

Each time he touched her in a new, more intimate place, she felt a surge of delight and discovery. Her heart beat violently; her body trembled. She realized now there were no limits to what a man and woman could feel together.

There would be no words of protest tonight. Tonight she would forget that Logan intended to make her his wife. Tomorrow was time enough to tell him the truth.

WELCOME TO...

SUPERROMANCES

A sensational series of modern love stories
from Worldwide Library.

Written by masters of the genre, these longer,
sensual and dramatic novels are truly in keeping
with today's changing life-styles. Full of intriguing
conflicts, the heartaches and delights of true love,
SUPERROMANCES are absorbing stories —
satisfying and sophisticated reading that lovers
of romance fiction have long been waiting for.

SUPERROMANCES
Contemporary love stories for the woman of today!

WHEN DREAMS COME TRUE

DIANNE KING

A SUPERROMANCE FROM
WORLDWIDE

TORONTO · NEW YORK · LONDON · PARIS
AMSTERDAM · STOCKHOLM · HAMBURG
ATHENS · MILAN · TOKYO · SYDNEY

Published February 1984

First printing December 1983

ISBN 0-373-70101-2

Printed in Canada

RAINBOWS

Be careful with rainbows
  they are an endangered species.
Arcing across our world
  they shimmer on the horizon
  promising hopes and dreams
  and wishes, too.
So, be careful with rainbows
  they are
An endangered species.

PART ONE

Washington, D.C.

CHAPTER ONE

STILL IN HER SATIN SLIP, Nicola Wynter Mather considered her wardrobe. Her slender hands, bare save for a thin platinum wedding band and a stunning six-carat diamond, seemed suddenly clumsy and slow as she searched for just the right thing to wear.

"Are you ready, Nicola?" Andrew asked, walking out of his dressing room.

"No, just a minute," Nicola answered distractedly. Usually she was decisive and organized. However, this morning she had tried on and discarded three blouses and two suits.

She slipped on yet another blouse and smoothed it over her gently sloping white shoulders, closing several tiny buttons and one stubborn snap. Then she stood back to look at herself in the wall of mirrors that ran along one side of the room.

The dark green silk blouse accentuated the sea green of her eyes and contrasted vividly with the pale porcelain of her creamy complexion. The expertly tailored beige linen skirt that she stepped into didn't quite hide the lush curves of her long-legged, graceful body. She was five feet seven inches tall in her stocking feet, five-nine in the heels she wore. She had learned long ago not only to accept but actually to enjoy being tall.

Her glossy, white blond hair, inherited from Swedish ancestors, was pulled back from her face. It hung just past her shoulders, and though it was baby fine and straight, there was masses of it. When she wore it loose, as she did sometimes to please Andrew, it was a shimmering thick mane of champagne and silver. This day she had it pulled back severely from her face, with not a strand out of place.

Slipping on the jacket that matched the skirt, she scrutinized herself in the mirror. *Well, it will just have to do,* she thought. *There simply isn't time to try on anything else.*

She felt a heady mixture of conflicting emotions— eagerness, determination, insecurity. This was the day she would give her closing arguments to conclude what the press were calling the "trial of the decade." An Arab oil billionaire, Faisal Gibran, had recently divorced his American wife and was refusing to pay more than token child support for their five children. If Nicola was persuasive enough, her client, Amanda Gibran, could win the biggest divorce settlement in history—and Nicola's career, which was already exceptional, would skyrocket.

Suddenly she noticed Andrew's reflection in the mirror as he walked across the room to stand behind her. She watched as his eyes took in her "lady-lawyer look," as he called it.

Andrew was of medium height, though he seemed taller because of the force of his imposing personality. His broad shoulders sagged slightly in a way they hadn't done in the early years of their marriage. The hair that had been salt and pepper for so long had recently turned silver. The ruddy face, deeply tanned by years as an avid golfer, was etched with furrows that came with age and career responsibilities.

But there was also a strength and vitality that infused his whole being. He was indomitable, a fierce individualist, robust and commanding. Somehow the lines that creased his handsome face only made him appear more dignified.

As their glances met in the mirror's reflection, Andrew gave a barely perceptible nod. "As usual, you look exquisite this morning." There was the merest bite to his words.

Nicola forced herself to smile at him. "Ah, but do I resemble a competent successful attorney?" She was only half joking.

"Isn't looking exquisite enough?" Andrew's wry smile touched only his lips. His eyes still evidenced the previous night's quarrel.

"Not today," Nicola answered, determined not to back down. She waited. Caring supportive consideration should be each partner's due in a marriage. She'd always sent Andrew off with her warmest best wishes. It was *her* turn now. *My turn. . . is that the problem,* she wondered.

She'd tried to make Andrew understand, but he'd refused to see her viewpoint. The previous night their discussion of the changes her case had brought into their lives had suddenly erupted into a battle of wills.

"Can't you see," she'd demanded, "*why* this case is so important to me? Finally I have a chance to be recognized for my own abilities." Then, trying to lighten the impact of her words, she'd finished, "It isn't easy being married to a living legend, you know. Everyone knows me as Andrew Mather's wife, not Nicola Wynter Mather."

But her attempt at humor had been quickly brushed aside as Andrew's eyes had narrowed and he'd responded curtly, "Nonsense! You exaggerate this business of being in my shadow."

"Well, it *is* a giant shadow," Nicola had commented, feeling her stomach tighten and her mouth compress into an angry line. They'd been over this too many times lately. With both of them used to their positions as mentor and protégé, he couldn't— or wouldn't—deal with the fact that she was becoming her own person, no longer blindly accepting of his judgments. As her law practice blossomed, she'd begun to have more of a sense of her own self-worth, and the role of student to Andrew's as teacher had become restrictive.

When they'd met seven years earlier, she'd been young and yielding. He had been her hero, bold where she was shy, wise where she was inexperienced.

Yet now, at twenty-eight, she was beginning to feel that perhaps she no longer wanted a hero but a man who could see her as his equal. Now, standing beside her husband in their bedroom decorated in pale blue and white—an old-fashioned, warm, romantic room—she wondered if it were possible for Andrew to view her as an equal. Perhaps he wanted her to remain an adoring acolyte, with views that always reflected his own. Instead of being proud of her growth as an attorney and as a person, he seemed threatened by her increasing competence and independence.

Still angry over Andrew's refusal to attend that day's session of the trial, Nicola's tone was cool as she said, "Today is the most important day of my life and—"

"Nicola," Andrew interrupted. "I didn't want you to take the case in the first place. I told you it would be a three-ring circus, bringing out just the kind of notoriety that it has. This sort of thing makes a mockery of the law. I accepted your decision, but don't expect me to be happy about it or participate in it."

He walked to the door and waited. "Are you ready now? Shall we go down to breakfast?"

Nicola picked up her handbag and walked past him. "I think I'll skip breakfast. There really isn't time."

Later, in the courthouse parking lot, she slammed the door of her bright red BMW, locked it and dropped the key into her purse. As she walked across the street, her leather briefcase swung just at the hem of her skirt. The Gucci case, made of the finest calf-skin suede, had cost all of the first paycheck she'd earned as a lawyer. That had been four years ago, and it still had more significance for her than the diamond she wore. Andrew had selected her ring, and she had been thrilled at his generous choice, but the briefcase represented *her* achievement, and especially on this day, it was important to her.

As she reached the sidewalk, Nicola paused to look around on this splendid April morning. Commuter traffic had been particularly slow that morning because Washington was even more crowded than usual with tourists drawn by its springtime beauty. The hundreds of cherry trees that lined the shores of the Tidal Basin were in bloom, their scent sweet and heavy. In the clear morning air the city was unbelievably bright and clean-looking. The buildings of grays and whites almost seemed to come straight from Athens, that city of white temples.

Nicola loved being in Washington. An intoxicating sense of power filled the air almost as pervasively as did the scent of the cherry blossoms.

Andrew had power. He was the senior partner in a prestigious law firm whose clients ranged from ex-presidents to the head of multinational corporations.

The memory of their disagreement still rankled as Nicola headed up the steps of the courthouse. Normally calm and composed, her heart was now beating furiously. Her large, almond-shaped eyes reflected her emotions just as the sea reflected the changing light. Usually a clear blue green, they darkened when she was excited or angry, as did the ocean on a stormy day. This morning they were pools of darkest green, lit by flashes of fire like that of the bioluminescence of tiny sea creatures carried on the cresting waves.

As she climbed the steps of the courthouse, she squared her shoulders determinedly. Whatever her feelings toward Andrew at the moment, she knew she would need her full concentration in court.

Deep in thought, she walked past the voice that said, "Well, well, a little preoccupied this morning, aren't we?"

"Lisa!" Nicola exclaimed. "What are you doing here?" She grinned, delighted to see her dearest friend.

"Are you kidding? You think I'd miss this circus? It isn't every day that my former roommate handles a case that's on the front page of the *New York Times*. I decided I just *had* to hear your summation. The Justice Department can get along without me for one morning." Smiling broadly, Lisa finished enthusiastically, "Oh, Nicola, you've really done a terrific job!"

"Thanks. I just hope the judge will share that opinion."

As they walked side by side, Lisa studied Nicola. "I don't understand how you can look so cool and confident. I'd be nervous as hell if my opposition were a battery of high-powered international attorneys."

Nicola grinned at her friend. "I'm nervous, all right. I've never been in a situation like this before, where so much is at stake."

"And the fact that you're really shy doesn't help."

"In a way it does. People often mistake it for calm!" Nicola answered with a rueful laugh.

" 'Ice princess,' " Lisa replied, quoting the press. "Little do they know that beneath that unruffled exterior is a heart that's beating a mile a minute!"

Nicola laughed with her friend. Though she didn't say so, she was aware she had Andrew to thank for her cool demeanor. When she'd first begun practicing law, she'd received a lot of press coverage because she was the wife of one of the foremost attorneys in the country. Andrew had told her to wear a mask, build a wall, so no one could see her fear and pain.

That was good advice, Andrew, Nicola thought now. *And not just for the press. This day won't be what it might have been because you refuse to support me. That hurts more than I can admit, even to Lisa.*

But she couldn't dwell on that. This day was one of the many times in her career when she must hide the vulnerability that was at the core of her personality. Instead she must call on the fierce competitiveness that reinforced her when she felt outmatched.

They entered an elevator, and Lisa pushed the fifth-floor button. "Is Andrew coming today?" she asked.

Nicola hesitated, then said with studied nonchalance, "No, he couldn't make it. An appointment he couldn't change."

"There's *no* appointment he couldn't change," Lisa replied tartly. "Clients wait for him, not the other way around. He's simply being self-centered again."

"Lisa, don't," Nicola said. "It doesn't matter."

But it did matter. And Nicola knew that Lisa was well aware of that. Despite herself, she had to admit that Lisa was right—Andrew was being deliberately self-centered, putting his feelings above her needs. *And not for the first time,* an insistent little voice reminded her.

As the elevator glided to a stop, Nicola realized what she had tried to avoid all morning: she was disappointed in Andrew. More than disappointed, disenchanted. And deep inside, she hated to accept that feeling because the awareness of it could never be erased. Allowing it into her consciousness was dangerous. *How will I smooth this wrinkle out of the fabric of my marriage,* she wondered as the elevator doors opened.

As Lisa and Nicola stepped out of the elevator, they were bombarded with a blaze of lights, cameras, reporters and photographers. Outwardly at least, Nicola seemed perfectly composed. Only she knew how much effort it took not to let her feelings show.

The questions flew so fast she had no chance to answer them individually.

"Miss Wynter, what do you plan to say during your closing argument?"

"Are you optimistic about your client's chances?"

"Is it true that your client has been offered a substantial out-of-court settlement by her ex-husband?"

As the questions came one after the other, Nicola made her way purposefully toward the courtroom, with Lisa beside her. At the door she stopped to say succinctly, "My client hasn't even considered a settlement because we feel confident we will win. The ultimate division of property is up to the court. As for my closing argument, you'll hear it soon enough."

"Has your husband given you any advice?"

Ignoring the question about Andrew, Nicola turned to enter the packed courtroom.

"She's a cool one, I'll say that for her," commented the reporter who had asked about Andrew.

"What would you expect from Andrew Mather's wife?" another responded. "He probably coached her every step of the way. Maybe he even used his influence somehow."

They didn't seem to care that Nicola heard every word. She was infuriated, and it was all she could do to fight back a tremendous urge to tell them just exactly how wrong they were.

Lisa touched her arm. "Hey, don't let those idiots get to you. Obviously, if you wanted to trade on Andrew's influence you wouldn't have chosen to practice law under your maiden name." As she stepped aside, Lisa added, "Go get 'em, tiger."

Nicola was grateful for Lisa's support, but as she joined her client at the plaintiff's table, she was still boiling, though she tried hard to conceal it. "How are you holding up?" she asked, sitting down next to Amanda, a rather plain woman in her early forties.

"I'm just glad it's nearly over," Amanda answered in her tentative way. "At this point, after all the publicity and pressure, it'll be a relief to have it finished whether we win or lose."

Squeezing Amanda's hand reassuringly, Nicola said, "I don't believe we'll lose. The law is based on male logic, it's true, which is often unfair. But this time I think it's going to work the way it should. Your husband owes you a great deal more than he's offering, and we're going to get it."

Amanda managed a slight smile, but Nicola could see she was far from optimistic.

As always, Nicola was struck by the difference between her and her client. A series of important victories in local women's rights cases had brought her to Amanda's attention. But from the beginning the two women were a study in contrasts. Twenty years of marriage to an insensitive man with old-world values had beaten down Amanda, destroying whatever spirit she might once have possessed when she was a young Washington debutante.

Only concern for her children's welfare prompted her to file suit against her ex-husband after he left her almost penniless. When Nicola told her what she should be entitled to in terms of dollars and cents, she was almost disbelieving.

Nicola herself was filled with outrage at Amanda's situation. Her husband held the money—the power—and thus controlled her life. Amanda Gibran was, like too many other middle-aged women, financially dependent upon her husband and had little sense of her own worth. The only difference was that Gibran had a great deal more money than most husbands. Nicola was determined that some of that money would go to Amanda.

The low buzz of conversation that filled the courtroom grew much louder when Faisal Gibran, flanked by four lawyers, entered and sat down heavily at the defendant's table. He was handsome in a dark smoldering sort of way. Nicola didn't care for his looks, but she could understand how Amanda might have found him attractive. There was a forcefulness about him and an exotic foreignness that could be irresistible to the right woman.

Gibran stared penetratingly at Amanda, who lowered her eyes. Nicola knew that Amanda had been obedient and awed by her ambitious handsome husband during the entire marriage. Somehow this made her even angrier.

As she waited for the judge to enter, Nicola glanced slowly around the courtroom. It was filled with reporters, as well as people who were merely curious about a financial disagreement that was measured in the billions of dollars. The case had dragged on for weeks, but this day was the last day of the trial. After this session, Amanda's fate rested with the judge. He would consider the evidence, evaluate the arguments presented, determine what was just. *He* would hand down the decision. Nicola hoped it would not take too many days. There was a tangible air of tension as everyone wondered how this story of power, passion and money would end. Nicola felt the tension—almost a living thing growing, expanding at a terrifying rate. She was so caught up in it, she started nervously when the bailiff announced the arrival of the judge.

As the courtroom rose in unison, then waited for the judge to call for the proceedings to begin, Nicola told herself to calm down. She didn't want to be like the racehorse that uses up all his energy in prerace jitters.

When she stood a moment later to give her closing argument, she was aware that every eye in the courtroom was riveted on her. There was no sound, not the slightest movement, as people waited to hear how she, a soft-spoken, vulnerable-looking young woman would wrap up this intriguing trial.

Quickly Nicola looked once at her notes, then laid

them down on the table. *Here I go,* she thought wryly, feeling the usual mixture of excitement, determination and fear that she imagined a parachutist must feel with every jump.

Her feelings were the same with every trial, never lessening even with time and experience. If anything, they were more intense this time. For now so much was at stake. She had planned a brief, objective, to-the-point summation of the facts revealed during the trial. But as she stood before the judge and began her speech, she found her low throaty voice growing impassioned. Suddenly her planned objectivity was replaced by an empathetic anger at the injustice Gibran was attempting to do his ex-wife.

"What law is there that says man is more and woman is less," she asked. Even as she spoke for her client, Nicola knew she was thinking of herself and Andrew.

Once she looked pointedly at Gibran, who was glaring intimidatingly at her. She wanted badly to say to him, "I'm not Amanda. My eyes aren't clouded by love or duty. I know you're a greedy, selfish, ungrateful bastard, and I'm going to beat you."

From time to time as she spoke, Nicola glanced at the judge. She carefully calculated her timing and was attuned to when the judge's interest had peaked and she should close. She felt a tremendous sense of confidence develop in the way she had been handling things so far, an almost instinctive awareness that she was doing it right.

As she went on to describe how her client had been thrown aside, her words dripped with scorn. Then she finished, "Your Honor, we have proven that Amanda Gibran has a legitimate right to a significant portion of Faisal Gibran's assets. It is up to this court to determine if Faisal Gibran will be allowed to perpetrate such an injustice, to callously discard the woman who helped make him such a success; who helped, for twenty years, to make the marriage a success. It is up to this court to determine whether twenty years has value—has worth. It is up to this court to determine if Faisal Gibran will be allowed to deny Amanda Gibran her rightful due."

When Nicola sat down, feeling drained, there was a soft collective sigh throughout the room. Somehow she sensed that her words had touched every woman there who had ever been financially dependent upon a man.

The judge, a stern-faced, elderly man who had betrayed no emotion or partiality toward either side in his handling of the controversial case, adjourned the proceedings for lunch.

Amanda, who hated facing the reporters, left immediately through a side door. Nicola met Lisa, and they made their way through the crush of reporters.

"Let's get out of here," Nicola told Lisa as the reporters closed around them, shouting questions and taking pictures.

Together the two young women raced to an open elevator, entering just as the doors closed, leaving behind a crowd of disappointed reporters.

"How about the Sans?" Lisa suggested.

When they entered the exclusive French restaurant a few minutes later, they received the usual looks from the other patrons. The two of them, so different in appearance, always created a stir of interest when they were together. While Nicola was tall and fair, Lisa was petite and dark, her "black-Irish" heritage showing in her onyx eyes and olive complexion.

They had met on the first day of law school, and their friendship had formed initially because there were so few other women in their class. Both had been more scared than either would ever admit, and they'd found tremendous support in each other. They'd even shared an apartment for a year before Nicola married Andrew.

Now, seven years later, Nicola and Lisa had the kind of friendship that was easy and comfortable, based on the certain knowledge that each could turn to the other in time of trouble.

When the food was ordered, Lisa leaned across the table, her round chin cupped in one hand. "So what do you think, counselor? What's the verdict going to be?"

Sighing, Nicola replied, "Honestly, I just don't know. But I do know we're right. Gibran has pulled every dirty trick in the book trying to cheat Amanda." She sighed again, releasing a long deep breath of tension. "After lunch we'll hear the other side, and then it'll be up to the judge. And unfortunately the judge is a man."

"You did a good job. There are several leaks in the dike. It'll take some fancy footwork now by Gibran's attorney, Krantz, to plug up the holes."

Nicola laughed at the mixed metaphor. "Thanks... I think...." She waited while the waiter placed their salads before them, then said, "Enough about me. What have you been up to lately? I haven't been able to reach you in weeks. Every time I call you're out. Are you in love again?"

"Yes, but not the way you mean." Lisa grinned hugely, and her dark eyes were afire with glints of joy. "Nicola, remember how I've always wanted to learn to fly?"

"Of course! You always said that as soon as you could afford it—"

"When we were in law school and long on dreams but short on cash, I couldn't afford it. Now I can." She grinned impishly and paused to eat a crisp cool asparagus spear. "My mother can't understand this attraction to danger, as she calls it. She keeps asking me why I don't fall in love, get married, have babies. Follow the family tradition, as she puts it. There's a long line of mothers in our family. I tell her, later. Right now I want to qualify for my pilot's license. Later I want to buy my own—"

"Lear jet?" Nicola interrupted with a laugh.

"I'll settle for a Cessna 182. To start with, that is." Lisa put down her fork and leaned forward. "Oh, Nicola, it's so exciting! Leonardo's right, you know."

"Leonardo?" Nicola interjected. "Is he your instructor?"

Lisa laughed, her face shining with pleasure. "Da Vinci. To paraphrase, he said after you've been up there—that's where you want to be. It's absolutely thrilling."

Nicola watched her curiously. She'd never experienced that kind of excitement herself, even during her courtship with Andrew. It was surprising that Lisa felt this way, not about one of the many men in her life but about a long-cherished dream.

Suddenly Nicola registered a chill deep inside. She said pensively, "You've been smart, Lisa. You gave yourself time to find out who you are and what you want."

"We're both smart," Lisa replied. "Look how far we've come."

"We've been lucky, too. Even when we had that small apartment we were lucky. We had control over our lives. Control...power...that's what this trial is about. Lots of women never have any."

"Right," Lisa agreed. Then she added, "But one day you came home quoting Blaise Pascal, determined to throw away your control."

"Ah, yes. 'The heart has reasons, which reason knows nothing of.' " Nicola smiled wryly at the memory. "Well, I thought Monsieur Pascal could explain my falling in love with Andrew better than I could."

Before Lisa could respond, the waiter came to ask if they'd like dessert. Noticing the time, Nicola pushed back her chair. She asked for the check, then turned back to Lisa. "It's awfully late. I've got to get back to nailing Faisal's hide to the proverbial barn door."

"Run along," Lisa replied, standing to press her cheek against Nicola's. "My treat today. I'm very proud of you. Win or lose, you've made your mark today." Then, grinning impudently, she added,

"Hang in there. And I still say Andrew's a rat not to have shared this day."

As Nicola's taxi sped toward the courthouse, she pushed Lisa's parting remark to a far corner of her consciousness. She needed to concentrate now on her client's problems, not her own.

BACK IN COURT, Nicola was surprised by the defense's closing arguments. She had expected them to be brief after the lengthy trial, but, apparently determined to lay out every possible piece of evidence in Gibran's favor, Simon Krantz spoke for more than two hours. He spoke persuasively, as the highest-paid divorce lawyer in Washington might be expected to do. Nicola had to acknowledge that Krantz was delivering a brilliant rebuttal to her own impassioned argument. Abruptly she came down from the high she'd been on.

When Krantz finally finished, the judge asked formally, "Has anyone any further evidence to submit?" There was no response, and he continued, "Ladies and gentlemen, the matter is under submission. You will be notified of my judgment."

As she and Amanda rose to leave, Nicola had the awful feeling that she had lost. Krantz had looked so confident...and something about the firm way the judge had said he would notify them of his decision made her feel that he'd already made up his mind. The thought of failing hurt even more than she had anticipated, especially since she had felt so confident about her closing argument that morning. Had she been persuasive, she wondered now.

Amanda seemed to share Nicola's sudden pessimism, for she said, "Whatever happens, I appreciate your hard work. I don't think anyone could have done a better job than you have."

"I hope I've been good enough, Amanda," Nicola replied, accepting the fact that there was nothing more she could have done to win the case. All that remained now was to wait for the judge's decision. She hoped fervently that he wouldn't take too long.

EXPERTLY, NICOLA GUIDED her BMW through the familiar streets of the exclusive suburb of Georgetown, past the immense federal and Victorian mansions of old wealth and new power on Dumbarton Street. The high-walled gardens and neat brick town houses of the upwardly mobile Washingtonians went past in a blur. For once Nicola didn't take note of the gently flowing Chesapeake and Ohio Canal as it meandered through the district.

Turning north on Twenty-eighth Street, the small car climbed easily up the gentle incline before passing through wrought-iron gates crowned with gold leaf. She drove past the tall old magnolias that were just beginning to bloom and stopped in front of the genteel Georgian mansion she'd left early that morning.

Deliberately putting aside her anger at Andrew, she composed herself and replayed in her mind the defense's final summation. She'd feel better after discussing it with Andrew. He had a marvelous ability to see both sides of a legal question. All at once she felt drained. She'd enjoy a hot bath and a leisurely dinner.

As soon as Nicola opened the massive front door, Thomas, their butler, came toward her. "I'm glad to see you, Mrs. Mather. Mr. Mather's dressing. He's been anxious about you."

Andrew dressing...then she remembered. The Kennedy Center Gala. Oh, damn! Surely Andrew would understand that she was simply too tired to go out this evening.

She hurried up the stairs to find Andrew standing in front of his dressing-room mirror, struggling to adjust his black tie.

"Hi, let me help you," she offered softly, walking up to him. She pulled the tie loose from its knot. Drawing the tie from his collar, she kissed him. "Since this isn't a command performance, let's stay home," she urged. "I'm so full of the trial, and there's so much I want to talk to you about."

At her mention of the trial, Andrew disengaged himself from her embrace and shook his head. His smile was pleasant enough, but the warmth that usually shone from his eyes wasn't there. "No, dear, we need to attend this gala. And you're already quite late. Please hurry, I hate—"

"Yes, Andrew," Nicola interrupted, furious at his lack of consideration. "You hate to make an entrance." Stung by his rebuff, she hurriedly pulled out a red taffeta evening gown from the closet. At the same time she grabbed a pair of silver pumps from the shoe rack. "I'll just slip into this and fix my hair."

Without looking again at Andrew, she undressed, then slipped on the evening gown. Dramatic and stunning, with huge sleeves, a deeply plunging neckline and a full skirt, it showed off Nicola's figure to perfection.

Andrew stood watching her silently as she sat down at the dressing table and twisted her hair into a chignon. Clearly trying to make amends, he asked, "How did the trial end?"

She recognized his effort at peacemaking. But it was too little and too late to make up for what had been lost that day. However, realizing this was not the moment for a confrontation, she forced a light touch as she answered, "With a whimper instead of a bang, I'm afraid. Why don't you go on downstairs. I'll just be a minute."

When he was gone, Nicola opened her jewelry case. She selected diamond earrings and a diamond-and-pearl choker from among the mass of glittering jewels. Then she rose, grabbed a beaded evening bag and mechanically transferred makeup and a comb into it.

As she left the room, she caught a glimpse of herself in the full-length mirror. Her hair shone pale gold in the soft lamplight, and her skin was ivory against the deep red of the dress. *The transformation's complete,* she acknowledged angrily. *The lawyer who plied her skills so adroitly just a brief time ago is once again the social butterfly, a fragile stunning creature suitable to adorn a possessive arm.*

When they walked into the red-carpeted grand foyer of the Kennedy Center for the Performing Arts, Nicola noticed with relief that everyone still seemed to be mingling outside the concert hall. Fortunately the concert hadn't begun yet. The formally dressed people who stood under the long sparkling chandeliers were among the most important in Washington. At one time Nicola would have felt a surge of pride at knowing that she was with one of the most powerful men in a town of powerful men. Instead all she could think of was her disillusionment.

A few minutes later, seated beside Andrew, Nicola listened to the rustling sounds of the audience settling itself—the soft whisper of silk, the muffled greetings, the discreet shifting to observe latecomers. Sitting there, she thought about Andrew.

As the houselights dimmed and the curtains parted, she realized that when she'd married him, she'd wanted someone to lean on, someone who knew so much more than she. Someone to make her feel important and loved and secure. Someone to come between her and the terrors of the long dark night.

A father.

Finally she had admitted what she had never been able to face previously. She had married Andrew for reasons that had very little to do with romantic love.

It was all too easy to see now how it had happened. Her mother, who came from a genteel but poor Virginia family, had married well. Edmund Wynter had had wealth and breeding. He didn't have sensitivity. When Nicola was eight, her mother did what was unacceptable in her social circle—she left her husband for a poor but immensely charming artist. She gladly gave up wealth and social position for love. But then her lover died, and she was alone. And Edmund Wynter wasn't the sort to forgive. He turned his back, not only on his ex-wife but on his daughter, as well.

Edmund Wynter wasn't the only member of this family drama who was unforgiving. In that year of being eight, except for her mother, Nicola lost her entire family—grandparents on both sides, aunts, uncles and cousins. She lost both her position in a secure family structure and her place, her home.

As she grew up, Nicola told herself she didn't miss her father or any of the rest of them, but she did. By eight, the imprint of belonging was indelibly stamped on her person. Her mother managed to provide adequately for the two of them, but the effort used up her energies. She simply was not prepared for the role life had handed her. The summer before Nicola began law school, her mother's car slammed into a stalled truck, and Nicola was left quite alone.

When Nicola met Andrew, it was as if a huge empty hole in her life had suddenly been filled to the brim. Voluminous copy, some of it harshly critical, was written about the surprising match between the beautiful young law student and the dynamic legendary attorney who was thirty-two years her senior. She married Andrew in the magnificent Washington Cathedral, with Lisa as her only attendant and a the-world-be-damned expression on her lovely face. Suddenly she went from the quiet obscurity of a first-year-law student living in a small apartment to a position as one of the brightest stars in the exclusive circle of the power elite in Washington. At first she hadn't minded being placed on a pedestal by Andrew, because at the same time she was at the center of his exciting life. But now she no longer wanted to be on the periphery of Andrew's career; she wanted her own glory.

She didn't understand why Andrew didn't want that for her.

Their marriage had worked well in the beginning, she told herself. The problems had developed recently, when their roles as mentor and protégé had changed. When one partner changed, the partnership changed, she mused. She was no longer the shy girl Andrew had married. She had become a confident independent woman. Why was he less than enthusiastic about her transformation, she wondered. Surely he wouldn't be threatened by her success—his was so much greater.

The pianist began the calm and flowing figures that open the romantic and bittersweet *Moonlight Sonata*—four groups of triplets against changing harmonies formed each measure of the introduction, and then came the gently melancholy song of resignation. As Nicola listened, her thoughts drifted back to the beginning of her relationship with Andrew....

Nicola, barely twenty-one, had been a first-year student at Georgetown University Law School. Andrew had come to lecture to one of her classes. She'd been overwhelmed by this multifaceted man. He was a courtroom genius, a best-selling author on the nature of the law—and even at fifty-three, still an undeniably attractive and most eligible bachelor.

Growing up in a small Virginia town under her mother's watchful eye hadn't prepared her for life in a city like Washington, where everyone else seemed so much more sophisticated and knowledgeable. When Andrew had actually seemed impressed at the quality of her questions, she was flattered. When he'd later asked her out to dinner, she was surprised. And when he'd proposed, she was deliriously happy.

The proposal came at the end of a day when they had been hiking in the mountains. When they returned to Andrew's magnificent home, Nicola felt out of place in her faded jeans and turtleneck sweater. Taking her gently by the hand, Andrew led her up the curving staircase to the master bedroom. For a long time he simply sat on the bed, holding her, as the evening light came through the tall windows, the dusky golden rays diffused through the leaded panes.

His voice, when he finally spoke, was reassuring yet tinged with passion. At the same time that he whispered endearments to her, his hands caressed her face, her neck, her shoulders, finally lingering softly on her breasts.

She didn't have to tell him she was a virgin. It was obvious in the way her body shivered at his touch, the way she watched him with both uncertainty and eagerness. She wished she could tell him how badly she wanted him, how much she wanted to please him, but she didn't know how to put this desire into words without sounding young and foolish.

So she said nothing, hoping desperately that her quiet pliability told him what her voice couldn't. At that moment, all she could think of was him, his feelings, his needs, his pleasure. She felt as bathed in the joy of loving him, being there with him, as the room was bathed in the amber light streaming through the window from the setting sun. It was for her a golden time.

In her silence she looked at him closely, observing everything about his face—his tanned smooth skin; the only wrinkles, squint lines at the corners of his pale eyes; iron gray at his temples; still black eyebrows that she lightly traced as he leaned toward her. . . .

"Don't be afraid," he said, smiling tenderly. "I'll never hurt you."

It was only slightly a lie. He was so patient, so gentle, that when the pain came it was fleeting, quickly superceded by a feeling so profound, so overwhelming, that even the memory of the pain was obliterated.

In the dusk her voice sounded soft and childlike, "Andrew?"

"Yes, little one."

"I love you."

There was a long pause, during which Nicola feared that she'd gone too far, saying words that perhaps Andrew didn't want to hear. The experience that meant so much to her might mean very little to him.

Then abruptly, as if he had made up his mind suddenly on a thorny problem and was determined not to turn back, he responded firmly, "I love you too, little one. With all my heart." Unexpectedly he finished, "And I want to marry you."

Nicola was stunned. Disbelief mingled with a tremendous sense of pride that this man whom she had idolized wanted her. *Her.* Realizing that her silence might mislead him, she answered quickly, "I want to marry you, too."

"Don't answer too quickly," he admonished. "Think about it. After all, I am a great deal older than you." Then he told her he had been married once previously—during World War II, in Paris after the liberation. "I loved her very much," he said. "And when she died after only a few weeks, I thought I would never feel that kind of love again." Then, turning to face Nicola squarely, he finished almost angrily, "But I have felt it again, with you. And I promise you—I will keep you happy and safe and secure for as long as I live."

After their wedding, Nicola continued attending law school during the day. In the evenings she and Andrew went to parties and concerts or enjoyed quiet evenings at home. As Andrew told Nicola of his important cases, she listened and learned. She had everything she thought a woman could possibly want: a stimulating career and an adoring husband. A princess in a fairy tale—she had expected to live happily ever after.

Now, seven years later, after the pressure of law school had been replaced by the frantic pace of actual practice, she was beginning to feel a vague restlessness, like a racehorse being firmly reined in when he longs to run full out. . . .

Nicola listened to the intricate pattern of the music, each movement independent, varying in mood and tempo, yet bonding, blending, to form the whole composition. This, she thought, was how a relationship between a man and a woman should be. Not predictable harmony, but distinct counterpoint, both equal, separate, yet coming together for a greater fulfillment than either could know alone. As she listened to the pianist evoke with wonderful clarity the structural themes of the fourth movement, she was entranced. Sometimes his playing was gentle, almost languorous, and sometimes it was bright with energy and he drew upon the full crashing powers of the piano.

Superimposed over the music were the happenings of that day—the quarrel with Andrew in the morning and his lack of caring in the evening, Lisa coming to support her and the excitement of delivering her final argument in Amanda's behalf. Like the music so had been the day. Some of the melody was bright with energy and golden with promise, but woven through the harmony and rhythm were passages of contrasting tempo and interpretation. If the performer was careless and struck the wrong note, the effect was discordant and the performance marred. Like the day. That day should have been a gloriously happy day, from early morning until that moment. It was her day to perform, and Andrew should have given her star billing. Wasn't that what he'd promised that first time? "I will keep you happy and safe and secure for as long as I live."

As the music ended, Nicola lifted her chin and squared her lovely white shoulders. Then she joined the audience in a standing ovation for the pianist. His had been a superb performance; he had lived up to his star billing.

At home Andrew declined anything to eat. He was tired, he said, and wanted to retire. Nicola stood a moment watching him climb the curving oak staircase to the second floor. He was, she knew, also declining any discussion of their differences.

It had been a long time since that lunch with Lisa. She was starving. In the kitchen she concocted a magnificent triple-decker ham-and-cheese on rye, topped with rare roast beef on whole wheat. She added a crisp dill pickle and two cherry tomatoes to the plate. Then she poured a tall glass of milk and carried the tray into the dining room.

This room and her bedroom were the two rooms Andrew had asked her to redecorate. It was a sophisticated yet somehow comfortable room. Pleated rosy-brown Suleido fabric covered the walls and swept across a corner of a mirrored wall. The oblong oak table was only one of the many priceless antiques Andrew had found in his world travels. The Louis XV chairs surrounding it were still covered in their original leather. And on the table was a vase of white freesias.

Nicola lit the white tapers in the Georgian silver candlesticks, then sat in solitary elegance. *There's something incongruous about this scene,* she told herself with a grim smile. *I hope it isn't prophetic.* Andrew used to enjoy having a late-night snack before going up to bed. As she bit into the sandwich, it occurred to her that this was his favorite. It also occurred to her that he'd been the one who usually made the sandwiches, telling her just to sit there and be beautiful. And after they'd finished, he would begin removing her jewelry and unfastening her buttons or unzipping her zipper as they made their way up the stairs.

When had all this change begun, she asked herself. With the Gibran case—that was when, she answered, realizing that indeed she had been wrapped up in the case. But she and Andrew had managed to survive several important cases that he had defended, her heart argued. Ah, but that was different, cautioned her head. That didn't count.

Sighing, she rose and went up to her bedroom. She sat in front of the vanity table. She wore only a lace-edged, peach-colored silk teddy. As she loosened her hair from the restrictive chignon at the base of her neck, she brushed it out slowly and methodically and watched Andrew sleeping.

Filled with a vague stirring that she was loathe to analyze, she hurriedly slipped out of the teddy and into a nightgown, a bare little wisp of emerald green silk. Then she slipped quietly between the sheets, pressing her body against Andrew, who continued to breathe with measured regularity.

After a moment she turned over onto her own side of the bed and sighed deeply. It wouldn't have changed anything, she knew, even if they had made love. They had crossed their Rubicon.

CHAPTER TWO

A WEEK LATER Nicola sat in her office, hurrying through her work so she could leave early enough to have plenty of time to dress for the ultraformal party at Beechwood estate. When the door flew open, her first thought was mild irritation that the person hadn't bothered to knock. But looking at the smiling excited face of her secretary, Cheryl, she realized something important was up.

"The *Post* just called," Cheryl announced breathlessly. "They've learned the decision in the Gibran case. You won, Miss Wynter! And they're saying it's the largest divorce settlement in history!"

Cheryl grinned happily when Nicola reacted with stunned amazement and relief.

"The judgment should be delivered any minute," Cheryl continued. "But in the meantime, do you want to talk to the reporters?"

As a wave of exultation washed over Nicola, her expression relaxed into a huge Cheshire-cat grin. "I certainly do! This is one time I can't wait to talk to them!"

After giving the *Washington Post* reporter her response to the news, she quickly scanned the opinion that arrived almost immediately. Amanda was awarded everything Nicola had asked for her, and the judge had denounced Gibran in scathing terms.

Awed by the magnitude of her victory, Nicola sat transfixed for several seconds. Then, grabbing her purse and ignoring the work that remained on her desk, she ran out of the office. She couldn't wait to tell Amanda the news, and she knew her telephone would be busy with reporters trying to reach her.

After a short joyous conversation with an immensely relieved and grateful Amanda, Nicola raced to Andrew's office. She was told he left early. *So he's heard,* she thought. *He's probably waiting for me with a bottle of chilled champagne. Now that I've won.*

She hurried home, leaving her car at the front door. She quickly looked in the living room and Andrew's den, then raced up the stairs to their bedroom. To her surprise, he wasn't waiting with champagne. He was dressing for the party and hadn't heard of her victory.

"Oh, Nicola," he began as she stopped in the doorway. "I'm glad you're early. We're supposed to stop by—"

"Andrew, the decision in the Gibran case was handed down today. I won!"

He hesitated, then in a tight voice said, "Congratulations, my dear. I'm sure this is just the first of many big victories for you."

His words were correct. It was his tone that was all wrong.

"Andrew!" Nicola protested, her voice shaking with outrage at his formality, his lack of enthusiasm.

"Why are you acting this way? My God, I've been so glad for you for everything you've achieved. Why aren't you glad for me?"

Walking up to her, he put his arms around her and kissed her. "I'm glad you won, Nicola. I'm not glad you took the case in the first place. I've made my position clear. Now let's put this whole thing behind us. Please hurry and dress. We're supposed to arrive in time for cocktails at Beechwood." He left then, saying he had a call to make and would wait for her in the den.

As he left, she felt torn between fury and resignation. A lukewarm congratulations and her big victory was dismissed—their big conflict was dismissed. Did he really believe he should tell her which cases to take? What had changed him so? Was he threatened by her success? If so, he wasn't being consistent. During the first years of their marriage, he'd taught, shared, encouraged. It couldn't be that he was threatened, Nicola decided. His own reputation in the legal community placed him far above her.

If I'm not threatening to him as a lawyer, am I threatening as a wife, she wondered. *Is his love for me conditional—if I assert my rights, will he withdraw his love?*

As she slowly undressed, then soaked in a hot tub, she felt her excitement wither and die. She thought of all the times she had toasted Andrew's brilliant victories. Even if he hadn't wanted her to take the case, since she had—and especially since she had won— couldn't he be generous?

Was the age difference between them troubling

him, she wondered. She had wanted to ask him that question but was reluctant to bring up a sensitive subject. Did he fear she was coming into her own power just as his was beginning to peak? But if he loved her, how could this be a problem? Nicola felt a chill at the possible answers. There wasn't anything either of them could do about the fact that she was twenty-eight and he sixty.

BEECHWOOD WAS ONE of the most magnificent of the old Washington estates. Located at the top of a hill in Georgetown, it was a huge red-brick manor house surrounded by ornate gardens. The long winding drive that led up to the house was lined with tall beech trees. The numerous mullioned windows on the front of the house were brightly lit, and formally dressed people were pouring in, laughing and talking happily. It was a happy festive scene, one that Nicola wished fervently she could avoid.

As they entered the foyer, with its terrazzo floor and ornately carved ceiling, Nicola said in a low voice, "Andrew, let's not stay late. I'm really tired. It's been a long day."

"You'll perk up when you've got some food in you."

Nicola didn't respond. Mary Jayne Wilson always served an interesting array of hors d'oeuvres at her cocktail parties. Nicola had tried to eat a hot crab puff, but it wouldn't go down. It couldn't get past the knot of anger that lodged in her throat. She'd accepted a glass of white wine and had carried it with her the entire time they were at the Wilsons'. She'd used it to fend off further hospitality.

The Wilsons were longtime friends of Andrew's and had children older than Nicola. They'd made the obligatory comment of congratulations on the Gibran case, but Nicola could sense they were as disdainful as was Andrew of the case. She wondered if it was the Arab connection and the nouveau-riche connotation of the trial that apparently offended the gentry, Andrew included. Or was it because Amanda Gibran's rightful due had become a focus for women's rights? Either way, Nicola was totally unprepared for the lack of warmth, interest, concern even, for the outcome of the trial. She had the distinct feeling that Mary Jayne would have much preferred the subject of the Gibran decision not be discussed at her party.

The entire time they were there had been awkward for Nicola. There wasn't one sincere exchange of conversation. It was for her a king-size example of cocktail-party superficiality. She made herself as unobtrusive as possible, kept a smile on her face and waited anxiously for time to leave.

For Andrew to say now that she'd perk up after eating was insulting. But Nicola knew timing was as important in social exchange as it was in courtroom drama. This wasn't the time for further dialogue regarding her need for Andrew's understanding.

They entered the ballroom, where a string quartet was playing softly and tables were covered with a dazzling variety of delicacies. After greeting their host and hostess, they turned as someone called, "Andrew, hello."

It was Harold Wellman, one of the most distinguished attorneys in Washington and a close friend of Andrew's. With him was his charming wife, Betsy. Unlike most of Andrew's friends, Harold treated Nicola as if she were an intelligent worthwhile person in her own right. In fact, when she graduated from law school near the top of her class, he'd offered her a position in his own firm.

But Nicola, not wanting to trade on Harold's friendship with Andrew, had turned down the offer that would have been irresistible to any other novice lawyer. "Harold...and Betsy," she said, "how nice to see you both. It's been a long time."

Andrew shook hands with Harold and kissed Betsy on her cheek, telling her how lovely she looked.

Betsy hugged Nicola affectionately and then stepped aside for Harold to do the same. They both offered such warm congratulations that Nicola felt tears sting her eyes. Other than the pleased cry from Lisa when Nicola had called from Amanda's before rushing home to Andrew, these were the first truly sincere felicitations she'd heard. She was deeply touched.

Then Harold told Andrew that he'd really appreciate a few minutes of shoptalk with him, if the ladies would forgive them.

"Of course," Nicola acquiesced. "Betsy and I will sit in the corner and catch up." But before they could turn away, she heard Harold tell her to wait.

"Nicola," he said, "I have a friend who wants to meet you. Thomas St. Ives. He's from England. Perhaps you've heard of him?"

Indeed I have, Nicola thought, intrigued.

Without waiting for her reply, Harold continued, "Well, he's going to drop in tonight, and he's hoping to see you. I told him I was quite sure you'd be here." Then he and Andrew excused themselves and left to find a quiet place to talk.

It was always a pleasure to spend even a few minutes with Betsy Wellman. And Nicola realized that a few minutes would be all she'd have. Betsy was greatly admired by both men and women. She was the epitome of what Nicola thought a mature woman ought to be—witty, attractive, accomplished.

"So, you are enjoying your well-deserved accolades?" Betsy asked. "Is Andrew being loving or hateful?"

Startled by the on-target question, Nicola answered honestly. "I'm furious at Andrew. . . and puzzled by his reaction. I was aware that he disliked my taking this case, but until last week, on the final day of the trial, we had no direct confrontations. Ever since, we seem to be on a collision course." She paused and gave a small rueful laugh. "I'd be embarrassed at such a revelation if I didn't need so much to share it. Forgive me, Betsy."

"No need to apologize, dear." The older woman drew Nicola to stand before one of the tall mullioned windows that overlooked the terrace. "Beautiful gardens, don't you think. And I love that fountain," she said. "Do you know Shelley's poem about Arethusa?"

Nicola knew that Betsy was giving her time to compose herself, and she was grateful. She was familiar with the fountain. It was constructed of stone and decorated with sculptured figures of a beautiful wood nymph and the river-god, Alpheus. Soft lighting enhanced its beauty, illuminating the figures and the dancing waters. ''Tell me the story,'' she said.

''Arethusa was an attendant of the goddess Artemis. One day while she was bathing in the river, Alpheus fell passionately in love with her. To save her, Artemis changed the maiden into a fountain. Alpheus still pursued her in the shape of a swift torrent. In pity, Artemis opened an underground passage for Arethusa's escape. She fled through it until she came again to the upper world on the plains of Sicily. But the god Alpheus followed her. Greek legend says the waters of Alpheus and Arethusa are contained in a sparkling fountain on the seacoast of Sicily.''

Nicola smiled at her friend. ''Are you telling me that things might be worse. Andrew could turn into a—''

Betsy interrupted Nicola with a wave of her hand. ''I'm not sure what inspired that yarn, dear. I just know you and Andrew have to work things out. These are changing times for both of you. I care about both of you. It's too bad that—'' She never got to finish her sentence, for a group of friends came to chat with her. She gave Nicola a fierce hug and whispered, ''Take time to work it out.''

Kissing Betsy on her cheek, Nicola thanked her and turned away to wander through the crowd.

The sumptuously catered party was well attended by the movers and shakers in Washington's power elite. They were all dressed in their glorious best— rich fabrics cut in elegant styles, glittering jewels, thick furs. Nicola herself was resplendent in a black, hand-beaded sheath that clung to her every curve. The pristine high neckline in the front was in stark contrast to the daringly low cut of the back. Aside from engagement and wedding rings, which were never off her hand, her only jewelry was simple pearl earrings. Despite the simplicity of her attire, she turned heads even in this room of beautiful, gorgeously dressed women.

As Nicola circulated through the large ballroom, the conversations she heard were all about politics and those in power. The talk was boringly repetitive. She had heard it all before at an endless succession of parties that were really just working occasions. The only concession to the hour was that people wore formal clothes and drank expensive liquor.

This party was no different from the others. There was the usual assortment of at least one senator, one congressman, several ambassadors, one member of the administration, one political columnist, one reporter, one good gossip and a variety of hangers-on who listened avidly to every word.

The women, most of whom were simply content to bask in their husband's reflected glory, hovered around the edges of the small cliques of men engaged in earnest conversation. Nicola had long ago stopped enjoying these affairs. This night she actively disliked them.

The music of the string quartet drifted softly over the insistent buzz of conversation. People bumped against her without apology. Apparently news of her stunning victory wasn't widespread yet, she realized. With a rueful smile, she thought, *I'm not yet* someone. The victory she had savored so deeply was beginning to seem hollow and unimportant.

"Mrs. Mather!"

Turning, Nicola saw a short, balding, elderly man with twinkling hazel eyes that seemed lit by a secret amusement.

"I was hoping to run into you here tonight. I'm Thomas St. Ives. I believe Harold Wellman spoke to you about me."

Surprised, Nicola barely managed a polite, "How do you do?" The little man, who was much shorter than she, seemed more like a kindly gnome than a renowned international attorney.

St. Ives gave Nicola a look so piercing and shrewd she immediately revised her opinion of him.

"I must say, I'm very pleased that our social plans coincided tonight," he began. "You see, I've been badgering Harold to arrange a meeting with you. I sat in on part of your trial and was most impressed with your handling of a difficult complicated case."

"Why, thank you, sir."

"You skillfully wove the emotional content of the case with the hard facts. And your understanding of the intricacies of Mr. Gibran's oil business was especially impressive. A client of mine who's in the oil business accompanied me to the trial, and he, too, commented that you definitely knew what you were about."

Looking vaguely around the huge crowded room, he finished, "He's here somewhere, I think, if he hasn't grown bored and left. I particularly wanted him to meet you, but he has a marked distaste for this sort of affair and may have run off."

"I couldn't blame him," Nicola replied, smiling. "It isn't my idea of fun, either."

"No, my dear, I'm sure it isn't," St. Ives answered perceptively. "I imagine your idea of fun is a difficult case where the odds are against you but you know you're in the right."

"There is a certain stimulation to such a challenge," Nicola admitted with a smile, liking St. Ives more and more.

"Perhaps we could find a more private place to talk," he continued, looking around the crowded ballroom. "I'd like to discuss a business matter with you. I wouldn't interrupt your evening, but you see I'm leaving for England tomorrow, and this is, unfortunately, the only chance I have to speak directly to you."

"Of course," Nicola said, intrigued. "There's a small library over there." She pointed to a door in the far corner of the room.

"Very good."

Formally offering Nicola his arm, he escorted her through the crowd, seemingly oblivious to the odd couple they made—she so tall and willowy, he so short and round.

The library was a small, book-lined room with several comfortable chairs and a briskly burning fire in a red-brick fireplace. It was specifically kept available for important guests who wanted to conduct private conversations away from the hearing of other guests.

As Nicola settled into a wing chair, St. Ives began easily, "Now, then, Mrs. Mather, I should like to get straight to the matter at hand. Are you at all familiar with my firm?''

"Of course," she replied matter-of-factly. "I'm aware that you have offices in several countries.''

"Six to be exact," St. Ives explained, "including the United States. I'm over here now to oversee some important business at our Washington office. We employ about two hundred attorneys. I should like to add you to that number.''

Startled, she responded, "What?''

"I'm sorry, was I too abrupt? I've always been under the impression that you Americans prefer to come right to the point. Let me put this as clearly as possible. I am offering you a position with my firm. I think you're quite an exceptional lawyer and would be an asset to us. Let me assure you that you would find the salary generous and the work interesting.''

"I'm sure you're right on both counts," Nicola managed to respond, recovering her composure with difficulty. Never in her wildest imaginings had she expected something like this.

"And if you're concerned about leaving your husband, we could arrange for your headquarters to be in our Washington office. Though, frankly, you would be required to spend most of your time in London.''

Her mind was in a whirl. The offer was both exciting and disturbing.

Watching her carefully, St. Ives continued tentatively, "I'm sorry, you don't seem too taken with the idea. Somehow I rather expected you would find it intriguing.''

"Of course I find it intriguing," she burst out. "I'm both surprised and flattered. It's just . . . so unexpected. And I have other things on my mind at the moment."

"Yes, I can see that you do," St. Ives replied curiously. Then he continued, smiling. "Well, young woman, I'm sorry I can't give you more time to think this over, but I'm afraid I must have your answer before I leave in the morning. You see, I have a particular spot that must be filled soon, and if you won't take the position, then I must find someone else who will."

Nicola's mind raced as she thought of all this would mean—leaving her own fledgling practice, spending a great deal of time in London, going into a new area of law. To her surprise, she didn't feel dismayed by any of it. She simply felt it would be an exciting challenge.

But there was Andrew to consider. And she knew he wouldn't want a "part-time" wife. But, she thought hopefully, she could discuss it with him. Maybe somehow they could work it out.

She knew immediately that she wanted the opportunity very badly. And then, just when she was about to say, "May I give you my answer in the morning?" a disturbing thought occurred to her. "Mr. St. Ives, are you making me this offer because of my husband?" Her voice was calm, but inside she was in turmoil.

St. Ives looked surprised, then amused. "I hadn't considered such a thing, but I can understand how you might. Your husband is an important person in legal circles. However, you are a lawyer and should be able to look at things logically. Do you really believe that your relationship with him will be of any substantial importance in any of the foreign countries in which you'll be working? Your husband's influence and reputation simply won't be felt. You'll be entirely on your own."

Nicola sighed with relief. For the first time in seven years she knew that someone was seeing her for herself and not as an extension of Andrew.

"In that case, I'll consider the matter and call you in the morning," she responded simply.

"Good. I'll look forward to hearing from you."

He escorted her back to the ballroom, where he left her to look for his client. Nicola's mind raced as she considered how she would approach Andrew on this subject. Across the room she saw him still deep in conversation with Harold.

She wanted time and privacy to think about this marvelous offer. Through the open French doors she saw the garden. Quickly she went outside. Daffodils, roses and clematis were blooming in glorious profusion amid the polished tumbles of old boxwood and forsythia in a tangle of golden chrome. There were rare Oriental magnolias, with their small white suede blossoms. The mingled scent of all these blooms filled the air with heady perfume.

Water splashing in Arethusa's fountain muted the sounds of the party.

Looking up, Nicola saw one star shining more brightly than the others. Suddenly she remembered a childhood rhyme: "Starlight, starbright, first star I see tonight, wish I may, wish I might, have the wish I wish tonight."

What do I wish, Nicola asked herself silently. And

suddenly she knew—adventure, romance, a knight on a white steed. On this beautiful, sensual, early-spring evening in this garden of earthly delights, she wished that all her most secret fantasies might come true.

"Hello."

The voice startled her out of her reverie. It was vaguely Southern, deep, rich and commanding. Nicola had a good memory for voices. This was not someone she had met previously. Looking around, she finally saw where the voice had come from. A few feet away a man stood watching her.

Nicola was struck first by the man's height, which was well over six feet. He stood straight and tall and completely at ease. His bearing was impressive even though his hands were thrust loosely in his pockets, and his ruffled white shirt was open at the collar, as if he could take only so much formality.

He stepped forward and held out his hand. "I have you at a disadvantage. I know you're Nicola Wynter. I'm Logan James."

Nicola took his proffered hand. "Mr. James," she acknowledged. Then remembering, she corrected, "I'm really Nicola Wynter Mather."

"My pleasure," she heard him drawl in a quiet voice. Though their handshake was certainly circumspect, Nicola noted a surety in his clasp. He obviously meant it when he shook hands. As she met his direct gaze, she was reminded of . . . something. She couldn't quite recall what it was.

In the light from the ballroom she could see the man was handsome. His hair and full mustache were a light reddish brown, but the symetrically arched brows were dark. His eyes were wide set, tawny brown, with black-rimmed irises. What unusual eyes, she thought. There was something unusual too about his expression—a directness, a boldness. Suddenly she knew what it was that she was reminded of.

The previous week she'd attended the opening of a new gallery, and the "best of show" for nature photography had been a large color photograph of a majestic lion. The photographer had caught the arrogant bearing of the animal as, seemingly at ease, it surveyed its kingdom, its gaze commanding and breathtakingly dangerous.

As she stepped back, he released her hand. She was just a bit surprised at herself. Betsy's story about the river-god pursuing the maiden must have gone to her head. There was no reason for this man to remind her of the photograph. He wasn't arrogant. He seemed the epitome of graciousness. From that accent, Southern graciousness, she'd bet.

She looked up into his face and saw he was watching her. The expression in his eyes betrayed a hint of amusement and curiosity. His features were clean-cut and strong, from the high cheekbones to the stubborn chin.

"Are you enjoying the party, Mr. James?" she inquired, appreciating this exchange.

"I am now." He smiled and asked her if she believed in serendipity.

"Serendipity?" Well, she thought, this certainly was turning out to be an interesting evening for cryptic conversations. First with Betsy, then Mr. St. Ives, and now this Logan James wanted to discuss "serendipity."

"That's an aptitude for making fortunate discoveries accidentally."

"Yes, I know.... Do you do that often?" she couldn't resist asking.

"Often enough. Every time I strike oil there's an element of serendipity in it."

"There's also a lot of money and tons of high-tech equipment, to say nothing of a fleet of engineers," she said with a grin.

"That's called 'backup.'" Once more he held out his hand to her. "I understand by the six-o'clock news that congratulations are in order. May I offer mine on a job well done."

She put her hand in his and again felt his gentle strength. After a moment she reluctantly withdrew hers. "Thank you. I must say I was relieved to receive the telephone call this afternoon. This has been a very long week."

"I happened to be in court on the last day of the trial. I wasn't surprised to hear that the judge found in your client's favor. I was impressed with you then. I'm impressed tonight, too." His expression changed from a light bantering tone to a deeper huskier register. "You're absolutely beautiful. That gown—your hair and skin so fair against that black. Very impressive." He spoke slowly, the southern cadence softening the edges of his boldness.

Well, Nicola told herself, *I did stand here in the moonlight and wish for adventure.* The cut of her gown was daring, and while the bold compliment took her by surprise, she was glad she'd chosen this particular dress. She hadn't planned to wear it. It just happened to be the first one she'd grabbed. Serendipity, she wondered, amused at her interpretation. She hadn't heard many compliments that evening. Now that she'd recovered from her surprise, it was most pleasant. Keeping her own tone carefree, she replied, "You're rather impressive yourself, Mr. James."

His appreciative laughter was pleasantly unaffected. "Actually, I hate wearing a tux—as you can tell by my rebellious collar. And please call me Logan, Nicola."

She noticed he didn't ask permission to use her given name, but somehow she didn't mind. Obviously he wasn't one to stand on ceremony.

"Congratulations aren't enough," he continued. "We need champagne to toast. . . ." He stopped and, as if he felt foolish, shrugged. "But of course you've been toasted. And, I'm sure, appropriately wined and dined. Well, again, please accept my congratulations."

Not really sure of her reasons, Nicola decided to be candid. "As a matter of fact, Mr. James, Logan, the momentous occasion has not yet been properly toasted."

He looked directly at her, a slight frown creasing his forehead. "Really?" he drawled.

"Really." And with that admission to this total stranger, Nicola admitted fully to herself how deeply angry—how very unhappy—she was with Andrew for both his lack of interest earlier and his lukewarm acknowledgment of her success.

Suddenly, with that admission out of the way, she

was aware that she was hungry. "Not only have I not been wined...I haven't even eaten tonight," she said, looking up at him. She'd surprised him as much as he had her with his compliment. She studied him a moment, then smiled warmly at him, feeling her full lower lip tremble slightly.

Nonplussed for just an instant, he recovered and grinned broadly. "Well, you just wait. I'll be right back." He disappeared into the house. In a few minutes he returned with a tray holding two plates heaping with food, two crystal glasses and a bottle of champagne.

He stood on the terrace steps for a moment looking around the garden. "Let's use that bench down by the fountain," he said, leading the way.

What fun, Nicola thought, *this is the kind of thing that happens in movies.*

He poured the champagne, set down the bottle, handed her a glass and raised his. "Here's to—" he paused, and Nicola watched him deliberate, pleasure dancing in his eyes and curving his mouth into a broad smile. She wondered what he would say. "Beechwood," he finished, glancing around.

"Ah, yes," she agreed. "Let's drink to Beechwood." Sipping her wine, she smiled back at him and proposed a second toast. "And here's to a perceptive, sensitive, fair-minded judge."

Logan touched his glass to hers and drank. "What were you seeing up there in the sky when you first came out onto the terrace?" he asked curiously.

"I was wishing on the first star. You know that old rhyme, 'Starlight, starbright....'" Raising her glass with a flourish, she said, "Let's drink another toast to hopes and dreams and to Amanda...to all the Amandas whose dreams come true," and then she drained the last of the wine.

Quickly Logan picked up the bottle and poured a bit more champagne into both their glasses. Then, standing there quite close to her, he gazed at her. It was the same way he had looked at her when they'd first met. This time she let her glance move over the angles of his face, noting the high cheekbones, the set of his jaw, the firm mouth. She wondered if his mustache felt as silky as it appeared. They had walked to stand near the fountain, and his face was clearly illuminated by one of the garden lamps. She could see not only the strange tawny color of his eyes but the black-rimmed irises, as well. There was no barrier between his eyes, clear and shining, and hers.

A tender expression came over his face as he raised his glass in salute. "Once more, Nicola, congratulations. And to the happy times when dreams come true...."

"When dreams come true," she echoed softly. As she lifted her glass to drink, he let his gaze travel over her face, from her eyes to her mouth, then back to her eyes again. Then he smiled—a warmly intimate smile. It was as if he'd touched her lips with his. She felt her heart fall with a thud to the pit of her stomach and her throat constrict. For a split second she stopped breathing and her entire body was still.

As he stared at her, she stared, enchanted, back at him.

Nicola felt she stood on the edge of a chasm that

stretched deep and dark and inviting. With an effort she pulled herself back. She was married, she reminded herself. She wasn't free. This delicious excitement was forbidden to her.

Trying to rationalize her rapid pulse and shallow breathing, she told herself it was just chemistry. For some reason this particular man made the neurotransmitters that governed her physical responses go crazy.

A couple came onto the terrace and stood chatting on the steps leading down into the garden. After a moment they returned to the ballroom. The spell was broken.

"I. . . ." Nicola looked toward the house, then noticed the plates of food that Logan had set down on the bench. "I did mention dinner, didn't I. This looks delicious."

She sat down on the bench, and after a moment, he sat down, too.

As she picked up her plate, he said, "Tell me about yourself. Not the stuff the newspapers print. Really tell me about yourself."

Nicola buttered a piece of muffin. "Um, delicious," she said as she ate the small toasted muffin. "They're lemon. Did you get one for yourself?"

"I'm not fascinated with lemon muffins," he replied. "I want you to tell me about yourself. I've been following this case, and frankly, I'm curious about you."

She wondered what to tell this charming stranger about herself that would be honest but not embarrassingly revealing. This wasn't her night to be glib and superficial. She'd already revealed a great deal to Betsy Wellman this evening. Andrew would be shocked if he knew.

Some lines from a poem came to mind. She couldn't remember them exactly but it was something like, "What would happen if one woman revealed the truth about her life? The world would never be the same."

Would that tell anything about her to this man who was looking at her with such intense interest? Anyone would expect her to be flying high with happiness this evening. Yet she wasn't. She had all the trappings of success, but this evening she'd had to face the fact that in some very important areas of her life she wasn't at all successful.

"I love being a lawyer," she said, surprising herself. "I'm a good one, and I expect to be even better. With a few more cases like this one we're celebrating...." Her voice trailed off as she searched for something else to add.

"And," he encouraged, "you like winning. How do you feel about losing? Sometimes even good lawyers lose."

Nicola laughed. "Well, as Lisa used to say, winning is more fun than losing. And gets you a better grade."

"Who's Lisa?"

"Lisa Halloran. She's my closest friend."

The minute she said that, she realized what it implied about her marriage. Continuing slowly, she explained, "We met when we were both first-year law students. We shared an apartment before I married Andrew."

"And now you live in splendor and power," Logan

finished dryly. "Interesting. And does Lisa also live in splendor and power?"

"No. Splendor and power aren't high on her priority list. Ambition and accomplishments are." Then turning to look directly into his eyes, she insisted, "Now tell me about you."

"We haven't finished talking about you yet. Are splendor and power high on your list? Or do they just come with the territory?"

Nicola hesitated. She didn't want to discuss Andrew with this man. Even discussing him with Betsy made her feel disloyal somehow. Finally she answered his question carefully. "No, they weren't what I was looking for. I certainly never expected to find them to the extent that I have."

Pressing, he asked, "Do you consider finding them serendipity?"

There was a teasing note to his tone, and a slight smile softened the impact of the very personal question. Still, she knew very well what he was getting at.

Almost in spite of herself she answered frankly. "I was looking for security, I think. I lost mine at an early age." She played with the food on her plate rather than look at him directly. "My mother was raised with the idea that she must marry well. Her family lived in what I guess you'd call genteel poverty in Virginia. They were aristocratic but poor. She did as was expected. She married Edmund St. Clair Wynter. If you've been in the Virginia hunt country, you'll recognize the name," she said with an attempt at grim humor.

Even as she spoke, she realized that either her

brain was addled by all that had happened to her that day or this man was the easiest man in the world to talk to. *Oh, hell,* she thought, for once throwing caution to the wind. *He seems so interested. And tonight that's more intoxicating than champagne.*

"Anyway, my parents married and lived unhappily ever after. When I was eight my mother did the one courageous independent thing she ever did. She fell in love with an artist—a painter—and ran off with him."

Logan's eyebrows raised quizzically. "A romantic at heart, eh?"

"Oh, yes. She gathered up her courage, her personal belongings and me and moved in with him."

"Did they live happily ever after? Did her dreams come true?"

"No. The painter died shortly of pneumonia. My mother was completely ostracized by her own family, as well as by my father's. Of course my father never forgave her. He said she hadn't honored her commitments. I suppose she hadn't." But, Nicola thought, remembering his absence from her life, his own record of commitment left much to be desired.

Setting down her plate on the bench, she folded the white linen napkin and placed it beside the dish.

The waters in the fountain jetted and splashed softly, their action lively and festive against the subtle lighting illuminating the basin and sculptured figures. As a soft breeze wafted past, a familiar sweetness mingled with the perfume of roses, and Nicola glanced around to see a blossoming cherry tree. A whitewash of moonlight added its touch of lambent beauty to this garden scene.

She sighed and, looking into the eyes of this handsome stranger, finished candidly, "Anyway, she was on her own, with a child to raise and very little money with which to do it. She took too great a risk, you see. And lost everything."

He studied her, then the expression in his eyes changed, and he held her attention with a confident, almost commanding stare. Deliberately he placed his hands on her shoulders and turned her toward him.

"You're wrong, you know." His tone was firm. "About your mother losing everything, I mean. She took a chance, gained something, lost something. I'll bet if you asked her, she'd say it was worth it."

He was right. Her mother had told her once, long ago, that she never regretted her decision. It only bothered her that Nicola had to pay a price, too, losing father, family and financial security.

Then the hands that were loosely holding her shoulders tightened, and he drew both himself and Nicola to stand. He gazed down at her, and the expression in his eyes, which had been intent but unreadable, changed subtly.

She looked into those eyes and saw raw naked desire dawning in them. Her breath caught as she realized that the same thing must be evident in her own expression.

And then, as if it were the most natural thing in the world, he pulled her into his arms and kissed her deeply.

CHAPTER THREE

THERE WAS NO THOUGHT, no reason, only pure physical sensation. . . his lips on hers in a kiss that was searing in its intensity, his chest hard against her full breasts, his arms holding her as if they would never let her go.

My God, my God, Nicola thought from somewhere deep within the center of her being. She felt the firmness of his lips, the silky bristle of his mustache. . . she'd never before kissed a man with a mustache. It felt wonderful. Hard hands spanned her shoulders. . . he smelled of lime after-shave. That pleasant scent registered as an after-shave her grandfather had worn. All these flashes of awareness and memory and pleasure caused desire to rise in Nicola until she was suffused with an answering passion.

My God, her heart cried in response to his kiss.

In one breathless instant he made her feel like a total innocent again, as if she knew nothing of sexual desire. What she had taken for passion before was a pale superficial thing compared to this—this fire and ice.

He stripped bare her senses as her body shuddered and pressed even harder against his hard muscled frame. The scent of him sent her blood racing through her veins, and she felt vibrantly alive.

This had never happened before. Everything about her that was careful, deliberate, guarded, evaporated instantaneously. She was utterly pliant beneath the bold caresses of his wandering hands. His fingertips traced the curve of her bare back, skin against skin. From the nape of her neck to the tiny hollow beneath her waist, they explored her. A frisson of desire raced up her spine.

She didn't want his hands to stop, for everywhere they touched, her body was awakened, alive, on fire. She wanted to give of herself totally, to hold nothing back....

And then, in one awful blinding flash, reason returned.

She mustn't desire this man, couldn't give herself to him. She wasn't free. This kiss, this embrace, was forbidden.

She jerked away, as if pulled by a rope.

Andrew... what if Andrew should see, she thought with a growing sense of horror at her wantonness. Oh, God, he would never get over the hurt, the humiliation.

Guiltily she flashed a quick glance at the terrace, but it was empty. No one was watching. No one knew about this mad impulsive thing she had just done. No one but this Logan James and herself. And she knew she would never forget.

She stepped back from this compelling man who suddenly frightened her so. But her heartbeat was still strangely erratic, and she knew it was not the man who frightened her, but herself.

Other women, she knew, had affairs. In Washington marital fidelity wasn't considered crucial. What mattered was public loyalty. Nicola personally knew several women who assuaged their loneliness or their sense of unimportance compared to their powerful husbands by looking outside their marriage for fulfillment.

But not her. Until this moment she had never been tempted. And even now she couldn't give way to this seductive temptation. It would hurt Andrew too profoundly. And even if he never found out, Nicola knew she couldn't live with any sense of integrity.

Looking into the golden glowing depths of Logan's eyes, she said, "I have to go back inside." She finished shakily, "My husband will be looking for me."

He understood. He said nothing, but his look revealed that it wasn't any easier for him than it was for her.

But he didn't apologize for what had just happened. And for that she was glad.

Trying to restore some measure of order to the highly charged atmosphere, she added, "I'm sorry we seemed to talk only about me. I wish we'd got around to discussing you." Her tone was wistful.

"There's not much to tell," he responded. It also took a moment for his voice to smooth out a revealing huskiness. He drew a deep breath and gazed hard at her. "I look for oil, enjoy serendipity and believe wholeheartedly in taking risks—calculated ones."

That one short sentence was very enlightening. Nicola hesitated, all too aware of the double meaning in his words.

Then she saw Andrew standing in the open French

doors. She waved at him to indicate she would be right there. Turning back to Logan, she started to say something, then stopped. She couldn't say what was in her heart, and anything less would be insufficient. Finally she said simply, "Goodbye, Mr. James."

He hesitated, and Nicola could tell by the fierce expression in his eyes that he was torn by a tremendous internal struggle. At last, with a world of regret in his tone, he said slowly, "Goodbye, Mrs. Mather."

She walked past him, hurrying up to Andrew. She hoped he would take her home immediately. Home, where it was safe.

AS SHE LAY IN BED that night, Nicola tried not to think about that disturbing interlude in the garden. "Interlude" was the perfect word, she decided. What had occurred was an interlude in an otherwise well-ordered existence. It could never be anything else. But she knew she'd learned something extremely important about herself that night. She had learned that until this evening she'd held herself in check. Until this evening . . . when she had—in that moment it took Logan James to draw them both to their feet—*known* he was going to kiss her. And wanted him to. She'd deliberately stepped across that boundary line that divided safe familiar territory from uncharted lands. She knew now that she was capable of far greater depths of desire . . . passion . . . sexuality than she'd yet experienced.

She turned to look at her husband sleeping beside her, the moonlight revealing his face at ease. He had been good to her and for her. She was his wife, she reminded herself forcefully. She had to honor that commitment. She wanted to honor it. Go away, Logan James, she thought. *We met too late.*

She spent most of the night staring into the dark hours, which passed so slowly. The more she tried to relax and invite sleep, the more tense she became. Perhaps her subconscious self knew best. If she dared to sleep, she would dream of the tall handsome man whose tawny eyes held hers as his firm sensuous mouth came closer and closer until it touched her own. The touch and taste of his lips against hers was exquisitely sweet and satisfying.

She thought about St. Ives's offer. Did she dare? She knew Andrew wouldn't be happy about it, but at this point in their marriage things were far from perfect.

As Betsy had said, they'd have to work things out.

Finally, as dawn began to replace the grayish dark, she made her decision that she would speak to Andrew about it in the morning. She couldn't tell him why, but she knew it would be good for her to be so channeled and challenged. Then she slept.

AT BREAKFAST THE NEXT MORNING, Nicola waited until they were having their final cup of coffee. "Andrew, did Harold mention anything about Thomas St. Ives to you last night?"

Surprised at her question, Andrew answered quickly, "Why, no. Although I recall now that he said St. Ives wished to meet you."

"Yes. He did."

"I beg your pardon?" Andrew was puzzled at her cryptic reply.

"He did meet me," Nicola explained. "We talked, and he offered me a position with his firm."

"Well, I'm sure that was very flattering. Of course you refused." Andrew sipped his coffee and watched her. "His headquarters are in London, right? You see, that trial did bring a certain amount of speculative interest in you. Probably all sorts of publicity-seeking firms will make you offers."

Andrew, Nicola thought, *you're missing the point of the trial and of me.* She surprised herself at the quiet calm tone of her voice. "I told him I'd discuss his offer with you. He said that while he prefers that I come to London, he could arrange for my headquarters to be in the Washington office. I'm going to call him this morning and discuss it further. It's a very tempting offer. Too tempting to refuse without very serious consideration."

"Very well. You do that, dear," Andrew remarked rising from the table. "Just don't commit yourself to anything. We'll talk later." And he was gone.

Before leaving for work, Nicola called St. Ives at his hotel. Just as she was about to give him her answer, he said, "I'm so sorry you didn't have an opportunity to meet my client last night. If you come to work for me, you'll be handling Logan's case."

Nicola was absolutely still for a moment. Then she responded in an odd strained voice, "Logan?"

"Yes, Logan James. He's the oilman I was telling you about. He's negotiating for drilling rights to a North Sea oil lease. But I digress, as usual. You've called to give me your answer. I hope it's yes."

Logan James. If she accepted this offer, she would

be working with *him*. She knew about oil-lease negotiations. She would be working with him for a long time, meeting with him, talking to him, spending a great deal of time with him.

She couldn't do it. It would be tempting fate, and she knew who would win.

"I'm so sorry," she heard herself say. "I'm afraid I have to refuse your very tempting offer. I simply couldn't be away from my husband that much."

She heard St. Ives sigh with disappointment. "I do understand, Mrs. Mather. I must admit, I rather expected this. But if you should ever change your mind, I hope you'll contact me. I shall always be interested in your services."

"Thank you, Mr. St. Ives. I appreciate the tremendous compliment you've paid me."

She hung up the telephone gently. For a long moment her hand rested on the receiver. It would have been so easy to say yes, to fly to London. . . to fly into Logan James's waiting arms. . . .

LOGAN SAT in his hotel room, waiting for Thomas's call. Thomas had said he would phone as soon as he heard from Nicola regarding the job offer. He looked at the clock on the desk for the tenth time in five minutes, then muttered impatiently under his breath, "Damn! What's taking so long?"

Unable to sit still any longer, he uncoiled his six-foot-three-inch frame from the chair and walked over to a window. But as he gazed out, his mind wasn't registering the cherry blossoms or the meandering Potomac River. He was remembering a garden and a star-filled sky—and Nicola Wynter Mather.

When he'd first seen her in the courtroom, he'd been impressed with her ability. When Thomas mentioned that he was thinking of hiring her, Logan immediately asked that she be assigned to his case. She was a damn-good lawyer, and at that point, that was his only interest in her.

Then he found himself free of appointments that last day of the trial, and he had returned to observe the bright young woman who'd been so disciplined in her presentation, arguments and rebuttals. When she was gathering herself together for her summation, he could almost see her passion for justice rise. In spite of an obvious shyness, there was a moment when those compelling aquamarine eyes swept across the court to zero in on that Gibran for a moment. As he'd watched her, Logan knew there was no way she had made eye contact with him when she'd turned back to the judge, but he had made contact with her.

Meeting her at Beechwood was no accident. As he stood by the window now, remembering, he smiled dryly at the effort he'd made in order to get an invitation to that party once Thomas had told him he'd try to contact her there. It had amazed Thomas, who was well aware of his dislike of huge impersonal social functions.

But Logan was driven by an intense desire to see Nicola again, to talk to her, to get to know her. He told himself he was being stupid, behaving like a lovesick adolescent. She was, after all, very married. But all the hard self-criticism in the world couldn't lessen that irresistible urge to see her again.

Once he got to the party, he felt even more like a fool. He was just persuading himself that he should leave, forget the whole ridiculous thing, when suddenly there she was, standing in front of him, a gift from the gods.

She'd looked like a dream come true...the moonlight turning her pale hair to molten gold, that magnificent gown revealing a figure so inviting that he felt the blood pound in his temples and his pulse race. He could no more walk away from her than he could stop breathing.

And then, when he introduced himself and she took his hand, acknowledging, "Mr. James," in a low confident tone, he suddenly felt as if he'd been hit with a ton of bricks.

It was all he could do to play it cool, make conversation, hide the fact that he wanted her more than he'd ever wanted any woman in his life. Her allure was not just her beauty, although she certainly was beautiful. It was not just because she was bright and accomplished, although she was that—in spades. It began that second time he observed her in court. And when he looked down into those lovely shining eyes in the garden, his heart recognized her as the one he'd been waiting for.

He shook his head ruefully now as he remembered that kiss. He wasn't cool then. All of that powerful feeling that had suddenly taken control of his senses was in that kiss.

Hell! he thought, *a man would have to be made of stone not to want her, to touch her, hold her, feel her softness against him. And I'm definitely not made of stone.*

When her husband had appeared and she'd said goodbye, it had taken all of his considerable willpower to let her walk away without a word.

I will *see her again,* he told himself now. *She'll come to London, and we'll work together. And somehow I'll find a way—*

The telephone rang.

He picked up the receiver before the first ring was over and said, "Hello?"

"Logan, it's Thomas."

"Yes, did you talk to Mrs. Mather?"

"I did, indeed. A remarkable woman," Thomas mused in his slow thoughtful way.

Get to the point, Logan wanted to shout, but he forced himself not to behave like a total fool.

"At any rate," Thomas finally continued after a pause, "she's declined my offer."

"What?"

"Says she can't be away from her husband that much. He'd not be pleased with such an arrangement. I told her I could appreciate her husband's sentiments."

When Logan didn't respond, Thomas continued, "Well, I suppose I'll see you at the airport."

"Yes," Logan finally answered in a voice that lacked his usual determination.

After hanging up, he stood there for a moment.

I could see her, personally ask her to take the job. She might very well do it, he told himself.

But he knew that what he was really saying was that he could take her away from Andrew Mather, if he tried.

"Damn!" he exploded. Why did she have to be married?

Morality and passion fought bitterly within him.

She's everything I want, he thought. *Beautiful, brilliant, proud. She fills an emptiness inside me that no one else has ever touched. And she wants me as much as I want her.*

But even as he argued with himself, he felt a growing sense of blackness descend on him. He'd known from the beginning that it wouldn't work. He couldn't take her away from Mather, who undoubtedly loved and needed her.

That was no way to start a life together. And he wouldn't settle for an affair with her, even if she could be persuaded to do it.

Logan James was a man used to getting what he wanted by hard work, determination, sheer effort of will. There had never been a woman he wanted whom he didn't have eventually. But not this one. This one was taken.

After so many years of playing the field, of having his fill of desirable women, Logan James had finally fallen in love. With a woman who was forbidden to him.

Poetic justice, he thought with a grim smile.

Walking over to the bar, he poured himself a stiff drink, then downed it quickly.

The many women he'd left by the way would find it amusing, he thought. Suddenly he laughed out loud. But it was a bitter sound, completely devoid of joy.

CHAPTER FOUR

FOR THE NEXT TWO WEEKS, Nicola kept herself very busy. Andrew, too, was especially preoccupied, with an important case that required several trips to Chicago. The hurried pace of their respective schedules bridged an awkward time.

One day, while Andrew was in Chicago, Nicola finished her work early. She called Lisa and arranged to meet later for dinner. Then she went home.

Leaving her car in front of the house, she started up the steps. She was surprised when, before she reached the door, it swung open, and Andrew stood there. He looked so incredibly tired and sad she was shocked.

"Andrew, darling," she said, hurrying toward him. "What's happened. I didn't expect you until tomorrow."

He didn't say anything. He just drew her inside and took her in his arms. He held her close, his cheek against her hair.

Nicola knew that something had touched him deeply. It couldn't be anything about his case, she told herself. He wouldn't react this way. Andrew might not be pleased with the court judgments he had to accept, but he was always philosophical.

No, she thought, whatever had shaken him so had

nothing to do with a legal decision. She leaned back in his embrace to look at him. "Andrew, please tell me what is wrong."

"I'm glad to see you, little one." Even his voice was subdued. "I don't know what brought you home early, but I'm most grateful to the Fates. Let's go upstairs."

Nicola caught the endearment. It had been a while since she'd heard that.

In their bedroom Andrew sat down in one of the wing chairs and looked out at the giant magnolia trees that dotted the estate. His expression remained somber.

Sitting across the small table from him, Nicola leaned her head against the back of the chair that matched the one he occupied and studied him. Obviously he needed time to sort out what he wanted to share with her.

Their room was a restful place, she thought. A cotton print in pale blue and white, copied from an eighteenth-century design, covered the walls and the bed. The round occasional table was draped in a deeper but complementary shade of blue. On the table was a lamp, a novel she was reading, and a crystal bud vase with a single long-stemmed rose. It was a Queen Elizabeth, delicately pink and very fragrant, her favorite, from their rose garden.

Late-afternoon light came through the tall windows, the dusky golden rays diffused through the upper panels of leaded panes.

"Did you see a ghost today, Andrew?" Nicola said with a small smile. When he continued to stare out the window, she urged, "Please tell me. Perhaps I can help. I know things have been—"

"I'm worrying you," he interrupted, turning to face her. Sitting on the edge of his chair, he leaned his elbows on his knees and laced his long fingers together. Tension whitened his knuckles. "Remember I told you about Gregory Dawson?" he asked.

"Yes. Your character witness." She did remember. Andrew had spoken to her about this affable man who was so crucial to his client's case. Dawson was testifying at risk to his own career promotion. But he'd told Andrew, "Hell, there's more important things to life than money." Andrew enjoyed the man and admired him.

"He's changed his mind?" she asked. "He's not going to testify?"

"We'd met for breakfast . . . and were to meet in court. Greg had an errand to run for his wife. There was an accident. His car was broadsided at an intersection. God, Nicola," he said, his voice breaking slightly, "he was only forty. Still had a son to raise . . . his wife. . . ." Andrew got up and walked around the room.

Nicola waited a moment before saying, "I'm so sorry, Andrew."

"I offered my help," he continued, "but there was nothing I could do. The judge gave us a postponement. Suddenly I couldn't wait to get home—to tell you I'm sorry about the quarrel between us."

Nicola rose from her chair and went to him. She put her arms around him and said she was sorry, too.

"I was wrong, Nicola. On the one hand I encouraged you as I did when you were first my student. As I still do those first-year students. 'Fight for what you think is right,' I tell them. Then, when you disregarded my wishes, I didn't like it. We were at cross-purposes on this Gibran case, but I shouldn't have let it threaten our happiness. Life's too short at best. And when, like poor Greg, your time's cut short...." He cupped her face between his hands and kissed her deeply. When he lifted his mouth from hers, he said, "I want to make love to you, little one. I want to be warmed by you. I've missed you these past weeks."

Later, as she lay in his arms, she heard him whisper, "You know, when you look like this, so very lovely, I wonder what I did to deserve having the winter of my life so blessed."

There was a note of love-sated huskiness in his normally deep commanding voice and something touchingly vulnerable in his eyes. He traced the contours of her face with his finger, just a light touching of love, now that his passion was spent.

"Remember that first time we made love here?"

Nicola nodded and covered his hand with hers.

"I told you I would be selfish to marry you, but I loved you. And wanted you."

"I know, Andrew," she broke in. "I wanted you, too."

"Change is inevitable," he continued. "There are some things we can't reverse. Like time...like Greg's time today." He turned his hand over and brought hers to his lips and kissed it. "I'm not being morbid, but what happened today made me think about things I should have said. Like never be afraid to reach out to all that life offers. That's what I did when I met you.''

A FEW NIGHTS LATER, dressed in an aquamarine-colored, pure-silk crepe-de-chine gown, Nicola walked with Andrew into the French Embassy. Her gown, cut on the bias, completely bared one shoulder. It was Andrew's favorite, and she'd worn it this evening for him. He said its blue green color matched her eyes.

Andrew quickly became the center of attention, as often happened. Harold was there, along with some other lawyers. Nicola joined in their discussion for a few minutes, then decided to look around for Betsy.

She wandered over to the buffet table. But the food didn't interest her. Accepting a glass of champagne from a passing waiter, she took a sip. The slight jolt of the bubbly liquid revived her, and she came to a decision. Purposefully she made her way through the crowd to the open French doors that led out to a deserted garden. Though it was late April, it was still cool, and no one else was strolling in the garden. For a few minutes, Nicola realized with relief, she could sit quietly, away from the noise and the pressure.

Voices rose and fell around her as she slipped through the French doors.

''Of course, she's known for years that he's unfaithful, but she's been the perfect little politician's wife, anyway....''

''He's really out, it's only a matter of time before he's fired, though they'll let him say he resigned.''

''While the Democrats are scrambling around looking for some sort of consensus....''

As Nicola gratefully left the noise behind her, making her way to a stone bench on the far side of the brick patio, she thought how similar these parties always were. The same things were always being said, only different people were saying them. Drinking in the cool night air, she was glad to be out of it.

"All alone?"

The voice was vaguely sarcastic and very familiar.

Looking up, Nicola saw Simon Krantz standing over her. She'd been so lost in her thoughts she hadn't even heard his approach.

Without being invited, he sat down next to her. Quickly finishing the tall drink in his hand, he set down the empty glass, then casually dropped his arm over the back of the bench, lightly brushing Nicola's bare back as he did so.

She shivered at his touch. It made her wish she'd worn something a little less revealing. In a courtroom, Simon Krantz was merely unpleasant, but alone in a dark garden, he was rather menacing.

When Nicola said nothing, he continued smoothly, "Somehow I thought you'd be here tonight. Everyone who is anyone is, I understand."

She'd have loved to quip then that she was surprised to see him there. She continued her silence, hoping this would discourage him and he'd simply go away.

"I've met your husband several times, but he never seems to know who I am. That surprises me. I would have thought you'd have mentioned me."

Andrew knows who you are, you fool, she said to herself. *He doesn't deign you worth acknowledging.* Aloud she commented, "I didn't discuss my case

much with him. He's been awfully busy this spring."
Nicola's tone was curt; she wished she had the nerve to
get up and leave.

"I've heard about the two of you, of course. The famous May-December romance."

Nicola felt a surge of angry defensiveness. She was
well aware that Krantz's remark was a thinly veiled in-
sult to Andrew.

Guessing Krantz to be in his early fifties, she said,
"He isn't so very much older than you." Then rising,
she finished, "I must rejoin my husband now. Goodbye."

But before she could move, he stood before her,
blocking her way. She looked at the lighted windows
and willed someone else to come into the garden.

"I'm only commenting on the obvious," he began,
his pale eyes raking her body boldly. Then he continued, "I should think you wouldn't begrudge me a
little conversation. It's the least you can do after the
way you stole that case from me."

Taken aback, Nicola asked, "What do you mean,
'stole' it?"

"Well, all that business about the poor discarded
ex-wife. It had nothing to do with the law involved.
You used it to persuade. . . to influence. . . rather than
to convince. To prove. The press coverage was unfair
to my client." With his thin lips curving in disdain, he
added, "Every feminist publication in the country
covered it."

Realizing that he was either a greater fool than she
had judged him to be or that he'd had too much to
drink, Nicola knew anger would not be the way to deal

with him. Raising one blond eyebrow quizzically, she commented simply, "So that's how you justify your defeat? It couldn't possibly be that I was the better lawyer or that my client was right and yours was wrong?"

"Oh, come on," Krantz responded, his voice tight with anger. "Everyone knows you've only got as far as you have because of your husband."

Furious, and tired of this exchange, Nicola replied, "Do they? Well, they're wrong! If you choose to believe that because it's easier on your ego than admitting that I did a better job than you did, that's *your* problem."

She stepped aside to walk past him, but once more he moved directly in front of her.

"Hey, I didn't mean to get in an argument with you," he said in a more conciliatory tone. "I think we've both had enough of that in court lately. You say you've made it on your own. Okay, I believe you. But you're much too young and beautiful to be tied down. I'm sure you must have needs...."

Suddenly he stepped close to her, and Nicola, reading his intentions, took one step away. "Mr. Krantz," she said, her eyes blazing like emerald fire. "I refuse to be insulted by you. You move out of my way, or I'm going to scream loud enough to bring the entire French Embassy staff out here. Then for sure you won't be invited here again." For a moment there was silence. Then he moved reluctantly aside, and Nicola strode toward the house without a backward glance.

As Nicola entered the ballroom, she noticed that

everyone was staring at the corner where she had left Andrew only minutes earlier.

I wonder what's going on, she thought.

Somewhere near her, a woman spoke in a high nervous voice. "It's Mather, I think. He's collapsed."

"Andrew?" Nicola asked softly, her voice catching in her throat as her body tensed. And more urgently, "Andrew!"

Suddenly a terrible sense of fear came over her. Her heart pounded, and her mouth and throat went totally dry. She struggled to swallow. Then, oblivious to the people, the noise, everything else around her, she ran across the huge room.

He's got *to be all right,* she told herself.

As she reached the crowd and was trying to force her way through, she suddenly felt strong arms on her shoulders, pulling her back.

"I'm sorry, Nicola, it's too late."

It was Harold Wellman.

Looking up into his kind familiar face, which was now drawn, she whispered, "No...it can't be. Andrew! I want...."

"He's dead, Nicola," Harold said, trying unsuccessfully to soften the impact of his words. "They've called an ambulance but...."

In that one awful, stunned, disbelieving moment, Nicola felt as if her heart had stopped beating, and her mind went blank as the shock washed over her like a huge battering wave. For an instant she fought for balance at the very edge of a perilous sea, resisting the pull of a dangerously dark whirlpool. Then abruptly, as if a spell had been lifted, she was aware once more of the people, the shouting, the atmosphere of tragedy. . . and Harold, his soft hazel eyes pained, awkward, sympathetic.

"No!" she cried. She didn't shout, but her voice was nevertheless affecting with its anguish and horror. Wrenching free, she pushed through the crowd ferociously, not caring whom she shoved aside, concerned only with reaching Andrew, with helping him. . . .

He lay on the floor, utterly still. Someone had placed a hastily rolled up jacket under his head, though it was horribly clear now that it wasn't necessary. Kneeling beside him, Nicola looked at him tentatively before reaching out to lightly stroke his pale cheek. It was already growing cold. The vitality, the fierce indomitable will were gone.

Then Harold was beside her, placing his determined hands on her shoulders once more. "The ambulance is here. They've got to take him," he said quietly.

Looking up at him, she nodded. Then she said in a barely audible whisper, "I'll go with him."

"That isn't necessary," Harold began gently, but she interrupted him.

"I want to be with him."

Harold started to argue, then stopped. Instead he put one arm comfortingly around her and told her he would follow in his car.

Though she felt a profound fear deep inside, she held her head high. With iron will she kept her legs from collapsing as she walked across the now silent ballroom. She went with a quiet dignity because she knew Andrew would have expected it of her.

THE CLOCK ON THE MANTEL ticked loudly in the silent room. Nicola sat in a large overstuffed chair in the den, staring bleakly out at the garden in the rear of the house. It was late in the afternoon, and the light was fading quickly. A blue jay and a squirrel fought on the lawn, but the noise was muted inside the room. Nicola barely heard it. Instead she found herself listening for the sound of Andrew's footsteps, his voice. . . .

And then she heard it, the sound of footsteps crossing the hall outside, moving purposefully toward the den. For a moment she held her breath, and it wasn't until the door opened and she saw Lisa's anxious face peering in that she relaxed.

"Would you like some more tea?" Lisa asked as she stood in the doorway.

"No." The word was more curt than Nicola intended. She didn't really want Lisa's company at that moment but wanted to be left alone in the room where Andrew's memory was strongest.

Clearly sensing what Nicola was feeling, Lisa answered gently, "Okay. Are you all right?"

"Yes. Really. I just need some time alone."

For a moment she had a feeling of déjà vu. She had said those words in almost exactly the same tone so many times before to her mother after her parents' divorce. She was aware of the difficulty of her mother's life and didn't want to add to her worries. So she was constantly reassuring her mother that she could handle whatever problems came up. At a young age she took on her shoulders the burdens that other youngsters would have transferred to their parents.

"Well, call if you need me," Lisa said, then closed the door behind her as she left.

Once more Nicola was alone in the silent room. She hadn't cried yet. Between Andrew's death and the elaborate formal funeral that Harold had insisted was necessary were three days of frantic, almost unreal events. Then had come the funeral itself. All Nicola could remember of it was standing beside the grave, holding Harold's hand tightly in hers. She still couldn't believe it was Andrew's body in that coffin that was lowered into the ground.

Afterward she had remained in the house, locked in the safe beautiful world that Andrew created for her, refusing at first to see anyone but Lisa. Then Andrew's personal attorney asked to meet with her to explain her "situation," as he called it. She barely listened to his quiet recitation of the fact that Andrew's will left everything to his "beloved Nicola." She was a wealthy woman, but it didn't matter to her. What mattered was that she was alone.

She set down the cup of tea that Lisa had brought a half hour earlier. It had long since grown cold. A fire crackled brightly in the small brick fireplace. Though it was spring and flowers were blooming in the garden, the temperature was cool, and the warmth of the fire was very reassuring and comforting.

She felt both tired and restless, as if she wanted to fall into a deep sleep, yet at the same time wanted to go riding, running, swimming—*anything* to get rid of the oppressive feeling that weighed her down.

Suddenly she couldn't sit still any longer. Standing, she glanced around the room, then began walking around it, touching the things Andrew had loved—heavy antique bronzes sitting stolidly on tables, sporting prints on the wood-paneled walls, an antique quill pen on his massive oak desk.

Nicola's eye was caught by Andrew's desk diary, lying open to the day he had died. Written in his bold scrawl was "embassy party with N." Something about its casualness, its ordinariness, made her feel for a moment that the past several days had been a bad dream. If she merely turned the page, she would see Andrew's writing on the next date.

But when she did reach down and turn the pages, they were all blank.

It was then that she cried. For Andrew, whose love of life and tremendous vitality hadn't been able to defeat death. For the awful inevitability of age and time and change. For the pain and loneliness he had left her to face.

"Goodbye," she whispered to the empty room, then hurried out of it.

IN A WAY those first few weeks were the easiest. There had been so much to do—the estate to be settled, working with Andrew's law partners to tie up his unfinished business. Then there were no more details to be handled, only an endless succession of long days and empty nights. Her work kept her busy, but she couldn't work twenty-four hours a day, no matter how hard she tried.

The huge house that had seemed comfortable when Andrew's dynamic presence filled it, now seemed as cold and inhospitable as a museum. Nicola dreaded going home at night. But restaurants, theaters, the Kennedy Center, the homes of friends—all reminded her of Andrew. The entire city was steeped in his memory. She began to feel she would spend the rest of her life being defined as Andrew Mather's widow.

Then one day several months after the funeral, Thomas St. Ives called. He had sent a touching note of condolence when Andrew died. Now he told Nicola he simply wanted her to know that the position he had offered her was still available, if she was interested.

By this time, she was sure, another attorney had been assigned to the Logan James case. The idea of working for St. Ives in London was still terribly appealing. Now there was nothing tying her to Washington. In fact, she felt more and more anxious to escape the city and its oppressive atmosphere of sad memories.

After mulling over the offer for two weeks, she called St. Ives back and told him she would be delighted to accept. They settled on August as the month for her to report in for her new job, because that would give her enough time to close up her Washington practice.

THE LAST GOLDEN RAYS of a late-July sun streamed through the west windows, burnishing the antique brass bowl on the coffee table and highlighting the patina of the ornately carved figures of the chessmen.

"You shouldn't have stayed in this big old place alone," Lisa said. "You should have come to stay with me, as I asked."

Lisa had just returned from spending several weeks in Los Angeles. She'd gone there to discuss taking over a law practice from an old friend of the family's who was retiring. She'd urged Nicola to come, too, or to use her apartment while she was away, but Nicola had refused.

Shaking her head now, Nicola responded, "No, this was my home, even with Andrew gone. Running away wouldn't have solved anything."

They were sitting in the living room, a high-ceilinged, richly furnished room done in deep shades of russet to match the russet-hued oriental carpet that covered most of the wooden floor. Rare prints and exquisite china figurines were everywhere. It was a beautiful, coldly formal room, and Nicola had never felt comfortable in it. Now she said to Lisa, "Let's go into the kitchen, and I'll make some tea."

As they entered the pristine white room, Lisa asked, "But where are the servants?"

"I let them go except for Mrs. Collins, the housekeeper," Nicola answered, filling a white enamel tea kettle with water and turning on the heat beneath it. Then, taking a deep breath, she said what she had found strangely difficult to say earlier. "I'm leaving tonight, Lisa. And since I don't plan to come back, I'm closing up the house, putting it up for sale, along with everything in it."

"Tonight? So soon?"

"Yes."

"But I thought you didn't have to report to work till later in August."

"I don't. But I'll need some time to find a place

over there and get settled. Oh, Lisa, I just don't want to stay here any longer. There are too many memories. I'll never be able to put those memories in the past, where they belong, unless I make a change as soon as possible.''

"I understand," Lisa said sincerely. Then hugging Nicola, she finished, "And I think you're doing the right thing. When you told me about St. Ives's offer, I was so happy for you. I just didn't think you'd be leaving this soon. I'll miss you.''

Nicola smiled warmly. "I'll miss you, too. But we'll keep in touch. And I don't just mean exchanging Christmas cards!''

Lisa laughed. Then she said, "Your life isn't over now, you know, Nicola. In so many ways it's just beginning.''

Forcing herself to smile, Nicola responded with a shrug, "I hope you're right." She took down cups and saucers and a tin of tea.

"When does your flight leave?" Lisa asked.

"Midnight. I'd have gone this afternoon, but I wanted to tell you what I was doing." She set the tea on the table. Then the two women sat down. "I'm just going to throw a few things in a suitcase and leave everything else. Mrs. Collins will pack up my personal possessions and send them to me. I've arranged for a realtor to list the house. Everything's taken care of.''

Shaking her head, Lisa said, "You're moving awfully fast. You're sure you're not just running away?''

"I don't think so. If I am running, I hope it's *to* something, not *away* from it.''

Suddenly a vivid memory assailed her—Logan

James and that kiss that had left her senses reeling. *No, better not think about that,* she told herself firmly. She wasn't going to London because of him. She wouldn't be working with him and probably wouldn't even run into him.

She continued, "Enough about me. Tell me about your plans? Did you find an apartment in LA? Interesting, isn't it? Suddenly I'm off to London, and you're off to LA."

The next hour passed quickly. Then it was time for Nicola to get ready for her flight. She declined Lisa's offer to see her off, saying she just wanted to fold her tent and slide away.

At the open doorway the two friends hugged each other, promising to stay in close touch. Then Nicola watched Lisa hurry to her car and, with one last wave, drive off.

In her bedroom Nicola changed from her jeans to camel wool slacks and a matching cashmere sweater. London was cool sometimes now, she knew. She pulled one large suitcase from her closet and filled it with suits, blouses, slacks and sweaters. From a drawer she grabbed a handful of lingerie and tossed it on top of her other clothes. Some shoes and a purse followed. Sweeping the makeup off her vanity table, she dropped it into a small bag and put that in the nearly full suitcase.

Opening her jewel case, she took out a few of the simpler pieces, leaving behind a fortune in emeralds, rubies, sapphires and diamonds. Almost as an afterthought, she took off her diamond engagement ring and wedding band and dropped them into the box.

With an air of finality, she closed and locked the case, then put it in the small safe hidden in a wall. The following day Mrs. Collins would take it to the bank for safekeeping.

Looking quickly at the clothes she had tossed into the suitcase, Nicola decided they would have to do. Whatever else she needed she would buy in London.

As she swung the suitcase off the bed, she was suddenly overwhelmed by a feeling of nostalgia. She'd enjoyed many luxuries being Andrew's wife. Travel, money, position. But she also knew that she'd paid a price...made compromises for Andrew she didn't want to make again.

She wanted to go to London and work for St. Ives. It occurred to her that for all her world traveling with Andrew, she had never toured the British Isles with him. For some inexplicable reason this reassured her. London would be a new beginning for her.

Andrew had said there would come a time for her to reach out for what she wanted. Don't be afraid, he'd said.

Unbidden, the image of a tall attractive man, looking intently at her across the rim of a crystal wineglass filled with champagne, contended for her attention. "I look for oil," he'd said, "enjoy wholeheartedly serendipity and believe wholeheartedly in taking risks...."

The discreet chime of the old clock reminded her of the time, and as she made her way to the door, her eyes blurred with tears. Only the fact that she knew the house so well kept her from stumbling.

Stepping outside, she shut the door tightly behind

her. As she stood on the broad stone steps, feeling the unexpected rush of cool night air and smelling the musky sweetness of the large white magnolia blooms, she thought how it seemed like years, not months, since she had driven up the drive and come running into the house, anxious to tell Andrew of her great victory. It didn't seem possible that so much could have happened in so short a time.

It is true, she thought, *time is deceiving. A moment can hold more meaning than a lifetime.*

As she walked quickly to the waiting taxi, a random thought passed through her mind: *when one door closes, another opens somewhere.* She didn't remember where on earth she had heard it. Smiling at the simpleminded optimism in it, she hoped it was true.

Who knows, she mused, and brushed the tears from her cheeks.

PART TWO

London

CHAPTER FIVE

NICOLA HURRIED THROUGH the Temple, one of the areas of London traditionally occupied by lawyers. An idyllic place, with courtyards, trees and gardens, it was quiet and peaceful. On this resplendent August day, the morning sun was warm through the thin silk of her turquoise blouse and beige linen skirt. As she walked toward Thomas St. Ives's suite of offices, she heard the echo of her footsteps on the flagstone paving. The rhythmic cascading of water from a nearby fountain also caught her attention. Pausing to glance at the small stone fountain, she was amused to see water shoot up from the open mouth of a cherub.

She stood watching the silvery column of water plume, then arch back down into the basin, dashing feathers of spray into the sunlight. Then subtly, unexpectedly, the image of another fountain superimposed itself onto this one—the fountain at Beechwood, where she and Logan James had toasted the success of her case for Amanda Gibran. That evening, the murmuring sound of the water as it recycled through an intricate course of rock and stone and concrete had provided a background of sounds that had muffled their voices and given privacy to their conversation.

It didn't bother her now to recall that evening. Quite often during the past few months something would trigger that memory. This day it was the play of the fountain and the echo of her footsteps. These were happy sounds. There had been enough silence, she felt. She was glad to be alive on this lovely morning, glad to have the memory of that arresting man who'd made her feel so special that evening by celebrating her victory with champagne.

That man, she thought, and saw again his firm, well-defined mouth curving into a tender smile under his luxuriantly full mustache. She could still remember exactly how he looked...his hair a warm reddish brown, thick and wavy; his eyes set wide apart under heavy symetrically arched black brows. They were a tawny golden brown rimmed in black. His was a strong face that just missed being handsome. His jaw was too firm, there was a hard set to his features and his cheekbones were just a bit too high, suggesting Indian blood somewhere far back in his ancestry.

She remembered his direct manner of looking at whomever he was speaking to. He spoke through his eyes, as well as his words, and when he smiled, he smiled with his eyes, too....

Yes, Logan James was someone she would never forget. With one last appreciative glance at the sparkle of sunlight on droplets of silvery spray, she turned away quickly and decisively. As she continued walking, she felt a sense of renewal and purpose. Lisa was right, she realized. In some ways her life *was* just beginning.

Passing under an archway, Nicola came to the

door of Thomas's suite of offices, located on the ground floor of an ancient building of rich brown brick. She had been there only once previously, when she had first arrived in London two weeks earlier. This was her first day at work, and she was both excited and a bit nervous.

As she entered, the receptionist, Gladys, a perky redhead with a friendly smile, said, "Good morning, Miss Wynter. Mr. St. Ives is expecting you. Go right on into his office."

Nicola paused just a moment to slip on the beige linen blazer she had carried from the nearby parking garage. Then she opened the door and stepped inside Thomas's large, wood-paneled office. Immediately her happy smile froze on her lips. Instead of meeting Thomas, she came face to face with Logan James.

She felt her heart stop. As if she were outside herself, she observed him standing there, tall and broad shouldered and strong...and herself facing him, stunned. Finally her heart began to beat again, its rhythmic cadence pounding against her breast. She was more than surprised; she was astonished.

Not ten minutes earlier she'd thought about him— enjoyed the memory as she'd enjoyed the bright sunlight creating diamonds of the sparkling drops of water. But it was one thing to recall an enjoyable memory of that dynamic man and quite another suddenly to encounter him.

He stood near a small fireplace, in the corner, one arm lying casually on the marble mantel, one black-booted foot resting against the low hearth. She noted his informal dress—dark slacks and a white pullover cut in a deep vee-neck that revealed a triangle of tanned flesh covered with dark hair. Those wide-set eyes glinted with golden highlights as they impudently surveyed her. He wasn't at all surprised to see her.

She had expected—at some point—to see him again. But not at that moment. And not without warning.

To her chagrin, her famous self-control deserted her. She simply stood there, with no idea what to say.

With admirable aplomb Logan rescued the situation. "Hello," he said softly, the hint of a smile playing around his appealing mouth. "It's good to see you again."

With an effort Nicola composed herself. "I was supposed to meet Thomas...and my new client."

"Thomas is in the office next door. He'll be right back. Since you'll be working on my case, he thought I should be here to go over things with you."

"You mean *you're* my client. But...I assumed Thomas would have given your case to someone else by now."

"Oh, no," Logan replied amiably. "There was no rush. These negotiations take a while. I told him to wait for you."

"Were you so sure I would come?" She raised her eyebrows quizzically.

"No. But I hoped you would."

Just then Thomas returned. "Nicola, my dear. How good to see you. Have you settled into your new home all right?"

"Yes, thank you."

On Thomas's recommendation, she had looked at

a house in Chelsea that one of his clients was selling. It was a charming red-brick Georgian town house near the river, and Nicola had fallen in love with it on sight. She bought it immediately and had spent the past two weeks decorating it.

"Good. I thought that place would suit you." He stood between them, a smile on his face, obviously pleased with the arrangement. "Have you and Logan had a chance to chat about this case?"

"Not really," Nicola replied, glancing hesitantly at Logan.

"Well, let's sit down, shall we, and get to work." Thomas motioned to Nicola to take a chair near his large oak desk. He continued, "As you may remember from our earlier conversation, Logan's company is only one of several vying for North Sea drilling rights. The British Home Office is handling the negotiations for the government. I'd like you to serve as Logan's legal representative. Basically it's up to Logan to convince the government they should award this very lucrative contract to his company, but it's up to you to steer Logan through the legal morass this involves."

"I understand," Nicola said, wishing fervently that she could decline the assignment but knowing she couldn't. It hardly would look good to refuse the first case Thomas gave her.

"Of course I'll help you with any questions about the intricacies of British law," Thomas continued. "But basically it will be you and Logan working together. Since the case is so complicated, it will be your only assignment until it's finished."

That tears it, she thought. For the next several months her life would revolve around Logan James. She would be at his beck and call professionally. And there was absolutely nothing she could do about it.

"Well, you may as well get to work now. Logan can give you the background information you need in your office. And I'll have Gladys bring you our files on the subject."

She rose, holding herself erect and proud. Still, Logan towered over her as they went to her office down the hall. They passed other lawyers, secretaries and law clerks bustling through the narrow corridor. This was an old building, housing as many people as it would hold.

Hers was a small but pleasant room. One wall was lined with bookcases filled with books on American and British law. Paintings of lovely pastoral scenes hung on two pale blue walls, and a lage window filled the fourth. Sunshine flooded into the room. But even though she was bathed in the golden glow of the sunlight, Nicola felt no warmth inside.

She sat down behind her desk, using it as a barrier between her and Logan, and opened her briefcase. As she busied herself taking out the papers and files, she thought about the arrangement.

"What is not wisdom is danger," she told herself, recalling the proverb. She was far too aware of the tall man standing just on the other side of her desk— filling the room with his presence. Sighing deeply, she said, "Sit down, please, Mr. James."

"Logan," he reminded her in that soft Southern accent. "Don't you remember? We agreed to first names." He stood waiting.

"Logan," she said, and gestured toward the chair.

As he seated himself, he asked, "How are you? And don't say fine if you're not fine. I want to know how you are."

Nicola was silent for a moment. She was beginning to get her bearings again; her defenses were quickly coming into place. Finally she responded, "Are you always so direct in dispensing with social amenities?" But even as she asked, she knew the answer. This man was always direct.

A warm smile touched the corners of his mouth and lit up his eyes. "I try to be. Otherwise a lot of time gets wasted. I spent two hours this morning with three double-dealin', smooth-talkin' attorneys. Didn't get one straight answer. Back home we call those fellows 'Philadelphia lawyers.' " He crossed his long legs and leaned comfortably back in his chair. "So *Nicola*, how are you?"

The way he'd spoken her name was a caress. For the second time that morning she thought of Beechwood. . . and the softness of his voice over the murmur of the fountain as he'd said, "Goodbye, Mrs. Mather."

Now, she thought, she was no longer Mrs. Mather. She was Miss Wynter. And she was there with him. Once again, like a traffic signal's yellow caution light, her mind registered a warning. Somehow she had to maintain a distance.

"Cross my heart I am all right." She steeled herself to smile noncommittally at him. "I took some time to sort things out. Decided I wanted a complete change of scene. Then Thomas called and once again offered me a position."

She didn't add that when she accepted the job it was because she wanted to be someplace on her own, no longer under anyone's shadow. Now, with this man as her client, she knew her new fragile independence was threatened.

"Nicola," he began, his voice low and husky, "I...." He paused, and a slight frown creased his forehead. "That night at Beechwood...."

Nicola had to stop him. For months she'd dealt with feelings, considered options, made decisions. She'd known instinctively that night that he'd been affected by her, as she had been by him. No matter how else they lived their lives, no matter what other emotional commitments they might have, that night she and this stranger had stood in an island of time, momentarily suspended from other commitments, and had *not* been strangers.

After Andrew's death she'd thought often about their encounter. She hoped Logan James wasn't burdened with any feelings of guilt. Certainly his letter of condolence had been sincere and circumspect.

Now she wanted to reassure him and to put that encounter into proper perspective. "Yes, that evening at Beechwood.... At that time, my husband and I were having a...." Nicola paused to search for the correct term. "A conflict of interest. Andrew had wanted me to refuse the Gibran case. He hated sensational publicity and felt I would risk my reputation as a serious lawyer."

Again Nicola considered her words carefully. She didn't want to reveal how painful the conflict had been for her. It had changed her feelings for Andrew.

But neither did she intend to forget how difficult it had been to follow the dictates of her own conscience—to take a stand in opposition to Andrew. His very strength, which initially had attracted her, ultimately threatened to overwhelm her. "I felt it would be good for my career. The case, not the publicity. Publicity goes with the territory of certain cases. Andrew called it notoriety, but I felt compelled to try. Amanda deserved to win. Faisal wouldn't suffer any hardship by having to provide for her. How much money does one man need?" She smiled, and Logan returned the smile. She felt more comfortable with him now. She concluded, "So please don't concern yourself about me. Andrew was a very special man. I truly mourned the loss of him." She sat quietly for a moment without speaking, then said, "Knowing Andrew, he would be the very first to tell me to get on with my life. And I'm doing that."

"I'm glad," Logan replied simply. But she was aware there was a world of meaning in those two brief words. He was glad guilt didn't mar the memory of that evening, glad she was there with him at the moment.

Seeing the hopeful expectant look on his face, she realized something more needed to be said. "Mr. James, I'm not at all sure I should be the one to handle your case." It was easier to say than she expected.

"Logan," he insisted, otherwise ignoring her last statement. "Did Thomas tell you I have a petrochemical plant in Baton Rouge? You see, that's my concern behind the negotiations for this contract to joint venture with Global Oil. Concern, hell, need! I *need* to co-venture with them. My plant has to have a steady supply of high-grade crude.''

"When I accepted the job, Thomas said only that his client had a plant in Baton Rouge that needed a supply of raw material.'' She didn't have to add that had she known it was his case, she wouldn't be sitting there at the moment. As she looked at him, she was aware that she was in some ways a very different woman from the one he'd met that night. Andrew's death and long months of self-scrutiny had taught her something about herself. She had been shaken to her very soul by her conflict with Andrew. She didn't intend to get into the same conflict, that awful tug-of-war over control, with another strong-minded man.

But even as she told herself she intended to resist the invitation to intimacy that was explicit in his every word, she was all too aware of how attractive he was.

"Nicola,'' he said, interrupting her thoughts, ''I think we're walkin' around something important. I think it has something to do with Andrew. Let's get it said and then forget it. I don't feel any guilt—if that's what you were trying to explain away. Guilt's a waste of time. There's an attraction between us— happened the first day we met. You can pretend you don't know what I'm talking about, if you need to. But, lady, you haven't been far out of my thoughts since that first time I met you. There's lots you need to know about me and lots I need to know about you. For different reasons, maybe, but we still need information.''

Overwhelmed yet amused, Nicola parried, "Are these questions relative to the contract we're trying to negotiate?"

"Well. . ." he drawled, grinning slyly. "They *are* a bit personal. But I think the relationship between client and counselor should be personal."

"Is your relationship with Thomas personal?" she quipped.

He laughed. "No. But he's the best there is for my business. I respect him and hope he respects me."

Suddenly he stood. "Because of my meeting with those lawyers, I didn't have time for breakfast. I'm starved. Let's go to lunch."

Nicola checked her watch and saw that it was nearly eleven. Glancing up at Logan, she noticed a look in his eyes that held such intensity and desire that she was startled. She knew her reaction showed in the flush she felt. Instantly the light left his eyes, and it was as if she were watching a blind being lowered. He glanced away for a moment, and when he once more gazed into her eyes, the man was safely private behind a closed door.

Ah, she thought, *he is wary of rejection.*

He held out his hand, saying "You and I will make a good team. Let's give it a try."

As at their first meeting, she felt an intensity about this man that astonished her. She knew she should refuse lunch, refuse to work with him, refuse to be drawn into the turbulent vortex of his powerful personality.

Knowing all this, Nicola still stood and took the hand he offered. "I'm hungry, too," she said, smiling up at him.

They ate at Harry's Bar on Audley Street. The name belied the Italian menu. It was Logan's choice, since he knew London better than she did, and she approved of it wholeheartedly. The decor was pleasant—Fortuny wall-coverings, Peter Arno cartoons, fresh flowers everywhere and Limoges china with a pattern of tiny bluebells. With the sunlight pouring in through the curtained windows, it was marvelously cheerful.

Logan and Nicola talked with an ease that surprised her, between courses of fresh spinach salad sprinkled with crisp bacon, rich fettucini and a sinfully delicious chocolate torte. Logan discussed the negotiations, the oil lease he wanted so badly, his competition. But even as he spoke, Nicola found herself wanting to know more about him. In fact, she wanted to know *everything* about him—what his childhood had been like, who his friends were, his likes and dislikes. It was all she could do to control her rampant curiosity about this man who intrigued her so. She hadn't felt such an intense curiosity about another person since she'd been twelve and just learning exactly how different boys and girls were.

Finally she couldn't resist asking, "How did you get in the oil business in the first place?"

"It's a long story." He paused to sip the hot dark coffee. "Basically I'm just taking over where my grandfather left off." As he mentioned his grandfather, his expression softened, and Nicola sensed his deep love for the man.

"I was named after him. He was a wildcatter... came up the hard way. He was young when the oil industry was young. Was in the right place at the right time. For men who were tough, indifferent to danger and independent, there were tremendous opportunities.''

"It sounds like a risky time," Nicola interjected.

Setting down the cup, he smiled and leaned forward to rest his elbows on the table. His eyes, like his voice, were animated with his story. " 'Risk' was the name of the game. In those days the men didn't wear hard hats, steel-toed shoes or safety belts. They used nitroglycerin to jug out the bottom of the well. There weren't any blowout preventers. They lived with gas and explosion and fire. Risk went with the work. In fact, the danger they were exposed to was a source of pride to them. I can still remember my grandfather saying, 'We weren't pencilpushers. We were men!' ''

As he spoke, Nicola couldn't help but think times hadn't changed much for Logan James. He, too, fitted his description of those early-day oilmen: tough, indifferent to danger and independent.

"So survival depended on sheer luck," she said, obvious disapproval in her tone.

Logan shook his head. "No. Not just luck. Competence. You had to know how to take *calculated* risks. My grandfather was one who knew how to calculate risk well enough to survive and prosper. He wasn't afraid to go after what he wanted.''

As Logan finished, he looked at her deliberately.

Before she could respond, he continued, "My grandfather was spudding in a well near Shreveport. He needed a loan, so a friend sent him to John Morgan in Baton Rouge. To make a long story short, he got the money, got invited to dinner and met Annabel, the banker's daughter.'' He grinned at her, obviously enjoying this story. ''Before dinner was over, Papa had made up his mind to marry her. He courted her and, a month later, sent her this telegram: 'The well came in. Get packed. I'll be on the noon train Thursday.' ''

Nicola couldn't help smiling at the blatant romanticism of the story. ''Did the banker's daughter and the wildcatter live happily ever after?'' she asked, already knowing the answer.

''Of course. She adored him. And to the day he died, he treated her like she was made of spun gold.''

''That's a nice story. But they don't write songs like that anymore.'' Nicola's tone was pensive. Immediately she realized her words were more revealing than she'd intended for them to be.

''Sure they do,'' Logan insisted gently, his leonine eyes locking with hers. ''You just wait an' see.''

For a moment Nicola sat utterly still. If there was any movement around her, she wasn't aware of it. She was aware only of the undisguised look of desire in Logan's eyes and her own rapidly pounding heart and shallow breathing.

Then the waiter quietly placed the check on the table, and reality returned.

''Your grandfather seems to have had quite an influence on you,'' she commented.

''I was ten when my parents were killed in an automobile accident. From then on I lived with papa and my grandmother.''

''Oh, I'm sorry,'' Nicola said with real feeling. ''That's young to be orphaned.''

"Except for losing my parents, I've had a good life. I grew up in a close family—aunts and uncles and cousins. My cousin Beau is my business manager. We've always been good friends."

After a pause he asked, "How about you? Do you have anyone besides your father? Your mother...."

Nicola shook her head. "No, I never see any of my relatives on my father's side. And my mother was an only child...remember I told you she disappointed her parents. I never got in touch with them. Nor will I." She couldn't help thinking how lucky Logan had been in a way. Always surrounded by family. She wished she'd known such closeness and security. Not wanting to dwell on her feelings of sadness and loss, she continued, "I can see why you were so influenced by your grandfather."

"He made me want to be just like him when I was growing up. And now I want children and grandchildren to remember me with the same regard I have for him."

"Are you a wildcatter, too?" Nicola asked with a teasing grin.

"If you call wildcatting hunting oil by drilling wells whose chances of productivity can't be completely accurately predicted, even with high-tech." He reached across the table and took her hand and held it captive between his two strong ones.

When he spoke again, his voice was tender. "Nicola."

She did not try to free her hand. There was a melodious cadence to the way he pronounced her name. Whether it was his soft Southern speech or the register of his voice, she couldn't tell, but for some reason, each time she heard him say, "Nicola," it seemed like a caress. And her awareness of this fact concerned her.

As if he sensed her sudden tension, he released her hand and leaned back casually in his chair, completely relaxed.

Continuing his narrative, he said, "I studied engineering in college. Then, when I was twenty-nine, my grandfather died, and a few months later, my grandmother. They left everything to me, including a petrochemical plant. I decided to expand and established a business building platforms for offshore drilling rigs."

Nicola considered the brief history he'd given her. In all his talk of family and work there was no mention of a wife. Could this charming, undeniably attractive, downright sexy man really have reached the ripe old age of thirty-six without ever having married? And if so, why? Was he a confirmed bachelor who enjoyed the chase but didn't intend to settle down?

Suddenly she realized she needed to bring this conversation to an end. "I've got to get back to work. It's my first day, and I've been in the office less than an hour."

Logan quickly paid the check, then escorted her back to his car. When he dropped her off at the office a few minutes later, he said, "I'll be seeing you."

"Of course," she replied, and thanked him for lunch. Her voice was not quite as impersonal as she would have liked. As she walked toward Thomas's office, she was fully aware of Logan's eyes following her.

SHE RETURNED HOME that evening just as the sun was setting. Chelsea was especially lovely on this Indian-summer evening. The Thames wound dark and placid beyond the Embankment, and the plane trees were lush and green. A pleasant residential district of old mansions and interesting newer town houses, Chelsea extended for one and one-half miles along the north bank of the Thames. For centuries it had been the home of many artists and had a bohemian atmosphere that appealed to Nicola, after the political stuffiness of Washington. Her own house was on Cheyne Walk, an attractive row of red-brick Georgian houses. Narrow public gardens separated Cheyne Walk from the Embankment. Black wrought-iron railings and a gate surrounded the small front garden. Windows only a foot above ground looked into the gleaming white-tiled kitchen.

The house was three stories tall and narrow. The first floor had a sitting room, formal dining room and kitchen. On the second floor were two bedrooms and a bathroom, and on the top floor a small attic study.

As Nicola walked into the cheerful sitting room, she felt her body relax. She loved the way this house had turned out. After two weeks of clutter and bustle, of boxes and packing crates, painters, paper hangers and assorted repairmen, the house was exactly as she wanted it to be. Glancing around at the bright-yellow walls and green-chintz-covered furniture, she thought how pleasant and cozy this room was. French doors opened onto a tiny, brick-walled garden. In the sunlight the garden was bright with pots of yellow marigolds, hanging baskets of star jasmine and green ivy. The previous owner had been an avid gardener, and Nicola was determined to keep the garden always looking as beautiful and rich as it did now.

A white wrought-iron table sat in the middle of the tiny brick patio, and Nicola had already established a habit of drinking her early-morning tea out there.

Compared to the magnificence of the mansion she had shared with Andrew, this house was little more than a cottage. But she loved it. It was hers—warm, cozy and unpretentious.

Dropping her blazer and briefcase on a nearby table, Nicola poured herself a glass of Perrier, kicked off her shoes and sat down on the comfortable over-stuffed sofa in front of the small, white-manteled fireplace.

"Hello, miss. I was in the kitchen an' never even 'eard you come in."

Nicola turned to see Mrs. Murdle standing in the doorway, drying her hands on the apron tied tightly around her ample stomach. She was short and plump, with graying brown hair and hazel eyes that sparkled with impudent humor. A charwoman, she had been recommended by Thomas. Nicola had taken to her immediately. Unlike the reserved, almost haughty servants at her old home, Nicola was relieved to find her funny, candid and cheerfully curious about Nicola herself. She was every inch a cockney, "Born wivin' the sound of Bow Bells," as she proudly told Nicola. At Nicola's look of confusion she had patiently explained, "Meanin' the bells of St. Mary-le-Bow, where cockneys 'ave always been."

Her accent was so thick, that even after seeing her nearly every day for two weeks, Nicola occasionally found her hard to understand. But she enjoyed their talks tremendously. Mrs. Murdle—she refused to let Nicola address her by her first name, Charlotte—liked to talk as she worked. Whenever she and Nicola happened to be in the same room, she would launch into a rapid-fire monologue about whatever happened to be on her mind at the moment. Often she spoke about the fluctuating state of her marriage to Ralph Murdle, a porter in the Smithfield meat market. The previous day she'd been fuming when she arrived and told Nicola she and the mister " 'ad 'ad a spat.''

"I threatened to go 'ome to mother, I did,'' she said. "An' 'e says, 'Well that won't take long, dearie, as she lives in the flat upstairs.' '' She'd marched into the kitchen muttering something about, "Showin' 'im.''

Now Mrs. Murdle beamed happily at Nicola and continued, "Lovely weather we're 'avin, ain't it, ducks? But we'll 'ave to pay for it, I warrant. It'll be a dreary winter.''

Nicola smiled. "Let's hope not. So far I've been pleasantly surprised by the weather here. I was prepared for rain and fog.''

"You'll get plenty of it, to be sure, miss. Just you wait.'' Glancing at Nicola's drink, she finished, "Must be dry work bein' a solicitor.''

Nicola couldn't help grinning in amusement. From the first moment they'd met, she had been a constant surprise to Mrs. Murdle. First, because she was American; second, because she was a young woman living alone, and third, because she was a lawyer. Even when Mrs. Murdle was especially angry at her husband, she made it clear that a woman needed a man around.

"Actually, it is rather dry work," Nicola agreed. Then suddenly realizing it had been an exceptionally long time since lunch, she asked, "By the way, what have you made for dinner?"

Mrs. Murdle came Monday through Friday in the afternoons. Before she left, usually at six each day, she prepared something for Nicola's dinner. Thus far, the meals had been delicious, though definitely not gourmet.

"Roast beef an' Yorkshire puddin'." Then she added slyly, "An' there's enough for two if you 'appen to 'ave a young man you'd like to invite."

Nicola laughed. "I'll be dining alone, thank you."

"You're sure? There's plenty."

"I'm sure, Mrs. Murdle."

"Well, I'll be goin', then, dearie. My bus is due down at the corner in five minutes." She untied her apron and stuffed it into a huge purse she carried. "Good night, then. See you Monday."

Even as she heard the front door close, Nicola's thoughts turned to Logan James. Mrs. Murdle would most certainly approve if she invited him to dinner, Nicola reflected, amused. But she absolutely had no intention of doing that. Once more she told herself all the things she'd been telling herself for months—that what happened between them that night in Washington was unreal. The combination of her disappointment with Andrew and a particularly romantic setting had created an ephemeral moment of awareness. They'd shared a kiss, a brief emotional connection, nothing more. She'd told herself that if ever she did run into him again, she'd be disappointed, would wonder what she'd seen in him.

Well, she thought now, she hadn't been disappointed in him. Exactly the opposite, in fact. And while his attention was complimentary, it was also intimidating. She could easily be engulfed in his overpowering personality, as she had been in Andrew's. She *couldn't* allow that to happen.

Finally, finishing her drink, she went to the kitchen, where her dinner sat warming in the oven.

NICOLA WAS JUST stepping out of the bathtub, when the phone in her bedroom rang. Grabbing a large bright-yellow towel, she wrapped it around her dripping body, then hurried to the phone. "Hello?" she said, wondering who would be calling her at ten o'clock at night. She knew very few people in London so far.

"Nicola, it's Logan."

Her heart raced at the same moment her fingers tightened their grip on the receiver. Finally she responded, "Yes?"

"I'm sorry to bother you so late. I had a business meeting that just broke up. Were you asleep?"

"No, I was just getting ready for bed," Nicola said, not wanting to admit that she'd actually just stepped out of the tub and was virtually naked.

"Just getting ready for bed?" he repeated. "Now that conjures up interesting images. I wish the visual telephone were perfected." There was a teasing suggestiveness in his voice.

Instinctively Nicola clutched the towel even tighter around her body. "If this is an obscene phone call, you're going about it all wrong," she said in a matter-of-fact tone. "You're not supposed to identify yourself. And you shouldn't pick a lawyer who recognizes your voice and is likely to sue you.''

Logan laughed, then replied, "So, you've memorized my voice already? And we've only talked twice. That first meeting of course, was special. Even though our exchange was so short. And circumspect. I'm flattered, Nicola.''

She heard that caressing drawl in the way he spoke the three syllables of her name. *"What is not wisdom . . . ''* she reminded herself. "You called . . .'' she retorted sharply. "Is there something you . . . ?''

"All right,'' he complied, "but I was enjoying our conversation immensely. I called because I've got to fly back to my headquarters in Louisiana. I'm taking the red-eye tonight. I'll be gone several days. I just wanted to let you know in case you need to discuss anything with me. Gladys has my number over there.''

"I'm quite sure I can handle things while you're gone. I don't expect I'll need to talk to you before you return.''

There was a sigh of mock disappointment on the other end of the line. "Hardhearted woman. I was afraid you'd say that. You're independent and self-sufficient to a fault, you know. Well, remember, if something does come up, Gladys has my number. I'll be back as soon as possible.''

"Take your time. I have lots of work to do to familiarize myself with your case.''

Logan laughed again at her not-too-subtle rebuff.

Obviously he was completely undeterred by her barbed responses to his innuendos. "Goodbye,'' she said, determined to end the conversation.

"Good night, Nicola. Pleasant dreams," Logan replied. Then he hung up.

Nicola replaced the phone just a bit harder than necessary, then returned to the bathroom. Toweling dry, she pulled on a soft cotton nightgown and went to bed. But she couldn't seem to get to sleep.

Damn Logan James, anyway, she thought. He always seemed to have the last word.

Not if I can help it, answered a little voice inside her head. And suddenly she felt much better.

CHAPTER SIX

A WEEK LATER, on Saturday morning, Nicola was
working in her tiny garden. She was dressed in faded
Levi's and a pale blue T-shirt. Her hair was pulled
back in a braid that hung down her back. Wisps of
pale blond hair had escaped from the loose plait and
lay softly against her cheeks. She hummed as she
worked—an innocuous tune she heard sometimes on
her car radio on her way to work. As she dug in the
rich dark earth, its smell filled her nostrils. It was a
natural pleasant odor.

She was just planting a small fern in a freshly dug
hole, when she heard the front doorbell ring. Quickly
brushing her dirty hands against her jeans, she hurried to the door. She knew she looked a mess and
hoped it wasn't anyone important.

It was Logan.

He stood nonchalantly on the red-brick doorstep,
one shoulder leaning casually against the doorframe.
On this mild sunny day, he was dressed simply in
brown slacks and a matching lightweight pullover.
Through the soft knit, Nicola could just distinguish
the outline of his hard muscled chest.

"Good morning," he said with a cheerful lilt to his
voice. "May I come in?"

Without waiting for a reply, he brushed past her and entered the sitting room. Glancing around the room, he continued, "This is sure nice. It suits you. And so does that charmin' outfit you're wearing."

His eyes rested on the curves of her hips in the tight jeans and on her full breasts thrusting against the thin cotton of the T-shirt.

Somehow Nicola felt she couldn't have been dressed more provocatively if she'd been wearing a black lace bra and panties.

Trying to sound nonchalant, she replied, "It's Saturday, in case you've forgotten. I'm gardening, not working."

She hadn't heard from him all week. Now he was back, walking into her life as if he owned it. Well, she wasn't about to be treated so cavalierly, she told herself with righteous indignation.

But there was something she didn't want to admit to herself, let alone to him, because it was too revealing. The fact that she'd subconsciously waited all week for his return, or even a phone call, was something she didn't want to think about. "Did you have a good trip?" she asked.

Ignoring her question, he said, "I'm glad to see you're not working. I'd hate to think you were becoming a workaholic. Actually, I tried to reach you last night, but you were out."

The sentence ended on a note of undisguised curiosity, but Nicola had no intention of satisfying his subtle inquiry. It was none of his business what she did on her own time. She was especially reluctant to answer his implied question because the truth was so innocent—she'd spent the evening having dinner with Thomas and his wife at their house just outside London.

When Nicola didn't respond to his statement, Logan continued, "Anyway, I do have some important business to discuss with you. The final presentation for contracts has been moved ahead. Now they're scheduled for nine o'clock Monday morning. There are some things you and I need to go over before then."

"Who's the meeting with?"

"The British government's chief negotiator, Gerald Laughton. I've met him before, of course, but this will be your first time. I thought we'd go over the information today."

Nicola sighed, exasperated. There was no way around it. Though she strongly suspected his motives for coming over, she couldn't argue with him.

"Very well," she agreed reluctantly. "I'll meet you at the office in an hour."

"Why waste time going all the way down there?" Logan asked in a perfectly reasonable tone. "I'll tell you what. In return for making you work on your weekend, I'll show you around London. You did say you weren't familiar with London, didn't you? I'm not a bad guide, if I do say so myself. We can talk about this meeting while we're sight-seeing."

"That isn't necessary..." Nicola began.

He interrupted her with a winning smile. "I know. But it would be very pleasant."

Before she could object, he walked over to where she was standing by the front door. When his hand reached toward her, she stiffened as every nerve in her body came alive. But Logan merely brushed his finger across the bridge of her nose and told her she had dirt on her face. His touch was unbelievably gentle and light, just the merest wisp of contact. Yet she could feel the adrenalin pumping through her veins, and something strange seemed to have happened to her heartbeat.

Looking down at her, he said in a curiously tender voice, "There's nothing to be afraid of, Nicola."

Instinctively, she believed him. She relaxed and suddenly became aware she'd been holding her breath, for she didn't know how long.

"So," he continued, his voice becoming autocratic once more, "get changed and we'll do the town. And while we're at it, we'll get this business taken care of."

He sat down on the sofa and crossed one long leg over the other. Obviously as far as he was concerned everything was settled.

Giving up, Nicola turned and walked up the stairs to her bedroom. She took a quick shower, then applied makeup lightly—a quick brush of lip gloss, some tawny brown shadow to contrast with the sea green of her eyes and a touch of mascara to darken her naturally light lashes. She undid the braid and brushed her hair until it glistened gold with white silver highlights. Then she pulled on gray linen slacks and a gray, boat-neckline sweater. She threw her wallet and a comb into a small clutch, then grabbed her matching cardigan. She wasn't sure where they would be going or how long they would be out. It could turn cool, especially in late afternoon.

When she returned to the sitting room, Logan was still comfortably ensconced on the sofa. He smiled appreciatively at her quick transformation. Before he could say something that would shake her self-control, she asked, "Where are we going?"

"I thought we'd go sailing," he said, rising.

"Sailing? In London?"

"Of course," he answered, leading her out the front door.

A half hour later they were in a small sailboat on the Serpentine, the lake in Hyde Park. Sea gulls floated over the glittering water, shrieking at each other in high-pitched tones, as the hired boat tacked along the lake. Its gaily striped sail filled by a cool breeze, the boat pushed along smartly.

"You didn't believe me when I said we'd go sailing, did you?" Logan asked.

"Well. . . ." Nicola hesitated. Finally she smiled and admitted, "No, I didn't."

"You should do that more often," he said. His voice was soft and husky.

"What?"

"Smile. It brightens your whole face and destroys that ol' sourpuss expression you try so hard to maintain."

"I'm not trying to look like an old sourpuss," Nicola insisted. "When I'm at work, I simply behave like the professional attorney I am. Which reminds me, we have business to discuss."

"Oh, *that*." Logan dismissed the subject. He kept one hand on the tiller and stretched the other comfortably along the edge of the boat.

"Yes, *that*," Nicola retorted in a tone that brooked no nonsense. "I've spent the week wading through the complexities of British law. But tell me—in your own words—what this contract means." She smiled at him to soften the edginess in her voice.

"Well, my firm is one of two finalists bidding on the tanker farm off Scotland's northern coast. It'll be a billion-dollar facility when it's done."

"Obviously an enormous undertaking," Nicola responded thoughtfully. As she looked at Logan, whose understated tone had indicated this was just one more job, she felt a renewed respect for him. He certainly wasn't given to boasting. He didn't have to be. Still, she was impressed. "It must've been hard to get this far—to be a finalist."

"Yes. There was an endless process of negotiating with the Department of Energy. By the time that was done, most of the original companies bidding on the contract were out. Only mine and Mannering Construction, a British firm, were left."

"And now the final presentations are due to start."

"Monday at 9:00 A.M. Laughton's the senior civil servant in the Department of Energy. Mannering's people are meeting with them next week, too. A decision should be made within the next couple of months."

Cocking her head to one side, Nicola scrutinized this ostensibly laid-back man. "You're very deceptive, you know," she said. Her tone was far less guarded than it had been.

Raising one dark eyebrow quizzically, he asked, "Oh? How so?"

"I do know a little about the oil business. I know how hard it must have been for you to get this far. Behind that air of casualness, you must be very driven, indeed. Just how did you persuade the British to consider you?"

He smiled disarmingly, and for a moment Nicola had the eerie sense that this was how his grandfather had looked when he was persuading a banker to bankroll his wildcat wells.

"Let's just say I was resourceful in producing modifications tailor-made to conform to British desires. In other words, I gave them what they wanted."

"In other words, you used that famous Southern charm?"

"And a great deal of engineering expertise," he added.

She laughed. "I'll bet all your life, Southern ladies have gushed, 'My, you *are* a wonder, Logan James.'" There was no edge to her voice. Beneath the sly teasing tone was real respect.

"What other ladies might have said doesn't matter now. It's your opinion I'm interested in, Nicola."

Once more those eyes held hers, as if she were a prey at his mercy. An electric silence fell between them. And even the splash of the water against the boat, the screeching of the sea gulls, the whistle of the wind through the nearby trees, seemed to fade into the distance.

No matter what we're talking about, she thought, *no matter what I'm feeling, it always gets back to this—this desire that has been between us since the first moment our eyes met. Since that night in the garden he has wanted me. And God help me, I want him.*

She looked away, concentrating on the lovely curve of the lake, the other sailboats racing past, anything but this profound feeling that she couldn't seem to control.

When they docked, Logan helped Nicola step out of the boat, holding her hand just a moment longer than was necessary. Now that their business was taken care of and the sailing finished, she assumed she would go home. As if sensing her thoughts, Logan said quickly before she could speak, "Now I've got something *really* interesting to show you."

"But..." she began.

"Don't argue. I'm the guide, remember?" he insisted as he steered her toward his car, a deep burgundy Jaguar sedan.

As he made his way through the crowded London streets, Nicola thought again about that night in the garden of Beechwood. She'd wished on the first star for a knight on a white steed, someone to make all her unfulfilled romantic fantasies come true. *Is this he,* she wondered now. *This confident man with his confident way?*

And then they were at Portobello Road.

In spite of herself Nicola was excited. She'd always wanted to see this famous outdoor antique market. As the crowd jostled her, she stood entranced, watching a street musician with a polyphone, an old music box playing perforated disks, and holding an brilliantly colored parrot on a stick.

Her attention was soon caught, however, by another musician. He held a long stick with half a dozen green and yellow parakeets on it. The birds ignored the man's commands to do tricks until the small audience gathered around answered his plea to shout. Then he sounded a police siren, and the birds rushed to a nearby cage.

Nicola laughed joyfully along with the other bystanders.

Watching her, Logan said, "Who'd have thought such a talented, high-powered attorney could be amused so easily?"

"There's a touch of the child in all of us, you know," she said with a smile. And, she thought, there had been little enough foolishment in her childhood.

He took her arm and led her down the street, which was crowded with stalls filled with an overwhelming variety of both junk and true antiques. "They're called buskers," he said, "these street musicians."

"Oh? Are you an expert on everything?" Nicola teased.

"Almost everything."

"Then tell me more about them."

"One of the men in my London office worked his way through school being a busker. The name comes from the French word *busquer*. Means 'beating the woods, making noises to scare up game for the hunters.' " He paused and looked around at all the commotion surrounding them. "Their quarry" he went on, pointing to the street musicians, "is you and me, the passersby with some extra change in our pockets. Each busker works his own pitch, or territory. Some of them have been in the same place for years. A few were headliners on music-hall stages.''

Eyeing Logan speculatively, Nicola commented, ''You must meet a lot of interesting people.''

''Well, getting around is part of my job. By the way, if you want to buy something, be careful. There are some valuable antiques here, but most of it's worthless junk.''

''Don't worry. I'm not easily taken advantage of.''

Logan sighed in mock exasperation. ''So I've discovered.''

Nicola grinned at his playful innuendo. ''I'm just looking today, not buying.''

''Careful as always. Do you ever take risks, Nicola?''

She looked at him soberly now, well aware of what he was getting at.

''When possible,'' she finally answered slowly, ''I prefer to eliminate risk.''

''So do I—when possible. That's what engineering's about. Making expert calculations to eliminate the danger from risk. But sometimes, depending on what's at stake, once you've made the calculations you have to proceed. And hope it will work.''

''You can get hurt that way.''

''You can also get lucky,'' he responded, eyeing her meaningfully.

Lost for a response, Nicola was silent. At last Logan took her arm and said, ''Let me show you something.'' He led her across the road to a jeweler's stall.

The pieces there were all old, ornate and beautiful, and the gold and silver gleamed in the bright midday sun. The seller smiled hopefully at them. He had a ruddy complexion, bright red hair and dancing blue eyes. And though Nicola suspected he would drive a sharp bargain, she liked him immediately.

"Afternoon, sir, miss. This is the finest collection of antique jewelry on the road. You won't find none finer. An' low prices, too. I'm practically givin' it away." He shook his head sadly. "Ah, well, but what can a merchant do in times like these? The pound's low, an' you lucky folks may as well take advantage of my vulnerable position."

Nicola grinned, then looked at Logan, who wasn't taken in, either. Her glance roamed over the lovely jewelry. Though she was no expert, the prices seemed awfully high. Then her eye caught an intricately carved gold ring that clearly had been someone's wedding band once. Its lovely yellow color shone with a soft glow.

Noting her look of interest, Logan reached down and picked up the ring. Without saying a word, he slipped it on the appropriate finger. It fitted.

"Interesting," he said. His tone was noncommittal, but the look he gave her was intense.

"Too expensive," Nicola replied, slipping it off and handing it back to the disappointed seller.

"But, miss, this is a valuable piece. Twenty-four carat. Worth far more than the pittance I'm askin'."

"He's right, you know," Logan said, surprising Nicola.

Surely, she thought, he must be aware that though

the ring was undeniably beautiful, it wasn't worth nearly what the man was asking. "But..." she began.

"The intrinsic value of the ring," Logan interrupted, "is worth more than the money you pay for the gold. My grandfather gave my grandmother a two-carat diamond when they married. He gave it in love. She wore it in love for more than fifty years. She'd have worn a cigar band with the same love. It isn't the price. It's what the ring means."

Nicola shook her head. "I'm not in the market," she said to the seller, who'd listened silently to Logan's speech. Nicola knew what the street merchant did not. Money had nothing to do with this.

As the man started to protest, she finished, "Sorry," and turned away. "I don't know about you, but I'm starved," Nicola said, facing Logan in an effort to break the far too personal mood set up by that dialogue over the wedding ring.

"I know just the place to eat," Logan responded, guiding her down the bustling street.

They ate at a French restaurant on the nearby Kensington High Street. As they enjoyed sole in mornay sauce, scalloped potatoes and crusty French bread, Nicola was careful to keep the conversation strictly impersonal. She wanted no more talk of risk, with its dangerous double meaning, or wedding rings and their more obvious one. They talked further about the meeting on Monday, and Nicola tried very hard to concentrate entirely on business. But occasionally her attention wandered, and she found herself remembering how it had felt when Logan had slipped that ring on her finger and looked down at her with bright promise in his eyes, for all the world as if they were standing before an altar. Shaking her head, she thought, *this won't do*.

"Is something wrong?" Logan asked.

"No. I was so hungry I ate too much," Nicola lied, pushing away her empty plate.

"What you need is exercise. There's still a lot more of Portobello Road to see."

"All right," she agreed. But this time, she told herself, she wouldn't stop at any jeweler's stalls.

They spent another hour wandering up and down the market.

"How about a quick drive through Hyde Park?" Logan suggested.

The park was lovely in the late-afternoon sunshine. The rich foliage of majestic plane trees was burnished green gold by the setting sun. Neatly turned-out riders cantered along the bridle paths, and on the shore of the Serpentine, fishermen sat patiently. A hardy swimmer with Spartan endurance dove into the chilly waters from a wooden diving board.

Sitting on the leather seat beside Logan as he drove, Nicola thought what a lovely day it had been. She enjoyed Logan's company immensely. He seemed at ease anywhere, whether an exclusive French restaurant or a noisy crowded outdoor market. He was like a chameleon, adapting to circumstances—he was impeccably well-mannered when it was called for, down-to-earth and friendly in less pretentious surroundings.

Andrew had been born and raised amid great

wealth and social prestige. He was always correct, always formal. It intrigued Nicola now to be with a man who had a self-confidence and assurance so well grounded that he could talk to a cockney vendor in a market as if they were on the same level. She knew from his business interests that he must be wealthy. Yet he didn't feel the need to proclaim this constantly. It was refreshing, especially after the rigid social stratification of Washington, where everyone stayed aware of who was above them and who below.

Back in Chelsea, Logan parked his car across the street from her house, next to the Embankment. Nicola saw swans gliding on the water, muted in the pearly mist of the late afternoon.

As Logan turned off the engine, he said, "I know a terrific place for dinner. Unfortunately it's rather formal, so we'll have to dress."

"I'm afraid—" Nicola began firmly.

But he adroitly cut her off. "You wouldn't leave me to eat a lonely dinner in my hotel room, would you?" Somehow he was able to invest his eyes with all the pathos of a basset-hound puppy.

Nicola couldn't help smiling. "I doubt that would ever be your fate, Logan James. You've spent a lot of time in London, so you've told me. I suspect there's more than one female dinner companion you could choose from."

"Ah, but you're the only one whose company I want tonight."

"Sorry, but it's been a long day, and frankly I don't feel up to going out."

"Right. We'll eat here. I can whip up a pretty

mean omelet,'' he replied as he opened the car door for her.

But spending an intimate evening alone wasn't what Nicola had in mind, either.

''I'll just run down to the nearest market and get some eggs and cheese and shrimp...'' he continued as they crossed the road.

''All right,'' Nicola capitulated. ''But we'll eat out.''

Logan's smile brightened his eyes. ''Great. I'll pick you up at eight.'' Still looking pleased with himself, he reached over to lightly stroke her hair. ''Leave it down, please.''

Nicola watched him stride happily back to his car. When he drove off, she sighed with exasperation, then unlocked the door and went inside. She told herself she was only going out with him to avoid argument. But as she ran a hot bath, then soaked in the water, she felt a pleasant tingle of anticipation.

CHAPTER SEVEN

SHE WORE A KNEE-LENGTH dress of layers of gossamer silver lace over a silk underdress of darker silver. The three-quarter sleeves were sheer, as was the top half of the bodice. Most of her full white breasts were revealed under the sheer lacy covering. Carefully she slid black lace stockings over her long legs, then slipped her feet into black satin pumps.

As Logan had requested, she left her hair down. It fell in a thick straight shimmer of silver and gold. She put on a little more makeup than usual. The dark eyeliner and mascara made her eyes stand out like brilliant turquoise gems set against white velvet.

At her throat she wore pearls, but she left her fingers bare. A ring might spark a renewal of that conversation they'd had at Portobello Road.

As she gave herself a final once-over in the mirror of her dressing table, she was startled by her appearance. It wasn't the gorgeous dress, a designer original that she'd bought in one of her rare moments of self-indulgence, that caught her interest. Or the pearls, gleaming porcelain smooth and white in the lamplight. It was the expression on her face.

In all the times she'd dressed in glamorous clothes

and stunning jewelry for an elegant ball or dinner party, she'd never looked quite this way before.

Excited. Expectant.

She glowed with a fire that had been firmly banked but now beginning to redden. An irrepressible light danced in her eyes, and her body felt as light as air.

At the moment she almost felt she could float down the stairs and out the door, her feet skimming the surface. She wasn't a flesh-and-blood person; she was a spirit—but a happy one. And in a few moments she'd be meeting the sorcerer who'd cast this enchantment over her.

Logan.

As his name filled her thoughts, the doorbell rang, shattering her mystical reverie. Grabbing her purse and a mink jacket—one of her furs sent from Washington, for nights were cold in London—she hurried down the stairs. She didn't quite float, but she was hardly aware of her feet touching the soft carpet.

She opened the door, then hesitated, feeling unaccountably nervous as he gazed at her. He looked absolutely marvelous in a gray tweed jacket and matching slacks and cream turtleneck.

As she returned his gaze, she knew no words were necessary. The approval in his eyes was so blatant it was as if he spoke every word of desire any lover had ever uttered. The unconcealed longing in those black-rimmed eyes made her breath catch in her throat and her knees grow weak.

Something in her expression must have told him how vulnerable she felt at that moment. In a husky voice he quickly asked, "Shall we go?"

She nodded, unable to speak. As they walked to his car, he didn't touch her. She was grateful, for she had a sudden unreasonable conviction that if he touched her, she would melt.

They had been driving for several minutes through the thick Saturday-night London traffic before either spoke.

"You're the most beautiful thing I've ever seen," he said gently, keeping his eyes on the road.

She glanced at him but did not say anything.

They drove around Piccadilly Circus, then turned onto Shaftesbury Avenue. After a few minutes she managed to ask, "Where are we?"

"Soho," he answered, his own voice under better control now.

"Soho," she repeated thoughtfully. "I've heard of it. But I thought it was..." she hesitated, unsure what word to use.

"Unsavory?" he finished for her. "It's been called that. And spicy, as well. And the words don't just refer to the cooking. Foreigners have always congregated here. Once it was the haunt of petty crooks and hardworking streetwalkers. Now it has striptease shows and tastefully furnished apartments for call girls." He added dryly, "So I've been told."

"An unusual place for a formal restaurant, surely."

He smiled. "Not really. Soho's become the culinary center of London. Especially for foreign restaurants—Italian, Greek, East Indian. It used to be known for grubby little hole-in-the-wall places that served delicious food. Then society discovered it, and

now the restaurants are elegant and expensive.''
Looking around at the flashing neon lights and crowded sidewalks, Nicola was surprised to find it a rather quiet place. If there were prostitutes on the streets, they were unobtrusive. And even the advertisements for the strip shows were high toned. One proclaimed its wares with blowups of photos of *Le Baiser* by Rodin, a bas-relief from the Hindu temple at Khajurao and a detail from a picture by Renoir.

As they came to the heart of Soho, the streets became more congested and the character decidedly cosmopolitan. Clubs and restaurants of every nationality sat next to one another.

Logan parked near Kettner's on Romilly Street. It was a beautiful, very formal restaurant. Crystal and fine china glistened on linen tablecloths. In a corner a young woman strummed languidly on a harp.

They were seated at a choice table in a quiet corner. As Nicola opened the menu, resting it on the thick white damask cloth, she saw that the restaurant was as expensive as it was elegant. Whatever her half-formed opinion of Soho had been previously, she realized this was no hole-in-the-wall place where streetwalkers might drop in to ply their trade. Around them the tables were filled with well-dressed people talking softly and eating delicious-looking food.

After they ordered, the waiter left, then returned almost at once with the soup Logan had specified.

At first they simply concentrated on the food, a delicious vichyssoise, followed by poached salmon.

Then Logan asked, ''Do you approve of my choice, after all?''

Nicola smiled. "Yes. The atmosphere's perfect. The food's terrific."

"And the company?" he wanted to know, letting the word trail off into a question.

She hesitated, then answered honestly, "And the company is very charming."

The simple compliment pleased him enormously. For a moment there was a warm dancing joy in his eyes. Then his expression sobered, and he said, "Nicola, there's something I want to talk to you about."

She hesitated, wondering what was coming. But she said nothing, and he took her silence for tacit assent.

"I'd like to talk about Andrew."

She felt herself withdraw almost imperceptibly. For some reason it bothered her to talk about Andrew with Logan. She thought they'd put that subject behind them when they'd spoken over lunch her first day on the job. It wasn't a subject she wanted to pursue again, and she didn't understand why Logan wanted to.

Suddenly he reached out, his hand covering hers on the table. He looked intently at her, penetrating the veil that had come down over her face. "I know it's been only a few months. It's still painful for you to discuss him. Your entire life's been through an upheaval. Everything's changed, and you're starting all over again."

She didn't respond. What he'd said was true. She had chosen to change her life, to move away from memories that were not only painful but threatened to overwhelm her attempts at independence. It had been a scary move. Perversely she often found herself missing all the things she had run away from—the things from her life with Andrew that made her feel safe and secure.

She smiled dryly. "Human nature is so contrary. We yearn for something at the same time we're running away from it as fast as we can." Realizing the significance of those words, how they summed up the ambivalence of her feelings about Logan, she pulled back abruptly, withdrawing her hand from his.

He wasn't put off. His smile was understanding. "You haven't put that other life behind you yet. You're still tied to it in a way, whether you think you want to be or not."

Nicola considered his statement. It was true. She said pensively, "It took a long time for me simply to accept that he was gone. I guess it will take even longer to let go."

Logan nodded. "I don't know if it's true that time heals all wounds. But it does make most things easier to bear. In time we learn acceptance, if nothing else. Then we go on from there."

She knew exactly what he was getting at. He hoped she would go on from Andrew to him. The thought sent two conflicting emotions raging through her body: a pleasurable thrill and a sense of danger. Logan was exciting, but he also was dangerous—she was sure of that.

"Why did you mention Andrew?" she asked when the waiter had removed their plates.

"Because there's a barrier between us. I felt it all

day today. Every time we began to get close, you backed off. I assume it's the memory of Andrew that's bothering you."

He was both right and wrong. She had put Andrew behind her, at least as the focus of her love and devotion. But the lesson she'd learned from her marriage to him was one she would never forget. Never again would she let herself be controlled by a man as she had been by Andrew. She knew instinctively Logan would take control if she let him.

Perhaps it was time, she thought, to tell him exactly how she felt. There was certainly no use denying the attraction between them. If she explained how determined she was to remain free, her own person, perhaps he would stop pursuing her and leave her in peace.

Her hands curved around the warmth of the white porcelain cup. Slowly she took a sip of the strong tea the English loved and she was only beginning to like. Finally she found the courage to raise her eyes to his.

Gazing directly at him, she said, "I was so very young when I married Andrew. I knew almost nothing about life, about people...especially about myself. Looking back on it now, I think Andrew represented the security I'd never had. And he was charming...a fascinating powerful man. Because I wanted to please him, I became socially adept, even though I hated those big superficial parties."

Logan listened intently, ignoring the coffee growing cold on the table in front of him.

"Andrew encouraged my law studies and was proud of my accomplishments...until I wanted to go my own way and do what I felt was right even when it differed with his beliefs. I'm nearly twenty-nine. Yet it's only been the past few months that I've felt grown-up, a free independent person, able to choose for myself, to be whatever I want to be. I want to live my own life now, Logan,'' she insisted, emphasizing each word carefully. ''On my own terms. I know what commitment means, especially marriage. I know the sacrifices of self that are involved. And I'm simply not interested right now in surrendering my freedom.''

For a long moment Logan said nothing.

Nicola sipped her tea and waited for him to speak.

Turning away, he motioned to the waiter, who came immediately with the check.

Silent, Logan helped her slip on the mink jacket. Outside, the cool night air made Nicola's skin tingle. Logan still hadn't spoken. Had she offended him so terribly, she wondered, anxiety building inside her.

In the car Logan turned on the heater. Still she felt a chill—of that apprehension, she guessed—as they sped through the dark quiet London streets. She had as much as told Logan she wasn't interested in him. Why hadn't he responded? Perhaps this blow to his ego had angered him. And yet when she stole a glance at his face, there was no anger there. His expression was unreadable; only a tightening of his jaw betrayed any emotion.

The uncomfortable silence continued until they were at her front door. As she removed her key from her evening bag, Logan reached for it and unlocked the door.

Looking up at him, Nicola felt a stab of remorse so

intense it jolted her. Should she take back her words? No, a stubborn voice insisted deep inside her. She'd spent seven years being someone's shadow. Now it was her chance to step out into the sunlight, to be herself and not a reflection of a more powerful personality. If she gave in to Logan James now, she'd never be free again.

His deep eyes surveyed her intently. The corners of his mouth crinkled in a gentle smile, infinitely tender and understanding. It occurred to her that he knew what she was thinking.

With a faint sense of panic she hurriedly said, "I had a lovely time, Logan. Thank you. I'll see you at the meeting Monday. Good night."

Before she could step through the door to close it securely behind her, he extended a hand and held her shoulder with a light, but irresistible touch.

"Maybe it's too soon," he said softly. "I won't rush you. You don't need that kind of pressure now. But I'm not about to let you run away from what's between us. You may as well face this now—I love you. I fell in love with you that night in Washington, even though you were married and I knew you were off limits. My feelings haven't changed, and they won't change. I want you . . . and I can wait."

He was so close to her at the moment she could feel his warm breath on her cheek, see the tiny points of gold in his eyes. Bending his head, he kissed her, pulling her into his arms. Her breasts were crushed against his hard broad chest. As before, his lips were surprisingly gentle as they touched hers. Yet behind the tenderness she sensed a towering passion barely held in check. Senses reeling, she felt herself falling, falling into a warm enveloping darkness of pure physical sensation.

She'd never dreamed it could be this way. On the level of pure instinct she had known there should be more to lovemaking than what she'd experienced with Andrew. Now she knew she could never have imagined this missing part...this complete giving way to desire so that even thought was extinguished.

What she felt now made it seem that until this moment her life had been empty. This poignant thought intensified her newly aroused passion, making her response to Logan full and uninhibited. She'd waited far too long for this delicious sensation of pure bliss.

Some part of her that remained rational, still aware of the danger this man represented, cried, *don't give way. Don't let him touch that part of you that's never been touched. Once you've tasted from that tree of knowledge you can never go back to innocence.*

It was too late. Her arms were around his neck, and his body fit hers as if it had been made only for her. That nagging fear, that voice of reason, receded into her dim unconscious as her body was shaken by new and overpowering sensations.

Logan was the one who finally drew back. His face was pale, his eyes dark with emotion. She could see that he fought with every fiber of his being to control his passion. She knew that he, too, had been overwhelmed by a tidal wave of feeling so intense it left him reeling. A part of her gloried in the knowledge that she could make him feel this way.

In a voice that was suddenly strange and unfamiliar he said, "Good night, Nicola." Quickly he turned and walked away.

Inside, she leaned against the closed door for a long moment, pulling herself together. What had happened was inevitable. She knew she had subconsciously been expecting it from the first moment they'd met again in Thomas's office. Yet she wasn't prepared for the almost terrifying response he'd awakened in her.

She knew he meant what he said. Logan James wasn't a man to be easily put off when he wanted something. And he wanted *her*.

Now she could no longer deny that she wanted him, too. Not only wanted him, she could love him.... It would be so effortless to take that one step, to let her heart lead her. But she was convinced that in that way lay danger—to her heart and to the fragile new life she was building for herself. Logan James was the kind of man who dominated all around him. Nicola didn't want to lose herself again to a dominating man.

As she finally climbed the stairs to her bedroom, her emotions were in turmoil, her mind and heart in a war as old as time itself. Would she do the safe thing, keep him at arm's length? *Could* she?

CHAPTER EIGHT

NICOLA AWAKENED EARLY. Beyond her bedroom window she saw a gray skyline. There was a decided chill in the room, and she burrowed deeper under the satin comforter.

Then she remembered that this morning was the meeting with Gerald Laughton. Although she would be present only in an advisory capacity and would have little to say, the gathering necessitated being with Logan. She'd have to face the profound response his presence evoked in her ever since his kiss had seared her very soul.

"Oh, well," she sighed aloud. Lying under the covers like a frightened child wouldn't solve anything; the situation had to be dealt with. She threw back the comforter.

Half an hour later, she was dressed in a pale blue tweed suit and matching cowl-neck cashmere sweater. Her hair was pulled back in a twist secured by a tortoiseshell pin, and her briefcase swung by her side as she crossed the street to her car. She hoped she looked every inch an attorney because that was precisely what she wanted to project that day...*all* business...no nonsense.

The office was already bustling when she arrived.

With a pleasant good morning to the clerks and attorneys she passed, Nicola hurried toward her office. Thomas's London office served a broad spectrum of clients doing business in Europe, and his staff was a very international group.

Gladys gave her a cheery hello. "There are hot cross buns and tea in the lounge, Miss Wynter."

"Thanks," Nicola responded with a grateful smile, for she had left the house without breakfast. She took a bun and a cup of tea into her office and sat down at her desk. Since she had gone through Logan's files thoroughly the previous week, she intended to take this time to brush up on some minor details.

"Good morning, Nicola." The sound of his familiar drawl at once set her senses tingling.

Glancing up, she met those marvelous eyes that were like no other eyes in the world. This morning their expression was carefully under control, betraying no hint of the rising passion she'd seen there the last time she looked into them.

"I thought I'd give you a ride to the meeting with Laughton," Logan continued easily.

He was dressed according to the strictest standards of British working regulations...a three-piece gray suit and white shirt closed firmly at the throat by a navy tie. With his hands thrust casually in his pockets, there was something about his attitude that revealed an unspoken mocking of convention.

Well, you can take the boy out of Louisiana... Nicola told herself, not bothering to finish the thought.

This must have brought a smile to her face, for Logan said, "Glad you're taking my suggestion to smile more." Before she could come up with a retort, he continued, "Well, we'd better be going. It'll take a while to get to Laughton's office, and it's nearly nine now."

The clock on her desk said 8:30. Surprised, Nicola realized Logan was nervous about this meeting. Clearly it meant a great deal to him. Picking up her briefcase, she rose. "I'm ready," she said brightly.

A half hour later they were sitting in a conference room at the Department of Energy. Across the table were the British representatives, Gerald Laughton, Lord Carlisle, as well as representatives from Her Majesty's Treasury and British Petroleum. To Nicola's amusement, they had all come in wearing bowlers and carrying tightly rolled umbrellas.

Laughton was a short slender man with thinning brown hair and a nervous manner. He perfunctorily disposed of the agenda, from the price-adjustment schedule to the import licenses. Nicola answered his questions succinctly, only rarely having to consult her notes and files.

At one point Logan flashed Nicola a look that clearly said, "I'm impressed. You're doing a great job."

For her part, *she* was impressed with Logan's composure. This contract was crucial to him. Yet he appeared perfectly calm.

When they adjourned for lunch, Logan and Nicola retreated to a small pub nearby that featured seafood. As the waiter served their clam chowder, Logan said sincerely, "You did a marvelous job."

"Thanks. But you're the one who came up with a solid bid. I think you stand a good chance of winning the contract."

His gaze revealed real concern for the first time all morning. "I hope so. The other bidder, Mannering, has a psychological edge. They're a British company, although they work worldwide, as we do."

"Do you think that really matters?"

"Being British?" He shrugged. "Who knows? We have the technical edge. We'll just have to wait and see. Our presentation will be finished this afternoon, and a decision should be made before too long. If we win, we'll be busy blocking out subcontract proposals."

From what she had learned in her recent study of Logan's files, she was convinced he was the best person for the job. His record as an engineer was impressive. He'd built port facilities in Kuwait and pipelines in Valdez, Alaska. On each occasion he had come in on time and under budget. Although he'd tackled these jobs with platoons of technicians and the latest computer equipment, not to mention a huge budget, it was obviously his personality that made the difference. He was a perfectionist who demanded and got the best, both in terms of people and material.

"What is going on in that legal mind of yours?" Logan asked, interrupting her thoughts.

"I was just thinking that you deserve to win this contract," she answered honestly.

"I'll drink to that." Logan smiled at her and finished his Perrier.

The waiter arrived with their entrée, lobster thermidor. As Nicola enjoyed the delicious dish, her thoughts wandered traitorously from the business at hand. *What if I'd met Logan before I met Andrew,* she wondered. *That night in the garden in Washington might have ended very differently if I'd been free. There'd have been nothing to stop him from pursuing me, and I doubt that I'd have resisted. At this moment we would be lovers, not client and attorney. I'd know more of him than just his kiss.* She felt her cheeks grow warm at the thought and pretended to concentrate on her food.

Those shrewd eyes that never seemed to miss anything about her had caught that look. "Nicola—" Logan began, his voice low and husky.

"We'd better hurry," she interrupted. "We're due back in half an hour." *Later,* she told herself. *Right now, we both need all our wits about us for this meeting.*

Walking back toward the government buildings under a cold gray sky, they came upon the first sidewalk artist Nicola had seen since she'd come to England. An elderly man with a thin face, wearing a black stocking cap, was kneeling on the sidewalk. The squares of pavement were his canvases, and he had already completed several pictures with his colored chalk. One was a lovely garden filled with bright red and blue flowers, framed by elaborate curlicues. Another was of clouds in a baby-blue sky. With deep concentration the crouching artist worked on a new picture—a spreading tree beside a gentle stream, with low lavender hills in the distance.

"How lovely," Nicola exclaimed.

"What's nice about these artists is that they're not elitist," Logan told Nicola as they watched the man's deft strokes. "They sell transient pleasure to anyone who wants it. All it costs is a coin tossed in a hat." He dropped a pound note into the man's upturned hat, where a small mound of coins had accumulated.

"Thanks, guv'nor." The man gave them a broad toothless smile and bent once more to his work.

"They'll be gone by tonight, I suppose," Nicola said, thinking that the pictures were as impermanent as happiness.

"Specially for you, miss," the man said, quickly adding an arch of colors to make a rainbow over the lavender hills.

"Perfect." Nicola's smile was rueful. "Like all rainbows, it's brief, beautiful—and not true."

Logan's tawny eyes held hers in an intense gaze. "It's true enough, Nicola," he said. "The rainbow's promise is real. . . if we let ourselves believe it."

GOLDEN SEPTEMBER ended summer. The last defiant green leaves on the trees finally turned russet, gold and orange before falling to the ground. English autumn began, unspeakably cold, gray and bleak.

After the meeting with the representatives from the English government there was nothing further Logan could do to secure the contract. His many other projects—among them, the petrochemical plant in Baton Rouge, construction of an offshore drilling rig near Santa Barbara—all required his attention. He was away from London most of the time.

Nicola told herself she didn't miss him, that it was easier to keep her life under control when he was gone. But the independence she guarded so jealously often seemed flat and empty.

On rainy nights by the fire in her sitting room she couldn't help thinking of him, wondering where he was, what he was doing, whom he was with. When Mrs. Murdle made transparent remarks about the need for "certain young people to get out an' enjoy themselves before they're too old," Nicola merely shook her head and smiled. The thought of dating any man—anyone but Logan—seemed an exercise in futility.

Logan found reasons to be in London as often as possible. When he was in town, they went out—to dinner, to West End plays, on short trips into the countryside. True to his word, he said nothing more about their future. Although his good-night kisses grew longer, more ardent, more difficult to end, he didn't press her.

One Saturday morning when London was thick with a proverbial "pea-soup" fog, Nicola received an unexpected phone call.

"Is this Nicola Wynter?" a very British voice on the other end of the line asked.

"Yes," Nicola responded, puzzled. The voice sounded vaguely familiar, but it definitely wasn't anyone from the office.

"This is Gerald Laughton, Miss Wynter."

Now Nicola remembered him. It was odd that he was calling her at home on a Saturday. And how did he get her number, she wondered.

Before she could ask, he continued in a brisk businesslike voice, "We're on the verge of making a decision, Miss Wynter, but we need a little more information. I understand that Mr. James is in the States."

"I'm sure his London office can give you a number where he can be reached," Nicola answered.

Laughton replied promptly. "Of course. But I thought that since you're here and you know a great deal about the situation, you could simply give me the information I need."

"I'll certainly try," Nicola offered. She wished Logan were there. It was rotten timing, having to be away just when they were apparently on the point of deciding.

"Good. Could you meet me at Lord Alfred Carlisle's residence in an hour? It's 9 Belgrave Square."

"May I ask why we're meeting at Lord Carlisle's residence? Wouldn't your office be more suitable?" Nicola asked, a faint twinge of apprehension threading through her mind.

"Lord Carlisle is with British Petroleum. He's actually the one with questions that require clearing up. And he's working at home today...a bit under the weather. I'll just be there to supervise, so to speak."

Nicola seemed to remember Carlisle being at the meeting. But he had said little and hadn't made much of an impression on her. Trying hard now to place him among the numerous British contingent, she decided he had been the tall, urbane-looking man who seemed almost a stereotype of a British aristocrat.

"Very well," she finally answered. Even as she

agreed, some inner warning buzzer sounded. *Damn,* she thought. This didn't seem proper, even if there was nothing overtly wrong about it. How she wished Logan were there. If only Thomas hadn't chosen this weekend to go to Paris. She really was on her own. "I'll see you shortly."

"Good. I'm terribly sorry to inconvenience you on your day off, but this should wrap things up nicely."

When Laughton hung up, Nicola stood for a moment by the telephone, trying to understand her concern. Was this a harbinger of good news or bad?

Belgrave Square was one of the oldest, most exclusive residential areas in London. Many of the stately mansions surrounding the beautiful sunken garden in the center were now embassies. Number 9 was imposing, set back amid a garden protected by a black wrought-iron fence.

A uniformed maid answered the door and showed Nicola into the sitting room, where a fire blazed cheerfully in an ornate marble fireplace. "His lordship will be with you in a moment, miss," the maid said primly, closing the door behind her.

Nicola set her briefcase on a table. She had stopped by the office to pick up her files on Logan, and now the case was heavy.

Almost immediately Lord Carlisle came in, followed closely by Gerald Laughton. "Ah, Miss Wynter. Lovely to see you again," Lord Carlisle declared jovially.

"Indeed," Laughton added politely.

Nicola shook hands with both of them, then said, "I hope you won't mind if I come straight to the point. How may I help you?"

"Oh, just a minor question about the convertibility clause. But as it's the last thing that needs to be clarified before we can come to a decision, I thought we might as well take care of it today." Carlisle walked over to a bar and asked over his shoulder, "May I get you a drink?"

"No, thank you." She wanted to add that it was hardly noon and rather early for drinking, but she couldn't. This man would soon be helping make a decision that was crucial to Logan's company, and she wasn't about to endanger his chances.

"I hope you won't mind if Gerald and I indulge," Lord Carlisle asked with a smile.

"Of course not."

After pouring two drinks and handing one to Laughton, Carlisle turned back to Nicola. "Please sit down." As she did so, he continued in a more businesslike tone, "Now about this convertibility clause...."

For several minutes they discussed the issue. Nicola looked through her files and was able to answer Carlisle's questions.

She had hardly been in his home for fifteen minutes, when he rose and said, "Well, that's all settled then. So glad you could come by and help us with this."

"I'll see Miss Wynter to the door," Laughton offered.

"Good. I do hope we meet again, Miss Wynter."

Nicola smiled noncommittally and followed Laughton out of the sitting room into the massive entryway, with its marble columns and marble floor. As Laughton opened the front door for her, he said unexpectedly, "I don't think there's any harm in telling you, it looks as if your client will win the contract."

Nicola paused, surprised. "Do you really think so?"

"Yes, indeed. Well, I really can't say more at this point. But we'll be in touch."

Hurrying homeward, Nicola felt exuberant. She wished Logan were there so she could share the news and relieve his worries. On second thought, she decided, maybe it was best he was gone. If something were to go wrong at the last minute, it would be too disappointing for him. But she couldn't entirely contain her sense of excitement.

On Monday morning, Nicola was sitting at her desk when Logan burst into the office. She hadn't been aware of his return from the States, and his sudden appearance startled her. "Logan!"

"Nicola!" His face was suffused with a huge grin, and his voice was nearly a shout. Coming around her desk, he pulled her to her feet, then spun around with her, laughing all the while.

"What on earth?" she gasped.

"We did it! We beat Mannering! The contract's ours!"

Impulsively Nicola hugged him, feeling a rush of joy and relief.

"I just got into the office an hour ago," Logan continued exuberantly. "There was a message for me to call Gerald Laughton. He told me they're awarding the contract to me. They'll make the announcement in a few days, after all the loose ends are tied up."

"Oh, Logan. . . I'm so happy for you." She started to tell him she'd been expecting this, but he interrupted her.

"Let's get out of here. We have some celebrating to do. Thomas will understand."

"I can't," Nicola protested as he grabbed her coat from the rack in the corner and put it over her shoulders.

"Of course you can," Logan insisted.

"Just let me talk to Thomas—"

"I'll talk to him," Logan said as he propelled her down the hallway. Stopping at Thomas's door, he knocked once, then flung it open.

Startled, Thomas looked up from his desk, where he had been perusing some papers.

"I'm kidnapping your prize attorney for the rest of the day, Thomas. I've got a lot of celebrating to do, and I don't intend to do it alone."

Thomas beamed. "I take it you won the contract, then?"

"I did, indeed."

"Well, forge ahead, then, old boy. Do bring her back sometime, though. We've come rather to depend on having her around, you know."

"I can understand why," Logan answered, looking warmly down at Nicola.

A moment later they were outside in the clear sunny autumn day. In his haste, Logan had double-parked his car on the side street close to Thomas's office. "Where are we going?" Nicola asked.

"Who knows?" he replied blithely as they hurried along the flagstone paving, ducking under arches and barely avoiding the branches of sprawling trees.

Nicola felt like a giddy schoolgirl playing hooky. Left behind was the quiet staid decorum of the Thomas St. Ives law office. Ahead of her was a day with Logan. And that could mean anything.

As they reached the car, Logan told her, "I've just landed the biggest contract of my career, and I intend to enjoy the triumph."

Surprisingly, he chose a small intimate restaurant overlooking the Thames. But he vociferously informed the waiter they were celebrating and ordered champagne.

"To us," he said, lifting his glass to her, looking deep into her eyes. "We make a great team."

Caught up in his warmth and excitement, all her doubts forgotten, Nicola returned his toast. "To us." For a long moment time seemed suspended, with the two of them drowning in each other's eyes.

All during lunch Logan made millions of plans. Nicola had to laugh at him when he ended by using his napkin to draw a long list of things to be done.

The champagne had made her dreamy, she thought, while sipping her coffee and staring out the window at the tourist boats heading up the Thames. Glancing up, she met Logan's eyes.

"Have you ever been up the Thames?" he asked.

"No." She smiled. "There's been so little time for anything but work since I've been here."

"Today there's time for everything," Logan announced as if it were a royal proclamation. "Let's go...."

Quickly he paid the bill, and they were off to yet another adventure.

They drove down to the pier, with Nicola laughing at his impulsive antics as they boarded one of the numerous boats anchored there. "Is this yours?" she asked in surprise.

"No. It belongs to a friend. He's away and told me to make use of it." He grinned at her. "Even this day was meant for celebrating. How many beautiful sunshiny days does London offer this time of year?"

While Logan unfurled the sail, Nicola sat down on a padded seat, observing his obvious capability. Was there anything he couldn't do, she wondered as he brought the boat expertly about and headed upstream.

As the boat moved smoothly upriver, they passed landmarks that Logan identified for her... Westminster Pier, the terraces of the Houses of Parliament, the old walls and towers of Lambeth Palace.

"All England awaits you, my lady," he announced, flourishing a wide gesture at the passing scenery. "Did you know English royalty once used the Thames to travel between palaces? You can be my queen... and I your gallant knight in Harristweed armor."

My knight, Nicola thought, smiling at him, *the knight I wished for on a star once in a garden that's now an ocean and a lifetime away.* Logan reached over and gently stroked her silken cheek. The Thames and all of London were forgotten as their eyes held for a long enchanted moment.

"My Nicola," Logan said almost reverently. In those two simple words he managed to convey a world of meaning. Unfortunately the sails required his immediate attention, and all too soon he was gone.

Nicola saw that they were traveling beneath the wide Victoria Railway Bridge, then the Chelsea Suspension Bridge. "There's my house," she exclaimed, pointing to the red-brick houses of Cheyne Walk, visible beyond the Embankment.

"This is the most picturesque stretch of the river," Logan told her, and casting her his most charming smile added, "But nothing can beat the scenery I have in my boat."

"I'm not sure that's a compliment," she laughed as they slipped past a stretch of gray and dreary-looking factories.

Then she saw the Surrey hills in the distance. Along the banks there appeared little parish churches and rowing-club boathouses. The terraces of 18th-century mansions faced the river. Richmond rose majestically behind a bridge, with formal gardens and grand houses barely visible through the trees.

Logan brought the boat around at the wooded riverbank and dropped anchor. A carpet of emerald green grass stretched down to the edge of the water. Weeping willows trailed slender bare branches in the gently moving river.

"A perfect spot to finish our perfect afternoon," Logan said, stretching contentedly.

Sitting in the rear of the boat, Nicola relaxed and smiled at him. Everything was still and quiet; the only sounds were the soft lap of water against the boat and birds calling in the distance.

Logan leaned back in the seat facing Nicola, his arm resting on the tiller as he thoughtfully considered her. "I have to fly to Scotland tomorrow to inspect the North Sea site," he said. "Will you go with me?"

Looking down at her hands in her lap, Nicola hesitated. She realized what this trip could mean . . . being alone with Logan with nothing to restrain the passion they felt for each other. She looked away, unable to meet his eyes.

"Nicola?" The word was spoken softly, each syllable a caress. It was as though he had touched her, arousing an undeniable yearning.

Her voice was barely above a whisper as she met his searching eyes. "Yes . . . I'll go with you."

CHAPTER NINE

NICOLA STOOD ON a bleak, stone-shingled beach on the northern coast of Scotland. She looked out at the gray sea stretching past barren rocks to an equally gray and forbidding sky. Squawking sea gulls circled overhead. The landscape was austere, broken only by the small village nearby.

This place was so different from the rest of Scotland. As they'd flown over the country earlier that morning, Nicola had found it enchanting...the gentle, lavender-and-blue hills of the Lowlands, the green woods and deep blue lakes of central Scotland and the heathery moors of the Highlands in the north. It was all wildly beautiful.

But this coast.... Nicola looked around in dismay. It seemed like the end of the world. Thinking of Logan working under such harsh conditions gave her a sudden insight into his character. He had to be hard in a way to make a living in places like this. The freezing cold of Alaska and the searing heat of Arabia had probably been even worse. A man who could shape the building of massive structures in such places must have an iron will, no matter how it was concealed by smooth Southern charm.

And here I am alone with him, she thought. *I doubt very much that my will is as strong as his.*

Suddenly she felt raindrops on her face. Looking up, she saw black storm clouds moving in.

Logan had warned her what to expect, and she had dressed warmly. She wore a heavy coat of gray and taupe over beige wool trousers, with an argyle turtleneck. Gray leather gloves and boots completed the warm outfit.

Even as snugly wrapped as she was, she shivered in the biting sting of the harsh North Sea wind. Her face felt as cold as ice. She'd forgotten to put on a hat or bring an umbrella. In the worsening rain, tiny rivulets of water coursed down her cheeks and soaked her hair.

Walking up behind her, Logan said, "We'd better get back."

"Yes," Nicola agreed, turning to face him.

They hurried to the small rented car they'd taken from the tiny airstrip nearby. In only a couple of minutes they were back in the village. When Nicola had first seen it, she'd thought it too small and unlovely to be impressive. Now, however, the old stone cottages and the ancient inn seemed a warmly welcoming respite from the storm and the dreariness of the countryside.

By the time they'd reached the shelter of the inn, a huddled ancient structure, rain was falling hard. Thick slanting sheets of water obscured everything beyond the distance of a few yards. When they entered the foyer, where coats and umbrellas were hung, Nicola thought how pleasant was the mingled scent of tangy sea air and burning driftwood. From somewhere back in the inn came the unmistakable thud of a dart in a cork board and a jubilant shout of, "Double-twenty!"

As they took off their dripping coats, Nicola wondered if they would still be flying back that evening as planned. Logan himself had piloted the plane up there. Nicola had learned enough from Lisa about flying to know she should be impressed with his ability. Surely, she thought, the best of pilots wouldn't go up in a storm like this.

Logan might have been answering her unspoken thought when he announced, "We can't fly in this weather. I'll call the weather station in Inverness and find out how long it's likely to last. When I phoned this morning, they said there should be only light rain at worst." He smiled, then added, "But of course the weatherman is always wrong." He disappeared down the hall, where there was a telephone.

Nicola seated herself at a wooden trestle table near the roaring fire in the ancient stone fireplace. Gratefully she felt the warmth seeping into her chilled body. Her hair hung wetly down her back, and she shook it out, spraying drops of water on the table.

The room was flanked with long settles and scented with hundreds of years of driftwood smoke.

"What'll it be, miss?" a smiling young waitress asked in an accent so thick Nicola could hardly understand her.

"Tea, please."

A moment later the girl returned with a brown pottery mug and a small teapot with steam rising from its spout.

"Do you have any idea how long the storm will last?" Nicola inquired.

"Hard to say, miss. Like as not 'twill go on all day."

Looking around the haphazard, low-ceilinged room, Nicola realized things could be worse. This was a warmly inviting place on a stormy day. Still, it wasn't really physical comfort she had on her mind. It was the thought of staying there alone with Logan.

Just then he returned with the proprietor of the inn. "They think the storm will die down by morning," he said. "In the meantime, Mr. McGregor's arranged for us to have a couple of rooms."

"Aye," the large jovial innkeeper replied. "Two o' the best rooms in the place. Ye'll be comfortable, miss, dunna' worry about that. Come now, an' I'll show ye to yer rooms."

"But I didn't bring any overnight things," Nicola protested, remembering she didn't have so much as a toothbrush with her.

"There's Gunn's Store just down the High Street that has whatever ye might need," McGregor assured her as they ascended the stairs and walked down a wide hallway. Opening a door, he said, "This is yer room, miss."

It was charming, with flowered wallpaper, white lace curtains and a huge old four-poster bed. A small fireplace was laid for a fire.

"We'll just take the chill off," McGregor offered, bending to light the fire. In a moment the wood was crackling cheerfully, and the room, which had been cold, indeed, began to warm up. Turning to Logan, he said, "I'll show ye to yer room now, sir."

The two men left, and almost immediately Nicola heard another door opening. Logan's room was nearby, probably next door.

A moment later Logan returned, alone. With a grin he asked, "Are you ready for our shopping trip to Gunn's?"

Gunn's turned out to be a general store with a little bit of everything. Because of the influx of American engineers and other people involved in oil drilling, it had stocked up on a few luxuries. Nicola located not only the necessary toothbrush and toothpaste, but a fleecy white nightgown with billowing sleeves and a lace ruffle at the neck.

When she took her purchases to the counter, she found Logan waiting with only a toothbrush and a razor in his hands. Obviously he didn't feel the need for pajamas. At the mental image of Logan without pajamas, she felt a slow flush creep up her cheeks.

After their dash back to the inn, Nicola's hair was soaking wet. Alone in her room, she took off her dripping coat and her sweater and trousers. Standing in front of the brightly burning fire, she shook out her hair, hoping the fire's heat would dry it.

A knock at her door startled her. Grabbing the folded wool blanket at the end of the bed, she wrapped it around her shoulders, then answered the door.

Logan smiled at her. "You look charmingly bedraggled." His eyes glinted mischievously. As they took in her bare shoulders, revealed under the hastily thrown-on blanket, he added, "I must say, that suits you." Before Nicola could reply he asked, "May I come in?" He stood in the doorway, looking incredibly attractive.

For a moment Nicola was tempted to respond with

a firm no. Her state of half undress, Logan's over-powering masculinity, the remoteness and isolation of their location, all made her feel more vulnerable than she had in a long time. More vulnerable, in fact, than she'd felt since that heady night in the garden in Washington, when she'd been so susceptible to his virile charm.

But she wasn't about to give in to these feelings of helplessness. Pulling herself together, she replied, "Of course," and stepped back to let him enter.

Glancing around the room, Logan saw a thick white towel hanging near a washstand that held an old-fashioned pitcher and bowl. "Here," he said, grabbing the towel. "You'd better dry off or you'll catch pneumonia." Without hesitation he began roughly to dry her hair.

Squirming, Nicola protested, "Logan, I'm perfect-ly capable of drying my own hair!" She pulled back. Her gleaming golden hair was no longer plastered wetly against her head but hung full and thick and disheveled. She tossed it back with a quick movement of her hands.

"You have no idea how charming you look right now," Logan said in a voice husky with desire.

At once Nicola was intensely aware that beneath the thin blanket she wore only a sheer silk bra and panties. One bra strap was visible, and she saw Logan's eyes fasten there.

She thought he would come to her then. Her body tensed with a pleasurable mixture of nervousness and anticipation, and her fingers tightened on the blanket. She felt a tingle deep in her stomach, and her lips parted slightly as her breathing became shallow.

He reached out one finger and lightly traced the narrow pink strap to the point where it disappeared under the blanket.

Nicola's entire being yearned for him. She stood rooted to the spot, unable to move, to speak, to deny in any way what she felt for him.

Then, to her surprise, he pulled back suddenly. His body stiffened perceptibly with the effort of maintaining his distance from her. "Mr. McGregor said lunch will be served in half an hour. I'll meet you downstairs." And he turned and strode from the room.

Nicola simply stood there for a moment. Then her body shuddered with both relief and disappointment. She realized that he wouldn't force her. He wouldn't even take advantage of her vulnerability. He wanted her to come to him willingly, knowing what was in store, so that afterward there would be no regrets.

Sighing, she moved back toward the fire and began to comb out her hair. When it was dry, she brushed it until it shone, then left it hanging thick and straight past her shoulders. She had only lipstick and mascara in her purse. After applying these, she put on her sweater and trousers, which had dried and warmed by the fire.

Downstairs, Logan was already seated in the small wood-paneled dining room. In his heavy white cable-knit sweater, dark wool pants and sturdy boots he might almost have passed for one of the locals who filled the room. A fire blazed in the massive old stone fireplace. The entire effect was cozy, peaceful and seductive in its simplicity.

As Nicola sat down, Logan eyed her appreciatively. "You look lovely," he said softly. "Not many women could go through a rainstorm like this one and emerge barely an hour later looking so terrific."

The obviously sincere compliment pleased her, but it also made her self-conscious. Before she could decide how to respond, Logan went on, "I'm afraid the menu's pretty limited here. Lamb or salmon. But they're both excellent."

Nicola watched as the waitress took a plate of steaming hot salmon to a nearby table. It looked utterly delicious.

"Mmm. Real Scottish salmon sounds good," Nicola replied enthusiastically.

Logan smiled, and she felt her heart soar. His smile took her breath away; it was that simple.

"Salmon for two, then," Logan said to the waitress who had served them earlier.

The meal was plain but delicious. Strong Scotch broth, thick slices of dark pink salmon that was succulent and tender, rich creamy scalloped potatoes. They finished with a delicious trifle made of sponge cake, pudding, raspberry jam and just a touch of brandy.

Nicola felt pleasantly relaxed. The good food, the warmth of the fire, the shelter of this quaint charming inn on this storm-tossed afternoon all combined to make her feel mellow and happy. For once she was at peace with herself, with no desire to argue with Logan or put him off with chilly politeness.

Looking at her intently, Logan said, "I didn't arrange the storm, you know."

She didn't pretend to misunderstand. "I know."

After a moment's silence, he continued matter-of-factly, "The weather report expects clearing by morning. Although the weather can be awfully changeable up here. I've seen it clear one minute, then quickly grow stormy the next. Right now I have to run up the coast to the construction site. Beau and my estimator, Sam Johnson, and a team of engineers are up there now, waiting for me."

Nicola smiled. "Oh, yes, that fleet of engineers...."

He smiled in return. "Well, it takes a fleet of engineers and high-tech equipment to make serendipity happen."

Turning to look out the window, Nicola saw that the storm was much worse. The rain fell so thickly it was impossible to see across the High Street. Thunder and lightning rumbled and flashed across a black sky. All her life she'd been afraid of such storms. They brought out her deepest insecurities.

Her apprehension growing, she looked back at Logan. "It's pretty bad out there. Do you really have to go?"

"That's why I came. I planned on taking you with me, but I think you'd better wait here."

Nicola frowned, wishing he would postpone the trip. "Where are you going exactly?"

"My people arrived yesterday and set up a camp on the planned construction site. I've got to go over the terrain and take a look at the places out in the bay where the tanker berths are to be built. I've been there before, of course, but then everything was theoretical. Knowing I'll be doing the job makes a difference.''

"You're going out on the ocean in this weather?'' Her voice was sharp with concern. When they'd been on the beach earlier, the ocean had looked ominous. Although she couldn't see it from the inn, she was sure it was much worse now. It would be dangerous.

"There are high-powered boats designed especially to travel in weather like this,'' he assured her.

Suppressing the urge to grab his arm and insist that he stay, Nicola reluctantly gave in. "If the weather's still bad when you get there, don't try to come back. Stay there. I'll be all right.''

His smile held a hint of passion. "Don't worry, Nicola. I'll be back.''

As he pulled on his heavy coat, Logan watched her. She knew her face must reflect her anxiety. Her every instinct advised her to stall for time. Quickly she discarded the thought, knowing it would do no good. This was simply part of his work. He would never give in to her fears for his safety.

Logan reached out one finger and lightly tilted her chin so that she was looking into his eyes. "I'll be back,'' he repeated. *And then we'll finally be together,* the expression in his eyes said clearly.

Nicola stood in the foyer, watching him through the leaded windows. Filled with trepidation, she continued to watch until his car was out of sight in the rain.

During the long lonely hours she spent waiting by

the fire in the lounge, she thought about Logan. *This is what he's all about,* she realized. *He'll always be rushing off somewhere, often to dangerous places. Do I want to live with this, going from one tense situation to another? And if I don't, can I back out?*

She knew the answer. When she made the decision to come up to Scotland with him, it was, in reality, a decision to give in to the love she felt for him. They'd both known that. At that moment she'd gone past the point of no return. Now she could only wait, hope and pray he would come back to her as he'd promised.

A KNIFING RAIN driven by black thunderheads spread across the horizon, spattered against the windshield. Logan fought the buffeting winds as he drove the twisting lane towards Spaniard's Cove, where Beau and the team of engineers and estimators were waiting.

God, he thought, this Scottish north country was a harsh one. Beaten down by rain and wind like this day's to a surly stubborn heath. Hostile to men like him who would dare to try to carve it to their needs.

As always when on a new site, he thought of Papa and Uncle Alex. They used to laugh and say that much of the time where they drilled for oil looked like the jumping-off place for hell. That description might have fitted the last construction site—the dry hot Saudi Arabian desert—but it didn't fit a place on the North Sea coast of Scotland with a name like Spaniard's Cove.

It was true what they used to say. The oil game was

one that would never have a frontier until the last porous layer of rock had been explored. Those pioneers left their trailmarks across a continent, from Pennsylvania to California, then across a hemisphere, to Mexico and Venezuela. Now he and Beau, traveling in jets, crisscrossed the world in the same exciting search.

The rain eased a bit as Logan drove the last mile over the rutted quagmire that served as an access road to the barren little harbor. Through the mist he could make out the dun-colored, prefab dormitory that housed the field team. A bluff-bowed utility launch rocked on its moorings in the lee of the wooden dock that thrust out into the dark churning ocean. Beyond the breakwater, the sea, taking on the hue of the angry sky, rolled in heavy gray swells.

Damned fine day for a cruise, he thought, pulling in between a battered four-wheel-drive vehicle and a mud-spattered pickup parked in front of the building. Zipping up his heavy parka, he stepped out of the car into the icy teeth of the wind.

Just then Beau and another man, similarly bundled in heavy-weather gear, stepped out of the dorm.

"Thought maybe you had sense enough to stay home by the fire." Grinning, Beau gave Logan a welcoming embrace. "Have we got a deal?"

"Looks like it. So let's get to work."

They made their way down to the pier and boarded the launch. The craft was pre-World War II vintage. Her iron work was scabbed with rust, and she was creaking deep in her bones even at anchor.

Logan noticed Sam Johnson, the chief estimator,

shaking his head. "Damn, you sure this thing'll float?"

In the pilot house an elderly dwarf of a man awaited them. There was a belligerent cast to his eye as he peered at Logan, and clamped between his teeth was the rancid stub of a pipe.

Beau laid his hand on the man's shoulder. "This is Dougal, Logan, our pilot and the proud owner of this splendid craft. Knows these waters like a Mississippi barge captain knows our wily river's changing channels."

Dougal snorted and removed the pipe from his mouth. "I know naught of any Mississippi barge cap'n. But ye'll not be compellin' me out among the islands today, lad. Yon storm looks to break in a fury by nightfall."

Logan had learned to be wary of local "authorities" who warned of various perils that would invariably rear up to confront the outsider. Moreover, he'd caught a radio weather summary that morning. He hoped that the ominous thunderheads were only the trailing flank of a front that already had passed through.

He considered strangling the pilot, who was eyeing him craftily from behind the wheel. Instead he put on his most engaging smile. "The trouble is, I don't have another day to spend up here. Maybe we ought to talk about a 'hazard-duty' bonus. If you're interested?"

Dougal's gnarled face split into a gap-toothed grin. "Aye," he said, and reached for the starter switch.

The old kettle bucked her way across the channel,

groaning from the depths of her keel. Beau spread his blueprints on the chart-room table, and they went to work.

Logan looked out at the godforsaken excuse of a harbor, dotted with small islands, that he and his men would have to transform into tanker berths.

As Johnson's flat voice enumerated in tedious detail the expenses involved in working there, Logan's mind began to wander. His eyes drifted to the rain-spattered windshield beyond old Dougal's hunched shoulders.

Nicola.

He'd deliberately avoided thinking about her and the feast of love promised for the night ahead. Never had a woman such as she crossed his life.

Though she was beautiful, it wasn't her beauty that drew him to her. And while he admired the efficient way she handled herself while retaining her alluring femininity, it wasn't that, either.

It was her integrity. She was cautious and honored her commitments. He knew how she had felt that night when he'd first kissed her. She'd known the same fire of desire as had he. But she hadn't been free to yield to it and had been wise enough to refuse St. Ives's first offer. That she'd honored her commitment to Andrew made Logan value her all the more. With a woman like her a man wouldn't need to keep looking over his shoulder.

Her vulnerability matched his own. Without taking pride or arrogance from the knowledge, Logan knew that he feared nothing outside himself. But deep within, a reserve of strength abided in him that he wanted to share with a woman—to love and protect her . . . and someday, their children. Without fulfillment of this, he feared his life would be incomplete.

He'd known a lot of women. But until Nicola, he'd never wanted to make a lifelong commitment. She was the one he'd been waiting for. Hers was the face that promised the love he needed to share.

Then, as the boat shuddered into another swoop, Logan's reverie was broken by a question from Beau. From that moment on, for the rest of the miserable trip, he was kept busy equating the physical geography of the site to the drawings and specifications.

Logan was relieved when the boat finally nosed into harbor. He'd had about enough of the stormy trip. And besides, Nicola was waiting. Suddenly he couldn't wait to get back to her.

As they walked off the dock, Logan told Beau and Sam he'd see them in a few days when he returned to Baton Rouge.

"I think old Dougal's right," Beau said, looking at the driving rain. "This storm is working itself into a frenzy. Better spend the night here with us."

"No," Logan declined. "I'll get back to the village. It's not far." He waved and made a dash to his car.

A few minutes later, as the countryside faded into darkness, he had to admit old Dougal had been right. The storm broke in a fury. The rain fell in sheets so thick he could see hardly more than a few feet. The road became treacherously slippery. Twice the car skidded around sharp curves and he barely managed to avoid going into the ditch that ran along one side of the road.

And then he heard a loud pop, and the car swerved sharply. With effort Logan brought it to a halt on the pavement. He'd blown a tire. *God,* he thought, *let there be a spare.*

Hurriedly he unlocked the trunk. "Damn," he swore, standing there in the pelting rain. He should have checked when he'd rented it. *Well,* he thought, *I'm not going to sit here—when she's there at the inn.*

Slamming down the trunk, he locked the car and struck out down the road, his shoulders hunched against the rain.

NICOLA WATCHED THE STORM all afternoon and evening. She couldn't believe how fierce it had become. Never had she seen rain as thick or heard wind roar as this wind did. She understood now why the buildings in the village were all made of stone. Wood homes might very well be blown away in weather such as this. And to think of Logan out in it. . . .

By ten o'clock that night, Nicola couldn't bear to sit in the lounge any longer. When the evening meal was served, she'd managed to get down a steaming bowl of potato-and-leek soup with scones and tea. While she ate, she could only wonder if Logan was cold and hungry. Her apprehension increased to the point where she could not sit still.

Going up to her room, she changed into the nightgown she'd bought and huddled in the bed, blankets pulled up to her chin. Every time thunder cracked or lightning flashed, she winced, picturing Logan out in the wild night.

She hoped he was staying at the construction site. If he was on his way back to her, it would be fool-hardy and dangerous, though very much in charac-ter. Damn that man! He would probably consider a drive on a rain-soaked, muddy country road in the middle of a gigantic storm just another calculated risk. *Dear God,* she prayed fervently, *don't let his wildcatter's luck run out now.*

When the knock at her door finally came, she was out of the bed like a shot, flinging it open without even asking who it was.

It was Logan.

Nicola breathed a silent thanks.

He stood there, water dripping from his soaking hair. His coat, which hung from one hand, was sod-den. He looked half drowned. Relief flooded through her so violently that she threw herself into his arms.

"Thank God you're back." She stifled a sob and pressed her face against the shirt that clung wetly to his broad chest.

He held her tightly against him, then replied with maddening calm, "I told you I would be."

She pulled back, anger following on relief. "Logan James, you've put me through hell tonight! Now you come traipsing in as if you've been for a pleasant stroll. I . . . I . . . ."

He laughed. "Were you so worried about me, then? *Good!*" His eyes narrowed appreciatively as he took in her nightgown. The front of it where she'd pressed against him was wet and nearly transparent.

Nicola's breath caught. Her whole body went still as she returned his look.

Logan's wonderful leonine eyes held hers. His voice was low. "Nicola...I've loved you since that night in Washington. If you hadn't been married, I'd have claimed you then. I've been patient, waiting all summer and fall until the time was right for you. But tonight, darlin', my patience is all gone. I walked the last three miles here because the damn car died. I can't look at you anymore without touching you. If you don't love me, say so now. Because its almost too late for protests."

With all her heart Nicola knew she could no longer deny him. Her eyes met Logan's. She smiled a slow smile of surrender. "I think you'd better come in where it's warm. Before we scandalize the other guests."

He hesitated for the briefest second. Then he pushed the door firmly closed with one booted foot.

Trembling, Nicola watched as he kicked off his boots, dropping his drenched clothes in a pile on the hearth. When undressed, Logan turned to her, enfolding her in his strong arms. His mouth claimed hers in a kiss telling her that that long-ago first kiss had been only the merest prelude to what they must ultimately share.

"Nicola," he whispered, his voice hoarse with passion. "My God, I want you."

Her reserve burst then. With both hands she pulled his head down to touch his lips again, pressing her body desperately against his.

Her inhibitions were completely gone now in the face of the overriding passion she felt for this man.

"I love you, Logan," she whispered, committing herself totally. "Oh, God, I love you so much."

Carefully, with a patience Nicola could tell was hard pressed, he pulled the damp nightgown over her head and dropped it unceremoniously on the floor.

The room was lit only by the flickering light of the small fire. For a moment they stood naked beside each other, their bodies gleaming in the firelight. Then Logan picked her up in his arms. With infinite tenderness, as though she were as fragile as porcelain, he laid her on the big four-poster bed. Tenderness and fierce desire mingled in his eyes as he looked down at her.

That burning, barely banked fire she saw in him stirred her own passion. For the first time in her life she felt a physical need so great nothing could stop it. The wonder of it all, this feeling that she'd caught only a tantalizing glimpse of that night in the garden, stunned her. The barriers she'd tried to keep between them had been breached by a love so profound it had to find complete fulfillment. Holding out her arms, she drew him with her beneath the thick wool blankets and crisp white sheets. His aroused body molded itself to hers, and his kiss obliterated all thought.

In the fireplace a small log broke in two with a sputter and fell onto the hearth. Nicola dimly heard it.

"Logan," she whispered, her voice husky with passion. She pressed close to him, her arms holding him, her body one long aching need that only he could fill.

Drawing back, Logan looked at her. In the semi-dark of the room, his golden eyes seemed to glow like a cat's.

There's nothing in me he doesn't see, she thought, returning his intense gaze. *All the barriers are gone. And it's all right because I don't want to withhold anything from him. . . not any part of my being.*

"I've dreamed about you every single night since we met," he murmured against her cheek. "Somehow, some way, I knew we had to be together." His lips were on her eyelids, her cheek, the racing pulse at the base of her throat.

Without knowing it, she had waited all those months for this moment—ever since that night in the garden, when his kiss made her realize for the first time what could be between a man and a woman. This night was the inevitable culmination of that kiss. This night there was more than just emphatic desire between them. There was the reassuring certainty of fulfillment.

Logan was gentle with her. Yet neither could deny their mounting excitement. There was no time now to be patient with each other, to pause and observe and explore each other. That luxury would come later, when their urgent need was met. At this moment they only wanted desperately to be part of each other.

The pleasure his sure touch gave her was so exquisite she thought she might die of it. She gloried in his lovemaking, knowing this was what they had both been made for. Her body fitted his too perfectly for them not to have been ordained for each other.

His strong tender hands were miracles, transforming everything they touched. As they explored her, firing every inch of her bare skin, she responded by nuzzling his ear and kissing the strong curve of his neck. She was filled with the inexpressible joy of wanting him, needing him, having him.

Each time he touched her in a new, more intimate place, she felt a surge of delight and of discovery, for she was learning surprising new things about her body and its responses. Her heart beat violently; her body trembled; her voice, as she murmured words of love to him, deepened to a duskier tone tinged with passion.

As she felt the texture of his skin, the strength of his muscles rippling beneath her hands, she had a sensation of tremendous bodily warmth, as if she were drunk with fine wine.

Being with Logan shattered her previous convictions about the limits of lovemaking. She realized now there were no limits to what a man and woman could feel together. Bliss was a word that had held no meaning for her previously. Now she knew its full meaning.

I am his and he is mine, she thought. *And together we are so much more than we could ever be apart.*

Then his roving hands and mouth carried her beyond all thought to a region of pure sensation, overwhelming ecstasy. Logan's need fed hers, like two fires coming together to form one raging inferno. Nicola gave herself to him completely, with boundless generosity, holding nothing back.

From her most secret depths came a response so intense it destroyed what little was left of her reason. Consciousness itself disappeared as her passion exploded like a white-hot nova, sending a thousand prisms of fire throughout her body.

THE STORM LASHED at the windows, rattling the tiny mullioned panes. The old inn creaked. In the ancient four-poster bed, Nicola and Logan lay entwined in each other's arms in sated fulfillment.

Sighing, Nicola turned to press her lips against the pulse beating at the base of his throat. "I wonder," she whispered, "how many lovers have known each other here in this ancient room."

"None like us," Logan answered, his compelling eyes searching hers. As his lips found hers again, he murmured, "My love...now and forever."

CHAPTER TEN

NICOLA SAT IN HER OFFICE, absentmindedly chewing on the end of a pencil. She had work to do, but she simply could not focus on anything but Logan. Memories of their night together teased at her mind. Outside, the day was gray and cold. Winter had definitely settled on London. But there in her office, thinking of him...the way passion deepened the warm amber glow of those fascinating eyes...it was springtime. She was in love.

As if in answer to an unspoken wish, he was there. "A penny for your thoughts."

When Nicola looked up to see Logan standing before her, smiling in that exact way she'd just been thinking of, her heart did a wild flip-flop. They'd flown back from Scotland the morning before. It had been only twenty-four hours since she'd last seen him, but considering how ridiculously happy she was that he was there, it might have been a year.

"Hi," she replied. Her voice was soft, and she knew her smile reflected the sheer joy his presence brought.

"Well," he teased in his charming lazy drawl, "I made you an offer."

Gladys came into the office to place a file on

Nicola's desk. "Here's the report you requested, Miss Wynter."

"Thank you," Nicola said, forcing herself back into her role as a lawyer. When Gladys left the room, Nicola realized Logan was watching her expectantly, waiting for an answer. "If I told you my thoughts, we'd neither of us get to work. Now I for one have to get busy."

"Didn't look to me like you were accomplishing much. Daydreaming, weren't you?"

Of course, she thought, *and about* you. *For a day and a night I've been unable to think of anything* but *you.* Aloud she said, "Actually, I was considering the contractual phrasing for a technical point."

Lowering his tall frame into the chair opposite her desk, Logan regarded her steadily. "I did come to talk business. I need to go to Baton Rouge for a few days. I'd like you to come with me."

Before Nicola could protest, he continued, "There's a lot of preparatory work for a project as large as this one. We could work on the flights over and back, as well as when I have some free moments over there. I've just seen Thomas, and he agrees with me. I have to get back to Scotland as soon as we return, so we'll save valuable time this way."

Will we, indeed, she thought. *Valuable time for what?* Suddenly, unreasonably, Nicola felt the winter chill there in the room and in her heart. *Wait one damn minute,* her mind argued. *I'm your lawyer. Don't come in here, smile at me and* tell *me you're taking me to Louisiana. . .to save time. Is that what we did in Scotland?*

"Is this trip strictly a business proposition?" she couldn't resist asking. She knew the underlying meaning of her words wouldn't escape Logan.

"Well. . ." he let the word trail off suggestively. All the while he offered that warm intimate smile that touched his mouth and lit his eyes with dancing magic.

God, he's beguiling, Nicola grudgingly admitted, steeling her heart to resist.

"Nicola, is there a problem? A conflict with something you've planned?"

She listened to the familiar cadence of his speech. There was no impatience in his tone. He was, as he said, a problem solver. How she wished she could make him understand *her* problem. It wasn't even his fault she felt so terribly threatened by this situation. . . trying to keep a balance between her being his lawyer and his being her lover. She felt as though she were a first-time performer on a high wire, inadequately trained and working without a safety net. She'd experienced this same inner warning the very first time she'd met this man. Nicola knew she needed time to think objectively about him and what she was getting herself into. But there hadn't ever been time. It had seemed so simple up there in Scotland. He wanted her, and she wanted him. Now it was suddenly complicated. Even so, in her heart she knew she wished to be with him.

Sighing, she gave in to the inevitable. "When do we leave?"

"Tonight. There's a flight that leaves at six. I made reservations for both of us."

Startled, Nicola said, "So soon? I'll hardly have time to pack."

"I know. I'm sorry. But I do have to get back as soon as possible. This project's the biggest thing I've ever undertaken. I've got a lot to do."

"Okay," Nicola agreed reluctantly. Would nothing ever happen leisurely with Logan James, she wondered.

"I'll pick you up at your place at four," he said.

"Then you'd better get going so I can finish up here," she said with a smile.

As he was walking out the door, he turned to say, "Oh, by the way. You'll get a chance to meet some of my family. Not only have I told you about them... I've told them all about you. They're looking forward to this."

So it's all arranged, she thought. His meaning was unmistakable. She was sure Logan didn't make a habit of introducing women to his family. If she'd had any idea that their night in Scotland was simply the beginning of an affair, it was destroyed now. The only question was, was she ready for the sacrifice involved in what he was offering?

THE COMPANY LEAR JET was waiting for them when they arrived in D.C. Whisking through the airport and then airborne again almost immediately, Nicola had only the briefest glimpse of the city that once involved so much of her life.

As they approached Baton Rouge, Logan spoke into the intercom, asking the pilot to circle the countryside. "I want to show my guest what she's been missing."

"Baton Rouge," he said, pointing out the capitol. "Capital of Louisiana, land of magnolias, lakes and bayous, antebellum homes, oil, sugar, Mississippi and gulf shipping."

When Nicola commented that the city appeared to be set in a forest, Logan told her the trees were mostly oak, elm and magnolia.

"Of course, we're in magnolia country," she quipped with an exaggerated Southern drawl.

Turning back from the window, he kissed her and returned the banter. "We have a sayin' down here, 'a whistlin' woman and a crowin' hen never come to a very good end.'"

Holding his face gently in her hands, Nicola kissed a trail across his mouth. "Translation, please," she whispered, her lips against his.

"Be what you're supposed to be," he whispered back.

Once again she yielded to the incredibly sweet touch of his mouth on hers. Lightly tracing her fingers along the soft edge of his mustache, she pursued the question. "Does that have anything to do with my being your attorney?"

"Ah, my love, you're not just my attorney." With a smile he leaned back in his seat, pressed a button and told the pilot they were ready to land. "I've asked Aunt Cordy to meet us this morning," he said. "I've told you about her, she's Uncle Alex's widow. She's going to be your hostess while we're here."

Damn this man, she thought. He should have told her he'd asked his aunt to put her up. She hadn't inquired about his lodging arrangements because she didn't want to appear suspicious. Still, she certainly couldn't stay with him and let all his family know they were sleeping together.

"Thanks for your consideration," she said with a wry smile. Then added, "Logan, I pride myself on being what you so charmingly call a 'high-powered lawyer,' but I'm not exactly well versed in the art of 'mistressing.'"

"Of course, honey," he drawled, a teasing expression in his tawny eyes. "And I know you're not the kind of lady a gentleman compromises."

Relieved, Nicola teased back. "And what about Scotland?"

His marvelous eyes turned serious. "No one knows about Scotland except you and me. I keep my personal affairs private. You're going to matter in my life. I'm not ever going to be casual about you."

As they descended the steps from the plane to the hangar apron, Nicola was surprised to see a red Mercedes sedan driving fast toward them. Logan grinned. "That's my Aunt Cordy, breaking the speed limit again." He took Nicola's arm. "You'll love her. She's my kind of woman."

The woman who stepped from the Mercedes into Logan's embrace was not at all what Nicola had expected. She knew the James brothers, Alex and Logan, Sr., who founded this dynasty, had been born in the 1880s. Surely Cordelia James must be in her early seventies. Yet she stood tall and straight. Her skin was smooth, lightly traced by lines, and her eyes were a clear light blue. She was a strikingly handsome woman who wore her years well. Even her hair, drawn back and twisted into a high knot, was still dark and shining, except for the dramatic white wings at her temples. She was elegantly dressed in a black Italian knit suit and a bright red wool cape.

Holding his aunt with one arm, Logan turned toward Nicola. "Aunt Cordy," he said, "this is Nicola Wynter. She's the one I told you about."

She held out her hand to Nicola. "Welcome, my dear." Smiling at Logan, she said, "You're absolutely right. She's lovely." Squeezing Nicola's hand, she added, "I'm so pleased you're to be my guest."

Drawn by the obvious sincerity of her greeting, Nicola replied, "Thank you, Mrs. James. I hope this isn't an inconvenience for you."

"Of course not. And please, if you're not ready to call me Aunty Cordy, then how about Miss Cordelia? Mrs. James is much too formal, and I hope we'll be friends. Of course, I'm simply too long in the tooth to be called Cordelia by anyone as young as you."

"You can drop me at the office downtown," Logan said as Cordelia expertly negotiated her Mercedes through the traffic. "I have a lot of things to go over with Beau." Resting his arm on the back of the front seat, he laid his fingers gently on the side of Nicola's neck. For a moment she closed her eyes, reveling in his touch.

"Will you need me?" she finally inquired.

Seeming to ignore her question for the moment, he said in a teasing voice, "You know, Aunt Cordy, I think my lawyer is suffering from jet lag. Could you tuck her in for a nap this afternoon so she can shine tonight?"

"Tonight? What about tonight?" Nicola asked, annoyed because she *was* tired and she was sure Logan James had never suffered from jet lag.

"Family dinner—I told you there'd be a chance to meet my family." He chuckled as Cordelia pulled over and double-parked in front of a glass-and-steel high rise. Logan got out of the back seat. He paused to stick his head in the front window and give Nicola a brief kiss before he backed away from the car. "Take the rest of the day off," he grinned.

"Thanks a lot," she replied mockingly. A car behind them honked.

Logan stepped back and waved a hand. "See you tonight."

Cordelia eased the Mercedes into the traffic flow, and the car moved along toward the Mississippi River, glistening beyond the streets of Baton Rouge. As she drove, Cordelia chatted easily about Washington, D.C. and London. Nicola found her easy to talk with, well informed and intelligent.

They had traveled upriver for several miles when Cordelia swung off the main road. As they followed a shady avenue of live oaks hung with soft Spanish moss, James's Oaks suddenly came into view, sitting on a small rise above long sloping lawns. Even in October there were shrubs clad with brilliant blossoms.

The house, like its mistress, was elegant, Nicola thought. Three large brick pillars were equally spaced at each end of the dazzling white oblong house. French doors opened onto wide brick steps and onto the second-floor balcony. The high flat roof concealed the chimneys. When she stepped from the car,

Nicola turned to see, beyond the house, through a tangle of huge live-oak trees, the Mississippi River flowing serenely by. Smiling, she remembered the colorful stories she'd heard of Alex sweeping like a tornado through the oil fields. She'd have thought Steamboat Gothic would suit him better than this neo-Grecian splendor.

"We'll have some tea," Cordelia announced after the houseboy and the maid had departed with the luggage. "Those James boys can wear a lady down."

She smiled at Nicola, leading her into the sitting room, where a fire blazed in the wide hand-carved fireplace. The room was furnished with priceless antiques, all in the most elegant taste, as befitted the mistress of the house.

As though summoned by telepathy, a maid appeared with a silver tea service. "I hope you like Earl Grey," Cordelia said, handing her a teacup of the finest Sevres china. "They tell me that in England it's considered *vin ordinaire* . . . but I love it."

Sipping her tea, Nicola leaned back in the soft down-filled chair covered with deep blue damask. Already she felt comfortable with Cordelia, as if they were old friends.

"Please tell me about this dinner party tonight," she said, adding with a rueful smile, "I'm afraid Logan didn't quite prepare me for it, although he did suggest I might meet *some* of the family. This was essentially supposed to be a business trip."

Cordelia smiled at Nicola, her blue eyes sparkling with obvious pleasure. "Well, to him business is pleasure, and family is pleasure. And it's all very clear, now that I've met you. Logan may enjoy working all over the world, but Baton Rouge is home... his people are here. And no matter what other reasons he has for this trip, he wants you to meet his family and see..." she paused a moment, then continued, "his place—and I don't just mean in a physical sense necessarily. I mean," again she hesitated, obviously searching for the right words, "where he belongs."

My God, Nicola thought, *Logan's arranged a family reunion, a command performance...all for me.*

"Don't look so horrified, my dear," Cordelia told her with a small laugh. "They're all wonderful people, and I know they'll love you. As I said, family is important to Logan...to all of us. He wants to make you welcome."

"Yes, I know. It's thoughtful of him. And gracious of you to arrange this on such short notice."

For Nicola, one of the most difficult problems of her childhood was coming to terms with the loss of family. That traumatic experience—during the year she was eight—left her bereft of people and the place where she felt she belonged. She understood what this gracious lady was trying to say. She understood, because she'd lost her place.

Quite suddenly she'd had only her mother, and after her mother's death she'd had no family at all. And so she'd married too young and really for the wrong reason. Dear as Andrew was, she had confused love with security.

I mustn't make that mistake again, she told

herself. *I mustn't marry except for love. Not for sexual attraction, not for the warmth a large loving family offers. Thank God, I don't need to marry for money,* she concluded, giving a deep sigh.

"Logan was right," Cordelia continued, giving her a searching look. "You are tired. Let me get a sherry for you. Then Lola will show you your room, and you can rest until dinnertime."

The sherry glass was antique crystal, thin as paper. As she sipped the wine, Nicola felt herself relaxing. She had been on a hectic schedule for the past week... and an emotional one. She was looking forward to a quiet time.

THAT NIGHT she was dressing when she heard a light knock and her hostess call her name. "If you're ready, I've come to take you to meet the family," Cordelia said.

Nicola opened the bedroom door.

"You look lovely. That's a beautiful dress," Cordelia added as Nicola fastened the last snap.

"It's the only formal thing I brought," Nicola replied, looking down at her two-piece silk crepe de chine with sheer black lace covering the bodice and a wide belted waist. She had pulled her pale hair back in a chignon and put a small black-silk flower behind one ear.

They walked down the broad graceful staircase and into the parlor. Like the rest of the house that she'd seen, this room was tastefully furnished. Nicola had only a fleeting moment to admire the elegant simplicity of colors and textures before Logan noticed their arrival and walked quickly toward her.

Nicola felt her heart lurch as she recognized once again what a handsome figure of a man he was.

She noticed his collar was properly buttoned underneath his correct black tie. No rebelling against formal dress this night. He smiled down at her as he bent to kiss his aunt's cheek. Then he tucked Nicola's hand into the curve of his arm and turned to introduce her to his family.

There were representatives of the Jameses from Beaumont, Texas to Shreveport in northern Louisiana. Nicola tried to concentrate on the names, matching them to faces, as she and Logan made their way around the room. Then Logan said, "And this is Beau and Joanna Sue."

Joanna Sue was a diminutive redhead with emerald green eyes. She was an interesting contrast to Beau, her darkly attractive husband. His ice-blue eyes contrasted starkly with his black hair and olive complexion.

"I can see why you've found it necessary to spend so much time in London lately, Logan," Beau said, taking her hand in both of his.

"Now don't you start. You'll embarrass her," Joanna Sue admonished her husband. Although her tone was firm, the look she gave him was so clearly loving, Nicola wondered if they were newlyweds.

Just then they were asked to come to the dining room and take their places.

Nicola was delighted to be seated between her hostess and Beau. It would give her a chance to get better acquainted with both of them.

Dinner began with hearts of artichoke soup. The table was beautifully set with finest china, heavy monogrammed silver and fragile crystal. Tall tapers, the same red as the American Beauty roses in the centerpiece, sat in silver candelabras. Logan's family proved to be interesting people. Everyone of them was well informed, involved, opinionated and witty. Talk at the dinner table made her Washington D.C. dinners seem boring by comparison.

Nicola enjoyed conversing with Beau and even enjoyed his teasing remarks about Logan being in London so often until he mentioned something about Logan leaving Scotland in a bad storm the other night.

Cordelia, the perfect hostess, must have sensed Nicola's discomfort, because she urged Beau to stop dallying and finish his soup.

Nicola was very aware of Logan seated at the far end of the table and was careful not to look across at him too frequently. It was too disconcerting.

Asparagus salad vinaigrette was followed by a delicious shrimp creole. Logan blew Cordelia a kiss when dessert was served. It was his favorite, pecan pie, she told Nicola. The coffee was hot and strongly flavored with chicory.

As coffee cups were refilled and conversation centered around some family plans for the holidays, Nicola turned to Cordelia. "I've been admiring your pearls. They're so unusual." They were baroque pearls, and their soft sheen glowed against Cordelia's midnight-blue velvet gown.

"Alex gave them to me when we were married," she said, touching them as though they were an amulet. Her expression softened and the blue eyes turned dreamy. She leaned forward in her chair and turned toward Nicola. This was to be a private conversation. "Nineteen pearls—" her voice was soft "—for the nineteen years we waited."

Suddenly she appeared to remember herself, but that didn't seem to stop her. With a deprecating wave of her long elegant hand she said, "Oh, well. . . you might as well hear it all. Even though my stepchildren don't know the whole story, Logan does. Unlike Logan, Sr., my Alex married much too young and married the wrong woman. Amy was a sweet complaisant woman, and he needed a wife who could challenge him. But the James men *stay* married."

She sighed and gave Nicola a faint smile. "I suppose that's why *your* Logan has waited so long. . . waited until he was sure he'd found the right woman."

Your Logan.

Suddenly Nicola felt smothered, drawn almost against her will into the enveloping warmth of Logan's family. None of them, except perhaps Cordelia, would even consider what her own sacrifice might be in their relationship.

"My father was a doctor in Beaumont, you know," Cordelia was saying. "As his only child I wanted nothing more than to follow in his footsteps. Women in the medical profession were unusual in those days, but I was determined. After my internship I joined my father's practice. That's where I met Alex. . . in Beaumont."

For a long moment she seemed to be staring into the past. "We were lovers for nineteen years. No one knew except Logan, Sr. Not Alex's wife nor his children...I took nothing from them. Amy died when Carter there was starting college.''

Nicola glanced across the roses to see Carter leaning forward to participate in a three-way conversation. The James family were all clearly great conversationalists.

What a fascinating dialogue this was to be having in the midst of a family dinner party, Nicola thought, as she turned her attention again to Cordelia.

"Alex and I were married then. He was nearly sixty-four and I was thirty-nine. But we had twenty-one wonderful years together. I left my practice in Beaumont and worked in the charity clinic here. When Alex was eighty-five, he flew to an oil-producers meeting in California. Coming home, his plane ran into a storm and his 'wildcatter's luck' ran out.''

She sighed as her clear blue eyes swept across the family she loved. "We belonged together, Nicola,'' she said, lightly placing her hand over Nicola's as it lay on the lace tablecloth. "None of it was easy, but all of it was worth the pain. It was an exciting life... being in love with Alex James.''

Yes, Nicola thought, *I'm sure it was. As it is with Logan. Falling in love with him is exciting, but it's also terrifying. I feel my life is being swept by a gale into great change. And I don't have control over the direction or velocity of the wind. Change without control is terrifying.*

She'd been through that before—both as a child and a woman. And it was very soon to contemplate even the possibility of another drastic upheaval in her life.

But even as she argued with herself she felt Logan watching her. She glanced down the long table, past his family gathered there to meet her. Then she let her gaze meet his arresting declaration of desire. She wished she could take a candid look around this table of Jameses to see if anyone else had tawny eyes with black-rimmed irises. If so, did the strength of the gaze come from the unusual coloring or from the presence of the person?

In the moment it took to think this, she watched his expression change from one of shocking intimacy to a softer one of loving. His pleasure and pride in seeing her there were present in his eyes, and the tender smile he gave her was for anyone to observe.

Nicola felt a rush of love for him that spread like a liquid warmth throughout her. It began in her heart, but it centered in her loins. Instantly, Logan recognized her silent communiqué and reciprocated.

The company limo arrived to whisk the travelers back to the airport after coffee and brandy. It was incredible, Nicola thought, as she told the family goodbye, that they would all come this distance at Logan's behest, just to meet her. The warmth of feeling they obviously had for one another reached out and surrounded her. By the end of the evening she was no longer a stranger.

Now only Beau and Joanna Sue remained with Logan and Nicola in the sitting room. Cordelia had retired, pleading weariness. Smiling up at Logan as he handed her a brandy glass, Nicola let herself sink into the softness of the blue damask chair, enjoying the crackle of the flames in the fireplace.

Logan set his brandy on the mantelpiece and loosened his tie. Looking up, Nicola met his eyes and felt her heart leap at the depth of desire she saw there. *He loves me,* she thought. *This incredibly wonderful man really adores me. And I adore him.*

When Beau spoke, Logan turned to look at him.

"So it looks like we've got the North Sea contract," Beau commented, sipping his drink.

"Sure does according to Gerald Laughton. We just have to wait for the official word," Logan responded. Flashing Nicola a smile, he added, "I think it was Nicola's persuasiveness that finally tipped the scales in our favor. We were running neck and neck with Mannering. Then Nicola talked to Laughton and Lord Carlisle, and that was all it took."

"All I did was go over some figures with them that you had prepared," she insisted. As always when she remembered that day, a deep sense of unease filled her. Now she thrust it aside.

"Well, however it happened, I'm just damn glad it did. We need a steady supply of crude. We never know when our supply from the Middle East is gonna' get shut off."

"You'll have to come over again to look over the site with me," Logan told Beau.

"Great. It'll give Joanna Sue and me a chance to take a little vacation."

Joanna said with a critical look in her lovely green eyes, "Now, Beau, my boss may not necessarily like it if I up and leave right now without warning."

"He'll understand," Beau responded blithely.

Joanna's mouth set in a surprisingly stubborn line.

There was more to her than the fragile Southern belle, Nicola realized.

Obviously trying to break up the argument before it really got started, Logan turned to Nicola and explained, "Joanna Sue is the personnel director for a refinery in Baton Rouge."

"Oh? So you're involved in oil, too," Nicola commented to Joanna Sue.

The stubbornness left her expression, and she replied ruefully, "Sure am. Seems like everyone around here is in one way or another."

As they talked, it became clear to Nicola that Joanna Sue was a great deal tougher than she looked. She clearly valued herself and her career goals as much as her husband and Logan valued theirs.

When Joanna Sue told Beau there were important personnel changes under consideration at the moment, he drawled, "Well, hell, honey, just tell your boss you'll be gone for a week or so."

He meant it as a joke, Nicola realized, but Joanna Sue wasn't laughing. "That's why I refuse to work for James Petrochemical Company," she insisted. To Nicola she added, "These two are out to take over the world, you know, an' they expect everyone else to just kind of get in line behind them." The indulgent look she gave them took the sting from her words.

Nicola glanced at Logan across the coffee table separating them. He returned her look, and the corners of his eyes crinkled in a smile. The camaraderie among the three of them was obvious.

Logan turned to Beau. "Come on into Cordy's study. I want you to check over some of the contracts Nicola brought with her." Then he addressed Nicola. "I just want to clarify a few points for Beau." He paused, then grinning, added, "Now that you've made them clear to me. I'll call for help if I need to."

"It's just like them to abandon us," Joanna Sue said. "Business first—*always*." Her tone was understanding, but there was an edge to it that made Nicola wonder.

Joanna Sue sighed. "Oh, well, it doesn't do any good to get mad. Beau just smiles at me, an' the next thing I know, I've forgotten entirely what I was mad about."

Nicola smiled knowingly. Beau wasn't the only member of the James family with that ability.

As if reading her mind, Joanna Sue said, "When they were passin' out charm, the James boys must've stood in line twice, cause they sure got more than their fair share."

The two women laughed together.

Then Nicola asked curiously, "How did you and Beau meet?"

"At Harvard, of all places. We were both in the M.B.A. program. I had no intention of getting married, and certainly not to a Southerner. I had enough of bein' put on a pedestal when I was growin' up."

"I know what you mean. I'm from Virginia."

"Are you? You talk like a Northerner."

Nicola smiled. "Eight years in Washington, D.C. had an effect."

"Well, you do know what I mean, then. Southern

men are raised to expect their women to be ladies in the drawin' room an' whores in the bedroom." Joanna Sue's green eyes sparkled merrily. "Well, there's nothin' wrong with that, as long as they let us be tycoons in the boardroom, too!"

Nicola was beginning not only to like Joanna Sue but also to respect her. She was pretty in a deceptively fragile way, but beneath that fragility she was proud and confident and nobody's fool.

"You know, Nicola, if I have one secret regret it's that I wasn't born a man."

"Why on earth would you feel that way? I'd say you have a lot going for you as you are."

"Oh, I love bein' a woman sometimes. But I want power and recognition, an' I'd be a lot more likely to get those things if I were a man."

"I don't think it really makes a difference nowadays," Nicola insisted. "I think we can accomplish whatever we want if we're determined enough."

"Oh, I agree. We'll get there in the end. It's just a bit slower going when you're a woman. I'm just short of scornful of women who don't hold their own.

"I'll bet you hold your own, even with Logan and Beau!"

Joanna Sue laughed appreciatively. "I sure try. But enough talk about me. Tell me about you. How in blue blazes did you get to be a lawyer in London?"

Nicola was speechless for a moment. Was it possible that Joanna Sue really knew nothing about her background? She was so used to being in the limelight in Washington that it startled her now to think someone might not know of her marriage to Andrew.

"Well..." she began slowly. "I went to Georgetown University Law School and practiced in Washington for a while before Thomas St. Ives offered me this job. I...I was married to a lawyer. He died earlier this year."

Joanna Sue stared at Nicola as if she'd suddenly sprouted a third arm. "Damn, if I'm not the biggest fool I ever did see! You're *her*."

"Her?" Nicola was completely puzzled.

"The girl Logan told Beau about last April."

Nicola felt a tiny thrill of pleasure at the idea Logan had been so taken with her that he'd spoken to his family about her.

"What did he say?" she asked.

Instead of answering her immediately, Joanna Sue leaned back on the sofa and stared at Nicola. Shaking her head, she said, "I should've known. The way he was lookin' at you tonight. I've never seen him look at a woman like that."

Nor has any other man ever looked at me like that, Nicola thought.

Joanna Sue continued. "He told Beau he'd finally met *the* woman. The one he could see livin' in his house an' havin' his kids. So Beau asked when the wedding was, and Logan just shook his head an' said, 'Probably never. She's married.' Well, it really shook up Beau. Logan's never been the type to mess with married women."

Suddenly realizing she'd made a faux pas, Joanna Sue went crimson. "I'm sorry," she stammered. "My stupid mouth is racin' ahead of my good manners."

"Don't apologize. It's all right. Really. Logan and I met...briefly. But as he said, I was married. I never expected to see him again. When I discovered I would be working with him in London, it was quite a surprise." *And that's quite an understatement,* she added to herself.

Joanna Sue continued to look at her intently. In a more sober voice she said, "I'm sorry about your husband."

Nicola wasn't sure what to respond to this, so she remained silent.

Suddenly Joanna Sue said astutely, "Logan swept you right off your feet before you knew what happened, didn't he? He and Beau are just alike that way. It's how they operate, you know. They don't give a girl a chance to think about things."

"Are you talkin' about us, sweetheart?" Beau gave his wife an irresistible smile as the two men returned to the room.

"Hell, no. We've got better things to do than waste time talkin' about you two," Joanna Sue replied tartly. But the way she smiled at Beau softened her words.

"We ought to be goin'," Beau said. "You ready, Logan?"

Logan had arrived with Beau and Joanna Sue, and they were to give him a ride home. Suddenly Nicola felt let down. This was not the way she would have chosen for the evening to end.

Beau and Joanna Sue discreetly stepped into the foyer while he went to get her mink. Logan closed the door behind them, quickly crossed the room to where

Nicola stood beside the fire. In his eyes she saw a reflection of her own desire. He pulled her into his arms, his strong masculine body pressed against hers. As Nicola yielded to his kiss, she thought, *Oh, God...I want you so. If only this night could be like Scotland....*

Logan drew away, his eyes looking deep into hers, and she knew he understood. "I know, darlin'," he whispered. "Me, too." Again his lips claimed hers, and she felt the effort to release her shake his body. "I'll pick you up at nine," he said in a husky voice. Smiling, he added, "Maddy, she's my housekeeper, can't wait to show off her Southern brunch for you. And I can't wait to show off my home."

She understood his obvious pride when he took her to his home the next morning. The long drive was lined with live oaks. Spanish moss moved gently in the soft breeze. "Like bearded old men," Nicola pointed out, smiling at Logan.

"There's an old Indian legend about the Spanish moss," he told her solemnly. "A young and beautiful Indian princess was murdered by an enemy tribe during her marriage ceremony. Her grieving lover cut off her hair and spread it over the limb of the oak tree above her grave. The hair blew from tree to tree until it finally turned gray. The oak trees carry it as a tribute to those who are fated never to live out their love."

Nicola shivered. Something in the innocent tale brought with it a sense of dread. Reaching out, she placed her hand over Logan's, needing to touch him, to feel close to him.

Just then the long avenue of oaks ended. Logan stopped the car. "There it is," he said proudly. "Magnolia Hill."

A circular driveway ascended a slight rise carpeted with emerald green grass. A grove of magnolia trees surrounded the house, their leathery green leaves shining in the pale winter sun. Nicola drew in her breath in surprise. She had expected another "Greek-revival" mansion along the lines of James's Oaks. The enormous house stood on brick pillars, with a long elevated veranda across the front and wide steps leading down to the driveway. Shuttered French doors lined the sides of the house, and the hip roof was crowned by dormers and several brick chimneys.

Logan started the car up the driveway. "This house," he told her, "is ante antebellum. I think it always pleased papa that his home was a hundred years older than Alex's place. Magnolia Hill was built in the 1700s, and it's really indigenous Louisiana Creole architecture. See—" he pointed "—the raised basement is built of brick, with white-plastered brick on the second and third floors. In a time when there was no air-conditioning that basement provided relief from the heat."

He smiled at her. "It was pretty run-down when papa bought it, but he modernized and refurbished it. Even put a billiard room in the basement. Of course," he continued, "I haven't made many changes since my grandmother furnished it fifty years ago because I'm traveling most of the time. I have a live-in couple who look after the place. "Do you like it?" He gave her an anxious look.

"It's lovely, Logan...magnolias and moonlight."
She might have known Logan's house would be
something out of the ordinary even for Louisiana.
He was no ordinary man.

"Wish I could show you the magnolias in the
moonlight," he grinned. "Maybe in the spring,
when they're in bloom."

As they mounted the wide steps to the veranda, a
small wiry woman dressed in a maid's uniform came
out to greet them.

"Brunch is ready, Mr. Logan," she said, eyeing
Nicola curiously.

"This is Miss Wynter, Maddy...and Nicola, this
is Maddy, who takes care of things around here."

Inside a large foyer, a curving walnut staircase led
to the upper rooms. Also in the foyer, a rich old
oriental rug lay on the polished floor and an antique
armoire stood against one wall. "In the breakfast
room," Maddy said, leading them quickly to the
back of the house. The table was set with creamy
linen and Spode china. Tall windows looked out on
lawns sloping down to a tree-girded lake. Two swans
glided across the water, followed by a retinue of
multicolored ducks. Weeping willows trailed their
graceful branches in the still water. It was so utterly
peaceful and lovely that Nicola sighed aloud. "Oh,
Logan," she said, turning to meet his pleased expression. "This is an absolutely heavenly place."

"*Now* it is," he replied, giving her a meaningful
look. Maddy bustled in carrying two crystal dishes
filled with fresh fruit.

Maddy's crab-meat omelet was as light as air, and

so were her fresh steaming popovers. She kept coming back into the room to observe their reaction to her cooking and to soak up their compliments.

When they had finished the hot chicory-flavored café au lait, Logan rose and held out his hand. "I want to show you the rest of the house."

He led her into the living room, huge and tastefully furnished with obviously expensive antiques. Over the marble-manteled fireplace was a large portrait of a stunningly beautiful woman with raven hair and enormous brown eyes.

"That's my grandmother," Logan said. "Papa hired a New York artist to come down here and paint her. He felt the mistress of the house should have her portrait done. She couldn't persuade him to do the same."

"She was beautiful."

"Yes. She was twenty-five when that was done. But even when she was eighty she was still beautiful. Her kind of beauty never ages, I guess, because it came from within as well as without. She was the gentlest woman I've ever known. Yet she could humble my grandfather with one look from those big brown eyes."

As always when he discussed his grandparents, Logan's voice softened. Nicola felt him take her hand in his as they stood together looking at the portrait.

Somewhere in the back of the house a telephone rang. In a moment Maddy appeared. "It's for you, Mr. Logan. Mr. Beau."

"Oh, yes," Logan said. "They're to meet us at the

airport this afternoon and pick up my car.'' Turning to Maddy, he added, ''Finish showing Miss Wynter the house, will you?''

''I'm proud Mr. Logan brought you to visit,'' Maddy chattered as they climbed the stairs to the third floor. ''This place gets lonely at times.''

''Have you been here long?'' Nicola asked, admiring the huge master bedroom.

''Since Mr. Logan's parents died and he came here to live with his grandfolks. Mrs. James hired me to look after him. Now me and my husband, Charlie, take care of the place for him.''

Gazing at Maddy's pale, almost unlined face and her white hair, Nicola couldn't guess her age. One thing was obvious: she adored Logan.

''This was his room when he was a boy,'' she was saying, pushing open the door to a small, obviously masculine bedroom. Banners from Tulane and MIT still hung over the oak desk. Nicola smiled, wondering if this was Maddy's shrine to the little boy Logan had once been.

''Ornery little devil, he was,'' Maddy chuckled. ''Always into everythin'. *Curious*, you see, not bad. Took everythin' apart to see how it worked. His granddad had to whop him more'n once for taken' apart somethin' he wasn't s'posed to touch.''

Nicola was not surprised. Logan the man was very much the same as Logan the little boy—given to direct action, intensely curious and not easily put off.

Continuing her reminiscing, Maddy led Nicola back downstairs. ''He was a handsome one, too. Lord, miss, many's the time I told Charlie that child would grow up to break a hundred hearts. He had a way with him that was well nigh irresistible to ladies."

Nicola smiled. Logan had a way with him, all right. She had cause to know how irresistible he could be.

"I suppose he had lots of girl friends," Nicola ventured, embarrassed by her own temerity.

"Well, not serious," Maddy replied. "Seemed like there was a different one every week. His grandparents wanted him to settle down and get married."

"Why do you suppose he didn't?" Nicola asked, trying without success to make the question sound casual.

Maddy's blue eyes sparkled with amusement. "We thought he was close once, with a girl from Baton Rouge. But it never happened. Guess he just didn't love her enough. He told me once he would bring only one bride to this house. When he does settle down, he means for it to last forever."

"I hope you're not giving away any family secrets, Maddy," Logan said as he rejoined them at the front of the stairs.

Maddy flushed.

With a wink at Nicola, Logan continued, "Beau just reminded me it's my turn to have the clan here for Christmas. Do you think you can handle it for me?"

"I always have," Maddy replied indignantly. "Miss Cordelia has already talked to me about it." She turned and started out of the room. "Just you get yourself back here from London in time."

"What do you think?" Logan asked when they were alone, a wave of his hand taking in the house.

"It's a very seductive place," Nicola replied. At the same time she thought that beautiful as it was, she would soon grow bored playing lady of the manor. She was a lawyer. It was not only what she did for a living, it was what defined her, gave her life meaning and structure. She'd worked hard and come far but was still finding her own sense of identity and self-worth. She couldn't give up her career then and there—even for all that Logan offered.

Would he even understand that, she wondered as she looked at him. In his experience, ladies were meant to be decorative. Their careers had to take second place to their husbands.

All those doubts flew from her mind as Logan drew her into his arms. The touch of his body against hers sent a delicious thrill racing through her.

"Nicola." His voice was low and husky. Gazing down at her he murmured, "I've imagined you here in this house so many times. I wanted you to like it...to like my family. They've all fallen in love with you. Just as I did."

She remained utterly still in his arms, content to listen as his voice caressed her, totally enthralled by the light in his eyes. His arms tightened around her.

"You belong here with me, my Nicola. Come back with me at Christmas time. We'll be married here... in our house on Christmas Eve, darlin'," he whispered. "Say yes."

For a moment Nicola had a vision of herself floating down the broad curving stairway in a flowing gown, holding a spray of lily of the valley. For a split second something inside her rebelled. Then she was lost in Logan's kiss. His mouth devoured hers; his embrace was no longer gentle but possessive. What few emotional defenses remained after their night together in Scotland slipped soundlessly away.

CHAPTER ELEVEN

WHEN NICOLA ENTERED the reception room early Monday morning, Gladys said anxiously, "Oh, Miss Wynter, thank God you're back! Mr. St. Ives has been trying to reach you all weekend."

Nicola had practically floated into the office, walking on air, overflowing with happiness. That incredible feeling of joy began to fade at the sight of Gladys's worried face. A faint premonition of disaster tinged Nicola's rosy glow with a darker tone.

"I was traveling from Baton Rouge to London most of the weekend," she explained. "I just got in last night. Is Thomas in his office?"

"No, miss. He isn't feeling well, and his doctor's ordered him to stay home for a few days."

Nicola's premonition grew stronger. Thomas wasn't young, and he drove himself awfully hard.

"I'll drive out to Longridge immediately," Nicola told Gladys. "If something comes up you can reach me there in about an hour."

She drove quickly through the thick London traffic, having learned her way around the city in the past couple of months. Soon she was in the countryside, speeding toward Thomas's country estate.

Longridge was a magnificent old Tudor mansion,

set in well-manicured gardens. Nicola had been there once—for dinner with Thomas and his wife. Parking her car now on the graveled drive in front of the broad stone steps, she realized her feelings had been quite different on that occasion. Then she had been filled with excitement about her new job and the new life she was making for herself in London. This day she was apprehensive. There was a cold feeling in the pit of her stomach, a sense of something gone wrong.

Thomas's butler answered the door. "Ah, Miss Wynter, Mr. St. Ives has been expecting you. He's in the library."

Nicola followed him down the wide entry hall to a door at the far end. Knocking discreetly, the butler opened the door and announced, "Miss Wynter, sir."

The library was a mellow room, lined with floor-to-ceiling bookcases filled with worn leather-bound books. Tall windows were draped with burgundy velvet. Comfortable leather chairs were placed around the room. In front of the fireplace, Thomas sat with a lap rug over his knees. Although he smiled at Nicola, his face was pale and the twinkle was absent from his hazel eyes.

Hurrying up to him, Nicola asked, "Thomas, are you all right?"

"Of course, my dear. Just my blood pressure acting up again. My doctor, who's a conservative fellow, insisted I take it easy for a while. I'll be back in the office by next week, I'm sure."

"Don't hurry it. We'll manage without you for a bit."

Thomas smiled ruefully. "I'm not sure that's at all

complimentary. I would much rather hear that the office couldn't possibly function without me.''

Nicola smiled at him with real affection. In the short time she'd known him, she'd grown very fond of him. ''The truth is, we all rely on your wise counsel, and you know it.''

He returned her smile, clearly very pleased. Then his expression sobered, and he said, ''I'm afraid there's a problem, Nicola. A very difficult one. I tried to reach you in Baton Rouge, but you'd already left.''

''Yes, Logan and I flew out of there Saturday. I feel as though I've been on airplanes for days.'' Seeing the seriousness of Thomas's expression, she finished soberly, ''What is wrong?''

''It's Gerald Laughton. He called me Saturday. Quite simply, my dear, he accused you of trying to bribe Lord Carlisle to influence the final decision on the North Sea contract.''

''What!'' Nicola couldn't believe what she was hearing. Surely there was some mistake.

''He said you met with Carlisle alone at his house in Belgrave Square and offered him an unspecified sum of money to award the contract to Logan James.''

''Thomas, this is insane. I met with Carlisle, it's true, but Laughton was there. He arranged the meeting. At the time he said they simply had some last-minute questions that needed to be cleared up.''

''Of course I believe you, Nicola. Let's understand that. I didn't believe Laughton for a moment.''

''But it doesn't make sense. He told me Logan was almost certainly going to get the contract. Why should I bribe Carlisle?''

"Well, according to Laughton, you approached Carlisle *before* Laughton had reached a decision. Carlisle said nothing to Laughton about your meeting, but when he learned that Laughton was going to award the contract to Logan, he felt duty bound to tell Laughton of the bribe attempt."

"That's ridiculous! The whole thing's a lie!"

"I'm sure it is, my dear. But because of that, Laughton is now saying he will award the contract to Mannering. In order to avoid any taint of scandal, you see."

Nicola leaned back in the chair, completely drained and horribly confused. Why would Laughton lie? Why had he arranged that meeting with Carlisle in the first place?

"If I tell the truth—"

"No one will believe you except the people who know you," Thomas insisted bluntly. "It's a case of your word against Laughton's and Carlisle's. Most people will believe them. They're English, and Carlisle's a highly respected aristocrat. You're an American interloper, and many people will assume Americans think they can buy anything, even government contracts."

Thomas's statement was completely accurate, she knew. Despite her confusion and anger, she was beginning to understand what must have happened.

"For some reason, Carlisle and Laughton want to award the contract to Mannering, not Logan. They've set me up so that Logan could be discredited." She shook her head. "I just don't understand why."

"That *is* the question. And we haven't much time to

find an answer. The government is supposed to announce its decision publicly next Monday. That's one week. Unless we can somehow clear things up by then, I very much doubt Logan will win the contract.''

Nicola felt utterly crushed. She understood all too well how this loss would affect Logan. He'd made it clear how important the contract was to him. She knew he'd already started preparation for the job on the perfectly logical assumption that the contract was his. Laughton had practically promised it to him.

"I wish Logan were here," Thomas said, sighing heavily. "He's got to be told as soon as possible."

"He flew straight to Scotland," Nicola told him. "But he's due back tonight."

"Good. I'll leave a message for him to call me as soon as he returns." Flashing Nicola that shrewd look she knew so well, he mused, "There are only three reasons Laughton and Carlisle would be doing this. . . revenge against Logan or you, or money."

"You mean Mannering must have bribed them?"

"Either that or, as I said, revenge. As far as I know, there's been no personal contact between Logan and Carlisle or Laughton. Nicola. . .'' he paused. "You're a very attractive young woman. Did Carlisle perhaps try to force his attentions on you?"

Nicola couldn't help smiling at his Victorian phrasing. "No. It can't be that. I met him only that once, and then we talked about the contract. He didn't do or say anything personal."

"Too bad," Thomas replied. "I was hoping it was a case of 'hell hath no fury like an aristocrat scorned'. Well, it must be money that's the motivation, then."

"But how on earth can we prove a bribe by Mannering? Especially in one week?"

Thomas shook his head. "I don't know, my dear. We can only try." He slapped the leather arm of the chair angrily. "I only wish I wasn't confined at home right now."

"Don't get upset, Thomas, please." Nicola placed her hand on his reassuringly. "I don't want this mess to make your blood pressure even worse."

He sighed. "Ah, my dear, your concern warms my heart. When it comes from my doctor, it's merely irritating."

Nicola stood up. "I'd better get back to the office and start trying to sort this thing out."

"All right. I'll do what I can, make some phone calls, that sort of thing." He smiled supportively at Nicola. "We won't go down without a fight, my dear."

She tried to smile back at him, but it was a weak effort.

BACK IN THE OFFICE, Nicola placed calls to both Gerald Laughton and Lord Carlisle. It didn't surprise her when both refused her call. Even if she could get through to them, she was sure it would do no good.

Thomas had given her the name of a friend who was a reporter from the London *Times*. Since he wrote for the business and finance section of the newspaper, Thomas had said, he might know something about Mannering Construction. When Nicola reached the man by telephone, he had little to tell her. Mannering was a new firm, the management was relatively young and unusually zealous for an English company, but there had never been any hint of scandal about them. Mannering's stock was traded publicly and was considered a good buy, since the company was expected to prosper.

Deciding to throw caution to the winds, Nicola asked bluntly, "Can you see them involved in bribery?"

"Goodness, no!" the reporter replied in shocked tones. "They're go-getters, as you Americans say, but quite honest. It simply wouldn't be in character."

Late in the afternoon, when a discouraged Nicola was about to give up for the day, Logan suddenly walked into her office, smiling happily. "I came back from Scotland early," he said. "I couldn't stand being away from you any longer."

Nicola felt sick with dread. She had left Logan the night before, convinced that nothing could threaten their newfound happiness. Now everything had changed. This contract meant everything to Logan, and she was all too aware of what her disheartening news would do to him. To think that somehow she was being used as a pawn to deny him the contract made her feel even worse than the attack on her professional integrity.

"Obviously you haven't talked to Thomas," Nicola began reluctantly as Logan leaned across her desk to smile into her eyes.

"No. Why, has he been trying to get hold of me?"

"Yes. Sit down please, Logan." Her heart sank as she anticipated the impact of her awful news.

"All right," he agreed, sitting down. "Now, then, what big news do you have for me? You look absolutely miserable."

"I'll tell you, and then you'll need to talk to Thomas. He isn't here. He wasn't feeling well, and his doctor ordered him to stay home for a few days."

To her relief, Logan didn't interrupt. He sat quietly, listening, his eyes intent on her face. Briefly and with a control that was purely superficial, Nicola repeated what Thomas had told her earlier.

To her surprise, he didn't react as she had done with anger and confusion. Instead he sat silent for a long moment, his forehead furrowed in sober thought. Finally he said, "Mannering's obviously bribed them. That's the only answer."

"You're certainly taking it calmly," Nicola responded, her emotions dangerously close to getting out of hand.

He flashed her a dry smile. "I'm used to these kinds of shenanigans. Bribes, industrial espionage, corrupt government officials...it's all part of the game. I must admit this is the first time I've seen anything quite so blatant."

Nicola's spirits rose. At least Logan had managed to keep it in perspective. That was something, anyway. He clearly had no doubts at all about her innocence.

"Well, this is Monday," he mused. "We've got a week to clear up this mess and get on with the job."

Nicola explained that neither Laughton nor Carlisle would talk to her and that the only information she had about Mannering wasn't helpful.

"I'd better call Thomas," Logan said, "and find out whom he wants to handle things now."

Confused, Nicola asked, "What do you mean?"

Looking at her directly, Logan answered, "I'm sorry, but it's clear you can't continue to represent me. I'll do everything I can to get to the bottom of this for your sake as well as mine. But in the meantime another attorney in the office will have to take over to avoid any appearance of impropriety."

"Impropriety!"

"You know what I mean, Nicola. You must understand."

All day a sick feeling had clung to her, covering her frantic efforts like a pall. Now it filled her, blurring her vision. Trembling, she stared at Logan, knowing that she didn't understand. She would never understand how Logan could turn his back on her when she needed his support most.

"I see." Her voice was cold and bitter. "You're cutting your losses, trying to salvage the contract by dissociating yourself from your crooked lawyer."

"Nicola, that's not fair, and you know it." His voice was angrier than she had ever heard it. She knew very well that if there was one thing Logan James prided himself on it was his loyalty. But where was his loyalty to her?

"Oh, it's fair all right!" she cried. "It isn't just your company at stake here, Logan, it's my career. If I can't prove my innocence, I'm finished as an attorney in London...and probably in the States, as well."

"I know that, Nicola. Hell, do you think I don't

care about what this is doing to you? Do you really believe I'm thinking only about my own company profits?''

Dear God, she thought, *that's exactly what I believe.* Without another word, she rose and grabbed her coat and purse from the rack in the corner.

"I'm leaving," she announced. "You and Thomas can do as you please about assigning another lawyer to your case, but I intend to try to clear myself." Holding herself with rigid pride, she tried to move past him where he had risen in front of her desk.

Logan grabbed her arm firmly. "Nicola!" Swinging her around to face him, he said, "We've got to talk about this."

"There's nothing to talk about." Nicola's expression was implacable. Wear a mask, Andrew had said, and that's just what she was doing. Nothing of the agony she felt was visible on her pale lovely face. "Would you dump Beau if he were in this position?" she demanded. "Why are you doing it to me?"

"Damn it! Don't be this way! Don't let those crooks come between us. I can't let my personal feelings about you jeopardize my company. Once this is settled we can work together again."

"Wrong, Logan! Once this is settled, I never want to see you again."

She felt abandoned and betrayed by this man to whom she had given so much of herself. She had ignored all the obvious conflicts between them and allowed herself to believe that somehow it would work. Now reality had set in with a vengeance.

"You don't mean that. When you've had a chance to calm down...."

She jerked out of his grasp. Though she felt a raging maelstrom of emotions inside, she forced herself to sound calm and deliberate; flying off the handle would just confirm Logan's feeling that she was being "emotional." Instead she was very much in control as she said, "I mean it, Logan. You'd like to think I'm upset over nothing, that I don't understand your position. Well, I understand it perfectly."

"Nicola, listen—"

"No, *you* listen, Logan James. What we're talking about here gets to the heart of who I am and what I do. If you genuinely respected my ability, you'd give me a chance to do the job I was hired to do. Instead, at the first sign of trouble, you want to put me aside and bring in someone else. Well, I won't be put aside that way. I've had enough of that for one lifetime, thank you."

"If you mean to compare me to Andrew—"

"I do, indeed," she interrupted coldly. "Andrew only wanted me to go so far and no farther. He couldn't give me complete encouragement to be everything I could be. He insisted on drawing boundaries around me. That's just what you're doing. But I'm not the same naive, easily influenced girl now that I was when I married Andrew. I know who I am and what I can do, and I won't be held back by a man who'd rather see me in his bed than in an office doing my job."

"Damn it, Nicola," Logan thundered, "think about what you're saying! Why on earth would I want to hold you back?"

"I don't know if it threatens you to see me so committed to my career, or if you plain don't believe a woman could honestly be good enough to handle a serious crisis like this one. Whatever is going on in that arrogant male head of yours, I'm not prepared to give in this time. I'll clear up this mess, *without* your help. I'll prove my innocence and win that contract for you, because that's my job. But afterward I never want to see you again. Because life's too damn short to make the same mistake twice."

Her voice had lowered to a whisper by the end of her impassioned speech. The turquoise eyes that had greeted him with love when he had come in only minutes earlier were cold with anger and disappointment.

He started to reach out to her; she pulled back. She was filled with a pain that left her reeling, but she pulled herself together and finished, "Now get out of my office. I have work to do."

He hesitated for just a fraction of a second. Then, with a lost expression on his rugged face, he turned and strode out of the room.

CHAPTER TWELVE

"WHY, MISS, you look fair done in. Was it a long hard trip, then?" Mrs. Murdle was solicitous as she helped Nicola off with her coat.

"Yes," Nicola replied in a thoroughly exhausted voice. "It was a very hard trip." *A hard trip back from fantasy to reality,* she thought.

"Well, I've a nice lamb stew simmerin' on the stove. A bit of food, a nice 'ot bath an' a good rest'll cheer you up. In the mornin' you'll be yer old bright self again."

I'll never *be that,* Nicola realized. She shuddered suddenly.

"Why, miss, yer cold as can be. Come in 'ere by the fire. I stoked it up good just a few minutes ago, knowin' you'd be 'ere soon."

In the sitting room Nicola sat down in a comfortable wing chair close to the fire.

"Can I make you a drink, miss?"

"Yes, a brandy, please," Nicola answered. Then, almost as an afterthought, she added, "And pour one for yourself. It is cold out there. You'll need something to warm you on your way home."

"Thank you, miss, but I don't partake in spirits. Not since Mr. Murdle an' me was married. He's a teetotaler, ye see. On our weddin' day he told me he wouldn't hear of spirits in the 'ouse, not even for medicinal purposes. It really put out my mother. She was used to nippin' of a bit o' brandy for her rheumatism, ye see.''

Cocking her head to one side, she eyed Nicola carefully. ''Is somethin' worryin' you, miss. You do look awful down.''

''Oh, it's just a case. It's. . . a bit complicated.''

''Has to do with money, I'll wager. Most things do, in one way or another.''

''Yes,'' Nicola agreed with a wry smile. ''It does have to do with money.'' The money Logan would get if his company won the lucrative contract. The money that had probably been paid to Carlisle and Laughton.

''A goodly sum, must be, to involve a big solicitor like yourself, miss.'' Mrs. Murdle's eyes sparkled with curiosity. ''Is it a big divorce case, miss, involvin' alimony an' all?''

''No.''

Mrs. Murdle was clearly disappointed. Nicola sensed that she'd hoped to get an insider's gossip about a divorce scandal.

''It's just that where money's concerned, there's usually a woman involved somewhere.''

Well, I'm certainly involved, Nicola thought.

''I'll be goin', miss. Me 'usband'll be waitin' for 'is supper. Trotters, it is tonight. 'is particular favorite. See yer tomorrow.''

''Good night, Mrs. Murdle. And thank you for everything.''

"My pleasure, I'm sure."

When the woman had gone, Nicola continued sitting by the fire, desultorily sipping the brandy. She had absolutely no idea how to go about proving Carlisle and Laughton were liars. But somehow that was just what she had to do.

That night she sat on the window seat in her bedroom, staring out at the glowering sky. It had rained all evening and looked as though it would continue all night.

It was hard to believe it had been less than twenty-four hours since she'd been with Logan, loving him, opening her heart to him. Their private world of intimacy had seemed so safe, so utterly impregnable. It must have been only an illusion. Otherwise it couldn't have been destroyed so easily.

Thomas had called her that evening, explaining that he had assigned another attorney to Logan's case at Logan's request. But he had little hope that would make any difference as far as the contract was concerned. It looked as if that would go to Mannering.

Nothing was going right. Lord Carlisle and Laughton refused to return the calls Nicola had placed repeatedly throughout the day. She had no idea what to do next, what line of inquiry to pursue.

The ringing of the doorbell interrupted her desperate thoughts. Even before she answered it, she knew who it would be. No one else would come so late at night.

He stood quietly on the threshold. For a moment neither said anything. Nicola was emotionally and physically exhausted. She wanted simply to tell him to go away, to leave her alone. But she knew they needed to talk, to finish their relationship once and for all.

"Come in," she invited.

She led him into the living room, pausing to turn on the light. The fire burned low in the fireplace now. Picking up a poker, she stirred the dying embers into small flames, then added another log. Turning, she faced Logan, who waited silently.

"We can't leave things where they were this afternoon," he said.

"I meant everything I said," Nicola replied. She was no longer angry, but her tone was absolutely unshakable. Logan moved closer to her, as if to take her in his arms.

"No," she insisted, moving back. "You can stop our argument with your kisses, Logan, but it won't change anything ultimately."

"I love you, Nicola, and you love me. That's all that matters."

"I wish it were." Nicola's tone was wistful. "Then we'd have a chance at real happiness. But it isn't all that matters, Logan. Not here, in the real world. When it's just you and I alone in a Scottish hideaway, it's pure bliss. But when we have to deal with our lives as a whole...." Her voice trailed off helplessly.

He shook his head. "I won't accept that. We can resolve this disagreement."

"No." Her voice shook, and she paused to get it under control. "It's not just a disagreement. I'm sorry I compared you to Andrew earlier—that wasn't fair. But what's happened between us today is very similar to what happened between Andrew and me. What I need to fulfill myself as a whole person gets in the way of the love we feel. People talk about women 'having it all'—a career, marriage, children. I used to think it was possible, but now I don't. Not for me. Not when the career demands so much commitment, and not when the marriage is to a man like you, who is equally committed to his career.''

"Nicola, you're being pessimistic," he insisted.

"I'm being realistic, Logan. The only way to work this out is for me to give in as I've always done in the past. But I'm no longer willing to give that way, because I end up being eaten up by resentment at the sacrifice I'm making. I have a pride now that I didn't have before. I have a sense of freedom—freedom to pursue my highest goal. I have more control over my life. More ability to be myself and use my own voice and be the person *I* want to be, not the person someone else wants me to be. I won't give that up.''

She stood with her back to the fire, facing him without flinching.

He shook his head. "I don't understand."

"No. I suppose you don't."

They continued to face each other helplessly. Nicola wanted desperately to reach out to him, to let him hold her and tell her that nothing else mattered but the way it felt to be his. But she couldn't do that. There was an invisible wall between them that she knew was impregnable.

Finally he said, "I won't pressure you right now. You've got enough to deal with. But it's not over, despite what you say. I've waited all my life for you, Nicola. When I found you and you were married, I felt desolate. I thought I'd lost my one chance at happiness. Then we met again, and you were free. Fate gave me a second chance. We were *meant* to be together. I'll *never* give up. Remember that when you go to sleep tonight and tomorrow night and all the nights to come. Somehow, someday, we *will* be together again—and forever.''

Then, without touching her, he turned and strode out the door. She heard the front door open and close, but she knew Logan meant what he said. He wasn't walking out of her life forever, no matter what she insisted.

LOGAN DROVE through the dark quiet London streets. He intended every word of his determined speech to Nicola; he wasn't a man who gave up easily. But despite his determination, he was more worried than he'd let her see. When they'd argued earlier, he hadn't taken it that seriously. She'd been naturally upset about the bribery charge, he'd thought, and when she'd had time to think things over, she'd change her mind about their relationship being finished.

But by the time he'd called on her she'd had several hours to think things through, to calm down, and she'd still been determined to end their relationship.

It was her calmness that had got to him. She wasn't being emotional. She was simply looking at the situation objectively and saying, ''This won't work.''

His hands gripped the steering wheel tightly; his

knuckles showed white with anger and worry. He didn't understand everything she'd said, but he knew she felt she was right. She was convinced their relationship wouldn't work—at least not alongside her career. Somehow he had to make her see that it not only *could* work, it *had* to. For without each other, both were lost.

TWO DAYS PASSED, during which Nicola accomlished absolutely nothing. Two days wasted, she thought, as she sat in her sitting room one evening. Three working days to go, not counting the weekend, and she had absolutely no idea what to do next.

The ringing of the telephone jolted her out of her growing despair. For a moment she hesitated to answer, fearing it might be Logan. Steeling herself for the impact of his voice, she picked up the receiver.

"Nicola!"

The voice was unmistakable. And as welcome as a brightly burning fire on a dismal winter day. "Lisa! Oh, it's *so* good to hear from you."

"What's wrong?" Lisa asked immediately, perceptive even on a transatlantic call.

"Nothing," Nicola lied, her voice sounding unconvincing even to herself.

"Come on, you sound like the world's falling apart around you. Hey, did that good ol' boy do something?"

"I. . . I'm not seeing Logan any longer," she said.

"What did the rat do?"

In spite of herself Nicola smiled. "You're a loyal friend—and for that I'm grateful. You automatically assume it's *his* fault."

"Of course." Lisa laughed, and added, "You're nice, intelligent, honorable—all the virtues dear to a Boy Scout's heart. If something went wrong, it's *got* to be his fault."

"Actually, *everything* went wrong, and Logan and I just sort of got caught up in it," Nicola said. Briefly she explained the situation.

"Oh, Nicola, I'm so sorry. What a mess."

"Exactly."

"But surely Logan doesn't believe you're guilty?"

"No. He knows me better than that. But he isn't exactly standing by me, either. He immediately replaced me with someone else. I wouldn't have minded so much if we hadn't—" Nicola stopped, suddenly feeling awkward.

"If you hadn't fallen in love," Lisa finished for her.

"How did you—"

"How did I know?" Lisa interrupted. "Well, for starters, I've had only short notes saying, 'Hi! I *love* my work. I *love* London. Love, N.' " Lisa tried again for levity. "That quick call from Baton Rouge certainly sounded as if you were on a high."

"I was then. I called you from the airport just before we left for Kennedy to catch our flight back to London." Nicola knew her voice was giving her away.

"Well, what went wrong," Lisa insisted. "I've never heard you sound so wounded—and we go back a ways together, Nicola. You did fall in love with Rhett Butler, didn't you?"

It was true—she had. And where Logan was concerned she reacted with her heart and not her head.

In all this awful situation it was what she experienced as his rejection of her that hurt the most.

"Is there anything I can do to help?" Lisa asked.

"No. I wish there were. But thanks, anyway."

"Listen," Lisa said suddenly. "Why don't you just say to hell with the whole damn place and come back to the States? There's a spare bedroom in my apartment and a spare desk in my office. We could be partners. Oh, Nicola, it would be fun! Halloran and Wynter, together again!"

Nicola laughed. "You're crazy. The last thing your firm needs is a lawyer with a shady reputation."

"Don't be ridiculous. Nobody over here would believe that of you for a second. Nicola, you know I was critical of your marriage to Andrew. But when it came to his stature as a lawyer, I had great respect for him. He had tremendous integrity and courage. What would he advise you to do now?"

Andrew. Nicola hadn't thought of him in days. Now a vivid memory came to her: Andrew lecturing to her first-year law class. "Always fight for what you believe in. It isn't only the victory that matters. It's the fact that you were willing to fight."

And Nicola realized that although Andrew was gone, he had left her a legacy of courage. He had fought all his life for the ideals and principles he believed in. The law, to him, was more than statutes; it was a commitment, an obligation for those trained to practice it.

For a while he'd seemed to have had tunnel vision when it came to applying this philosophy to her own ideals and principles. But he'd overcome that, and by the end he had once more encouraged her to do what she believed she should.

Realizing now how close she'd come in the past few days simply to giving up and feeling sorry for herself, she felt guilty. Andrew would have expected more of her.

"You're right, Lisa. Somehow I've got to clear this up."

"And when you do?"

Nicola noticed that Lisa had said, "when," not "if." She deeply appreciated her friend's confidence in her. In response she added, "And then I'll consider that offer."

"All right!" Lisa exclaimed happily. "Hey, I'm sitting here with a lapful of travel brochures. I'm going to give myself a ten-day cruise somewhere. I've worked nonstop ever since I came here. I was thinking about a trip up the Rhine. But why don't I invite myself over to London, and then we can travel home first class on the Queen Elizabeth II. The last sailing from Southampton is sometime in November, I think."

"Whoa." Nicola laughed. "I'm still not sure what I'm going to do. But I've got to get busy now. Thanks, Lisa. Your call was just what I needed."

After hanging up, she phoned Thomas.

"I'm glad you called, Nicola. I want to talk to you about Logan. He had no choice, you realize, in asking me to assign another attorney to his case."

"I understand," Nicola answered, though she didn't. "But I don't want to talk about that. Where can I go to find out everything about Lord Carlisle?"

"Try *Debrett's Peerage*. I believe it would be the

best book available. And Somerset House would have a copy of his father's will, which would show everything he inherited. That would give you a good idea of his financial situation.'' He added happily, ''I must say, my dear, you sound most determined.''

''I am.''

Thomas tried again to speak of Logan and his position, and again Nicola blocked his effort to discuss the painful situation. She'd told Logan that he and Thomas could do as they pleased about assigning another attorney to the case; she meant to try to clear her name. And without Logan's support. Somehow—someway—she would do it...and then she and Logan James would be even. She'd have her standing as a reputable attorney again, and Logan would have his damn contract.

A half hour later she was in a bookstore buying a copy of *Debrett's Peerage*. The information about Carlisle was brief and depressingly unhelpful. He was the second son of the Duke of Cumberland, a graduate of Cambridge, active in the government in a variety of posts, married to Letitia Conrad, whose father was Sir Sidney Conrad, a world-famous engineer who had died recently. It was all perfectly innocent, even admirable, and thus far Nicola could see nothing that would indicate why Lord Carlisle would lie about her.

From there she went on to Somerset House, where wills were filed. For a small fee anyone could read anyone else's will. Looking up the Duke of Cumberland's will, she discovered that the duke had not been a wealthy man. His estate had been entailed and had gone to his elder son. There was very little left to Lord Carlisle. It was the common story of the aristocratic house having fallen on hard times.

And yet, Nicola considered, Carlisle lived in a magnificent house in the most expensive area of London. He had a staff of servants—which was certainly not cheap these days. His government salary couldn't possibly amount to that much. How, then, she wondered, did he afford that lavish life-style.

Suddenly Mrs. Murdle's words came back to her: "Where money's concerned, there's usually a woman involved." Was it possible he was living on his wife's money? Surely the daughter of an engineer, even a famous one, couldn't have inherited *that* much money, she thought.

Then she had an inspiration. She was not sure what prompted her to do so, but she asked to see Sidney Conrad's will, also. As she read the long complicated document, she felt her enthusiasm fading. There was nothing there that shed light on the problem. Conrad had left his limited holdings to a variety of relatives and charities. His daughter, Letitia, had been given a great deal of stock in a firm called Wagner, Inc., but very little cash.

For some reason the name Wagner struck a dim chord in Nicola's memory. Where had she heard it previously? She sensed it was important, and she wracked her brain trying to remember.

And then it came to her. The reporter at the *Times* had mentioned that Mannering Construction had grown by clever takeover bids of other companies, including Wagner, Inc., a successful engineering firm.

Though she would have to check it out, Nicola was sure the stockholders in Wagner had probably been given shares in Mannering.

Thunderstruck, Nicola sat back in the chair. *So that's it*, she thought. She understood it all now. Through his wife, Carlisle had stock in Mannering. If Mannering won this lucrative contract, its stock would certainly soar. Nicola had no doubt that Carlisle badly needed the money he would then receive.

But how to get proof to validate this theory? Hopefully Thomas could help her there.

She drove straight to his house. This time she didn't notice the quaint charm of the house or the beauty of the grounds. When the butler opened the door, she asked to see Thomas, immediately. The butler took her to the sitting room, where Thomas was reading the paper before dinner.

When he looked up at her in surprise, she said, "I know why Lord Carlisle lied!" She proceeded to tell him everything she'd learned. Then she finished— less confidently, "But I have to prove that his wife still has the stock."

"That's easy enough to do," Thomas said, smiling broadly. "Leave it to me." He added wonderingly, "So that explains it. I must say, I'm astonished. He comes from one of the best families. But no matter. He's in for it now, my girl."

"Oh, Thomas, do you really think so? Is this enough to clear me," Nicola asked, betraying more anxiety than she wanted to.

"Yes, my dear. There's no doubt of that. By to-morrow afternoon Lord Carlisle's reputation will be shot and yours will be restored. And Logan will win that contract Monday.''

Nicola sighed with relief. Impulsively she leaned over and kissed Thomas's cheek. "Thank you. For everything. Especially for not doubting me.''

"Oh, there was never any question of that, my dear. I'm just glad it's all going to be cleared up.'' His usually twinkling eyes held a look of compassion. Taking her hand in his, he asked, "Now about Logan....''

"I know you're concerned, Thomas, and I appreciate that. But I'd rather not discuss him now.''

"Very well, Nicola. I understand. Well, my dear, this calls for a celebration for you and an early return to the office for me. But be sure you're in bright and early in the morning. We've got a lot of loose ends to tie up if we're to get this contract for Logan and restore your good name.''

Nicola smiled brightly at him. For the first time in a while she was looking forward to the next day.

ON MONDAY AT NOON, Nicola sat at home waiting impatiently for Thomas's call. During the past few days she and Thomas had worked feverishly to clear up the mess Carlisle had so cleverly created. Thomas had gone over Laughton's head to his superior in the government with proof of Laughton's and Carlisle's wrongdoing. Laughton was fired, and Carlisle was forced to resign in disgrace. The Mannering Company insisted it had no knowledge of the affair. Nicola didn't believe this, but it didn't really matter.

She was vindicated, but there was still the contract

to be awarded. The announcement was to be made that morning. Nicola had declined to go with Thomas, for she knew Logan would be there, and she simply couldn't face him. Thus far he'd respected her wish to be left alone, but she knew that wouldn't last long.

For the tenth time in an hour, Nicola picked up, then put down a brief she'd been trying to read. She simply couldn't concentrate on anything. Why hadn't Thomas called, she wondered. Surely the announcement would have already been made.

When the doorbell rang, it jolted her already jangled nerves. As she went to answer it, she thought perhaps Thomas had come to tell her the decision in person.

Logan stood on the doorstep, holding a magnum of Taittinger champagne. At her startled look he explained, "I won."

She felt her heart turn over and knew it wasn't entirely because of the successful bid for the lucrative contract. Logan was *there*, at that moment, after she'd spent long lonely days and nights without him. Flashing him a rueful smile, she opened the door farther so he could enter. In the sitting room, she led him to the bar, and watched while he opened the bottle of champagne.

He poured two generous glasses, then handed one to her. Holding up his glass in a toast, he said, "To you, Nicola. It's *your* victory. I would never have won this contract without you."

She didn't reply. Instead she sipped the delicious bubbly liquid and tried not to think about how close Logan was, how desperately her body yearned for his. After a moment she said, "I know how much this contract meant to you, Logan. I'm glad you've won. I mean that."

"Nicola...." He set down his glass on a table, then moved to take her in his arms.

It was what she wanted more than anything. But she knew that if she let him touch her, she was lost. Stepping back quickly, she insisted, "No, Logan. Please."

He looked at her with a pained vulnerable expression, and her heart went out to him. At that moment she realized there was no way she could continue to remain in London. Their relationship was impossible, but being near him without being involved with him was also impossible. She had to leave, to get as far away from his overpowering presence as she could.

She made a sudden decision. "Logan, there's something I have to tell you. I'm giving Thomas my resignation today. I'm leaving London."

"Leaving!" He was stunned.

"I'm going into partnership with Lisa, the friend I told you about once. She has an office in LA."

"Damn it, Nicola," he exploded, "you can't do this!"

"I can do as I please," she shot back. "I don't belong to you."

For a moment they stood glaring at each other, blue green eyes meeting brown ones stubbornly. But the longer she looked at him, the more she felt herself drawn irresistibly toward him.

Finally she whispered helplessly, "Oh, Logan, don't you see, this situation's hopeless. It's far better for both of us to end it now—a clean break. If we drag it out, we'll make each other miserable."

His voice was tender as he asked, "And just how happy do you suppose either of us will be apart?"

She didn't answer. It was pointless to argue. She knew what she had to do, and she intended to do it, no matter how deeply it hurt.

In one swift unexpected movement, he took her into his arms. He held her firmly against him. Startled, she stared up into his intense gaze. "You can run away, Nicola. Hell, you can run halfway around the world. But it won't do any good. Because you can never run away from what we feel for each other."

With that he kissed her deeply, sending shock waves of desire and longing flowing through her quivering body. When he finally let her go, he finished breathlessly, "Remember that when you're in Los Angeles!"

CHAPTER THIRTEEN

NICOLA AND LISA stood on the deck of the Queen
Elizabeth II as the ship sat docked at Southampton.
It was Saturday, November 5, and in a moment the
ship would depart. The atmosphere was hectic, gay,
noisy. Passengers crowded near the railings to wave
down to friends and relatives on the dock below.
Streams of serpentine showered down on everyone,
and the ship's horn blew loudly.

The two young women waved at their own small
group of well-wishers. Thomas and his wife, Mr. and
Mrs. Murdle, even Mrs. Murdle's venerable mother,
had come to bid them bon voyage. It had been an
emotional leave-taking for Nicola. She knew she
would miss these people, especially Thomas. She had
come to London alone. But she had made good
friends. *And* found a rare love. Now she was leaving
those friends—and her love—to start all over again
elsewhere.

As the ship slowly pulled away from its berth, Nicola couldn't help but think it was symbolic of her
life for the past year—she always seemed to be leaving.

"Let's get down to our cabins and see what they're
like," Lisa suggested gaily.

Nicola nodded and turned away from the railing—away from England and from Logan James.

Nicola's cabin wasn't terribly large, but it was comfortably furnished with a double bed, dresser and a table flanked by two easy chairs. Two porthole windows would make it sunny and cheerful during the day, she knew, and there was a private bathroom.

As she opened the suitcases the steward had left on a luggage rack at the foot of the bed, she listened to Lisa's excited chatter through an open door that led to the adjoining cabin.

"You'll see, Nicola. A little champagne and caviar will improve your mood one hundred percent. What you need right now is a little luxury, maybe even downright decadence. Leisure time without obligations. You need to relax."

"Well, five days at sea with nothing to do but relax should be adequate," Nicola replied.

She hung her evening gowns in the small closet. First-class passengers on the QE2 were expected to dress for dinner, so she had brought several gowns.

Lisa came into the room. "Let's do a quick tour of the ship."

"Okay," Nicola agreed, hanging up the last of her clothes.

The ship was massive, a fabulous floating city. There were sun decks, indoor and outdoor pools, nightclubs, bars, a casino, movie theater, shops and restaurants and a health spa.

As they walked around the ship, Lisa read aloud from a brochure. "'The QE2 stands thirteen stories tall, measures 963 feet from stem to stern.' "

"Lisa, enough already!" Nicola responded.

"Okay, if you don't want to hear any more fascinating statistics, we could stop by the casino and take on the roulette wheel."

Nicola laughed. "Not yet. Why don't we have dinner first?"

Glancing at her watch, Lisa said, "Oops, you're right. I made reservations for us at the Princess Grill in half an hour."

They returned to their cabins. Lisa finished dressing first. She lounged on Nicola's bed while Nicola combed her hair.

"There's something about the ambience of a transatlantic crossing," she mused. "It's terribly glamorous—dressing for dinner and all that. There'll be music floating out on the evening breeze, moonlight trailing a silvery path on the water, strolling on the decks...."

"Forget the romance," Nicola cut in. Her tone was too adamant to brook arguing.

Tactfully Lisa changed the subject. "Well, enjoy being pampered, anyway. You deserve a little self-indulgence."

"What on earth are we going to do for five days?" Nicola asked.

"You have no idea how much time it takes to be blissfully relaxed," Lisa replied with a grin. Picking up the ship's newspaper, the *QE2 Times*, she recited a list of activities: games, bridge, lectures on everything from flower arranging to commodities. "And if you're determined to be doing something all the time, you can exercise all day. Start with a run on the quarterdeck in the morning, then work out in the gym. Personally, I plan to eat my way across the Atlantic. Did you know there are three first-class restaurants?''

Nicola smiled in spite of herself.

"See," Lisa said triumphantly. "You're feeling better already.''

But she wasn't. She was only learning to live with the pain of missing Logan. Still, she had to admit Lisa was right in one way. She did need to relax after the pressure of the past two weeks in London. And this was a good way to do it. If only she could put Logan out of her mind....

She had told him she never wanted to see him again. And yet perversely, when he left her alone, she felt bereft.

Well, it's over, she told herself bluntly. *Forget him.*

Thinking about Logan made her feel tense. And her hands were suddenly clumsy as she tried to twist her pale golden hair into a chignon. "Why don't you go ahead to the restaurant?" she suggested to Lisa, who was fidgeting impatiently. "I'll join you in a few minutes.''

Lisa left, and Nicola finally managed to get her hair just right. Then she changed into a white cashmere evening gown. Its soft simplicity was broken only by a diamond-studded belt. The gown was high necked and ankle length, ostensibly demure. Yet the way Nicola looked in it was anything but demure. It hugged her lush curves, and the pristine white made her golden blond loveliness even more stunning.

She clipped on dangling diamond earrings, then slipped her narrow feet into the silver evening sandals. After putting a comb and lipstick into a silver beaded evening bag, she was ready.

She was pleasantly surprised by the Princess Grill. It was relatively cozy—not the cavernous barn of a dining room usually found on cruise ships. The plush burgundy red color scheme was sumptuous.

Nicola immediately spied Lisa sitting at a table for five in a corner. A white-uniformed waiter was bending toward her solicitously. He smiled broadly, murmured something, then left just as Nicola sat down.

"I ordered caviar," Lisa explained. "The waiter said we can have it every night if we wish, and I said we definitely wish."

Nicola grinned. "Aren't you being greedy?"

"Of course. For the next five days I intend to be greedy, self-indulgent and lazy. And I advise you to be the same."

Looking at the three empty chairs at the table, Nicola asked, "Do you know who will be sitting with us?"

"No. I asked the waiter, and he said it's *very* interesting. Whoever they are, they weren't on board when we left. They chartered a helicopter and are flying out to the ship right now. Must be nice to be so rich."

"Mmm," Nicola agreed, not really interested.

At that moment the waiter returned with a silver bowl filled with a rich black caviar and a tray covered with a variety of thin crackers. He took their order for dinner, then left.

Somehow Nicola couldn't summon up much of an appetite. Watching Lisa enjoy the caviar, she wished she could join in the spirit of the occasion. But the heaviness that had weighed down her heart ever since her argument with Logan wouldn't go away. By the end of the meal, when Lisa ordered crepes suzettes for dessert, Nicola felt she couldn't pretend any longer.

"Lisa, I'm sorry, but I'm awfully tired. I'm going to take a walk around the deck, then turn in."

"But I thought we'd try out the casino tonight," Lisa said, clearly disappointed. "I feel lucky."

"I'm sorry. Tomorrow night for sure, okay?"

Lisa flashed an understanding smile. "Sure."

Returning to her cabin, Nicola put on a full-length white mink cape to protect her from the chilly Atlantic breezes. Then she went out on deck. It was all just as Lisa had described earlier. There was a faint streak of moonlight from a pale quarter moon, the sea stretched endlessly into the night and the strains of a romantic melody drifted out from a nearby piano bar.

Listening intently for a moment, Nicola finally identified the music as a popular theme song from an old classic movie. As she listened to the song, she looked out at the expanse of sea and sky. It was as if this huge ocean liner, this floating resort hotel, were sailing toward an unknown destination where there were no boundary lines, no borders, no edges to define time or place.

Leaning against the rail, with the heavy fur cape protecting her from the cold wind, she listened to the sounds of the night and the sea. There was tremendous force in those unplumbed depths, alive with constant motion and surging power. She stared into the limitless darkness.

God, she thought, *I feel so lost. Not just because of the vastness of the empty space beyond the lights of this ship. No, lost because no matter what else I might see on the horizon tomorrow, I won't see Logan.*

Once Lisa had arrived in London, they'd been on a whirlwind tour of the city. Then Nicola had had to close her house and arrange for her things to be shipped to Los Angeles. It had been a hectic time, and she had been able to push Logan from her thoughts.

But out on the ocean, alone in this night, sailing away from where she'd known such joy and pain, she let the memories of him wash over her... Portobello Road; Logan slipping the beautiful gold ring on her finger... after dinner that night in Soho; Logan telling her he'd fallen in love with her in Washington, that he wanted her and would wait until she was ready... and that night in Scotland, Logan returning to her through a fierce storm and their waiting no longer.... She remembered Logan's tender sweet smile, the way his lips curved beneath that luxuriant silky mustache.

Oh, Logan, her heart sighed in longing as she looked up at the sky. It was alive with thousands of stars pinpricking the blackness.

Well, she thought, *I've learned one thing. I know better now than to wish on a star. In the garden at*

Beechwood I did that, and like King Midas, I re-ceived my wish—adventure and romance and a white knight.

Midas had wished that everything he touched would turn to gold. But when he couldn't eat or drink or even hold the maiden he loved, the wish be-came a curse. To break the curse, he bathed in the river Pactolus. He lost the magic touch, and the sands of the river turned to gold.

Where is the river Pactolus for me, Nicola won-dered. How would she remove the pain from her aching heart? For that brief time with Logan she'd felt incredibly alive—shining like the glittering stars above—with joy and expectation. She'd made her de-cision to trust him *and* the love he'd declared at that inn in Scotland. She'd reveled in the sight, touch and taste of him. She'd yielded her heart to the promise that had begun at Beechwood over champagne and toasts to "when dreams come true."

All relationships hold a promise, she thought. *If the promise isn't fulfilled, the relationship withers. And the promise, unfulfilled, becomes a bitter lie.*

Nicola shook her head. She'd thought enough of Logan for one night. Sighing, she turned away from the rail.

And then she saw him.

A tall man in a black tuxedo, his hands thrust casually in the pockets of his black slacks, which seemed molded to his long sinewy legs.

Logan.

He wasn't a figment of her overwrought imagina-tion. He was real, and he was there.

She said the first thing that came into her mind. "You're supposed to be in Baton Rouge."

He smiled, and she felt her heart lurch. "I *was*. Then Beau and I had to go to Scotland. Joanna Sue came with us. When I got back, Thomas told me where you'd gone. So I chartered a helicopter to get us here."

"But why?"

"Isn't that obvious? I wanted to see you. To talk to you. I knew if I tried that in London, you'd just tell me to go to hell and run away. You can't do that in the middle of the Atlantic. You'll be stuck with me for five days, whether you like it or not."

"And exactly what do you think that will accomplish?"

"This," he answered.

He took her into his arms and kissed her. He did not begin with a light tease of a kiss as he often used to do. He crushed her against him and brought his mouth down full on hers. She felt the soft bristle of that mustache she'd just thought about, and she felt the familiar rush of warmth from her head to her heart to a secret place deep inside her.

A wave of desire swept over her. Her heart betrayed all her firm resolve. She reached her arms up around his neck to draw him closer. When he finally lifted his mouth from hers, she drew a long shuddering breath and laid her head against his chest.

"It's not fair," Nicola said, her voice muffled. "You use airplanes and helicopters and mint-julep charm. Logan James, you don't fight fair!"

He pulled away. Cupping her face in his hands, he

looked deep into her eyes, shimmering translucent aquamarine with tears. "You know what they say, 'All's fair in love and war.'" Then he lowered his lips to hers again, this time in that sweet teasing way he had. He kissed each corner of her mouth, the tip of her nose.

As she closed her eyes, she felt the barest touch of his lips on each eyelid. The fierce anger she'd felt toward him, her conviction that he'd abandoned her, was no match for this far headier emotion. As his arms encircled her, pulling her tightly against him, her body molded to his instinctively.

This can never work, she told herself desperately.

But to her yearning body it didn't matter. She might be determined to be master of her fate, but Logan was master of her body and her heart. Under his touch her entire being dissolved into a quivering sensuousness, and the flickering ember that had always been between them was ignited into a raging inferno.

Finally he released her. And when she looked up into those compelling eyes, her own held no anger, only intense desire.

"Nicola," he whispered hoarsely.

He was no more in control of his own senses than she was.

She stepped out of his embrace. She had to be in control, she knew. Because the alternative was to be hurt again as only Logan could hurt her.

"You told me once you would wait until I was ready." She drew a long steady breath. "I want you to wait now. All this is moving too fast. Too much of my life has moved too fast lately."

"But you want me."

"Yes, and I want to put the past aside, to come to you right now. But for once in my life I'm going to take the time to consider my actions. I can't forget that when I needed your support in London, you weren't there!"

Logan reached out to take her firmly by the shoulders. Even through the thick mink cape Nicola could feel the electric thrill of his touch.

"Listen to me, damn it! I did not abandon you. You knew my schedule. I had to return to Baton Rouge."

"But you hired another attorney."

"I had no choice, Nicola! There was a lot of money behind that project, other people's money. I can't be emotional about conducting business. You took a necessary business procedure as a personal rejection. It was simply a matter of protocol. I had to honor my commitments to the people I work with."

Nicola was silent. In her mind she knew Logan was right, but in her heart she still felt betrayed. Reluctantly she admitted to herself that she'd allowed her personal feelings for Logan to interfere with her professional attitude. Perhaps because Andrew had let her down when she needed his support most, she was too ready to believe the same of Logan.

Looking at him, she said, "Everything you're saying is right, but it doesn't change the fact that we have problems, Logan. Our careers will always create conflicts between us. I still need time to think. I fell in love with you in London before I had time to get to know you. Now I want to get to know you and to have you get to know me. That's the only way we can avoid conflicts like this one.''

He took her in his arms and said tenderly, ''I've said it before, and I'll say it again now. You're worth waiting for. We've got five days and nights, love. You tell me when you're ready.'' He smiled down at her. ''Now, then, I'll walk you to your cabin and kiss you good-night at your door like an understanding and patient suitor.''

He was as good as his word. When he left her alone a few minutes later, she felt relieved, as if the world had been whirling around violently and had finally slowed to a pace she could handle. And yet, at the same time, she felt a thoroughly contrary sense of disappointment that Logan was, indeed, a man of his word.

THE NEXT TWO DAYS and nights passed quickly. Logan was always there, joining Nicola at breakfast, jogging on deck with her, dancing with her in the nightclub. Beau and Joanna Sue and Lisa were there, too, but to Nicola they seemed almost like figures in the background. She could focus only on Logan.

''Now I see why you've been thrown for a loop,'' Lisa said to her after meeting Logan. ''That guy's not someone you'll ever forget.''

Nicola just smiled. No, Logan wasn't someone she could ever forget, whatever happened between them now.

As they spent every waking moment together, they learned about each other...their feelings about family, their values, their likes and dislikes. Nicola discovered that this man she loved and desired was someone she also liked.

One afternoon there was a brief rain. When it was over, Nicola and Logan walked out onto the deck.

Logan pointed to the horizon. "Look."

Turning, Nicola saw a rainbow arcing across the ocean.

"In London you said that rainbows are brief, beautiful and not true. You don't believe in rainbows, do you?" he asked softly.

She shook her head. "No. They're an empty promise."

"Well, I believe in them. I believe in the pot of gold in the same way I believe in serendipity. I read a poem once I've never forgotten." He quoted:

> Be careful with rainbows
>   they are an endangered species.
> Arcing across our world,
>   they shimmer on the horizon
>   promising hopes and dreams
>   and wishes, too.
> So, be careful with rainbows
>   they are
> An endangered species.

He hesitated, then finished in a husky voice, "We must make the most of what we find. You're far too young and beautiful to be so cynical. A rainbow is a bonus, and the poem's right. We do need to be careful with its gift."

She was silent, still unsure and afraid.

"Did Aunt Cordy tell you the story of her and Uncle Alex?" Logan asked suddenly.

"Yes."

"You know, her necklace has nineteen pearls—nineteen years of waiting. Let's not waste precious time that way." He took her into the circle of his arm. He didn't kiss her. He simply held her patiently.

And suddenly she knew she was ready. . . .

She dressed with special care that night; her most beautiful outfit—a maroon velvet dinner suit with a sheer, lacy white blouse. . . her most enticing perfume sprayed behind her ears, between her breasts. . . . As she left the cabin, she had a thoroughly feminine smile on her lovely face.

Later, when Logan walked her back to the cabin, she said in a voice brimming with feeling, "Why don't you come in?"

He met her direct gaze. Then a slow sensuous smile spread across his handsome face. He followed her inside.

He crossed the few feet that separated them and took her face in his hands. As she looked up at him, his fingertips lightly traced the curves of her cheeks. Their eyes clung for one timeless moment.

His fingers moved down to stroke the long slender line of her throat. She felt the muscles in her abdomen tighten. Logan bent to kiss her, his warm breath caressing her face before his lips met hers tenderly.

The gentleness with which he held her made her pliant beneath the expert touch of his hands. Nicola responded with all her being. All her inhibitions were gone, leaving only a breathless joy.

Slowly her hands twined around his neck. She loved the feel of the dark silky hair that curled over the collar of his formal white shirt.

Logan's hand slid along her shoulder, and the maroon velvet jacket of her dinner suit fell unheeded to the floor. With infinite tenderness his touch moved beneath the white blouse to rest just under the swell of her breast. Carefully he unhooked the clasp of her silky bra. His fingertips moved in sensuous circles around one breast, while his other hand held her waist possessively.

Nicola leaned into his touch, her whole body quivering with erotic anticipation. When his fingertips touched her taut nipple, she gasped with pleasure. Her mind no longer had dominion over her body. She couldn't have resisted him now if she'd wanted to. "Oh, Logan," she moaned deep in her throat, pressing herself tightly against him.

From the moment on deck when he'd kissed her she had yearned for the sweet release only he could give her. Until Logan made love to her in Scotland, Nicola had only faintly realized the intense compelling bond that can exist between a man and a woman. She wanted to renew that bond again and again. All thought vanished in her imperative need to be joined with him.

Instinctively, without realizing what she was doing, she began to move her hips rhythmically against his lean body.

"Nicola!" Logan groaned passionately. Suddenly he picked her up and carried her to the bed. Propping himself on one elbow to look down into her dreamy eyes, his own eyes were aflame with desire.

As she twined her fingers in his thick hair, then ran them lightly along the nape of his neck, he whispered, "God, I've missed you!" His mouth sought hers once more as his hands molded her body to his.

Locked in that fierce embrace, Nicola hoped this moment would never end.

Gently Logan released her, looking at her with eyes dazed by the intensity of his desire. Then his lips traveled down her cheek to gently caress her throat.

Nicola sensed that this time, unlike Scotland, he wanted to go slowly with her. Together they would experience every facet of physical pleasure. That first time they'd made love they were both overcome by ravenous desire. Now they had time...all they needed.

In a movement that was remarkably smooth and quick, he slipped off her blouse and skirt and the fragile undergarments she wore. Lying naked before him, Nicola tried to restrain her rising excitement. She wanted to take the time for an exquisitely measured exploration of mutual pleasure. Yet her need for him grew more demanding by the moment.

Pale moonlight came through the porthole windows, making the room dim rather than totally black. In the diffuse lighting Nicola could see Logan's face—that face she had dreamed about every night they'd been apart. She knew the love and desire she observed there were reflected in her own expression. "I want you," she whispered unashamedly.

With hands and eyes Logan began exploring her

eager body. He traced the gentle swell of her full round breasts with a touch as light as down and as electrifying as a live wire. The pink nipples, still erect, responded again to his fingertips. Every nerve in her body was alive and tingling. "I need you, Nicola," he murmured, his raw voice revealing his vulnerability. "Without you I'm only half alive."

"Logan, my love, my *only* love..." she whispered, her throat tight with emotion. Her arms tightened around his broad shoulders.

With tantalizing purposefulness his hands moved along the sides of her body, following the hollows, the curves, the flat plane of her stomach and the fullness of her hips.

"I'm gong to kiss every inch of you," he promised. "There won't be a part of you left unclaimed. We belong together, darlin'. *Never* forget that."

"Yes...oh, yes!" she answered. Since their first kiss, she'd known she could never really belong to another man.

Gently Logan began to fulfill his promise. His lips lingered on the pulse at the base of her throat, then moved to the deep valley between her breasts, finally capturing her aching nipples.

Nicola moaned, clutching him closer, burying her fingers in his silky hair. Wave after wave of ecstasy poured over her, until she felt she was drowning in a sea of pleasure so exquisite she never wanted to come up for air.

His smooth dinner jacket and crisp white ruffled shirt moved sensuously against her bare skin. She was trembling now with desire.

Logan continued to kiss her, flaming her passion. His lips traveled lightly, deliberately, across her tingling skin, searching out every sensuous intimate place. No part of her body missed his touch. She had no secrets from him as his lips and fingertips roamed possessively past her hips and thighs to the very tips of her toes.

Her need for him was so urgent she felt she could no longer bear the suspense of waiting for ultimate fulfillment. "Logan...now..." she whispered, her voice catching in her throat.

Quickly he stood up, taking off his clothes. Nicola's eyes blazed with passion as she gazed at that ruggedly masculine body, well muscled, with broad shoulders and sinewy thighs. His sheer physical power was overwhelming. Yet she was not afraid. There was only this undeniable need to possess and be possessed. She wanted to touch him, to caress him, to make him feel what she felt when he touched her.

When Logan lay naked beside her, she began her own exploration. Tenderly, boldly, her hands moved over the hard smooth planes and angles of his body. His provocative lovemaking, gentle yet passionate, had brought her to a fever pitch of desire. She wanted to give him that same intense experience.

As she caressed him lovingly, he took her into his powerful arms. Trembling, she reveled in the touch of skin against skin along the full length of their bodies. At that moment there was nothing in the world she wanted more than Logan James. She wanted to meld her body with his, to become one being.

As he moved over her, she felt her body throb with almost unbearable excitement.

"Nicola...my Nicola," he murmured with infinite tenderness in his voice.

"Oh, Logan," she breathed. "I want you... Logan...."

He waited no longer.

By the dim moonlight filtering through the porthole window, Nicola gave herself as she had done only once before in her life—in a romantic old inn in Scotland.

In the part of her mind that was still rational, Nicola realized this man was the other half of her heart. She would love him forever.

Instinctively her body moved with sensuous abandonment beneath him. With fierce, yet gentle passion Logan responded. His body united with hers in the ultimate intimacy. Soaring in almost unbearable rapture, Nicola cried out at the moment of fulfillment. For one timeless moment she felt their bodies, their heartbeats, their very souls become one....

ON FRIDAY NIGHT, they all sat over after-dinner drinks in the Club Lido. A steward approached to tell Logan there was a call for him from Baton Rouge.

"C'mon, Beau," he said as he rose to follow the steward. "You'll need to hear this, too."

Nicola and Joanna Sue were left alone at the table. Idly they watched Lisa dancing with a handsome young officer of the ship.

"Your friend seems to be having a marvelous time," Joanna Sue commented.

"Lisa generally manages to enjoy herself," Nicola responded. "She never lacks for admirers."

Joanna Sue looked thoughtful. "She's exactly what I always saw myself being...a carefree independent career woman going my own way. Then I met Beau, and that idea went out the window."

Nicola smiled in sympathy. "The men in the James family have a way of changing women's lives."

"They take a lot for granted," Joanna Sue continued with a shrug. "Remember when you were in Baton Rouge. We talked about this trip. I told both Beau and Logan that my boss wouldn't appreciate my taking a vacation at this time. But Beau told me this would just be a quick trip, so I went ahead and arranged the time off. Then at the last minute Logan decided on this cruise. Beau called my boss—*then* told me." She shook her head helplessly. "Sometimes I feel I'm in a powerplay."

"Yes," Nicola agreed. "I know." She thought of London and that argument Logan still didn't understand.

"Now Beau wants me to take a year or two out to have a child. I want children, but that will mean a sacrifice in terms of my career, and I'm just not ready to do that yet."

Nicola smiled dryly. "I don't suppose it occurred to him that perhaps *he* should take off some time to help you with the baby?"

Joanna Sue laughed. "Oh, no! That's 'women's work,' you see."

She continued in a determined voice at odds with her fragile appearance. "I mean to stay married to that man—and have his children. But on *my* terms, as well as his."

"Good luck." Nicola raised her glass in salute.

"Luck's got nothin' to do with it, Nicola," Joanna Sue returned with a wry smile.

Nicola looked up to see Beau and Logan walking across the room, laughing together.

Logan stood behind her chair, and she felt his hands touch her bare shoulders, the warmth of that touch sending a flame through her body. He eased her mink cape off the back of the chair and around her shoulders. "Let's go for a walk on deck, honey."

The cold Atlantic was relatively calm. Nicola hugged the mink around her, looking up at the brilliant stars.

"We'll be docking tomorrow morning," Logan said.

Glancing at him, Nicola couldn't quite make out his feelings. "Yes," she replied noncommittally.

"Damn it, Nicola, you know what I'm getting at," he exploded. Grabbing her shoulders, he turned her to face him. "In Baton Rouge I asked you to marry me. Now I'm asking you again. We can be married as soon as we dock in New York, or we can go home and have a big wedding. Whatever you want. I just don't want us to be apart again."

"Logan, think about what you're asking," Nicola replied, trying to choose her words carefully. "I've made a commitment to join Lisa's firm. Do you expect me to turn my back on her and go flying off to Baton Rouge with you? And what then? Do I play lady of the manor while you go traipsing off to the four corners of the earth?''

"All right. You made a deal with Lisa. That's no problem." He was unexpectedly compliant. "I'm going to be working in Santa Barbara a lot for the next year on that offshore platform. Santa Barbara's only a couple hours drive from LA and an even shorter flight." He drew her into a close embrace and rested his face against her hair. "I just want us to be together, Nicola. We can find a way to reconcile our careers."

She hesitated. It was an extremely tempting idea. With all her heart she wanted to believe it would work. At this moment believing was all that mattered.

"Okay," she said with a sigh. "But we've got a lot of talking to do, Logan James."

Held tightly against him, even in the chill of the night air, his touch stirred fires deep within her. As his lips touched hers, she heard him whisper, "Let's talk later, love. Right now I've got a better idea."

EARLY THE NEXT MORNING, Joanna Sue stopped by Nicola's stateroom. She sat on the edge of the bed and watched Nicola pack.

"Are you going straight back to Baton Rouge from New York," Nicola asked snapping a suitcase shut and locking it.

"I am. Beau's going with Logan up to Valdez."

"Valdez," Nicola asked in surprise.

"Valdez, Alaska. You know...where the pipeline is. There's some kind of repair work needed to be done. And proposals for some new facilities."

"But I thought Logan was going to be concentrating on the Santa Barbara job for the next year," Nicola frowned, trying to assimilate this new information.

"Oh, sure. When he isn't in Scotland or Alaska or whatever other place turns out to need him. Where he goes, Beau goes. Well, you can see why I'm not ready to give up *my* career yet."

Nicola stood stock-still in the middle of the room, an icy feeling creeping down her spine.

"Well, I've got to finish my packing," Joanna Sue said, rising from the bed. "I just wanted to tell you I'm glad you and Logan patched things up. He's been an absolute bear since you two had your big blowup." She hugged Nicola. "Take care. I hope we see you again real soon."

When Joanna Sue had gone, Nicola continued to stand staring at the closed door, her mind in turmoil. Logan had given her the distinct impression he was going to be in Santa Barbara for a while. But instead he was going to be traveling back and forth from one part of the world to another. How could they talk about reconciling careers. They didn't even use the same language.

And it would always be this way. The wildcatter in Logan would never settle down. Yet he would expect her to sit in Magnolia Hill, waiting patiently for him. She'd had to give up her career in London because of her relationship with him. Santa Barbara was just another whistle-stop on his itinerary. Baton Rouge was only his headquarters and only because that's where James Petrochemical Company was based.

Is this *what loving him means,* she thought bitterly. *Giving up what makes me . . . me? Doing what's convenient for* him? "Damn!" she said aloud.

NEW YORK HARBOR came into view, and the ship slid by the Statue of Liberty. Her packing finished, Nicola dressed in a russet wool skirt and matching sweater with a lacy jabot. She was about to don her camel's hair coat when there was a knock at her door. She knew who it was and steeled herself for what was to come.

Logan walked in. When his eyes fell on her, his grin widened. Taking her face in his two hands, he kissed her possessively. Then looking around the room, he said, "You've already packed. There's no hurry, you know."

"I told the steward to send my suitcases on to the airport. My flight leaves early afternoon." Nicola kept her voice deliberately flat.

"What flight?" Logan asked, taken aback.

"To LA. I'm flying out with Lisa."

A frown creased his forehead; he was clearly puzzled. "I thought we were going to spend some time together before you went there. To decide *if* you were going there."

"Where? Where were we going to spend this time? Valdez? Alaska tomorrow . . . where next week?" Nicola fought for composure. He was perplexed, and she was angry . . . angry that Joanna Sue had been the one to tell her he was off to—God knows where next.

He kept declaring his love, but he didn't declare his flight plan.

"Nicola," he began, his tone placating, "Valdez is no big deal. I'll be gone a week at the most."

She looked at this man who affected her so deeply, and she sighed. "And what do I do while you're off 'taking over the world' as Joanna Sue so aptly put it?"

He stepped toward her. "Don't be afraid, Nicola. We can work this out if you won't be afraid."

How could she convey to him what she was afraid of. It was terribly ironic that in this age of advanced technology she couldn't find words to communicate her fears. Satellites were used to beam images and words across the world. Yet she was at a loss. She lacked the words—simple English words—to declare: *Logan, I love you, but I'm afraid to give up what I am to be what you want me to be.*

Aloud she said, "It takes a lot of courage to risk one's self in a relationship that's supposed to last forever. With Andrew when he protested in his silent way my involvement with Amanda Gibran—our relationship changed. I resented his attitude and lack of consideration. I love you, but I'm afraid I might learn to hate you if our life is based on your career at the expense of mine."

"Don't give in to that fear, Nicola," he urged. Clasping his hands on her shoulders, he looked deep into her eyes. "We can work things out. These problems are nothing compared to how we feel about each other."

"Logan. . . I can't be your camp follower!"

Sighing, Nicola closed her eyes, summoning up all her resolve. Her heart told her she couldn't live without this man, while her rational mind told her to end it immediately.

She put her hands on his face and drew his lips to hers. "I can't sit in Baton Rouge—at this stage of my life—and you can't sit in Los Angeles. I have my life and you have yours." The salt of her tears mingled with the sweetness of his kiss.

"I *won't* give you up, Nicola," he said. "You can run away a million times...but someday you'll realize our love is the only thing that matters."

Pulling away from him, she grabbed up her purse and coat and ran from the cabin. But even as she hurried on deck to join Lisa, his words echoed in her mind. "Our love is the only thing that matters."

PART THREE

Los Angeles

CHAPTER FOURTEEN

NICOLA HURRIED THROUGH the stained-glass doors of Halloran and Wynter, Attorneys-at-Law. In a raw silk jacket and matching skirt with peach-colored, crepe-de-chine blouse, she looked every inch the competent young attorney in a flourishing practice. Though both she and Lisa had to work long hard hours, they were thrilled with the steadily growing success of their partnership.

The office attested to the two women's new found prosperity. It was furnished in lovely antiques and original oil paintings that she and Lisa had chosen together. It was a small suite, but growing. Already she and Lisa had had to take over the office next door and hire another attorney to handle the work they simply didn't have time for. In only a month and a half Halloran and Wynter had become an upwardly mobile partnership.

She and Lisa had chosen Century City, an enclave of office buildings and condominiums surrounding an exclusive shopping center, because of its central location. It was near Beverly Hills, Santa Monica and Bel Air and only a short freeway drive to the courthouses in downtown Los Angeles.

Both women lived near the office. Lisa had a high-rise condominium right in Century City, and Nicola had a small house on the beach in Santa Monica. It was a contemporary redwood-and-glass structure that was nothing like her house in Chelsea. She had purposefully chosen something very different because she didn't want to stir up painful memories. The Chelsea house had been leased to a client of Thomas's. Because she loved the house, Nicola was loath to sell it. Someday, she hoped, she might be able to put those same painful memories behind her and use it again.

Memories...they came less often now, usually at night, when she was alone and her mind wasn't engrossed in a book or television show. Whether she remembered a place, a sound, or a feeling, all the memories had one thing in common: Logan had been there with her.

He hadn't contacted her those past six weeks. She told herself she was glad, but there was an emptiness, a yearning, that all the work in the world couldn't erase.

This day was Christmas Eve, and she and Lisa had taken their secretaries and the office receptionist to lunch. They'd spent a pleasant two hours at the Brown Derby. Then everyone but Nicola had had things to do—Christmas things, such as last-minute shopping, taking a gift to a friend, catching a plane back to a hometown. As Nicola returned alone to the office, she felt a reassuring sense of accomplishment in her work. *That's the important thing,* she told herself as she set her briefcase down on her large cherrywood desk, which was polished to a lovely sheen. She slipped off her beige camel's hair coat and hung it on the brass coatrack in the corner.

For a moment she paused to look out the large floor-to-ceiling window. Her office was twenty-two stories up, and the view on a clear day such as this was magnificent. It was a corner office with large windows facing both east and west. On one side she saw the Beverly Hills Country Club stretching narrow and green toward the Hollywood Hills in the distance. On the other side were skyscrapers of Century City. Beyond that, only a few miles away, the Pacific Ocean glistened baby blue on this sunny winter day.

Checking her watch she saw that it was three thirty. And suddenly for some reason the thought occurred to her that it was five-thirty in Baton Rouge.

Now why on earth did I have to think of that, she asked herself angrily.

Because it's Christmas Eve, an irritating little voice deep inside responded. *The day that would have been your wedding day.*

Stop it, she told herself. *God, it's hard to live with this continual anger. It drains my energy, and it doesn't change anything. It's over with Logan. I've got to learn to live with that.*

She turned away from the window and opened a file she'd left on her desk. This was a new client, one engaged in very complicated negotiations. She forced herself to concentrate and began to outline procedures. She had several hours to kill before she was due to meet Lisa and some other friends, all young single professionals. They all had one thing in common: at a time that is meant to be shared with families, they had nothing but loneliness to fill their holiday.

At six o'clock she finally left the office and went home to change. By eight o'clock she was having dinner with Lisa and the others at an intimate little French restaurant in Beverly Hills. She talked and laughed and told herself she was having a wonderful time, but late in the evening, when the others decided to go on to Lisa's house, Nicola finally admitted to herself just how miserable she was.

Nicola told Lisa she was tired—which was true—and started home. As she was driving down Wilshire Blvd., she saw a crowd of people entering a brightly lit church for candlelight service. She and Andrew had often attended such a service. Suddenly she felt a need for the serenity she knew she would find there.

When she entered the sanctuary a few minutes later, she was handed a small white candle. She found a seat and sat down. The congregation remained silent as the choir, in hushed voices, caroled an ancient air that recounted that holy night when a special star's light pierced the darkness.

As the minister spoke about what had brought each member of the congregation to the church on this night, Nicola thought about her own reasons for being there.

Logan.

She was there because she missed him so; the longing was a pure physical ache in her heart. Years earlier she had read a poem by Emily Dickinson about heartbreak. She could still remember some of the lines:

This is the Hour of Lead—
Remembered, if outlived,
As Freezing persons, recollect the Snow—
First—Chill—then Stupor—
    Then the letting go—

But I can't let go, she acknowledged honestly.

She kept hearing his voice: "You belong here with me, my Nicola. Come back with me at Christmastime. We'll be married here. . .in our house. . . ."

One by one, all lights in the church were dimmed, until the only gleam in the darkness came from the altar, where, before the bank of poinsettias, five tall white tapers and one large red candle burned.

The minister summoned four choirboys. Handing each of them a taper, he took the last one and lit it from the flame of the red candle, then gave each of them the light.

In their turn, they accommodated first the choir, then in silent accord proceeded up the aisles, giving the light to each person in the aisle seat, who passed it to his neighbor.

The person with the flame held his candle upright. The receiver tipped his taper to it.

When all the candles were lit, the congregation stood and sang "Silent Night, Holy Night."

This is why I came, Nicola thought. *I've hated everything about this Christmas. It's been full of pain and loss and unbearable memories. I came here to rid myself of the bitterness I've felt.*

As she watched the minister walk down the aisle and out into the night, followed first by the choir, then the congregation, Nicola knew she felt better. Something of the peace of this special night and this special place had soothed her weary heart.

She walked out with the others. Outside the church, she paused for a moment on the steps and gazed at the twinkling lights of the candles dispersing into the neighborhood.

Then she blew out her own candle.

Logan, my love, she thought, *I think I can bear living without you now. But I still can't help but hope that, wherever you are tonight, you miss me as much as I miss you.* . . .

LOGAN SAT IN the living room, watching Beau and Joanna Sue decorating the tree. It was a huge fir, nearly ten feet tall, and Joanna Sue laughed as Beau lifted her up to place decorations on the tallest branches.

It was nearly eleven o'clock. At midnight he and Beau and Joanna Sue would share a Christmas toast. Then the next morning the entire family would be there for Christmas brunch and the exchange of presents.

Normally he enjoyed all this ritual. The little boy in him loved Christmas, enjoyed giving and getting presents. But this year he felt nothing of the Christmas spirit. When Nicola went out of his life, joy went out, too.

At first it had been relatively easy not to think of her. There was the new contract to concentrate on— the biggest thing he'd ever attempted. There was so much to do he had hardly had time for anything else.

But as Christmas grew closer, his office shut down, and suddenly things were very quiet. He had time to think. And all he could think of was Nicola.

Damn, he grumbled to himself for the hundredth time. Why did she have to be so impossible? He had offered her the world, but all she chose to see were the conflicts that occasionally marred the perfect thing they shared. He finished the brandy and poured himself another.

"Hey, Logan, get off your duff and help us," Beau shouted from behind the tree.

"In a minute," Logan responded in a flat voice. This would have been their wedding night, he thought, if only she weren't such a proud, independent, stubborn creature. How was she spending this night, he wondered. Who was she with?

Slowly an encouraging idea took shape in his mind. If Nicola were as lonely as he, if she were thinking of what this night might have been....

He rose and went into the library next door. Picking up the telephone, he dialed the number he'd got from Thomas. Smiling, he remembered something his grandfather had said to him once: "Never tell me the odds. If I don't know how tough it is, I won't have any reason to doubt that I can do it."

I'll get her back, Logan promised himself as the phone began to ring. *To hell with the odds! That woman and I were meant to be together.*

But as the phone rang and rang in Nicola's empty house, Logan's smile began to fade. Finally he slowly put down the receiver. She wasn't there.

CHAPTER FIFTEEN

THE NEW YEAR BEGAN with an unusual system of storms that originated far out in the Pacific and swept in to batter the entire Southern California area. No sooner would one storm spend itself in a frenzy of wind and rain, then another would be forecast as on the way. The natives complained that if this weather kept up, sunny California's reputation for blue skies and balmy days would be ruined. But Nicola enjoyed the stormy weather, relating to the turbulence.

Finally January passed and February progressed to its halfway mark. Nicola kept as busy as possible. She came to the office early and left late. She overloaded her schedule, telling Lisa not to worry. She'd worked her way through loneliness before; she'd do it again.

On the morning of February 14, she awakened earlier than usual. When she'd dressed warmly for a walk on the beach, she glanced at the digital clock and noted the time—and the date.

As she walked briskly along the hard wet sand, she told herself that she'd survived Thanksgiving, Christmas, New Year's Eve and Lincoln's birthday without Logan James, and she most certainly would survive Valentine's Day.

Andrew had always sent her a dozen long-stemmed pink roses. This would be the first time in eight years that...she stopped and stood watching the early-morning surf build and break against the beach in a froth of foam.

She didn't allow herself to think of Andrew too often. She didn't regret her years as his wife; they were good years and had helped to develop her into what she was. For the hundredth time she gave silent thanks that she'd not defiled her commitment to Andrew. That she'd been honorable made it easier when she'd had to mourn the loss of him.

Standing there now, across the continent from where she'd lived with him, she thought again of what he'd said that day they'd reconciled their differences over the Gibran case. Andrew believed that one should always look forward to the next day and what it might hold. And for the most part she was able to do that. Her memories of their life together didn't actually hurt her. She could objectively contemplate them and then either file them away for safekeeping or simply let them go.

But it wasn't like that with Logan. He'd literally swept her into a storm of awareness...of herself and her capacity for loving and passion and desire. She *mourned* the loss of *their* tomorrow. Most of the time she kept her grief over Logan under control with work; work was her safe harbor. But sometimes she recalled how he made her feel when he looked at her, held her, kissed her, and there simply was no way to protect herself from the ensuing pain.

Deliberately she emptied her mind of a tall, lean,

silky-mustached Southerner. Deliberately she blanked out the sweet softness of a beguiling drawl. Deliberately she thought about the ambivalence of a prospective client and decided against taking the case.

She was almost back to her house when the question would no longer be denied. What would have been Logan's way with valentines?

NICOLA WAS SITTING IN HER OFFICE when Lisa poked her dark head in the open doorway. "Got a minute?" Lisa asked.

Putting down her pen, Nicola replied, "Sure. What's up?"

"Well, you know that Bennet trial."

"The policeman versus the newspaper publisher?"

"Exactly. The opposing attorney's doing far too good a job. He cross-examined my client, the policeman, yesterday and tore him to shreds," Lisa said, frowning.

"Mmm, that doesn't sound good."

"No. I'm convinced my guy's innocent, but after that grilling even I began to have some doubts."

"Your opponent must be some attorney," Nicola commented thoughtfully. Lisa was a brilliant attorney. It would take someone even more talented to fluster her so. "Do you think you'll lose?" Nicola asked.

"I'm afraid there's a good chance. Anyway, last night he called and suggested a settlement. I'm inclined to consider it. My client's more interested in money, frankly, than moral vindication. What do you think?"

"That depends on what they offer, of course. Why don't you ask him to come in for a meeting?"

"I already did. He'll be in at twelve o'clock. Could you sit in on the meeting with me?"

Glancing quickly at her desk calendar, Nicola nodded. "Sure. I'm having lunch with Stan at one, but that should leave plenty of time for the meeting."

"Stan's like an old hound. Ever faithful, ever patient, hanging around hoping you'll throw him a bone occasionally." Lisa's playful smile took the edge off her words.

"Lisa!" Nicola warned. The fact that Lisa's appraisal of Stan was accurate only made Nicola more irritated.

Stan Englund was a former client, an extremely wealthy young businessman. Nicola had successfully negotiated his financial separation from his very young, very greedy, live-in girl friend.

From the beginning it was an odd relationship. Normally Nicola would have been representing the woman in a case such as this. But when Stan explained the situation, she saw that this time it was the man who was being taken advantage of. The young woman had lived only six months with Stan. During that time he had showered her with money and luxurious material possessions, including a new Porsche and expensive jewelry. When he found out she was having an affair with one of the security guards at his lavish Holmby Hills estate, he told her to leave. At that point she filed a lawsuit asking for a great deal beyond the car and other gifts she took with her.

Nicola made short work of the case by proving that

the young woman had tried the same thing with three other wealthy men she'd lived with.

Now Nicola said defensively, "Stan's nice. An interesting conversationalist, attentive escort...."

"And thoroughly safe," Lisa added bluntly. Before Nicola could reply, Lisa finished, "Okay, I know, drop it. Consider it dropped."

"Good. Who is this lawyer we're meeting with today?"

"Michael Jardine. You've probably seen him around. His office is in the building." When Nicola didn't appear to recognize the name, Lisa added, "He walks with a cane."

"Oh, yes. I have noticed him before. A tall attractive guy. I've wondered why someone who looks so strong and healthy otherwise has to lean on a cane."

"I heard he was wounded in Vietnam," Lisa answered. "At least that's what another lawyer who knows him said. Well, I'll let you get to work. Will you drop by my office about noon?"

"Sure. See you then."

When Lisa had gone, Nicola continued to sit thoughtfully at her desk. She knew Lisa wasn't enthusiastic about her relationship with Stan. Not that she disliked him. He was terrifically charming and thoroughly likable. But he was, as Lisa said, not someone Nicola would ever be serious about. He was a determined playboy who went through women the way some people go through different brands of toothpaste. He wasn't quite thirty, but was already a millionaire many times over. He'd founded a video-games company that was extremely successful.

Nicola didn't know what Stan saw in her. She certainly wasn't his usual type. Normally he preferred very young, beautiful but not particularly intelligent actresses or models. "Why on earth are you interested in me?" she'd asked pointedly when they first dated.

"Because you're different. I can actually talk to you—which is nice for a change. And you're a challenge. You're so cool and reserved you make me want to get past that wall you've built around yourself."

A challenge.... Well, she thought dryly, it was a challenge he had failed. Not that he wasn't attractive. Most women would have found him impossible to resist, with his dark good looks and slim muscular build. But Nicola found it easy to resist him for the simple reason that he wasn't Logan.

At that moment her secretary buzzed her to say there was a delivery for her. Walking out to the front desk, Nicola found a man from an exclusive Beverly Hills jeweler's waiting for her. Without bothering to take the package back to her office, Nicola opened it there. It was a stunning emerald necklace. The large green stones were surrounded by sparkling diamonds. The attached card read, "Happy Valentine's Day from your not-at-all-secret admirer."

Closing the case with a snap, Nicola handed it back to the man. "Take this back, please."

The man looked startled. Obviously, Nicola thought, few gifts like this were returned.

"But..." he stammered.

"I can't accept it," she insisted. "Don't worry. I'll explain things to Mr. Englund."

"Okay," the delivery man said, shaking his head perplexedly. He and the young receptionist exchanged a glance that obviously meant, "Can you believe it?" before he left.

Back in her office, Nicola immediately called Stan.

He said brightly, "Hi, love, did you get the bauble?"

"Stan, I'm no expert, but that 'bauble' must have cost at least fifty thousand dollars. We've been through this before. I returned it."

He sighed. "I know. Sapphires and rubies didn't work, but I was hoping you might have a soft spot for emeralds."

Nicola laughed. "You're impossible."

"No, you're impossible. But I adore you, anyway."

"I know you have a lot of money—you don't have to prove it. But I can't be bought. So why don't you stop trying?"

"All right. How about dinner Friday? As a penance I'll even let you pay half the tab."

She laughed again. He really was charming in his own thoroughly decadent way.

"Very well. Pick me up about eight."

"Great. I'll see you at lunch."

"'Bye."

When she hung up, she continued to smile for a moment at his breezy charm. *He* is *good for me,* she thought. *He's tremendous fun when he isn't confusing me with one of his usual conquests, and I'll never have to worry about being hurt by him. Because I will never feel anything more for him than mild affection.*

Unlike Logan, her irritating inner voice reminded her.

Her good mood suddenly shattered, she put Stan out of her mind and settled down to work.

At noon she went into Lisa's office, where Michael Jardine was already waiting. Nicola had noticed him in the parking lot and the tiny snack bar in the basement of the building, but this was the first time they'd met.

As they talked about the case, Nicola was very impressed with him. She could understand why Lisa, a tough attorney, was finding him a formidable adversary.

"My client's position is that he stands behind the freedom of the press," Michael said, watching Lisa carefully.

"And my client's position is that he's been libeled," Lisa retorted. "His reputation has been irretrievably damaged."

"We have a great deal of proof that he accepted bribes."

"You have circumstantial evidence, not hard proof. And bribery is a serious charge to lay on a policeman. As it is, he's left the force—"

"Because he was guilty and didn't want to face a departmental hearing," Michael finished. Though his expression was stern, amusement glinted in his cool gray eyes.

Somehow Nicola found herself thinking what a striking couple Michael and Lisa would make—she was so dark, and he was fair, with blond hair and a light complexion.

Dismissing the irrelevant thought, Nicola interrupted, ''Why don't you two save your impassioned oratory for the courtroom? Since there's no judge or jury here to impress, let's get down to specific figures that both sides might find acceptable.''

Michael smiled, and suddenly he looked very attractive, indeed. Flashing a quick glance at Lisa, Nicola was surprised to find her nonplussed.

Michael said, ''The company that provides libel insurance for my client's newspaper is willing to pay five thousand dollars to get this hassle over with.''

''Five thousand? No way,'' Lisa replied firmly, coming to her senses. ''My client needs enough to support him while he finds a new career. I was thinking more along the lines of fifty thousand.''

For twenty minutes Michael and Lisa argued back and forth. But it was clear that everyone concerned wanted a quick settlement rather than a drawn-out court battle. They finally settled on twenty-five thousand dollars for Lisa's client.

''You're a tough negotiator, Mr. Jardine,'' Lisa commented.

''Michael, please,'' he urged with a flash of that endearing smile.

''Michael. Well, I'm glad we've reached an agreement. With appeals this thing could have gone on for years, and my client needs the money now.''

''I have to tell you, I advised my client to continue fighting this. He's right, and I know we would have won eventually.''

''You would have won!'' Lisa said hotly. ''The trial has barely begun, you know. I still have a few tricks up my sleeve if you'd like to continue.''

He replied evenly, "I wouldn't be surprised. So far you've been a lot tougher than I expected."

"You mean, for a *woman* lawyer?" Lisa asked tartly.

Nicola could see that Lisa was warming up for a fight. Criticizing her ability as a lawyer simply because she was a woman was the surest way to get her Irish temper up.

Nicola intervened quickly, "Now settle down, both of you. This isn't an ego contest. It's *over*."

"All right," Lisa agreed reluctantly, but anger simmered in her dark eyes.

"If you'd let me explain," Michael went on, "I was going to say that you surprised me because you're so young. Being a good trial lawyer usually requires a lot of experience. Frankly, you haven't made a mistake yet. You've asked only questions you obviously know the answers to, and the way you've kept my client from explaining his position has been brilliant, if irritating."

Mollified, Lisa murmured, "Thank you." As she looked at Michael, something in her expression altered significantly. After a pause she said, "Why don't we continue this discussion over lunch? There are still some details to be worked out. Such as, who pays court costs."

Michael frowned. "Wait a minute. Obviously, your client should pay, since he's getting a great deal of money he doesn't really deserve."

"That's *your* position. Ours is, needless to say, quite different. But as I proposed earlier, why don't we talk over lunch? I'll bet by dessert we'll work out an agreement."

To Nicola's surprise, Michael hesitated and actually looked rather flustered. He'd been confident and self-assured thus far. Nicola wondered at the fact that an invitation to lunch by Lisa could bother him so.

"Come on," Lisa urged, smiling. "I'll pay."

"I'll pay," Michael insisted.

"Even better." Lisa stood up. "I'll just powder my nose. Be right back."

When she was gone, Nicola looked at Michael, who in turn looked as if he'd been steamrollered. Shaking his head, he smiled ruefully. "Something tells me she'll be even more formidable over lunch than in a courtroom."

Nicola grinned. "You're right. But when her hackles aren't up, she can be quite reasonable."

"Of course," Michael replied. It was obvious that he was more than a little disconcerted. Then he added, "After all, it's just a business lunch."

Before Nicola could decide how to respond to this, Lisa returned. Nicola noticed that she'd quickly freshened her makeup and brushed her dark hair. And added a touch of perfume.

Michael rose and walked with Lisa to the door. When they reached it, there was an awkward moment. Nicola could tell that Lisa wasn't sure whether, because of his disability, she should let him open the door for her. Michael handled the situation with practiced ease. Leaning heavily on the cane, he reached out with his free hand and pulled the door open, stepping aside slowly to let Lisa pass through first.

Uttering, "Thank you," Lisa went out, followed by Michael.

Nicola felt that she'd just witnessed something significant. Something about the way Lisa had looked at Michael in that moment when he'd complimented her had struck Nicola. She would swear she had seen in Lisa's dark eyes that moment of first attraction, that spark of chemistry, that is the beginning of romance. "Mmm," she said thoughtfully before returning to her own office.

AFTER HAVING LUNCH with Stan, Nicola decided to do a little window shopping before returning to the office. For once her schedule wasn't crowded and she actually had a little free time. She headed toward the shops of Century City.

The weather that had been clear earlier had suddenly turned cloudy and threatening. Glancing up at the now glowering sky, Nicola thought that the weather was the way she felt—uncertain. She'd been unsettled and disconcerted, almost melancholy, ever since Logan came into her thoughts earlier that morning.

As Nicola rode an escalator to the main open-air shopping level, she saw lightning streak across the sky in cloud-splitting zigzags. Moments later, the thunder rolled across the heavens in booming reverberations, and suddenly the rain fell hard.

Nicola sprinted into the first shop near the escalator. It was a bookstore, decorated for Valentine's Day. Red satin banners lettered with Give your love a love story were strung above tables of books. Valentines were scattered everywhere—old-fashioned ones, blatantly sentimental, decorated with lace and streamers of narrow ribbon; slick contemporary ones; even comic valentines for those who could only say, "I love you," tongue-in-cheek.

Well, Nicola told herself dryly, *out of the frying pan, into the fire, so to speak.* At the same time she was firmly trying to put love out of her mind, she was in a veritable "hotbed" of romance.

As she stood there, she noticed one of the books on a table displaying secondhand books. Bound in maroon, hand-tooled leather, obviously old, obviously wellread, it was a copy of Longfellow's *Evangeline*. Picking it up, Nicola opened it, and there on the flyleaf in fine Spencerian script was written, "To my valentine, Mary, on 14 February 1900. Forever yours, G."

In an instant Nicola was back on the Queen Elizabeth telling Logan that Aunt Cordy had offered to take her to Evangeline country one day.

"I'll take you, if you want. I didn't know that interested you," he'd responded.

He had pulled her in his arms and kissed her in that sweet tantalizing way, his lips barely touching hers, and said, "I'll take you to St. Martinsville. Hell, I'll even sit under the Evangeline oak with you. We're not going to be tragic lovers like they were in the poem."

Damn you, Logan James, she thought now. Before she could argue herself out of it, she took the book to the desk, paid for it and arranged that it be mailed to Logan in Baton Rouge.

"Would you like to include a card, miss?" the clerk asked.

"No, that won't be necessary. Just mark the package Please Forward."

As Nicola left, she was relieved to find that the rain had stopped—at least momentarily. As so often happened in February, the sun suddenly came out and the day was sunny once more. Just then, Nicola saw the most incredibly beautiful rainbow appear in the cloud-spattered sky. It arced across the gray skyscrapers of Century City.

Tears stung Nicola's eyes as she stood mesmerized by the rainbow. *I won't cry,* she told herself.

But by the time she returned to her office, the tears refused to be contained. The moment she shut her door they began to stream down her face, and she stood there weeping as if her heart were breaking. As, indeed, it was.

Finally she wiped her cheeks with the back of her hand and sat down at her desk. Hopelessly she faced her dilemma. She loved him so. Her heart literally ached with all the truth the valentines had proclaimed.

How bitterly ironic that on this day of all days she'd stumbled into rain, valentines, Evangeline and one of Logan's rainbows.

"Be careful with rainbows...."

Remembering the poem, the ship gliding through the night, Logan's embrace, Nicola allowed her memory to sweep her away. Instead of sitting at her desk in Los Angeles, she was in London, seated across a table from Logan. He was telling her the story of the wildcatter and the banker's daughter. And when she had said "They don't write songs like that anymore," he had captured her attention—and her heart—by locking his leonine eyes with hers and answering, "Sure they do. You just wait and see."

Then the memory faded, and Nicola was back at her desk, alone, tears streaming down her face once more. She wanted to pick up the Steuben paperweight and slam it against the wall. But if she did, Lisa or Marsha would come rushing in, wondering what on earth was wrong. And Nicola couldn't possibly tell them.

WHEN SHE ARRIVED home that evening, she found a specially delivered package shoved through the mail slot. It was a tiny box wrapped in silver foil, from a Beverly Hills jeweler. Another one of Stan's extravagant gifts, she thought. A box of chocolate just wasn't his style, apparently.

But when she opened the box desultorily, she found nestled on a bed of soft white velvet a single baroque pearl. It was lustrous, beautiful and pierced for stringing.

CHASEN'S WAS AS CROWDED as usual on Friday night. But also as usual, Stan managed to get a very good table without waiting. As he and Nicola made their way through the room, led by the maître d', people turned to stare at them.

When they sat down, Stan said, "We make quite a striking couple, you know. I'm darkly handsome and you're a beautiful blonde."

Nicola smiled at him over the top of the menu the maître d' handed her. "You're also becomingly modest."

"Well, someone has to point out my tremendous assets to you. You seem blind to them."

As she looked at him quizzically, she thought, *he is handsome, with that black hair and those appealing dark brown eyes. And he's boyish in a way that can be captivating.* Aloud she said, "I'm sure more than enough women have told you you're attractive. You don't really need one more testimonial, do you?"

"It wouldn't hurt," he replied with an engaging grin.

"If I were a psychologist, I'd say you have a neurotic need for praise. Either your mother didn't love you enough, or your father expected too much from you."

Stan sighed. "Actually, my mother spoiled me rotten and my father thought I was God's gift to the world." Looking at his menu, Stan continued, "What shall we have? Chasen's famous chili?"

"Mmm, no, I'll have shrimp. You feed me so well I'm gaining weight."

Stan eyed her approvingly in her sunset-striped, silk-chiffon dress. "You look just fine to me."

Glancing at him, Nicola caught the look of undisguised desire in his voice and in his eyes. But she felt no quickening of her pulse, and her heartbeat remained steady. *I wish I could want him,* she thought hopelessly. *It would make everything so much easier.*

"Sorry," he said unexpectedly.

Nicola smiled at him warmly. "No, I'm sorry."

Then before he could respond, she said, "You know, Stan, beneath that dissolute playboy exterior beats a gentle and considerate heart."

He feigned a scandalized expression. "Don't tell anyone. You'll destroy my hard-earned reputation."

The waiter arrived then to take their order, and for the rest of the evening they talked of impersonal matters.

After dinner they went to a private club for dancing and some spirited games of backgammon. Finally, at nearly two in the morning, they drove down the Santa Monica Freeway toward the beach. Behind them the lights of the city stretched up the hills that ringed the LA basin and seemed to go on into infinity.

There were few other cars on the freway, and the night was dark and quiet. Nicola sat silently next to Stan in his silver Porsche. She'd enjoyed herself this evening. She always did with him. He was tremendous fun. But she was tired now and looked forward to getting home and into bed.

It took only a few minutes to reach Nicola's house on the beach opposite the palisades of Santa Monica. As Stan pulled into her narrow driveway, she couldn't conceal a yawn.

"I know I'm not a scintillating conversationalist, but I didn't realize I put you to sleep," he teased.

She smiled. "A long day at the office, then dancing, then several games of backgammon are putting me to sleep."

He got out and opened the door for her. As they walked up the short brick path to her front door, she took her key out of her evening bag. After unlocking the door, she turned back to him. "Thanks for a wonderful evening, Stan. I mean it."

He looked into her eyes and suddenly his expression was no longer light and teasing. Pulling her into his arms, he kissed her deeply.

It wasn't the first time they'd kissed. Each time Nicola had been half relieved, half disappointed when she'd felt no stirring of passion. It had been pleasant; that was all.

And that wasn't nearly enough.

She had tasted pure ecstasy with Logan. Now nothing less would do.

As she pulled away from Stan, his dark eyes narrowed in bitter disappointment. "Who is he?"

After a moment's hesitation, Nicola asked, "What?"

"The man you think about when you're with me."

"Oh, Stan, don't," she began.

"I'm not being masochistic. I honestly want to know. Maybe if you talk about him, we can exorcise his hold over you."

"You know I was married. Andrew's been gone only a year. Not even that, really."

"It isn't Andrew's memory that haunts you," Stan interrupted. "I may act like a fool much of the time, but I'm not. I've always known you were getting over someone else. I thought in time.... But it's been weeks now, and nothing's changed."

She tried to lighten the somber mood. "I know you sleep with a lot of women. Surely one less won't hurt your ego that badly?"

But he didn't respond to her teasing tone.

"It does matter. Because you're the only one I really want."

She didn't know how to reply to this. She hadn't expected such serious talk from him. Up till that moment he'd made it clear he wanted to make love to her, but she'd assumed she meant no more to him than any other sexual conquest.

Now. . . he looked at her with real feeling in his eyes, and she knew what it had cost him to ask who she was thinking of when they'd kissed.

"I'm not involved with anyone else," she insisted.

"Not now. But you were. I don't know when or where, but there was someone."

She knew that to talk about Logan would only make the dull ache in her heart grow sharp, so she answered evasively, "There was someone, but it's over."

"Okay," Stan finally said, sighing. "I won't press you."

With one finger he tilted her chin up so that she was looking into his eyes. The movement was so much like something Logan had often done that for a moment she thought she might cry.

"Good night, Nicola. I'll call you next week."

When he was gone, she went inside. But she wasn't alone. She had her memories to keep her company all through the sleepless night.

CHAPTER SIXTEEN

NICOLA AND LISA were sitting in Lisa's ultramodern high-rise condo overlooking Century City. Nicola was curled up in a corner of the off-white Haitian cotton sofa, watching an old Humphrey Bogart movie on television, while Lisa made popcorn in the kitchen.

"He's really very nice," Lisa said cryptically as she came into the living room and sat down on the sofa. "Have some popcorn," she added, setting the bowl on the coffee table.

"Who's very nice?" Nicola asked, confused. Obviously Lisa was thinking out loud, and Nicola didn't follow her train of thought.

"Michael Jardine."

"Did you two reach a settlement?" Nicola asked.

"Of course," Lisa replied as if that were beside the point. "He lives near here, you know," she continued musingly.

Realizing that Lisa wanted to talk, Nicola rose and turned off the TV. "Okay," she said, taking a handful of popcorn, "tell me everything."

"What do you mean?"

"You're obviously dying to talk about him. And since this isn't one of Bogie's better movies, I'm willing to listen."

Lisa grinned and happily proceeded. "He's the first man I've ever met who complimented my ability as a lawyer before complimenting my looks."

"Here we go again," Nicola responded matter-of-factly. "Number 112 in the long line of Lisa Halloran's beaux."

To her surprise, Lisa didn't join in her good-natured teasing. Instead her dark, heart-shaped face colored with a rare blush, and her voice had a serious note that Nicola had never heard previously. "He isn't interested in lining up for my attentions. I haven't had word from him since we had lunch last week."

"Now that's strange. He looked interested when you two left."

"That's just it! He was attracted to me. I know it. And that's not just my considerable ego talking. I've asked around, and he doesn't seem to be dating anyone else." She was thoughtful for a moment, then continued, "I used to believe I fell in love easily. Now I'm beginning to believe I didn't know the meaning of the word."

Nicola understood all too well what Lisa meant. She had thought she knew what love was. But when she met Logan James, she realized there were depths to the subject that she'd never even dreamed of.

Sighing, Lisa said, "Listen, how about some chocolate croissants? I got them fresh from La Boulangerie."

"No, thanks," Nicola replied, her thoughts far from food. "I'd better be getting home, actually. It's late, and I have an early court appearance tomorrow."

As she grabbed her purse and headed toward the door, Lisa followed. At the door Lisa asked tentatively, "Nicola, can you understand an attraction so instinctive that you can't explain it in words?"

"Yes." She paused, then finished, "I'd better go. See you tomorrow."

A few minutes later she was on Pacific Coast Highway. As she drove past the ocean, she remembered another time when she had looked out at the sea, glistening silver and ebony under a November moon. Then Logan had stood beside her on the deck of the QE2. Now she was alone.

Yes, Lisa, she thought dryly, *I can understand perfectly what you mean about an instinctive attraction. The problem,* she concluded as she pulled into her driveway, *is what to do about it when it goes wrong....*

THE NEXT DAY Lisa came into Nicola's office. With its pale yellow walls and lush plants, it was a cheerful place. But Lisa seemed immune to the sunny room at the moment. She plopped down in a chair and sighed heavily.

When Lisa just sat there silently, Nicola finally asked, "Okay, what's wrong?"

"I think I'm losing my sex appeal," Lisa replied forlornly.

Suppressing an impulse to laugh, Nicola said, "I doubt that very much."

"Then why won't Michael Jardine have anything to do with me?" Lisa exploded. Clearly she was frustrated and baffled. "I ran into him in the snack bar at lunch. I practically threw myself at the poor man. And believe me, that's not something I'm used to doing. I usually have to beat men off with a stick.''

Nicola smiled at her friend's unconscious vanity. ''Maybe he's involved with someone else?''

''Nope. I've checked. I even had my secretary pump his secretary over a lunch *I* paid for. He's divorced, and as far as anyone knows, he isn't dating anyone.''

''Well, that leaves one possible alternative. . . .''

''No way! That man is one hundred percent heterosexual, and he's attracted to me. I know it. Whenever we run into each other, he smiles so big it's obvious he's glad to see me. And when we happen to be in the snack bar, like today, he always talks to me. He enjoys my company and looks at me with plain old lust in his eyes. So why isn't he asking me out?''

Nicola was thoughtful for a moment. Michael had appeared to find Lisa very attractive that day he came into their office. ''What else do you know about him?'' she asked slowly.

''Well, his secretary thinks the divorce hit him pretty hard, though he doesn't talk about it. As far as she can tell, it happened right after he got back from Vietnam.''

''Was the divorce his wife's idea?''

''Of course!'' Lisa's dark eyes opened wide in sudden understanding. ''I'll bet his wife left him when he was wounded. He's had a rough time—in and out of hospitals for years. When he was in law school, he was in a wheelchair. He's only been able to walk again for a year or so.''

"Well, he may feel that if his wife couldn't handle his disability, no woman could. His ego is probably badly bruised."

"Oh, Nicola, I'm sure you're right," Lisa said enthusiastically. "It's all her fault."

"Now, Lisa, his ex-wife might not be to blame. Considering what Michael's been through, it's understandable his marriage might not have survived the strain. In fact, our whole attempt at 'pop' psychology may be wrong."

"You're trying to be fair, but I don't agree with you. The poor guy's simply afraid to ask me out. The question is, what do I do about it?"

"Well, you could ask him out."

"Right!" Lisa said, jumping up. As she headed for the door, she called over her shoulder, "Thanks." To herself she added, *Michael Jardine, you don't know what's about to hit you.*

Nicola smiled. Lisa could be incredibly stubborn when she set her sights on a goal. Michael didn't stand a chance.

Lisa was waiting for her when Nicola returned from lunch. Her dark eyes were shining like Fourth of July sparklers, and she wore a huge Cheshire-cat grin. "Ask me what I'm doing Saturday night?"

"Going out with Michael?" Nicola ventured, sitting down at her desk.

"Right! Oh, Nicola, you should have seen the look on his face when I cornered him in the elevator. I said, 'Where would you like to have dinner Saturday night?' Well, he just about fainted. But I've got to give him credit. He's quick. He answered, 'Is this a proposal or a proposition?' I told him I didn't work that fast. For now we'd just call it a date and take it from there.''

Nicola laughed. "Lisa, you're an inspiration to every woman who's ever waited helplessly by the telephone.''

"Well, why not take the bull by the horns, so to speak. If I were to wait for him to work up the courage to ask me out, I could end up an old maid. Anyway, it's for his own good. That man needs me—and wants me.''

Her voice was triumphant, and Nicola felt glad for her. She suspected there might be deeper problems regarding Michael's disability than Lisa was facing at the moment, but they had all the time in the world to deal with that.

THE HELICOPTER SWOOPED OUT of the sunny Southern California sky and low over the deep green swells of the Santa Barbara Channel, closing rapidly on platform one. Logan tried to control the anger he felt rising within him. Something was very wrong down there, and whatever it was had very little to do with the capricious fortunes of oil drilling. *Too many accidents in too short a time,* he thought grimly.

His young pilot, showing off a bit, slung the helicopter past the spars of the derrick in a looping arc, tilted over on one skid and then slipped her down on the transit pad.

But Logan was in no mood to applaud the young man's expertise. *Too many accidents,* he thought again. The only question was whether incompetence was the problem, or whether someone was intentionally trying to sabotage the co-venture. Logan's eyes took on a hard cast as he stepped out of the helicopter to meet his foreman.

"Morning, boss," Bud Cook said, extending a hand.

As Logan shook hands, his experienced eyes scrutinized the construction site. Everything appeared to be in order, from the big stacks of heavy steel plating and heavier construction pipe to the bustling roustabouts, pipefitters and welders at work on the main engine housing.

Logan nodded, a bit reassured. Bud Cook was a good man, and the job was clearly being run with a firm hand. The problem, he decided, lay elsewhere.

"You look tired, Bud," Logan said, clapping the man on the shoulder. "Ease up a bit. I'm counting on you."

Bud's heavy features broke into a smile. "Let me show you what we've got."

Logan examined the job from top to bottom. From the huge iron-beam underpinnings beneath the deck, fifty feet above the sea, to the ventilating ducts in the nearly completed galley and dormitories, the rig was first-class construction all the way. It met Logan's tough standards.

Briefly Logan spoke with Hudson Klein, Global's liaison man on the project. Because he was a Global employee, Logan didn't know him as well as he knew Bud Cook. But Global thought highly of him, and so far Logan had to admit the man seemed competent.

Like everyone else Logan questioned, Klein had no ready answer about the accidents.

"But frankly, my bosses are getting worried," he told Logan. "We're behind schedule, as you know. They want to start pumping oil out here."

Logan said nothing. He merely nodded noncommittally. He was well aware that Global was worried about meeting the production schedule. That was precisely why Logan had left Scotland and come to Santa Barbara at this time—to find out what was going wrong. He couldn't help suspecting industrial sabotage, but he had no idea who might be responsible or why it would happen.

As the day wore on, he began to reconsider. Perhaps the accidents had been simply that—accidents. He'd had a long run of relatively trouble-free projects, and maybe the law of averages was merely catching up with him.

Bud was walking him back to the transit pad, passing between high stacks of heavy construction pipe, when it happened.

Logan felt the shifting of the pipe even before he heard it—and the massive avalanche of heavy pipe began. "Look out!" he bellowed as instinctively he lunged into Bud Cook's back, hurling him clear of the falling iron.

But in the instant it took to push Cook clear he realized that he himself would never make it, and suddenly a stunning blow on his head slammed him to the deck. He saw the heavy iron plating rushing up to meet him just before the blackness overtook him. . . .

NICOLA WAS DRIVING home from work that evening when she heard the news about the oil-rig accident. The radio announcer said briefly, "And now for the latest bulletin regarding that accident on the offshore drilling platform near Santa Barbara. Three men have been hospitalized with serious injuries. Their names are being withheld pending notification of relatives, but it is known that the rig was a joint venture between Global Oil and James Construction."

Oh, my God, Nicola thought as her heart sank to the pit of her stomach. *It can't be Logan. Dear God, don't let it be him,* she prayed desperately.

As soon as she got home, she called Beau's house in Baton Rouge. Joanna Sue answered on the first ring. The anxiety in her voice confirmed Nicola's worst fears.

"Joanna Sue, it's Nicola. I just heard about the accident."

"Oh, Nicola! It's horrible! Beau flew out as soon as we heard. He should be there by now."

"Was Logan injured?" Nicola interrupted. She heard the shrill note of anxiety in her own voice.

"Yes, I'm afraid so. I don't know what to tell you. The doctor I spoke with over the phone said he should be all right, but they're not sure of the extent of his injuries."

"Where is he?"

"Cottage Hospital in Santa Barbara."

Thanking Joanna Sue, Nicola hung up. In less than a minute she was back in her car and headed north on the Pacific Coast Highway toward Santa Barbara.

Two hours later she drove into the parking lot at Cottage Hospital. A mobile unit from a local news show was parked nearby, and Nicola knew they must be waiting to hear about the injured men.

She hurried through the entrance doors up to the information desk. There she learned that Logan was in room forty-three. A moment later Nicola arrived to find a No Visitors sign hanging on his door.

She stood there, a lump in her throat and her knees weak. Two hours of driving with nothing to do but worry about how badly Logan was injured had left her nerves frazzled. Now to be stopped by a sign. . . .

"Nicola!"

Turning, she saw Beau walking toward her.

He hugged her quickly, then asked, "How did you hear?"

"The radio. I called your house, and Joanna Sue told me where he was. Oh, Beau, how bad is it?"

He put one arm on her shoulder and gently led her to a sofa nearby. As they sat down, he said, "He'll be okay. A slight concussion and a bad gash on his forehead. . . some bruises. . . . If it weren't for the concussion, he could leave. But the doctors want to keep him under observation for a while. Concussions can be tricky."

From sheer relief, Nicola began to cry. Wrapping his arms around her, Beau murmured, "It's all right, sugar. He's gonna be okay. He's damn tough, you know."

Brushing the tears from her pale cheeks, she asked, "But how did it happen?"

"That's the sixty-four-thousand-dollar question. I

haven't been able to talk to Logan, and the men on the rig all have their own version.''

"I heard other men were injured.''

"Yes, two. But they'll both be okay.''

"Can I see Logan?''

Beau shook his head. "The doctor gave him a pretty strong painkiller and it knocked him out. The damn fool kept insisting he was going back to the rig to figure out what happened and to assess the damage. Rather than argue, the doctor just gave him a shot, and Logan's out for the night.''

"Oh, Beau, while I was driving up here all sorts of horrible thoughts went through my head.''

She began to cry again, hating herself for her weakness but unable to stop.

"It's all right, Nicola, let it all out. I can imagine what you went through. I felt the same way during the flight out. At that point I didn't know if I'd get here and find him alive or dead.''

Looking at him, Nicola could see the lines of strain on his normally bright face. "Poor Beau,'' she whispered.

"You can peek in on him if you want.''

Beau led her to the door and she stepped inside quietly. Only a dim light near the bed relieved the darkness of the room. Logan lay there under a white sheet, wearing a hospital gown. There were several small bandages on his arms and a large one on his forehead. His face was pale, haggard. One lock of reddish brown hair fell over the bandage on his forehead.

It had been four long months, and yet now as she

looked at him, it might have been the day before that they'd parted. If anything, her feelings were even more profound now. She knew what life without him was like, and it was bleak, indeed.

Gazing at him, her heart swelled with emotion, and she wanted to stroke his face and murmur words of reassurance and love. *What a fool I was to think this feeling would ever die,* she thought. *It will be part of me as long as I live.*

Suddenly, as she leaned against the bed rail his eyelids flickered and opened. For the briefest moment he seemed to look at her. Then his eyes closed again.

Nicola couldn't resist. Leaning forward, she whispered his name. But he did not respond. She brushed the back of her fingers down his face in the lightest possible touch. She watched the rise and fall of his chest, his breathing, which was now deep and regular. Thank God, she thought, his wildcatter's luck hadn't run out. "I love you," she said softly to this sleeping Logan.

Beau touched her arm. "Come on, sugar," he murmured.

Reluctantly Nicola left the room and watched as Beau shut the door softly.

"You're exhausted," he said. "Why don't you let me get you a hotel room. Then you can come back in the morning."

Nicola shook her head. "That would be too hard on both of us, Beau. I just had to see him...to know he was okay. But now I'm leaving."

Beau started to protest, then stopped. Finally he nodded. "Okay. I don't know what went wrong with you two, but I know Logan's been in hell since you broke up. You're right. Unless you're gonna stay for good, it would hurt him too much to see you again.''

"Will you call me tomorrow? Let me know how he is?"

"Of course. But don't worry. Like I said, he's tough. Are you sure you don't want to spend the night, then drive back in the morning? You don't look any too well yourself right now."

"I'm okay. I'll stop and get some coffee somewhere." Opening her purse, she took out one of her cards. "This is my office number. Please call me as soon as you talk to the doctor. I'll be waiting to hear."

"Sure." Beau hugged her tightly for a moment. "Take care of yourself, Nicola," he finished when he'd pulled away.

"You, too. It's good seeing you again. I'm sorry it had to be this way."

The drive back seemed interminable. In the darkened car, Nicola kept seeing Logan lying in that bed. With every ounce of her being she wanted to turn around and go back to him, to sit beside him, be there when he awakened in the morning. But as Beau said, if she couldn't stay, it would only hurt him. And she couldn't stay.

LOGAN SLOWLY OPENED HIS EYES and found Beau watching him anxiously. Despite the pounding pain in his forehead and the incredible aching feeling that suffused his entire body, he managed a smile and a weak, "'Mornin'."

"'Mornin', yourself. Want me to open the drapes. . . let in a little more light?''

Logan winced at the thought. "No. I think I'd better wait till I get used to this pile driver that's working in my head."

Beau laughed. "Now before you start asking questions, everything's okay. The other guys who were hurt are gonna recover."

"What happened exactly?"

"A cable came loose and a bunch of pipes took a dive into the ocean." He tried to keep his tone light, but Logan could tell that it was more serious than Beau wanted to pretend.

"Another delay," he replied, frowning.

"Now don't worry about that. Just concentrate on getting well. Then we'll see what has to be done on the rig."

Logan looked at Beau a moment, hating to appear a fool but needing to find out. "I don't know what that doctor gave me, but it sure produced some strange dreams. I thought I saw—" He stopped, suddenly reluctant to continue. What if it had been only a dream?

Beau finished for him, "You thought you saw Nicola. It wasn't a dream, Logan. She was here last night."

"She was here? Then why the hell didn't you tell her to stay?"

He knew he shouldn't be angry with Beau, but the thought of being so close to Nicola, then losing her again was too much.

"Logan, I told her that unless she was here to stay, there was no point in talking to you. She agreed. She just came to make sure you were all right. I'm sorry, but it seemed the best thing at the time.''

Logan, who had raised himself up slightly, fell back against the pillow wearily. Beau was right.

Beau continued. ''She left her card so I could get in touch and let her know how you're doin'. You look exhausted. I'd better let you rest now. The doctor said not to talk too long. I'll head on out to the rig to see how things are.''

''Okay,'' Logan answered absently. For the first time since the accident, something besides the job was paramount in his mind: Nicola.

When Beau had gone, Logan thought long and hard about her. He'd never seemed able to put her completely out of his consciousness in all the time they'd been apart. Sure he functioned, worked, ate, went to bed at night and got up in the morning. But she was always with him. And God, he missed her.

At first he'd been determined to speak to her. But Joanna Sue had convinced him that Nicola needed time alone. So with tremendous impatience, he'd waited. During all the long lonely weeks apart he'd thought about their disagreement, the things she'd told him in London and on board ship, and gradually he'd begun to understand how she felt.

He was still right, though—their love was all that mattered. But he could appreciate her concern over what might happen to her identity if she became part of his on-the-move life. He had been selfish, assuming he would continue running around the world while she, as she so scathingly put it, ''played lady of the manor at Magnolia Hill.''

That was unfair of him. Especially since what had

attracted him to her in the first place was her tremendous ability—actually, brilliance—as an attorney. To ask her to give that up, or even to make sudden changes in her career, merely to suit his own, was arrogant at best, insensitive at worst.

Now, as he lay in the hospital bed, he realized just what it had meant to her when he'd replaced her with another attorney in London. Technically he had done the right thing. But theirs wasn't a technical relationship. It was highly personal. Hell, they were lovers. And because they loved each other, he owed her more consideration than he'd given. Even if it meant risk to his company.

Nicola.... God, how he loved her, missed her, wanted to feel her against him. Without her, his work, which had once been everything to him, was merely an empty exercise that filled his days and made him too exhausted to think at night.

He had to get her back. It was time. Somehow he had to convince her that he understood her feelings now and was willing to respect them. But how?

That evening Beau came to see him again. He looked even more worried than he had that morning, and Logan immediately sensed something critical was at hand. "What is it?" he asked, getting straight to the point. Before Beau could be evasive, he insisted, "I've got to know."

After a moment's hesitation, Beau nodded. He began reluctantly, "I talked to Global. They're going to sue for noncompliance. Their position is it's your fault the delays occurred, and they want you out of the deal."

Logan wasn't really surprised. He'd seen it coming when he'd talked to Global's foreman, Hudson Klein, and when he'd looked at his own estimates of the time the delays were costing. Global wanted to get the platform built and to start drilling for oil. Until that point, they wouldn't be making money on the deal. If Logan couldn't hurry up the job, they'd find another partner who could.

Beau continued angrily, "Damn it, Logan, I told them the delays weren't our fault. But they say their foreman, Klein, says they are, and we can't prove otherwise."

Logan thought intently for a moment. Without bothering to look at the contracts, he knew exactly what was at stake. In pure and simple terms, *everything* was at stake. If Global sued and won, he'd lose not only this job but his company, as well, for he'd gone far too heavily into the deal. He could lose everything his grandfather had so painstakingly built, and everything that he, Logan, had worked hard to add.

"Well, Beau," he said with a shake of his head, "I've got nothing better to do than lie here and worry about it. You go get a good night's sleep. You've been pushin' hard for days."

When he was alone again, he stared out the window at the night. There had to be a way to make this right . . . there was something somewhere that was the key to this mess. He knew the contracts were well prepared. Nicola had worked hard on them, and the responsibilities of each participant were very clear. Nicola had . . . *Nicola* . . . .

Suddenly it came to him. He knew what he had to do to try to get Nicola back—and to try to save his company. It meant risking everything in a way he'd never done previously. It was a gamble. The biggest gamble in a life full of gambles. And the odds were stacked against him, both to win back Nicola and to win this lawsuit. But the more he thought about it, the better the idea became. After all, nothing risked, nothing gained, and Logan knew he stood to gain far more than he could ever risk—Nicola.

A WEEK LATER Nicola was sitting at her desk, when her secretary buzzed her on the intercom. "Yes, Marsha?" Nicola responded, her mind on a divorce case she was handling.

"There's a man to see you, Miss Wynter. He doesn't have an appointment. I told him you're busy, but he insists."

"Tell him I can't possibly see him without—" Nicola began. But her words were cut short when the door was thrown open and Logan James strode in.

He was followed by a flustered Marsha, who persevered, "Sir, you *can't* do this."

"It's all right, Marsha," Nicola said slowly. "I'll handle it."

Seeming confused and curious, Marsha left, closing the door behind her.

Logan stood there for a moment, saying nothing. He appeared very different from the pale exhausted man Nicola had visited in the hospital. Only the bandage on his forehead was a visible reminder of the accident he'd been in.

He looked magnificent, and Nicola thought she had never been so glad to see anyone in her life.

When she spoke, her voice was calm and cool, but her heart was beating a mile a minute. "Hello, Logan."

"Hello, Nicola," he said in that familiar voice that sent shivers down her spine. The expression in his eyes made her wish they were alone in a bedroom somewhere, not in her office.

Damn the man, she thought irritably, her happiness at his being there quickly dissolving into anger. She couldn't look at him without wanting him. Trying to hide that was almost impossible.

"I'm glad you're up and around," she finally said.

He sat down languidly in a chair and crossed one long leg over the other. "Yes. The last time you saw me I was in a hospital bed." At her surprise, he added, "Beau told me about your visit. Pretty quick, wasn't it? You might have waited until I'd woken up."

"I didn't think that would be wise. I just wanted to find out how you were. When Beau assured me it would take more than a piece of steel pipe to have any effect on you, I left."

He smiled at the sarcasm in her tone. That smile made her heart plunge, and she was glad she was sitting down.

"What do you want, Logan?"

She was afraid of the answer he might give. But the answer he gave surprised her.

"I want to hire you."

"Hire me? What on earth for?"

"To represent me, of course. Global Oil is suing me for noncompliance. As prime contractor on the platform, it was my responsibility to make sure it was finished on time. After that accident it won't be."

"Oh, Logan," Nicola whispered. "But how...."

"Global is saying the accident was my fault. Poor management, shoddy construction...you name it, and they're accusing me of it."

"What happened exactly?"

"The cables securing the drilling pipe to the platform broke, and the pipe rolled into the ocean." He looked at her intently, and his voice gained a new strength. "My specifications were right, Nicola. My people are the best. I don't know what went wrong out there, but it wasn't my fault. I need to prove that to stop Global."

"How much is at stake?" she asked pointedly.

He hesitated, then said in a determinedly matter-of-fact voice, "Everything. I've put all my assets into this venture, and I won't make any money from the North Sea contract for several months."

"Logan, you don't realize what you're asking. This is serious."

"I'm well aware of that," he said with a hard smile.

"You need a good lawyer...."

"Exactly. One who will dig deep, who won't give up in the face of overwhelming odds. *You.*"

"No."

"Why? Because we had an affair and it ended badly? I have more to complain about than you do as far as that goes. You walked out on me, remember?"

For once Nicola's cool demeanor was shattered.

"I couldn't be objective! Surely you can see that!"

His eyes narrowed thoughtfully, "Well, at least you didn't tell me to go to hell."

"Logan, you must understand. There's been too much between us. I couldn't think straight. My emotions would interfere with my ability as a lawyer. It wouldn't be in your best interests—"

"It's in my best interest not to go bankrupt," he interrupted icily. "I've got to find out what really went wrong out there. And prove it. Or Global will send James Construction into receivership."

Nicola hesitated. She knew what it would do to him if he lost his business—the business his grandfather founded. This vital, commanding, energetic man who was used to roaming the world would be destroyed. It was that simple.

"I'll recommend someone else. There are a lot of excellent attorneys...."

"Don't run away from this, Nicola," Logan said, his voice sharp. "The last time you ran away only my happiness was at stake. This time it's everything that matters to me and to my family."

She went cold inside as the truth of his words spoke directly to her heart. A tense silence followed.

"I'll accept your case," she finally said.

"Nicola." The way he said her name made her knees weak. He leaned forward in the chair, and his brown eyes were warm and tender.

But before he could say anything further, she interrupted firmly, "This has to be strictly business. For both our sakes. My mind has to be clear. There can't be any confusion, or Global's attorneys, who I'm sure are very sharp, indeed, will eat me alive. I'll be your lawyer but not your mistress.''

She expected her blunt words to make him angry. Instead he smiled. It was only a trace of his former devil-may-care grin, but nevertheless the effect on her was awesome.

"We've worked together before. We managed pretty well then. We will now.''

She had a strong suspicion he deliberately included the double meaning of his words, but she didn't feel up to challenging him at this moment. She buzzed Marsha on the intercom and asked her to come in with her stenographer's pad.

When Marsha entered, Nicola said to Logan, "Tell me everything about this case—from the very beginning to the last accident. Marsha will take notes.''

He talked for more than an hour. Nicola asked endless questions, but Logan had a ready answer for all of them. There was no area where he was hesitant or unsure. Except when Nicola asked why the accidents happened. He simply didn't know.

When she had got every bit of information she could from Logan, Nicola felt she had a good overall picture of the situation—and it didn't look promising. "I'll need to see your contract with Global," she said.

He nodded. "I'll send a copy to you tomorrow.'' Watching her carefully, he asked, "Well, counselor, what do you think of my chances?''

Nicola wanted to reassure him, but she knew he wouldn't be fooled by polite words that lacked real conviction. "I'll have to see the actual contract before I can say."

"In other words, it appears hopeless." He smiled suddenly, then continued, "Don't look so glum, Nicola. It'll be all right. I have a much better lawyer than those guys."

But Nicola couldn't return his brave smile.

Logan rose and walked toward the door. In the open doorway he paused and said, "By the way, thanks for the valentine present."

She hesitated. Then with a semblance of her old cool demeanor, she replied, "And thanks for yours."

"That was just the first," he said. "There'll be more."

Then he left.

CHAPTER SEVENTEEN

NICOLA SAT ON THE SOFA in her living room, staring out at the ocean through the floor-to-ceiling windows that faced the beach. It was night, and the water was a massive dark expanse, broken only by a thin line of silver where the low waves played along the sand.

On her lap was the file on *Logan James v. Global Oil*. Sighing, Nicola closed the folder and placed it on the coffee table. Then she tucked up her legs and hugged her knees through the thin silk of the white caftan. *It doesn't look good,* she thought. *Oh, God, it sure does not look good.*

According to the contract, Global had the legal right to sue Logan for noncompliance. They could terminate their agreement with him, force his company into receivership.

And Logan would lose *everything*.

Just then the doorbell rang. Glancing at her watch, Nicola saw that it was past nine o'clock. *Who on earth,* she wondered, *would be visiting here at this hour?*

At the door she paused to glance through the peephole. It was Logan. For a minute she contemplated not letting him in, but deciding that was childish, she opened the door.

He just stared at her for a moment, at her hair falling like a golden cloud around her face and shoulders and at the caftan that clung sensuously to her body.

She felt a flush creep up her cheeks. Embarrassed, she looked down. Then, feeling silly, she forced herself to meet his gaze.

"Sorry to bother you at home," he said, "but I've just got some information that's important."

"I see. Well, come in," Nicola invited reluctantly.

Logan, there in her home at night, brought out feelings she didn't want to deal with. Reminding herself that she was this man's attorney, she said in a more controlled voice, "Would you like a drink?"

"A coffee, if it isn't too much trouble."

"No trouble."

There was coffee already perking in the kitchen. Nicola poured a cup for Logan, then brought it into the sitting room. Handing him the cup, she asked, "What's happened?"

He appeared to be under even more strain than when she'd first seen him in her office. Whatever his news, it must be bad, she realized.

"I've just heard from Thomas. He picked this up from someone else in London and passed it along to me. It isn't public knowledge, but apparently Mannering, my old nemesis in Scotland, is negotiating with Global to take over my interest in the Santa Barbara job once Global gets rid of me. Mannering wants the job badly and is offering Global more favorable terms than they currently have with me."

"I see."

It was all too clear. Global had even more reason

for pressing the lawsuit against Logan and forcing him out of their partnership. Logan's company would go into receivership, and Global would recoup their losses through Mannering's more favorable terms. Nicola didn't have to spell it out for Logan. He obviously understood precisely what was happening.

Logan walked over to the window and stood staring out at the ocean, slowly sipping the coffee. With his back turned to her, she could look at him closely without maintaining that distance that was essential if she was to work with him.

She let her gaze linger lovingly over his thick hair, which brushed the top of the dark green sweater he was wearing...then his shoulders, the muscles hard and tense through the thin sweater...his narrow waist...lean derriere and long sinewy thighs in tight-fitting jeans. She remembered something Lisa had said once. "The real test of a man's attractiveness is how he looks in jeans." Well, Logan passed the test with flying colors. He looked irresistibly virile. Unbidden, memories of his naked body lying with hers came into her mind.

Suddenly Logan turned and caught the expression in Nicola's eyes before she could alter it. Trapped by his compelling gaze and the knowledge of what he read in her face, she stood there immobile, utterly incapable of movement.

In that timeless moment she felt again what she had felt from the very beginning with this man...a desire so profound that everything else paled in comparison. Where he was concerned, she was no more in control of her destiny than was a tiny boat adrift on a restless sea.

"*Nicola* . . ." he whispered. As always, her name was a caress when he spoke it in that hoarse impassioned tone.

In a second he would cross the room and take her in his arms, and she would be lost. Because if he touched her, she couldn't possibly resist. Her body yearned for his touch as a parched mouth yearns for water.

But she couldn't let that happen. Not for her own sake—her heart was broken and past mending—but for *his* sake. If she didn't maintain her professionalism, she wouldn't be able to be effective as his lawyer. She would need every ounce of her skill and all of her concentration to save him from disaster.

And so, with an effort that was herculean, she disengaged herself from that mesmerizing gaze and forced the yearning softness from her own eyes.

He saw immediately that she had withdrawn. Without saying a word, he downed the last of the coffee, set down the cup on a table and strode out of the house.

Nicola continued to stand there for a moment, before quietly giving way to tears.

"So TELL ME about your date with Michael," Nicola said as she and Lisa had lunch on Monday.

"Well," Lisa drawled in a conspiratorial tone, "I made my famous fettucini à la Halloran, bought *two* obscenely expensive bottles of wine and finished the evening with Napoleon Brandy."

"The poor man didn't stand a chance," Nicola chided teasingly.

Lisa sighed. "Actually, he managed to escape with his virtue intact. But we're going out Saturday, so I'm full of hope."

"Going out Saturday? You must have got to him if he worked up the courage to ask you out."

"*I* asked him out again," Lisa admitted with a rueful smile. At Nicola's look of surprise, Lisa explained, "Well, he was just going to let it end there. So I told him he owes me a dinner, and I suggested how he could repay me. We're having dinner at the Cock n' Bull on Sunset."

"Ah, soft lights, a cozy table in a secluded corner...."

"You got it, kiddo."

Gazing at Lisa thoughtfully, Nicola said, "This isn't just another fling, is it?"

Lisa shook her head negatively.

"Why Michael?"

"I honestly don't know."

"Are you sure you don't feel sorry for him?"

"No," Lisa answered firmly. "I'm sure of that. Of course, that's what he thinks, I know, though he'd never admit it. I'll have to talk to him about that when we go out."

"Lisa, I've known you for eight years. You've always had a string of boyfriends and never wanted to get serious—even with the two or three I'm aware of who wanted to marry you. You've only known Michael a couple of weeks and already—"

"Already I know I'm in love," Lisa finished. "It's

crazy. I've never felt the slightest need to settle down. I've had crushes, infatuations. I've known wonderful men who would have made terrific husbands. But I didn't want that. *Now....*'' Her voice trailed off wistfully. All trace of a smile was gone now.

Looking at her, Nicola was struck by how serious she appeared. Her flippant, wisecracking, good-time-loving friend was very serious, indeed.

Lisa continued, ''Part of it may simply be timing. I'm nearly thirty...I've had ample opportunity to explore sexually, to pursue my career, to travel, to account to no one but myself. Maybe now I'm no longer afraid of 'losing' myself by getting into a committed relationship.''

''You mean 'losing' yourself in the way I did with Andrew.''

Looking at Nicola with real affection, Lisa admitted, ''Yes. That way. Well, I can see giving up some freedom in order to get other things—real intimacy, emotional intimacy.''

''You know who you are. You don't have to be afraid of losing your identity,'' Nicola said.

''Exactly. And I want to be with someone who knows who *he* is.''

Logan certainly knows who he is, Nicola thought pensively. *But if I were with him,* I *wouldn't know who I am. For the second time in my life I would just be an extension of a very powerful dominating man.* Aloud she asked, ''Why Michael, though? He isn't anything like the men you've been interested in before.''

Lisa smiled. ''I know. He doesn't pursue me. I

have to pursue him.'' Before Nicola could respond, she said, ''I know what you're thinking. But it isn't my ego that's involved here. It's my heart. Every time I look at him I feel an overwhelming urge to touch him, to hold him, to be held by him.''

Nicola had never heard such tenderness in Lisa's voice before. ''But there are obviously problems...'' she ventured tentatively.

''Of course. There are always problems. His physical disability seems a lot worse to him than it does to me. Did you know that man hasn't dated anyone since his divorce? He honestly has no idea how sexy he is.'' Then she finished, ''But enough about my love life. Tell me about Logan.''

''Oh, God, what can I say,'' Nicola responded, shaking her head miserably. ''He's back in my life again, just when I thought I was learning to live without him.''

''But you're not—involved with him?''

''No! I'm his lawyer, and you know what that means. Besides, nothing has changed, really. The same old problems are there.''

''The course of true love...'' Lisa quoted softly, letting the hackneyed phrase trail off without finishing it. ''Look at us. I'm in love with a man who doesn't think he's lovable. You're in love with a man who roars through your life with about as much subtlety as Sherman showed on his march through Georgia.''

Nicola laughed in spite of herself, but it was a bittersweet laughter.

''So where do we go from here?'' Lisa asked.

"I don't know. All I know is that I've got to win his case. Anything else is unthinkable."

"And I've got to persuade Michael Jardine that he is still very much a man and is definitely the man for me," Lisa replied determinedly.

"Why don't you take him flying with you?" Nicola suggested. "You've got that marvelous new Cessna you've been boasting about. Take him up with you. When you're up in the air, he won't have to use a cane and might not feel awkward about his leg."

Lisa grinned. "That's a fantastic idea! Why didn't I think of it? Oh, Nicola, you're brilliant! Flying doesn't require two perfectly functioning legs."

"And when you've got him up there alone in a tiny airplane, he will be very vulnerable to all your persuasive techniques."

"And if that doesn't work, I can always put the plane into a stall."

"Knowing you, I wouldn't put it past you." Nicola commented quickly checking her watch.

"Well, we'd better get back to the office. It's nearly two and I have a meeting then with the investigator I hired to check into the oil-rig accident."

"What's he looking for?" Lisa asked as they rose and picked up their purses and coats.

Nicola laid a ten-dollar bill on the small tray that held their check. "*Anything*. Somehow I've got to prove the delay isn't Logan's fault."

Lisa watched her carefully. "Do you really think you can?"

Nicola hesitated for a moment. Finally she admitted reluctantly, "No. I haven't told Logan, but frankly, our chances of winning this case are slim to none."

"Well, counselor, that's better than less than zero," Lisa quipped. "You've been outgunned before, Nicola, and won. I'm still betting on you."

Nicola smiled gratefully. "Thanks."

But as they left the restaurant, she knew Lisa's confidence in her came from friendship—not from a realistic appraisal of the case.

"So THAT'S IT," the investigator, Harry Tornino, finished a half hour later, handing her his report.

He was a middle-aged, balding man who looked thoroughly unprepossessing as he sat in Nicola's office. In his business, doing investigations for attorneys, his appearance was an advantage. He could question people without intimidating them, and he could blend in easily with a crowd when necessary.

Nicola sat behind her desk, nervously tapping a pen on the blotter. Finally she threw down the pen in frustration. "You got *nothing*?" she asked for the third time.

"Nothing that would work in your client's favor," Harry said. "There've been an unusual number of accidents on this job, but nobody seems to know why. Mr. James's men say it's the fault of Global's workers, of course. And the Global workers say it's Mr. James's fault for pushing too hard, trying to get the platform finished too fast. One guy named Klein said Mr. James takes too many chances, but he didn't have anything to back that up."

"Klein is the liaison man for Global, isn't he?"

"Yeah. He's been with the company for several years. They seem to think pretty highly of him."

"Damn!" Nicola exploded. When she saw Harry stare in surprise, she remembered he'd never heard the cool lady lawyer swear previously. "I'm sorry," Nicola continued. "It's not your fault. You can't manufacture evidence in my client's behalf."

Harry raised one eyebrow thoughtfully. "No. It's been done, but not by me."

"I know. That wasn't a subtle attempt at bribery, Harry," Nicola reassured him.

He smiled. "I didn't think so, Miss Wynter."

"Well, thanks, Harry. Give my secretary your bill."

"Sure. Sorry I couldn't be of more help," he finished as he left.

I'm sorry too, Nicola added to herself miserably. *Sorrier, Harry, than you can possibly imagine.*

The case looked hopeless. She didn't know how she would tell Logan. She could drag things out, use every talent she possessed for delays, but in the end the result would be the same: Global would win.

Pushing the intercom button, Nicola asked her secretary to get Logan on the line. She knew he was staying at L'Hermitage Hotel in Beverly Hills. Then suddenly she changed her mind and told Marsha to cancel the call. She owed it to Logan to give him this news in person, and he would certainly want to see the report Harry had put together.

Glancing at her watch, she saw that it was nearly six o'clock—almost time to go home. She could stop by Logan's hotel, give him the bad news, then go on home. Maybe if she spent the evening going over the case from the beginning again, she'd find something she'd overlooked. But as she grabbed her coat and put Harry's report in her briefcase, she knew that was a forlorn hope.

L'Hermitage was the most exclusive hotel in Beverly Hills. Yet as Nicola drove her car into the underground parking garage, her mind was oblivious to the lovely brick building with its tree-shaded patios and terraces. She was thinking about this meeting with Logan. She would have to tell him that he faced financial ruin. She didn't know how she would get through that, but somehow she had to.

She went directly up to the second-floor town house. When she knocked on the door, it was only a moment before Logan answered.

His eyes widened in surprise. "Nicola." Then holding open the door, he said, "Come in."

As she brushed past him, she tried to keep her expression perfectly neutral. What she had to tell him was hard enough, without giving way to emotion.

Logan had a two-story, town-house suite, with a living room and kitchen on the first floor and a bedroom and bath on the second. It was lavishly furnished and as big as many luxury apartments.

"To what do I owe this totally unexpected pleasure?" Logan asked, shutting the door, then turning to face Nicola.

She stood in the middle of the room, reluctant to sit down. In a firm voice she explained, "I have my investigator's report. I'd thought you'd like to see it."

"From the look on your face, I suspect it confirms my own investigation." Walking over to a bar, he asked over his shoulder, "Would you like a drink?"

"No, thank you," Nicola responded. She needed to keep her wits about her, she knew. Logan was being far too calm about this. Inside he must be like a quiescent volcano that could erupt at any moment.

Pouring himself a generous amount of brandy in an exquisite, cut-glass crystal brandy snifter, he said, "Well, I hope you don't mind if I have something. I think I'm going to need it."

As he turned to face her, she shook her head to indicate she didn't mind.

He stood sipping the brandy, watching her expectantly.

Opening her briefcase, she took out the report. She held it for a moment, then set it down on the coffee table. "There's no point in my reading the whole thing to you," she began, squaring her shoulders purposefully. "The bottom line is, we have no proof of industrial sabotage. Nothing to indicate that fault for the delays is anyone, but yours. And I've gone over the contract with Global again and again. There are no loopholes. They can sue you for noncompliance, as they are doing, and they will almost certainly win."

She was amazed at how calm she sounded as she told this man she still loved desperately that he was about to lose everything he and his grandfather before him had worked so hard to build.

Logan didn't even blink.

He expected it, Nicola realized. *Otherwise he'd be*

angry or disbelieving or something. She almost wished he would explode. Anything would be better than this dead silence.

Logan turned away to stare out the window. Dusk had fallen, and the myriad lights of Los Angeles were beginning to twinkle. Only the rigid set of his broad shoulders revealed the depth of his emotion at this moment.

Without looking at Nicola, he began speaking softly. "My grandfather nearly lost everything at one point. It was when he went for the loan to the banker. If the man had turned him down. . . well, he had no place else to go. No one else was willing to take a chance on him. When he applied for the loan and waited for the banker's decision, he said it was the worst moment of his life. Then by that night he had the loan, he'd met the banker's daughter and he knew he was in love. He went from the blackest time of his life to the happiest—all in the space of a few hours."

"I told you once they don't write songs like that anymore," Nicola responded, her voice poignant. "I'm afraid I was right."

Logan downed the last of the brandy, then set the glass on a small table in front of him. He continued to stand there, still not looking at Nicola.

I've just told him he's ruined, Nicola thought, *and he's taking it like. . . like the man he is,* her heart finished for her.

And suddenly she knew she couldn't pretend any longer simply to be his lawyer. She felt such pride in his courage, such profound sympathy for his pain, that she couldn't resist going up to him.

She put her arms around his waist and leaned her cheek against his back. His sweater felt soft against her cheek. Her hands were clasped in front of him. He reached down and covered them with his own, gripping her fingers tightly.

"Oh, Logan, I'm so sorry," she whispered. Her voice was bitter with the sense of her own impotence in the face of this threat to him.

He unclasped her hands and turned around to face her. She gazed up at him, her lovely aquamarine eyes bright with tears, her lower lip quivering softly.

His eyes searched her face urgently. "You still love me," he said. It was a statement, not a question.

She smiled through her tears. "Of course, but...."

"Say it, then," he commanded.

"I love you. I always have, and I always will."

He relaxed. Pressed against him, she felt the tenseness in his body ease as something hard and wretched left it.

He held her even more tightly and kissed the top of her head as she buried her face against his chest. "Nicola, my Nicola..." he murmured.

Then illogically she asked, "Why didn't you call me, or write. Why did you let me leave?"

"Joanna Sue told me to give you time. She said I could force you to give in because you loved me so much, but in a way you would never forgive me. So I waited...and it was the hardest thing I ever had to do."

She looked up at him. "Did you love me so much then?"

"Enough to let you go when, with every ounce of my strength, I wanted to force you to stay. But I must admit, I weakened on Christmas Eve and called you."

"Oh, Logan."

But her words were lost in his kiss. Her senses were assailed by him, his special scent, the feel of his rapidly beating heart as his chest pressed against her breasts, the taste of his mouth on hers. Insistently his lips parted hers, and his fingers gently kneaded her back.

A feeling that she couldn't possibly get close enough to him washed over her. *Oh, God, I want him so,* she thought before all awareness of everything beyond his kiss was extinguished. Wrapping her arms around his neck tightly, she returned his kiss with a passion fed by far too many lonely nights.

The eagerness of her response brought an equal response from Logan. Suddenly he picked her up as if she were as light as a feather and carried her up the stairs to the bedroom.

The room was dim, lit only by the light of a half-moon shining through an open window. As he lay her down on the bed, she saw the look on his face and felt her pulse race and her heart swell. His desire for her was so intense it was almost frightening. Yet at the same time she felt a thrill of fear, she also felt an equal desire for him.

"Oh, God, Nicola, it's been so long and I've

missed you so much,'' he whispered in a voice rough with hunger for her.

"For your sake, I want to go slow, but . . . ."

"Hush," she whispered, putting her fingertips against his lips. She smiled a slow seductive smile. "Don't worry about hurting me, Logan. You could never do that. Just love me."

The fragile hold he had on his passion snapped then.

Somehow, she wasn't sure how, their clothes were gone and they lay naked together under the blankets. His strong arms held her tightly. He kissed and caressed her with a need so profound it seemed to engulf her in intense intimacy. His lips tasted; his hands searched, electrifying her, until she felt drunk with loving him.

He did as she had asked him to do. He loved her. He was at once tender and passionate. Wherever he touched her, her body responded. Her heart seemed to explode with love as her body was ignited by a hot fire. She shuddered against him, clinging to him desperately. At the same time, he thrust so deeply that she felt he had touched her very soul.

As the fire died slowly within her, as she felt the overpowering tension slowly seeping from his body, she thought, *I will love him forever. . . I will belong to him forever. . . .*

Afterward they lay in each other's arms, barely moving. Only the soft rise and fall of Nicola's breasts and Logan's broad hard chest revealed there was life left in them. They were silent for a long time.

Finally Logan spoke. "What happens now?"

She knew what he was referring to.

"I can get postponements, try to delay the trial as long as possible...."

"There's no point in that, is there?"

"No," she admitted.

"Then let's get it over with. I'll go through with the trial because I won't give up without a fight. But when it's over, Nicola...."

She felt an awful blackness descend over them. "Logan..." she began.

"No! Don't argue. You know as well as I do what I'm facing. I'll be left with nothing, Nicola. I won't have anything to offer you but poverty. I'll have to start all over again, and I won't make you go through that...."

Rising up on one elbow, she looked down at him and asked angrily, "Do you think I love you only for your fine Southern mansion, your company jet, your money!"

To her surprise, he smiled. It was bittersweet and held only a trace of his reckless charm. "No, I think you love me because I'm so terrific in bed."

She sighed in mock exasperation. Then, as she gazed down at him, he reached up with one fingertip and traced the curve of her breast, finally pausing to lightly stroke a taut rosebud nipple.

"Well, maybe you're half right," she teased dryly.

"Oh? Let's see," he replied drawing her toward him.

But as they made love again, her heart and mind

were in turmoil, for she knew he meant what he said—he wouldn't stay in her life if he had nothing to offer her but a long hard climb back from failure.

CHAPTER EIGHTEEN

NICOLA WAS JUST LEAVING THE OFFICE when she ran into Stan. She was surprised and not at all happy to see him.

"Looks like I just caught you," he said, smiling. "I was in the neighborhood and thought I'd stop by and take you to lunch."

"Oh, Stan, another time, perhaps. I'm just going to grab a sandwich in the snack bar. Then I have to rush off to a meeting." At his look of disappointment she added, "I'm sorry. Why don't you call me...."

"I've been calling you, Nicola. And you always seem to be busy."

"Well, I've got a tough case right now," she explained. But as she gazed at him, she could tell he wasn't buying her excuse. The normally happy-go-lucky expression on his handsome face had been replaced by a soberness she'd never seen previously.

He put his hands on her shoulders and looked at her intently. "What is it? What's suddenly gone wrong between us?"

The hallway outside her office was no place for a personal confrontation, Nicola thought, but she knew she couldn't put off Stan any longer. The moment Logan walked back into her life again she had shut out Stan. She'd avoided seeing him, using one excuse after another. It wasn't fair. "Let's go down to the patio," she said softly.

Stan nodded, and they took the elevator down to the ground floor. Behind the building was a huge patio area that extended behind all the skyscrapers on Century Park East. There were trees and flowers and stone benches. On this bright, early-spring day, the flowers were a glorious riot of color and the trees were green with new leaves. It was the middle of March—three weeks since Logan had come back into her life on a cold, late-winter day.

Odd, Nicola thought. *Logan returns and suddenly it's spring.*

As she and Stan sat down, she decided to come straight to the point. He deserved the truth. "I'm sorry. I can't see you anymore."

He said nothing for a moment. She realized he'd been expecting this.

"He's come back, hasn't he? Your mysterious old flame," he finally managed.

There was a ghost of a smile on his face that tore at Nicola's emotions. She felt guilty and angry: guilty because she was hurting him and angry that Logan's mere presence could make her do this.

"Oh, Stan, you're terrific, and I wish...."

"If wishes were gold, we'd all be millionaires," Stan finished in an attempt at humor.

Nicola looked at him with real affection. He *was* terrific. For several long lonely weeks he'd kept her enjoyably busy, and if she had any sense at all, she'd give him a chance to win her back from Logan. *But where Logan's concerned, I don't seem to have any sense,* she thought miserably. "I'm sorry," she offered, immediately hating herself for repeating the lame phrase.

"If I said I wouldn't give up without a fight, would that impress you—or merely clutter up your life?" Stan asked with that disarming charm that Nicola liked so.

She smiled but shook her head. "I'm afraid it would impress me, but it wouldn't work in the end."

Again he was silent. He looked out at the flowers and the trees and the clear spring sky.

Nicola watched him, wishing with all her heart that things were different.

Finally Stan turned back to her. "He must be quite a guy, Nicola. I hope he makes you happy."

So do I, she thought. But she didn't say so aloud.

Leaning over, he kissed her tenderly. Then he whispered, "If it doesn't work out, you know where to reach me." Then he rose and, with touching dignity, walked away.

Nicola felt tears stinging her eyes. "Damn!" she said so loudly that a passerby stopped to look at her curiously. Pulling herself together, she grabbed her purse and went back into the building. She had no desire to eat at the moment, but she did want a strong hot cup of coffee.

In the snack bar she paid for her coffee. Then, as she turned to look for an empty table, she spotted Michael sitting in a corner. At the same time he noticed her and beckoned to her to join him. Taking her cup and saucer, she did so.

It was nearly one o'clock, and the tiny snack bar was full. Nicola edged past other people and at last sat down opposite Michael at the small table that had one chair on either side. She'd run into Michael often since he'd come to her office for that first meeting with Lisa, and they'd quickly developed a comfortable friendliness.

Looking at Nicola's cup of coffee, he asked, "Is that how you stay so slender?"

"Oh, I just don't have much of an appetite," she replied.

"Beautiful day, isn't it?" he commented. "Spring sure came suddenly."

"Yes."

As they made the usual small talk, Nicola sensed he was preoccupied. She suspected there was something specific he wanted to talk about but wasn't sure how to go about it. Finally, with studied casualness, he said, "Lisa's asked me to fly down to Baja with her."

"Mmm, sounds great. It's beautiful down there. Especially in the out-of-the-way places the tourists haven't got to yet."

When Michael looked less than enthusiastic, Nicola asked, "Do you like flying?"

He hesitated, then replied, "Not particularly."

"Lisa loves it, as I'm sure you've discovered. She's taking off this four days so she can do some real flying instead of 'poking holes in the sky,' as she puts it." Nicola smiled, then added frankly, "She told me she was going to proposition you."

Michael grinned, half embarrassed and half pleased. "She scares me, you know. I consider myself hell on wheels in a courtroom, but around her I feel about fifteen, with a bad case of acne and two left feet." He shook his head. "I don't know about this trip."

"Does it bother you to fly? Or that Lisa's flying is so important to her? I think she's as likely to end up running a flying school as a law practice."

Her joke seemed to fall flat. Michael didn't smile, and suddenly Nicola sensed that it was the prospect of flying that was bothering him so much. "I'm not saying this right at all," she began.

Michael interrupted. "No, I know exactly what you mean. She loves to fly. It's part of what she is—independent, bright, adventurous. I admire her more than I can tell you, Nicola. She knows who she is and what she wants, and she isn't afraid of challenges."

Nicola smiled warmly. "She's something, all right. A funny mixture of tough and tender. She can explode—there's definitely an Irish temper there. But she has more moral and emotional courage than almost anyone I know."

Nicola wanted to say, "She has enough courage to deal with your handicap," but she couldn't bring herself to verbalize it. She hoped that Michael understood what she was driving at.

Apparently he did, because he replied thoughtfully, "She's loyal. I can see that."

"That's for sure. You can make a damn fool of yourself, but if you're her friend, she'll stick by you. She and I have had our differences. I've done things she thought were big mistakes. But when I needed her, she was there. She helped me start all over again here, and I'll always be grateful."

For a moment Michael fell silent.

Deciding to throw caution to the wind, Nicola added, "The man who gets her will be lucky."

Michael smiled. "You don't have to tell me that. I know what you're getting at, Nicola. I may as well stop pretending my relationship with Lisa is casual."

"Michael, I hope you won't be offended if I speak frankly. But if you're concerned about your disability, don't be. As far as Lisa's concerned, it simply isn't a problem."

To her relief, he seemed glad the subject was out in the open. "Lisa's told me that. Man, that lady doesn't mince words. She told me she wants a man as strong as she is. She said I'm it."

Nicola smiled. That certainly sounded like Lisa.

"You're strong inside, where it counts, Michael. Or you wouldn't have come as far as you have. I'll tell you something. Lisa always tells the truth, whether you want to hear it or not. If she says she cares about you, then you'd better believe she does."

The smile faded from his engaging face, and there was a wistful look in his soft gray eyes. "I'd like to believe that."

"But . . ." Nicola finished for him.

"But . . . ." He let the word trail off.

Nicola could tell he was reluctant to admit the reason for his self-doubts.

"Michael, you know how close-knit the legal fraternity is. Lawyers tend to talk about one another. There are very few secrets.''

''In short, you've heard about my divorce.''

''Yes. You can tell me to mind my own business, if you want.''

''No.'' He sighed. ''It's no secret.'' Then he added quietly, ''I was a fighter pilot in 'Nam.'' Nicola's surprise must have shown, for he added, ''I don't talk about it very much. I was shot down, injured. I was married to a girl who was my high-school sweetheart. It was tough on her. Hell, I guess it was tough even before I was hurt. Being married was very different than we imagined it would be. Neither of us was ready for the sacrifices, the compromises—the hard reality. When I was in the hospital for so long, it just blew to hell any love that was left.''

''If that's so, then your marriage was existing on borrowed time, anyway,'' Nicola commented bluntly.

''Yeah, I guess so. But I got married with the idea it would last forever. I don't like making 360-degree turns. In my work and in my personal life I've always wanted to build something that would last. Can you understand that?''

Can *I,* Nicola thought bitterly as Logan's face flashed through her mind. She nodded, saying nothing.

''Lisa is so bright and beautiful. She makes me think of grace notes played on a flute. 'Quixotic,' I guess, is the word I'm looking for. She came dancing into my life, flirting outrageously with me, conning me into taking her out...conning me into *feeling* again. God, she's the happiest thing that's happened to me in years.''

He looked away, suddenly embarrassed. ''I want her so much I can't stand it. But I keep thinking—what if this is just 'be-kind-to-a-cripple month' for her?''

Nicola shook her head and said, ''One thing Lisa isn't is quixotic. I've known her for nine years, Michael, and I've seen her go through a lot of infatuations. She's never been serious about anyone the way she is about you.''

He was silent for a moment, thinking hard about what she was telling him.

Suddenly a voice cut in brightly, ''Hey, you two, what is this, a secret conference?''

Looking up, Nicola saw Lisa standing there, holding a tray with a salad and a glass of iced tea.

''Of course not,'' Nicola said with a laugh. Glancing at her watch, she noted, ''Damn, I'm going to be late. Here, you can have my seat.''

As Nicola rose, Michael remarked, ''It was nice talking to you, Nicola. Hey, I'll bring you something from Mexico.''

Nicola met his eyes and smiled.

Looking both surprised and pleased, Lisa said, ''So—you've decided to accept?''

As Nicola walked away, she heard Michael reply, ''Sure.''

NICOLA WAS HARD AT WORK on the following Monday when Marsha buzzed her. ''Yes?'' she answered absently, her mind on Logan's case.

"Miss Wynter, Rhonda asked me to find out if you know where Miss Halloran is? Her ten o'clock appointment has been waiting twenty minutes for her."

If Lisa was going to be late, she would have called her secretary. "Did Rhonda phone her home?" Nicola asked with a vague sense of misgiving.

"Yes. There's no answer. What shall we do? The gentleman's getting impatient."

"You'd better reschedule the meeting," Nicola finally answered. She was thoroughly puzzled. Lisa had never been late for an appointment as long as Nicola had known her. If she'd decided to stay down in Mexico longer than she originally planned, she would have called Nicola and her secretary.

Nicola was sitting at her desk, growing rapidly more worried, when Marsha buzzed her again.

"It's for you, Miss Wynter. A Mr. Donaldson from the Civil Aeronautics Board."

Oh, my God, Nicola thought, stunned. She knew Lisa had given the CAB her name and number as a person to contact in the event of an accident. Hoping against hope that this sick feeling in the pit of her stomach was wrong, she answered the call.

"I'm sorry to have to tell you," Donaldson began immediately, "that Lisa Halloran's plane has gone down."

No! Nicola wanted to scream. Instead she marshaled every bit of calm at her disposal and asked, "Where? What happened?"

"She fueled up at the airport at Santa Rosalia, a small town on the eastern coast of Baja, California. It's about halfway down the peninsula. Anyway, a couple of hours later she radioed the airport that she was losing fuel and encountering unusually strong headwinds, and they were turning back. But they didn't make it. The airport didn't receive any further transmissions, and we can only assume the radio was destroyed when they went down.''

"Have they. . . have they found the plane?" Nicola fought down the nausea that threatened her. *Oh, God,* she prayed. *Don't let it be so.*

"No. The Mexican authorities have started a search, but it's a big desert down there. It could be hours, even days, before they find anything."

Anything, Nicola noted that he used a purposefully vague word. From his tone she sensed he had wanted to say, "Bodies."

"I think I'll fly down," Nicola began.

But he interrupted firmly, "I can't emphasize how futile that would be, miss. I'm sorry about this. Believe me, I know what you're going through. But you couldn't do any good down there. Everything that can be done is being done. I'll get back to you as soon as I hear anything at all."

When she hung up, Nicola felt the same sense of disorientation she'd felt when Andrew died. *It can't be true,* she kept saying over and over to herself. But it *was* true.

Finally she grabbed her purse and went out to the reception area. In a dull monotone she explained briefly to her secretary what had happened and told her she was leaving.

"Where can we reach you, Miss Wynter?" Marsha asked.

Nicola paused to think. Where, indeed? The thought of going home and waiting alone for another call from the CAB was horrible. Suddenly she wanted Logan, *needed* to be with him. If only he were still at his hotel.

She gave Marsha Logan's number and told her she would either be there or at home. Then she hurried out, praying that Logan would be in.

A few minutes later she stood at his door, knocking on it for the third time. There was still no answer. He was gone, possibly to Santa Barbara, possibly even to Baton Rouge. She hadn't seen him since the night they had made love. It had been only a few days, but it seemed like an eternity now as she wished desperately he were there to hold her.

She knew why he hadn't contacted her these past few days. He didn't want to make it even harder for her if he did lose the case. Now the case appeared almost unimportant. Nothing mattered but feeling his arms around her as she cried for Lisa.

She leaned her hand against the door for a moment. She felt exhausted and bereft of hope. Lisa's plane was down. She might very well be critically injured—or dead. And Michael...almost as an afterthought, Nicola remembered that Michael was with Lisa. And all because she had urged him to go.

"Nicola!"

Whirling around, Nicola came face to face with Logan as he stepped off the elevator.

"My God, what's happened, honey? You look awful."

She flung herself against him, burying her face in

his chest. For a moment she couldn't speak. Then briefly she explained what had happened.

"Let's get you inside," Logan replied when she'd finished. Unlocking the door, he drew her inside. He led her to the sofa, and while she sat down, he poured both of them a stiff brandy. "Drink this," he ordered. Then he sat down beside her and took her into his arms. For a long while they sat that way, silent. Finally he said softly, "There's still hope, you know. Don't assume the worst until you have to."

"Oh, Logan, *I* persuaded Michael to go. If he'd refused, Lisa wouldn't have gone, either!"

"Stop that!" Logan commanded in a stern voice. "It isn't your fault. It isn't Lisa's fault. It just happened. But she's a good pilot, you said."

"Oh, God, I hope so."

"If the plane went down because they were out of fuel, then there needn't have been an explosion. It's desert, so probably she was able to find a place to crash-land. She and her friend would have been prepared for the landing. There's every chance they could survive it."

Nicola didn't know if it was his words or his arms holding her tightly that was responsible for the upsurge of hope she felt. But it didn't matter. She knew only that she felt infinitely better. He was right, of course. Lisa *was* a good pilot. If anyone could survive a crash, she could.

Sitting up, Nicola wiped the tears from her swollen eyes. "Okay. I'll believe that she's all right...that they're both all right. Until I have proof otherwise."

"Good girl," Logan said, kissing her softly on the forehead. "Come on, I'm taking you home, and then I'll arrange for some of my people to join the search team."

As they rose, Nicola asked tentatively, "Will you stay with me? Lisa is very important to. . . ."

"Of course, love. For as long as you need me. I know what Lisa means to you." The expression in his eyes was tender and so full of concern that her battered heart beat stronger.

For as long as I need you, she echoed in her thoughts. *That will be forever.*

Logan remained with Nicola the entire time. They spent the slow-moving hours talking. He helped her prepare their meals; he made endless telephone calls to monitor the progress of the search. He constantly reassured her, realizing that there'd been a series of losses of people dear to her—father, mother, husband. He knew how frightened she was about Lisa. When they went to bed at night, he held her, sharing his very physical strength with her.

It was a bonding time, and Nicola was reminded more than once of what she had learned on QE2. This man was someone to *like*, as well as to love.

Then, late in the afternoon of the second day, Logan was in the kitchen making coffee when the phone rang.

It was Donaldson.

Nicola said, "Yes? Have you heard—"

Before she could finish, Donaldson said quickly, "They're all right, Miss Wynter. Your friend and her passenger. They were picked up this evening. Apparently they weren't seriously injured. They'll be coming back to LA tonight."

Thank God, Nicola thought. Suddenly she felt lighter than air. "Thank you. Oh, thank you so much!"

He laughed. "Hey, it's okay. This is one of the nicer moments in my job."

Looking up at Logan standing in the kitchen doorway, Nicola saw him breathe a deep sigh of relief.

"When will they arrive, do you know?" she asked Donaldson.

"They've chartered a plane and pilot to bring them back. It seems Miss Halloran's plane is badly damaged. I'll call you as soon as they're here."

Nicola hung up, then said, "They're okay."

Logan laughed. "I gathered," he replied. "I'm glad, Nicola."

As he held out his arms to her, she rushed into them and wept with relief. The knot of fear that had settled in her stomach since Donaldson's first call finally began to unwind.

Later, drinking their coffee on the deck and watching the sun set over the Pacific, Logan tilted her chin up to look in her eyes. "You're a tough lady. You hung in there. See—" he paused, then continued, "—you must believe."

Something about the sober tone in his voice alerted her. "Logan—what is it?" Before he could answer, she knew. "You need to get back to Baton Rouge, don't you?"

"I put it off because I wanted to be with you, but

now that Lisa's okay...and you're okay...." He left the sentence unfinished.

She understood. "When will you be back?"

Shaking his head, he said he really didn't know. "But I'll be here for the trial. It's one spectacle I wouldn't want to miss."

She said nothing for a moment. Then her luminous sea-green eyes met his mysterious tawny ones. "In that case," her voice a soft sensuous whisper, "let's make the most of the time we have." Slipping her arms around his neck, she raised her lips to his, and as she felt their tantalizing pressure, she tried not to think that this might be the last time they loved....

CHAPTER NINETEEN

TWO DAYS LATER Nicola was seated in Lisa's living room, listening to the story of that remarkable weekend.

"It began great," Lisa said as she sat next to Michael on the sofa. "We went to Mulegé, which is on the Sea of Cortez. Nice quiet little place, very colorful and not too touristy. Flying over it, it looks like a green oasis in a huge brown desert."

"Sounds like you experienced the quiet before the storm," Nicola commented.

"Exactly," Lisa answered with a grin. "One day we were enjoying lazy days and tropical nights and watching dolphins leap out of that incredibly blue sea. The next we were stranded in the desert."

"How did it happen?"

"A leak in the fuel tank," Michael replied. "Then we encountered unusually strong headwinds out of Santa Rosalia that exhausted our fuel even faster than would have normally happened."

"I discovered Michael really has a sense of humor," Lisa said, shooting him a wry look. "When it became clear we weren't going to make it back to the airport in Santa Rosalia, he just said, 'Well, I've walked away from one crash. After this, I'll be an expert at it.' "

Nicola laughed along with Michael and Lisa, but she knew that beneath the light banter, they were still recovering from the shock of the experience.

"I would have been scared senseless," Nicola admitted.

"I *was*," Lisa replied. "I kept sending our position to the airport and at the same time trying to remember everything that had to be done. Michael just kept saying, 'You can do it, don't worry.' But there were so many things to remember. I had to trim and set up for a normal landing, watch the airspeed so we didn't go too slow and keep the wind direction in mind. Michael talked me through it. And just before we came in for the crash, he reminded me to cut the master switch."

"Just in case there was any fuel left," Michael explained. "I didn't want an explosion when we hit."

"When the engine quit, it was so quiet," Lisa said. "Scary quiet. I told Michael I had just found him after years of looking and now we were going to crash." She flashed him a look of profound tenderness. "He told me this was simply part of flying, what I had been trained to do. He was so calm, so brave."

"Well, you did it," Michael said, clearly proud of her.

"Except for one big mistake. I was trying to come down on a plateau so the radio could transmit. But a downdraft grabbed us, and we ended up awfully close to a pile of boulders. At the very last minute I braked a hard left to miss the boulders, but we landed in a canyon. The radio couldn't transmit from there."

"That's why it took so long to find you."

"Yes. If it hadn't been for Michael, I would have panicked. I don't mind admitting I was terrified. In a courtroom I'm anyone's equal, but in a desert...." She made a face of distaste. "Did you know there are lizards and snakes out there?"

Nicola smiled. "I've heard."

"Palm Springs will never again seem inviting."

Michael put one arm across the back of the sofa and squeezed her shoulder reassuringly. "It's all right now, hon'. It's all over. Something to tell our kids about."

The mention of children and the look of adoration on Michael's face were very revealing. *Tropical nights, indeed,* thought Nicola. *So* that's *the way it is.* She'd sensed a difference in the couple as Lisa talked. Obviously they were very much in love.

"Speaking of kids," Lisa said to Michael, "why don't we go ahead and tell Nicola now?"

He smiled in agreement.

Lisa explained to Nicola, "We had a lot of time to talk out there. And we decided...." For a moment she was uncharacteristically hesitant.

Nicola grinned broadly. "When is the wedding?" she asked.

"Immediately!" Lisa answered. "I'm not giving him any time to back out. We're getting married in three weeks at the Wayfarer's Chapel in Palos Verdes."

"Oh, Lisa, I'm so happy for both of you!" Impulsively Nicola jumped up and hugged first Lisa, then Michael.

"I know you two will be very happy."

"I'm sure we will," Michael replied.

"Nicola, what would you say to Jardine, Halloran and Wynter, Attorneys-at-Law?" Lisa asked. "I suggested to Michael that he join our firm."

"Sounds great. It will be nice to have you on our side. You're far too formidable an opponent."

"Thanks, Nicola. But I don't think my name should come first," Michael demurred.

"Only because it's more euphonic," Lisa insisted. "It has nothing to do with who's the best lawyer."

"Well, I think this calls for a toast," Nicola said. "You don't happen to have any champagne around here, do you?"

"I do, indeed."

Lisa went into the kitchen, then returned a moment later with a tray. On it were three wineglasses and a bottle of Dom Perignon.

"Mmm," Nicola murmured, looking at the expensive champagne. "You weren't perhaps anticipating this moment, were you, old friend?"

Lisa laughed. "Of course I was. I bought this the day after Michael and I went out for the first time. I was determined that sooner or later we would have something to celebrate."

Michael uncorked the bottle and poured a generous amount in each glass. "What shall we drink to?" he asked.

"To you two, naturally," Nicola answered.

They touched glasses, then sipped the smooth golden liquid.

"Nicola, we've done nothing but talk about ourselves all evening," Lisa perceptively interjected. "Tell me what's been happening with Logan's case?"

"Not a great deal," Nicola answered evasively. She didn't want to dampen Lisa and Michael's celebration, so she quickly added, "Let's not go into it now. I'll tell you all about it when you come back to the office."

"Well, I'll be back tomorrow. I'm not wasting any time. I've got a lot of business to clear up before the wedding."

Lisa looked warmly at Michael, and for a moment Nicola knew they had almost forgotten her presence. Feeling that three was beginning to be a crowd, she took her leave.

As she drove home, she thought how glad she was for the two of them. They both deserved all the happiness in the world. Now, Nicola knew, she needed to concentrate on Logan's case. But it, she suspected, might not have such a happy ending.

EARLY THE NEXT AFTERNOON Lisa and Michael came into Nicola's office.

"I was just showing Michael around. We're going to rent that office next door and put in a connecting door."

"Good. When do you officially join us?" Nicola asked. She tried to sound bright and welcoming, but her mind was on the files that covered her desk—files on Logan's case.

"Next month," Michael replied. Glancing down at the desk, he added, "Is this material on the Logan James case Lisa's been telling me about?"

"Yes. Mostly files on the workers on the platform. Harry Tornino, the investigator we use, did background profiles on all of them. I've gone through them over and over again, looking for something that might point to industrial sabotage. That's the only thing that will clear my client of responsibility for the delay in construction."

While Nicola talked, Michael casually glanced at the files. Suddenly he picked up one. "Hudson Klein? Is he one of Global's workers?"

"Yes. He's their liaison man on the project. Why?"

"I knew a guy by that name in 'Nam. It's an unusual name, not one you run across too often. Mind if I glance at the file?"

"Of course not," Nicola answered. "If I remember correctly, he did serve in Vietnam."

Michael was reading the file intently. Something in his look alerted Nicola. "What is it?" she asked.

"It's the same guy, all right. He was a bad case in 'Nam. Into black-market activities, drugs, you name it. He finally got kicked out—a dishonorable discharge. The thing is, Nicola, that guy would do anything for money."

"Even industrial sabotage?"

"Exactly," Michael answered, meeting her eyes.

"Now calm down, you two," Lisa intervened. "I don't want to play the devil's advocate, but don't get too excited yet. You've got to make sure it's the same guy and that he's up to his old tricks."

"At least it's a lead," Nicola responded, unable to contain her rising optimism. She felt as if she'd been lost in a dark tunnel and finally could see a ray of light at the end. "Until now there's been nothing concrete we could follow up. Michael, if you're right . . . ."

"I'm sure it's the same guy. I heard he settled in California when he left the army. How many guys named Hudson Klein can there be in this state?" Michael was thoughtful for a moment. Then he asked, "Is he still up in Santa Barbara?"

"As far as I know," Nicola answered.

"Tell you what. Why don't I do a little sleuthing? Hell, after that little adventure in Mexico, I feel like taking on the world. I'll go up there, find out where Klein hangs out and 'accidentally' run into him. He doesn't know I'm a lawyer. We haven't seen each other since 'Nam. We weren't exactly friends then, but I can play up the 'old army-buddies' routine. I'll buy him a few drinks and see what he has to say. The guy drank like a fish."

"Oh, Michael, I'd be forever grateful!"

"No problem. If I'm going to be part of this firm, I want to do what I can to see we win all our cases," Michael replied with a grin.

Nicola hugged him. "Oh, I *am* glad you're going to be with us."

"Hey, hands off," Lisa teased. "This man is taken."

"Do you want to let your client know what we're up to?" Michael asked.

"No," Nicola answered quickly. "I don't want to get his hopes up. If this doesn't work out . . . ."

She let the sentence trail off. If this didn't work out, Logan's case was as good as lost.

THAT WEEKEND, Nicola, Lisa and Michael went up to Santa Barbara, where they checked into a popular ocean-front hotel. Harry Tornino had given Nicola a list of places in which the Global oil workers were known to hang out.

"It's Friday night, R & R time," Michael said after dinner. "Surely there'll be some lead to old Hudson. He's smart, but not low-key. I'll mosey around to the various watering holes in the immediate vicinity."

After he left, Nicola and Lisa walked across the street to look out across the water. They could see the lights of Stearns Wharf, an extension of the city's main street that jutted out into the Pacific.

In the moonlight a fleet of pleasure crafts and fishing vessels anchored in the harbor bobbed restlessly to the motion of the wavelets. And farther out were the offshore drilling rigs. Nicola studied the monstrous behemoths of steel and power, so lit with lights she could see both the tending and exploration ships outlined against the sea and the night.

"That's his world out there," Nicola mused softly. "There's got to be some way to save it."

Back in the hotel suite, the two young women tried to set aside their anxiety. They talked some of Lisa's wedding plans, but it was difficult for Nicola to concentrate on anything except how much depended on Michael's locating Hudson Klein.

It was after two in the morning before he returned, dead tired and with nothing to report. No trace or clue of any kind.

The next night was the same. Nicola felt her early

optimism begin to fade. If they couldn't even find Klein, let alone get him to admit to any wrongdoing, the situation was hopeless.

On Sunday, after a late brunch, Nicola told Lisa that she was going to explore Santa Barbara and "worry in private." "That way," she said, "you two can have some time alone. I'll be back for dinner." It was a beautiful balmy day, too beautiful to spend in such anxiety, she thought. Damn Global Oil...and damn whoever was responsible for sabotaging Logan's work.

Driving around the city, she admired the plainly discernible Spanish motif—red clay tile and adobe—Hispanic architecture in modern-day form. Spanish street names—De La Guerra, Carrillo, Cañon Perdido, Indio Muerto—honoring pioneer families or events added to the early-California ambience.

Taking the scenic drive, Nicola followed the shoreline along the cliffs until the road looped back to where she could turn east through the Santa Ynez Mountains. As she drove, she thought about this country. The entire south coast was spectacular. At its northern end, a forest of derricks stood in the pounding surf and pumped the oil from deep in the earth. And off the Santa Barbara coast were the offshore drilling explorations—Logan's hope...his wildcatter's pot of gold.

She traveled through the quiet hills of the San Marcos Pass. Spring sunshine brightened the green, oak-covered hills where sleek horses grazed in open pastures and dairy herds followed the contours of the slopes as they foraged. She would love to explore this country with Logan the way they had explored London.

Late afternoon found Nicola back in Santa Barbara, standing on a knoll overlooking the city. She'd enjoyed her visit to the Mission Santa Barbara and, since she still had an hour to kill before meeting Lisa and Michael for dinner, had decided to look around in the historical park which had been built around the mission.

From the ruins of the old waterworks and grist mill, she looked down green weedy slopes and through olive trees to the great chapel's twin towers.

As she strolled slowly back to the mission yard, she reflected on Logan's ante-antebellum house and how he valued it all the more because his grandfather had so cared for it.

Earlier, when she'd stood inside the mission observing the altar candle whose significance reached back through history to the first candle lit at the mission's dedication in 1786, Nicola had thought about continuity, sequence, progression.

Would there be no way for her and Logan to live in love as had that first Logan James and his Annabel...so that someday their progeny would value *their* lives and love.

Nicola sat on the edge of the stone basin of the large Moorish fountain that graced the courtyard. A gentle breeze set in motion the draping branches of an old pepper tree and carried to her the delicate fragrance of the water lilies floating in the basin. She watched two of the fathers walk out of the mission, stride across the courtyard and disappear out of sight. One of them was old, the other young. Nicola remembered that small flickering light whose continuous burning symbolized constancy.

Aunt Cordy's words, "the James men *stay* married...*your* Logan has waited so long...found the *right* woman," came to mind. Whatever else their differences might be, Nicola knew Logan's love would be constant. The flame that burned so intensely between them had been kindled spontaneously but set aside—banked—denied—almost a year ago beside another fountain. But the flame had refused to die and had leaped to a gloriously burning fire again and again. *And now what,* she wondered.

The early settlers of this beautiful city called it *la tierra adorada*, "the beloved land," after their Mediterranean homeland.

Baton Rouge—Magnolia Hill—was Logan's *tierra adorado*. His place. Again Nicola thought of Aunt Cordy and remembered her bright blue eyes shining with kindness as she'd explained why Logan had brought her there to meet his family. It was his heritage that he wanted to share with her.

Dear God, she prayed, *please let Michael find Hudson Klein.*

MICHAEL LEFT AS SOON as they finished dinner. To fill in time, Nicola and Lisa strolled around the hotel grounds and along the sidewalk above the beach. Before returning to their suite, they had a drink in the lounge and looked out the big window at the harbor.

Later they watched the late news—and waited. Two o'clock passed, then three and four. At dawn,

Lisa and Nicola were on the verge of calling the police. Lisa looked more worried than Nicola had ever seen her. And Nicola felt guilty for having allowed Michael to do such a foolhardy thing. If anything happened to him, she would never forgive herself.

And then the door to the sitting room of the suite opened. For a moment both women sat tensely on the sofa. Then Michael was revealed standing in the doorway. After a moment he limped in, supporting himself heavily on his cane.

Lisa rushed to him. "Thank God. I was so worried!"

Michael leaned on her arm as he came into the room. He said nothing as he sank into a chair and dropped his cane on the floor. Still not speaking, he took a tiny tape recorder out of his breast pocket. He pushed a button, and in a moment Nicola could hear a muffled sound.

Gradually it became clearer. Two men, one of them Michael, were talking. The other man was very drunk.

"I always knew how to get mine," the man was saying. "There's big money to be made if you know what to do."

"Yeah, you always were clever," Michael was agreeing. "The rest of us were just stupid grunts, taking our miserable pay. But you had plenty of money, Hud. Looks like you're still doing all right, ol' buddy, for an oil worker."

"Damn right. But I didn't get all this on that little salary Global pays me. Hell, that wouldn't pay my liquor bill for a month." He laughed unpleasantly.

"You got somethin' going?" Michael was asking in a conspiratorial tone.

"Hell, yes. Don't I always? There are people willin' to pay for what I can do for 'em. Willin' to pay big."

Sounding impressed, Michael continued, "But aren't you worried about someone finding out?"

" 'Course not, Mike, old pal. The army couldn't get anything on me. They kicked me out just from spite. Nobody's gonna get anything on me now. I know how to make things look like accidents, y'see."

His drunken voice went on and on, explaining how clever he was in sabotaging Logan's work.

At that point Michael switched off the tape recorder. He smiled an exhausted but thoroughly pleased smile. "And that, ladies, is what is known in our profession as admissible evidence."

Nicola didn't know whether to laugh or cry or hug Michael. Finally she did all three.

NICOLA AND LOGAN met with the head of Global Oil's legal department in a wood-paneled conference room high atop the towering Global Oil Building in downtown Los Angeles. The attorney, Howard Kessler, was a stern, middle-aged man famous for his tough legal tactics. As they all shook hands, then sat down, Nicola caught the amused glint in his steel-gray eyes.

He thinks we're here to capitulate, she realized. *To offer an out-of-court settlement. In short, to beg for Global's mercy. Well, Mr. Kessler, you're* dead *wrong.*

She gave him her most brilliant smile. For the

briefest moment, he looked flustered. She could almost hear him thinking, *something is wrong here*. Then he reverted to his iron countenance. "What can I do for you, Mr. Logan, Miss Wynter?"

From her briefcase Nicola took out a copy of Michael's tape recording, a transcribed copy of that conversation, a voice expert's deposition stating it was Hudson Klein's voice and a report by Harry Tornino. With Michael's information, Harry had been able to investigate Klein thoroughly. He'd found proof that Klein had met with a representative from Mannering Construction, that he'd been spending far more money than Global paid him and that he'd been present on the platform before each accident.

When Nicola began talking, Kessler looked angry and disbelieving. But as she placed the evidence before him and described it in detail, his expression changed. He was beaten, and he knew it.

When Nicola finished, Logan, who had been silent until then, said, "As you can see, Mannering bribed Klein to sabotage the project so they could step in and take over. But Klein is still your employee, and you're responsible for his actions. I intend to file a countersuit against you, charging sabotage."

His voice, which was quiet, held a ruthless note that Nicola had never heard previously. Logan James was no man to cross. Though he didn't articulate it, it was obvious from his tone that he would thoroughly enjoy beating Global into the ground.

Kessler hesitated. He was furious at the turn of events, but he was too good a lawyer to waste time in a futile argument. He said slowly, "I think, Mr.

James, we'll consider dropping our suit against you."

Logan smiled. "I'm afraid, Mr. Kessler, that's not good enough. I expect Global to reimburse me for the losses I suffered because of Klein, and I want a revised schedule that will allow me to finish construction."

Before Kessler could respond, Logan rose, followed by Nicola. "Now if you'll excuse me, I've got work to do. Let my attorney know what you decide." And he and Nicola walked out, leaving Kessler open-mouthed with impotent fury.

Outside, Nicola and Logan stood in front of the towering black-glass Global building.

Looking at Nicola, Logan said, "We did it, counselor."

She smiled. "We did, indeed." Then she added quietly, "Thank you, Logan. You trusted me with everything that matters to you. I'll always remember that."

"I hired you because you're good, Nicola."

"And also because you wanted to make up for what happened in London when you turned to another lawyer?" she asked. Her tone was light. The past was buried now.

And then, as they stood on that crowded sidewalk in downtown Los Angeles, with towering skyscrapers surrounding them, Logan told Nicola what she had been half waiting to hear. "I love you, Nicola. I've said it every way I know. And I know that you love me. Sure, we have problems. But we can work them out. My grandfather settled down for the woman he loved. I can do the same. I'll have to travel some-times, but I'll cut down as much as possible. The house in Baton Rouge will be our home, and I'll only leave it when I have to."

"I have a career, Logan...."

"I know. At the same time I admired your ability as a lawyer, I guess I always assumed you'd give it up to be my wife. I know now how selfish that was. I want you to be whatever *you* want to be, Nicola. But you know, sweetheart, Baton Rouge, sure could use a terrific lawyer like you."

He smiled mischievously, much as he must have done when he was a small boy and was trying to talk his way out of trouble. The smile was as irresistible now as it must have been then.

By putting himself in her hands, he had validated the importance of her career. With two people as am-bitious as they both were, there would inevitably be conflicts. At least now she could see the possibility of overcoming them.

As those leonine eyes looked down at her, she said softly, "Just give me a little more time, Logan. You're asking me to make another new beginning. I need some time to think about it."

"All right, Nicola. A *little* more time. But don't take too long, or you'll find yourself with a second pearl ready for stringing."

CHAPTER TWENTY

NICOLA AND LISA sat in Nicola's living room, watching the sunset's last tinge of color fade into twilight. It had been a particularly beautiful sky—like the day. Special. She and Lisa had met for brunch, then gone to the airport to pick up Lisa's parents. Her mother was ecstatic about the wedding and chattered happily on about it as they drove to Lisa's condo. Michael, along with his parents and brother, was waiting there. It was a happy hectic afternoon as everyone went over the plans for the wedding, which was to take place the next day.

Then, leaving her parents to do some last-minute shopping and Michael and his brother to their own private bachelor's party, Lisa had come home with Nicola for a quiet dinner and chat.

The sky had been filled with sweeps of deep pink and soft tangerine. A broad swirl of purple had faded to lavender streaks and was now feathered into mere wisps of palest amethyst. A wash of gold lay over the sky and across the ocean.

"Your last day as Miss Halloran is ending in a blaze of glory," Nicola said, smiling.

Lisa returned the smile, then took a sip of the iced tea the two women were drinking. Leaning her head against the chair back, Lisa closed her eyes for a moment. When she opened them, Nicola said, pointing, "Look."

In the sky, the evening star had appeared

"Starlight, starbright..." Nicola quoted, then stopped, remembering when she'd last repeated that old refrain—in the garden at Beechwood, just before meeting Logan for the first time.

God, he came unbidden so often to her heart and her mind.

To avoid disturbing thoughts of him, Nicola asked, "Are you nervous about tomorrow?"

"Yes," Lisa admitted with a little laugh. "I think I've actually got stage fright. The idea of being the center of attention in a courtroom doesn't bother me. But in a wedding chapel...."

"Just don't trip coming down the aisle," Nicola teased.

They both laughed.

Then, after taking another sip of tea, Nicola asked softly, "Lisa—are you sure about what you're doing? It's happened so fast."

"I know. But I'm *very* sure. I heard once that the three most common times to get married are right after high-school graduation, college graduation and when you turn thirty. Well, I'll be thirty next month. But I'm not getting married out a sense of fear of growing older. I just know I've found the right man."

"I think you have, too. I like Michael," Nicola responded sincerely, "and admire him tremendously."

"I know. And I'm glad. That reinforces my conviction that I've chosen well. I love him more than I ever dreamed it was possible to love someone. But even that isn't the crucial thing. The fact is, I know we'll be good for each other and be able to make a good life together.''

Good for each other. . . yes, Nicola thought, seeing Lisa's eyes so bright with joy. Lisa and Michael *were* good for each other. And they would make a good life together, supporting each other in their work, as well as emotionally.

''That's what marriage should be about,'' Nicola mused as Lisa listened quietly. ''Not one person giving up what matters to him. . . to her, in order for the other person to be happy, but both people encouraging each other, trying to bring out the best in each other.''

''To be honest, I don't think most marriages are that way,'' Lisa said. ''Especially for women, marriage usually means giving up your identity to support your husband's. We're supposed to be nurturing and caring. Yet men aren't expected to be the same. That's why I waited so long to marry. I wanted to be sure I could still be all the things that make me *me*. Do you understand?''

Do I, Nicola thought wryly. Aloud she said, ''I think you and Michael will make a terrific team in every sense of the word. He was worth waiting for, wasn't he?''

Nodding, Lisa smiled gratefully. Then her smile turned into a frown of concern. ''Nicola. . . there's something I'd been wanting to talk to you about, but I haven't known how to broach it.''

"Well, why not just come right out with it? Lisa, it's not like you to be less than blunt," Nicola teased.

"Okay. Here goes. What's happening with you and Logan?"

"Oh, that," Nicola responded with a sigh.

"If I'm getting too personal, just tell me to mind my own business," Lisa said quickly. "It's just that, well, after the Global business was resolved, I kept waiting to hear that your relationship with him was resolved, too."

Nicola shook her head. "I don't know what to say. When he hired me to represent him in the Global case...well, it erased an old debt, let's say. But there are so many problems. Logan James isn't an easy person to be involved with."

And what she feared, but didn't say, was that she wondered if he *could* honor his promise that she could count on his support for her own career. If push came to shove, would she have to fight, as she had with Andrew?

Lisa smiled. "He does tend to sweep through your life like a whirlwind, doesn't he?"

"Indeed, he does."

"Nicola, is part of the problem the fact that you'd have to move to Baton Rouge and leave our practice?" Lisa asked directly.

"Yes, that's a big part of it," Nicola admitted, meeting Lisa's steady gaze.

"Well, I want to tell you here and now to forget about that. We've been good business partners, but we're even better friends. More than anything else, I want you to be happy. Because I know—better than anyone, maybe—that you've never really been as happy as you could be. You've been on the edge of happiness. I know that now because of how I feel about Michael. If Logan James can do that for you, the more power to him, I say. Now that Michael's joining the practice, you won't be leaving me in the lurch, you know.''

''That's generous of you, Lisa, and I appreciate it. But I've uprooted my life twice in the past year. I don't know if I want to do it for a third time.''

''But this would be the last time, wouldn't it? I mean, if you've finally found what you've been looking for.''

I have definitely found it, Nicola thought. *God knows, I love the man to distraction. There will always be problems trying to combine our lives—we're both very strong, independent—we test each other. But judging by his behavior toward me with the whole Global case, obviously he's more sensitive now to my feelings and needs. So why do I hesitate?*

She was still asking herself that question after Lisa left later that night.

She wondered if he would come to the wedding the following day. When she'd told him the time and place, she'd said she would understand if he was too busy to make it. He was pushing hard on the Santa Barbara project, now that everything was straightened out with Global.

It would soon be a year since they'd met that night in Washington. That year had taught her a great deal about herself and about love. She used to think love was a safe secure place. She'd learned that at least with Logan, it was a time, a happening, an ever changing state that was never safe. It was like a flash of lightning splitting the sky of her world for a brief moment. In the years ahead, this year, even with its pain, would hold a radiance that would color her life like that glow across the western horizon she'd seen earlier.

Logan was always in her heart and mind, even when half a world separated them. And she knew it was the same with him.

When they'd left Global's office that day, she'd asked for time—time to think, to consider. She was on hold, she knew, as was he. And that wasn't a situation he would allow to continue for long.

As the stars lit the night sky, Nicola sighed. *Logan.* Always Logan. She didn't know how to resolve their conflicts. She knew only that she couldn't live without him.…

LATE THE NEXT AFTERNOON, Nicola waited with Lisa and her father in a small room at Wayfarer's Chapel on the Palos Verdes Peninsula. Called the "glass church," it was a combination of glass walls and redwood beams. Built atop a steep bluff overlooking the Pacific, it was set against a background of cedar, pine and eucalyptus. It was gloriously beautiful.

As was Lisa. She wore a street-length, ivory crepe dress with long sleeves and a mandarin collar. The simple, close-fitting dress was perfect for her petite figure. On her head was a circlet of lilies of the valley, and she carried a bouquet of the same. Nicola wore a street-length dress of lavender chiffon that swirled softly around her knees. There was a matching lavender ribbon on her broad-brimmed straw hat.

Outside, a light spring rain fell from a sky that was alternately dark and bright.

"Wouldn't you know it would rain on my wedding day?" Lisa commented wryly.

"It doesn't matter," Nicola assured her. "Everyone will be looking at you, not the sky. And you're gorgeous!"

Suddenly the music began. A musician friend of Michael's sang "The Wedding Song" and "You Light Up My Life." Then the organist began the wedding march.

"Are you ready?" Nicola asked.

"As ready as I'll ever be," Lisa answered, smiling nervously.

Nicola hugged her quickly, then went into the chapel.

As she preceded Lisa up the aisle, she swept her gaze across the gathering of friends and relatives. She didn't see Logan. Trying to quell her intense disappointment, she told herself he obviously couldn't make it.

Then she spotted Michael waiting by the altar. Nicola only half noticed his cane now. What captured her attention was the expression on his handsome face. Michael clearly had no doubts about the rightness of this ceremony. When he saw Lisa, his face lit up with pure joy. *He doesn't hear the wedding march,* Nicola thought. *For him, silver trumpets herald her approach.*

Turning to look at Lisa, Nicola saw that her eyes were shining with the same joy, the same magic, as were Michael's.

When Lisa reached the altar and her father stepped aside, Nicola saw Logan.

He was seated in the first pew behind Michael's parents. A momentary stream of light from the sun fell across his face. In that instant, Nicola stood in a garden—where light streamed through tall windows illuminating Logan's wide-set eyes as he offered a toast to when dreams come true.

She smiled, and across a chapel of wedding guests, he returned her smile. The love he offered shone as brightly in his eyes as that she'd seen reflected in Michael's. As before, in the garden, she felt her heart fall with a thud to the pit of her stomach and her throat constrict with a feeling so intense she could hardly bear it.

In his charge to Michael and Lisa, the young minister spoke of trust. "It is the basic link that holds two people together. It does not spring up only in isolated or dramatic moments, but is a constant thread that runs throughout the fiber of the partnership between a man and a woman."

Michael and Lisa listened intently as the minister continued. "If communication is the stimulus of true intimacy, trust is the cement that bonds the relationship."

Nicola hardly heard the minister's words. As she stood by the altar, her mind was on Logan. For so long they had seemed fated just to miss each other; to come together, then part. Each time they parted, she died a little. And yet at the same time her love for him never died, never even weakened.

We have what Michael and Lisa have, Nicola thought. *A love so right, so powerful, nothing can destroy it.*

And as she heard Michael and Lisa repeat their vows, she knew it might have been her and Logan, she thought with bittersweet poignancy, if so very much hadn't happened.

Reflecting on what the minister had said about trust, she thought, *if I want to live with Logan, I must trust him enough to cross the chasm that divides our lives. My love for him is* everything, *and is worth the risk I have to take.*

Suddenly she knew when you gave everything, you risked everything. There was no safe middle ground.

The minister went on, "Dearly Beloved, I charge you both to remember that love and loyalty alone will avail as the foundation. No other ties are more tender, no other vows more sacred, than those you now make."

Nicola listened as Michael and Lisa vowed to take each other...to love...to comfort....

The spring storm clouds had blown capriciously across the sky all during the ceremony. When free of cloud cover, the sun shone brightly and its rays sent fingers of prismatic light through the glass walls to dance over the friends and relatives gathered there.

At the conclusion of the ceremony, the sun, as if on cue, broke through the clouds in a radiant burst of energy. And Nicola thought, *happy the bride the sun shines on!*

Smiling, Lisa and Michael hurried down the aisle. Outside, they stood on the steps of the chapel to receive the embraces and good wishes of their families and guests.

Tears of joy spilling down her cheeks, Lisa's mother kissed her daughter and son-in-law. Then she herded the wedding party back inside the chapel for a short session with the photographer.

Amid a shower of rice, the bride and groom ran to Michael's car for the drive back to Lisa's condo, where the reception was to be held. Everyone else followed.

From the moment Nicola knew Logan was there, it had been difficult to keep her mind on her duties as Lisa's attendant. Though a group of people separated them, she felt incredibly close to him as he bent to kiss Lisa tenderly on the cheek and wish her and Michael happiness. She remembered how strong and sure his handclasp felt.

Now as Nicola stood on the steps of the chapel watching the last car drive away, she heard that familiar voice that had the power to turn her knees to jelly. "You're even more beautiful than the bride."

She turned to smile up at Logan.

"Walk with me," he invited.

She nodded and took the hand he held out to her.

They stopped at the balustrade at the edge of the cliff. While Logan looked out at the ocean, Nicola watched him, wondering how to tell him what she'd been thinking during the ceremony.

Trust. That was what it was all about. The one

thing she had never given him. The one thing their love needed to grow.

Then, as she gazed past Logan toward the southern line of the coast, she saw a shimmering of color begin along the horizon. As she watched, the shimmering emerged into an arch of misty red, yellow and blue, with delicate shadings of orange, green, indigo and violet.

Her head acknowledged scientific data of refractive dispersion of sunlight in drops of mist. Her heart saw a glorious display of iridescence in the rain-washed sky.

"Logan! Look!"

He looked down at her and smiled tenderly. "What do you see, Nicola?"

"A rainbow."

"Tell me about it, love," he urged.

"It's beautiful...." She hesitated for just a second, then added, "And it's full of bright promise."

"Do you believe that promise now, Nicola?" he asked, tipping her chin so that she looked up at him.

She knew there was much to be worked out between them, but she could only trust that somehow they would do so. Even love, she knew now, was a calculated risk.

Finally she whispered, "Yes, Logan. I believe in rainbows."

ABOUT THE AUTHOR

Dianne King is actually a writing team hailing from Fresno, California.

Both career women, wives and mothers, one-half of the team teaches creative writing and the other half is a well-known romance writer who has published ten books in the past six years.

The two met at writing classes and decided to combine their considerable talents to work on *When Dreams Come True*.

Their efforts have been so successful they are already planning their next Superromance, to be set in the dazzling world of feature filmmaking, Hollywood, California.